"If you are looking for a character-driven, slow-burn romance based on a compelling tale of deceit, love, sacrifices, trust, secrets, blackmail, kidnappers, mafia bosses, assassins, and tycoons, Jodie Leigh Murray's *The Gangster's Daughter* is just what you should be looking for. Jodie unfolds the intriguing plot using a dual timeline and featuring a fascinating group of participants. The storyline had me hooked and on edge. Just when I thought I knew where the story was headed, I would be treated to an ingenious plot twist. The well-crafted protagonist's emotions were depicted engagingly and in a down-to-earth manner. This coupled with the vivid depictions of the scenes made the reading experience feel as if I was right there next to the role players, watching the story unfold. This amazing page-turner has suspense, action, and humor."

Keith Mbuya for Readers' Favorite

"*The Gangster's Daughter* by Jodie Leigh Murray is a compelling, exciting, and suspenseful romance novel. It was fast-paced, and I was hooked from the start. I could not turn the pages fast enough, and the events kept me on the edge of my seat. I could not put it down until I found out who Regan was going to choose-the man she loves or the man she is promised to marry. The attraction between Regan and Cameron was almost palpable, and a relationship was inevitable. The romance was a great addition to the nonstop suspense and action. The author is excellent at developing the characters, and it was interesting to get to know each one. The story was superbly written, and I was in for a big surprise."

Alma Boucher for Readers' Favorite

"Jodie Leigh Murray built suspense steadily throughout the story. The details of every moment were vivid. The amazing sunset and the sounds of the waves were easy to envision. I liked the unpredictable plot twist in the middle of the book. It glued me to every page, trying to figure out how Regan might conceal her ties to the mob. The conclusion was a shock. I recommend *The Gangster's Daughter* to fans of mafia-style romance novels."

Stephanie Chapman for Readers' Favorite

The Gangster series is best enjoyed in order:

The Gangster's Daughter
The Gangster's Mistake
The Gangster's Game

The Gangster's Daughter

The Gangster's Daughter

Jodie Leigh Murray

Jodie Leigh Murray Books

Book design by Jodie Leigh Murray

Published in the United States by Jodie Leigh Murray Books
Printed in the United States

Paperback ISBN: 978-1-968598-00-6
eBook ISBN: 978-1-968598-01-3

First edition: June 2023
Second Edition: June 2025

www.jodieleighmurray.com

For Joe,
For your unwavering trust in my ability to to see this through,
and your incessant pushing to pursue my dream.

Chapter One

I killed someone for the first time at the tender age of twelve, just shy of my thirteenth birthday. It had been self-defense, or so I was told, but I didn't believe it. I knew what had happened. After that, I was a tool. I had always been a tool, but hadn't understood it until I saw the pride shining in Pops' eyes after the incident. That should have been my first sign to worry about my future. I was the daughter who should have been a son, and I was a killer. He thought I wasn't afraid to take someone's life.

Except I was. And I wasn't the same person after.

He promptly enrolled me in classes meant to turn me into a fighting machine. I was an awkward kid, very much a loner, and the classes were not exactly honing my skills. I had expressed an interest in dancing and that was where I found my niche. Dance classes and practicing Jiu-Jitsu molded me into the person I am today. I don't like what I have become, what my father has made me into, but there was no point in blaming him. He wasn't the one who pointed the gun and pulled the trigger.

I was cunning, stealthy, and ruthless, and I would never be weak again.

At first glance, I was a well-put-together woman with an intelligent mind and a decent body that I'd earned.

Now, I stood on the thirty-fifth floor of a Miami skyscraper in a large, glassed in conference room, staring down a long conference table at several people given important titles they didn't earn.

Mark McCarthy, owner of several boating companies, was not looking happy, and I watched silently while he waved away the room's other occupants. Quickly, they gathered their things and filed from the room, leaving just him and me to stare at each other.

"I know why you're here, Ms. De Luca."

I feigned surprise and carefully set my papers down, eyes bold and challenging. I perched on the table's edge, crossing my legs and leaning toward him. Intimidation was my favorite–a trait I inherited from my father.

"You hired me."

"Exactly. I hired you to do a job, not try to buy me out."

I laughed haughtily, head tilted back slightly. He wasn't wrong. Mark had hired me to do a job. As a strategic consultant, a career I had worked extremely hard to build a strong reputation in, he had hired me to analyze everything about his businesses. He was in trouble, and he was looking for me to help him identify solutions. It wasn't my fault I found a solution to one of them.

"Your father has been after me for years to smuggle drugs out of South America. I'm not getting involved."

I could see his staff looking at us through the glass in curiosity. I raised my eyes, only to see them scamper away as soon as they saw me notice them. Good, let them think I would eat them alive.

"Mark, look at the documents again. Do you see the name Gavriel De Luca anywhere on them?" I kept my voice level and calm. "I shouldn't have to remind you these are legal. Drawn up by my lawyer and reviewed by yours. You are selling to me, not my father."

He looked up at me, his eyes still trying to intimidate me. Except I wasn't easily daunted. If there was anything I learned from being the daughter of a gangster, whether people knew my name, let no one see you sweat. Mark wasn't about to see any nervousness from me, and I wasn't about to let him know how much I wanted his boatyard.

When I found out that Mark McCarthy was in financial trouble with his boat businesses, I investigated immediately and found financial struggles he wouldn't be able to get out of easily. I contacted him, and although he was reluctant to do business with someone that carried my last name, he agreed to meet with me. He knew my reputation as a consultant, knew I could give him what he needed to turn him back around, and although I came with a hefty price tag, I agreed to lower my fees to help him.

Of the boatyards and marinas that he owned along the southeast coast, the boatyard he owned on the island of Cape Haven off the coast of South Carolina, was my goal. Cape Haven was the location of one of my family's homes, where we visited often when I was younger. It was a place where I escaped when I needed peace, and a place where if I had the option, I would settle down. Even if I never put down roots there, to own a business there that would thrive, and help the community flourish, I would achieve something on my own. Pops couldn't take that from me.

"His name, absent from the documents, means nothing. He could be a non operating owner. I'm not selling."

I tsked-tsked him and leaned back, tapping my finger against my lips while staring him down. "What *are* we going to do about that?" I emphasized the word 'are' for dramatic effect, and the sinister smile that curved my lips made him falter.

"You aren't going to scare me."

"Aren't I?" I challenged. "I have spent hours analyzing all your businesses, coming up with some very stimulating solutions to your issues, even lowering my fees substantially to help you. Taking one business off your hands is not the worst thing you can do, Mark."

Breathe in, breathe out, I reminded myself. Calm is what I needed to be. Calm and careful with my choice of words. There were few who I could trust with family intel. Very few.

"Let me tell you something, Mark. Something very few people

know about me." He leaned back in his chair, folding his arms in front of his burly chest. "I may carry the De Luca name, but my business is my business. Gavriel De Luca has no part in what is mine, and I have no part in what is his."

It was only part of a lie. Pops wouldn't have any part of this. This was mine. And this would be my key to finally settling down into a calm life. Eventually. Someday I would meet someone worth my time. My current relationship was going nowhere, but that was okay. It wasn't much of a relationship. Our careers were more important right now.

His eyes narrowed. "Is that true?"

I nodded. "I promise you it's the truth. What can I do to prove to you that you are selling to me, and only me?"

Before he could give me a response, the conference door opened, and the receptionist poked her head in. "I am so sorry to interrupt. Ms. De Luca, there's a phone call for you."

"For me?"

I always turned my cell phone off during business meetings. Not on silent or facing down. Off. There wasn't anyone that would know where to reach me unless someone had a tracker on me. I looked back at Mark, but it was too late. He had already seen the worry in my eyes. Inwardly, I swore.

"The gentleman said it was urgent that he speak with you."

I nodded, trying to calm the anxiety that bubbled up inside. Something was wrong.

"I'll be there in a moment." I turned back to Mark. "Think about it."

Mark excused me with a nod and I walked gracefully out of the conference room and to the receptionist's desk. The pretty receptionist sorted papers and tried to look busy. When she looked up, I gave her a quick smile and a wink.

"Line one."

I picked up the receiver and punched the button. "I'm in the middle of a meeting," I said, trying to sound annoyed instead of anxious.

"Regan, it's Giovanni."

Uncle Gio! How on earth was he able to track down where I was? I was also curious to know why he would track my whereabouts.

"Gio. I'm in a meeting. What's wrong?"

"Your father's taking a sabbatical. He asked me to call you, and urge you to take one yourself. No, not urge. You will take one yourself."

I measured my words carefully. Thoughts were racing through my head. "Why would I do that? And why would he do that?"

"He was making another Columbian deal, and something went wrong. He didn't give me all the details, but it's enough to make him go away for a little while. He wants you to do the same, since you carry his name."

"And you?"

"I'm handling things while he's away."

"How did you know where to find me? My cell phone is off. I'm in a meeting."

At the silence that followed, I knew I had triumphantly busted him. "Come on. You don't really think your dad doesn't track where you are? His only daughter and heir to his fortune?"

Gio knew me well enough to know I didn't give two shits about Pops' fortune. If Pops didn't leave anything to Gio, and to his long-time girlfriend, they would receive plenty from me. If he did, then I would give a lot to charity. My salary was enough to pay for my beach condo in Malibu and a comfortable lifestyle. It was enough for me.

"Fine," I said, seeing Mark getting restless. "I have to go."

"Where are you going?"

"I can't tell you that. If all goes well here, I'll be fine."

"Call me as soon as you get to wherever you end up."

"No," I snapped. "You tell Pops to call me. Tonight."

I heard Gio laughing right before he disconnected the call,

making me smile as I handed the phone back to the receptionist. Pops was extremely careful, being a man of great importance in the game of illegal and underground activities. Gavriel De Luca ran a tight ship and was a fair and rational man, but was someone no one thought about double-crossing. Double-crossing meant they find your body in a freezer or never found at all.

There were big names in these games, and if he was doing business with another boss that he had business dealings with in the past, and possibly double-crossed, he wasn't thinking straight. If he wasn't thinking straight, it meant he was getting old. I was grasping, not knowing what he had really been up to.

I smoothed down my suit jacket and skirt and returned to the conference room to resume my discussion. Mark fidgeted with his tie when I stepped in front of the table, summoning my best intimidating posture. He wasn't going to win this.

He leaned forward. "I will sell it to you under one condition. You keep the staff. Especially the senior boatbuilder."

Elation struck me. That was quite the ultimatum to consider, without knowing the work ethics of the staff. If I accepted his counteroffer and kept the staff, I wouldn't have to waste time on the long, tedious hiring process. I had seen the financials; it wasn't the staff bringing him down, but there were some very odd things in the financials that didn't quite add up that I would need to dig into.

"The boat builders there are some of the very best. It would be a shame for you to lose them."

"I can appreciate that, Mark. I accept your counteroffer. Are you accepting my price?" He nodded. "Good. Now, let's get these papers signed."

"Regan."

I looked at him, surprised at the sudden hitch in his voice. Here comes the sentimental side, I thought, and hoped that he wasn't about to get teary-eyed on me.

"Mark?"

"Please promise me that your father is not involved in this."

My eyes caught his full on. "I promise you; he is not involved."

∞

It was evening when I finally returned to my hotel room, immediately removing my heels as I moved across the living room of the suite. The entire corner of the room was windows that showed the ocean and beach. It was a beautiful view. Nothing but the best, and I would never settle for less. I dumped my bag on the couch before turning to the bar and pouring myself a glass of wine.

Sipping the indulgent alcohol slowly, I dialed the airline to see when flights were leaving for Myrtle Beach International Airport. I could have gone online, but I didn't want to waste time with technology, preferring to speak with someone who could get me dialed into my options for traveling quickly.

As soon as I'd booked my flight, my cell phone vibrated with an incoming call. I set my wine on the glass coffee table and sat on the black leather couch, tucking my leg beneath me.

"Pops."

"My darling, girl."

Pops had a soothing, calm voice. I recalled only one time when he was angry, his voice raising beyond his normal, calm voice. I challenged him during my teenage years. It was good to hear his voice.

"Gio said you are taking a sabbatical, that you're in danger," I said.

"I'm taking a vacation for a little while, yes. We won't speak after we hang up. Not even Gio can reach me. It's better this way."

"What about Gio?"

"Will remain at the house. And you are to go somewhere that you'll be safe, somewhere no one will know where you are." I opened my mouth to interrupt, but he sensed it. "Regan, you will do as I say. Trust no one."

That wasn't true. There were people in my life that I could trust. Tatum and Jazz, my two best friends, were trustworthy. They knew nothing about my family history, or Pops' business dealings. They knew the name, of course, but they never asked questions, and I offered no information. In fact, Tatum was such a good friend that she had moved into my condo in Malibu about a year ago. Part of the reason was to have someone there since I traveled sometimes. The other part was Tatum needed a place to stay, and her salary was not allowing her to afford a decent place on her own. It was nice to have someone there when I couldn't be, and it was nice to have someone there when I was home.

The argument with Pops wasn't worth the energy. Agreeing was the best thing I could do now. If he was in danger, the worry about me wouldn't do him any good. So, I agreed I would go somewhere, and I knew the perfect place.

"I bought the boatyard in Cape Haven today, Pops."

"Did you? I am delighted for you, my darling girl. Cape Haven is such a wonderful community. I miss visiting there. I know a young man that lives on the island. His name's Cameron. Nice, young man."

"Mmmmhmmmm," I said.

"You're twenty-seven now." Pops might have a soothing and calm voice, but I could tell when there was an edge to it. He was about to broadside me with something. "You're my only daughter. I need you to partner with someone who will take my place."

"Pops." My voice clipped with warning. My life was not a business arrangement.

"I've told you again and again that if you don't find someone suitable, I'll find someone for you. This has been a long time coming now."

I snorted, but said nothing. This was nothing I hadn't heard before. It was an idle threat he had brought up many times, usually when I was dating someone he didn't like, which was every time I met someone. Michael was a doctor, not an entrepreneur, and the most straightlaced person I knew. Michael would never break a rule in his life. He was incapable of replacing Pops. Not even close.

"The time has come now. You'll be married in March."

"I have a boyfriend."

The reminder wasn't enough. I knew it before I said it. "Michael doesn't have the backbone for this business. And your relationship isn't going to last."

None of them ever did, I thought to myself. Odd how they never worked out. It made me wonder if Pops had a hand in that. I wouldn't have put it past him to make sure my relationships didn't work out to make sure I married the right man. I shook my head, even knowing he couldn't see it. He wasn't wrong, though. My relationship with Michael was entirely too casual to last much longer. He was too involved in his career as an orthopedic surgeon, and mine had me traveling a lot. It had been good for us, the space. But it was too much space.

I didn't love Michael. It was the thought of settling down I loved. Having a family, maybe a dog. The idea of settling down with Michael would have been a possibility if my feelings for him were stronger. But they weren't. They would never be. I couldn't picture it with him. He deserved better.

I needed to admit it to Pops, but I couldn't if he was threatening to pick someone out for me. There was no humor in this. He couldn't force me to marry someone of his choosing, anyway.

"I had a contract drawn up years ago when you were a baby.

With a family friend who I've known for many years. You're to marry their oldest boy."

Silence fell between us while I thought about it, and Pops waiting for my reaction. I laughed, then laughed harder and harder until my whole body shook. A contract. Drawn up when I was a baby to marry me off to some family friend's son. Medieval bullshit is what this was, I thought. The threats over the years had never ceased, but a contract?

"And what if I don't marry this man you've picked out for me?"

His voice turned low. As devious as I had turned on Mark earlier. "Don't forget who helped you get where you are in your career. I can take it away as easily as I helped you achieve it. I have more connections than you think I do."

That rankled me. I had never asked him to get me a part-time position at a firm as a consultant while I was going to college. The position had been too good to pass up, and I still took my courses. I busted my ass, but it gave me the experience besides the education to get me where I was today. I did everything I could to make sure I would never be under Pops' control.

"You also forget that I keep tabs on your friend, Jake. Would be a shame for something to happen to him." I gasped at the threat. "Seems he has a stronger mentality than his father."

It was one thing to threaten my career, but to threaten Jake was a new low. I would never risk Jake. Jake was the friend Pops never wanted me to have. The friend I still had today.

I held onto hope my reputation in my work was enough to keep my career strong without interference from Pops, but I couldn't risk it. He could ruin me. He had enough connections. I knew he did. He had me right where he needed me to be.

I wanted to yell. I wanted to scream. Most of all, I wanted to throw something. But I couldn't. All I could do was sit there, frozen. My mouth couldn't find words to argue with him. Never once had I thought his threat had meaning behind it. He would never make me marry someone against my will. Gio could take over his business, fill his shoes. Gio could have all his money. I didn't want it. Except that wasn't what Pops wanted.

"Regan, I don't want to argue."

"Then don't make me do this," I choked out. "Don't make me marry someone I don't know. You are taking away every single choice for my future."

"I've told you many times before, I will protect you at all costs. You need someone to shield you. And he will do this. You'll have your career. Regan, you will be fine. Keep an open mind."

"Who is it?"

"I can't tell you that. I'll tell you when the time is right."

Dear God, this was getting worse. Choosing someone for me to marry, and not giving me the courtesy of telling me who I'm marrying, was too much to swallow. When I hung up with him, I was going to drink the rest of the bottle of wine and I was going to regret it, but I needed it.

That wasn't going to happen. Suddenly, I was exhausted. The argument with Mark had taken its toll, albeit a triumphant ending to it, but this wasn't one that I was about to win, and the energy was draining from me.

"Regan, please be well. I'll talk as soon as I can."

"Love you, Pops," I said, resigned.

"I love you, too, my darling girl."

I disconnected the call and tossed my phone onto the couch. It took a moment for me to collect my disarray of thoughts. Too many things were happening at one time. The glass of wine with the deep red liquid beckoned me, and without hesitating for another second, I grabbed it and took a few healthy gulps. Normally, I liked to savor my wine. I felt a pull for something stronger.

Marriage to an unknown man? My future tied to someone that I had never met? It was crazy. I'd never given marriage much thought, having built up my career in the last few years. I shook my head, wondering how I was going to end my relationship with Michael. It wasn't like I could be honest. Tying up my future with someone chosen for me was completely asinine.

Chapter Two

Where was Nicco? I looked down the street, craning my neck to see past the other vehicles in the pickup lane. There was no sign of the black Cadillac.

Nicco was never late picking me up from school. For the two years I'd been in middle school, he'd always parked and waited for me at the curb just beyond the tennis courts. Today, he wasn't there.

I adjusted the weight of my backpack, shifting my feet to take another look. I wondered what could have possibly delayed him. He would never forget about picking me up from school. Nicco was usually reading a newspaper or magazine when I got out of school. I always figured he got there early enough to make sure he was there waiting for me.

The minutes dragged on and on as my classmates, cars, and buses were slowly beginning to clear away. I didn't have to stand on my tip-toes to see the cars coming down the street. There were no cars lined up to pick up kids.

A black car pulled up, but it wasn't Nicco or his car. It came to a stop exactly where Nicco would always park. A dark-haired man with diamond studs in both ears climbed out of the passenger side. He motioned me forward with two fingers.

I took a step forward, then stopped. I didn't recognize this man. I leaned to get a look at the driver but didn't recognize him either.

"Your father sent us to pick you up," he said, his voice firm. "Come along, Regan."

He knew my name. I walked toward him but stopped when I was just out of his reach. Alarms resonated in my ears. Pops' words echoed in my ears that I should never, ever go with anyone other than Nicco unless he specifically told me that someone else would pick me up from school.

Sensing my hesitation, the man lunged, grabbing me and forcefully walking me to the car despite my protests. His hand clamped down over my mouth just before I could scream. He tossed me effortlessly into the back seat of the car and slammed the door, leaving me to believe that no one had even noticed.

I pinched my eyes shut against the memory and rested my forearms against the ferry's railing. Even though thoughts of that day resurfaced infrequently, they made me sick to my stomach. I had never wanted to end someone else's life, but I had no choice. Every time I thought about it, I considered what I could have done differently to escape the situation. But there was nothing. If it hadn't been that day, it would have been another.

The waves slapped against the boat, cutting through the blue water of the Atlantic. I stared ahead at the dot on the horizon that was my destination. It had been a few years since I had been to this house. While Pops had gotten me the job with the consulting firm during college, as grateful as I had been for the opportunity, I had only stayed for another six months after I earned my Master's degree before I took the risk of going out on my own. I hadn't planned on working for someone else, especially not for Pops. I had taken a brief vacation in Cape Haven before I delved into my independent consulting. My reputation for being the best strategic consultant took off quickly, and I hadn't had time to come back since.

I sighed, forcing my memory back to the island. During the spring, summer, and fall months, the island's small community of businesses relied heavily on tourism. The island had the beauty of sandy beaches, lush green trees, and very few major roads. The town itself was on the southwestern part of the island, providing everything a vacationer might need—a coffee shop, bike shop, and a hotel owned by a friend of my family. There was a police station, albeit on the small side, as they had few noteworthy crimes other than a fender bender or an occasional shoplifter.

The main road traced the coast from southwest to northeast and was littered with resorts. Many boasted small cabins and a few family restaurants.

I was too young to remember when Pops had built a house right on the beach about a mile from the town. It hadn't taken long before there was a row of houses up along the beach. As I grew older, visits became much more infrequent. It had been quite some time since Pops and I had been to this place together, the last time being shortly after I was thirteen. I suppose he thought a vacation would help me heal from my ordeal, but it hadn't, and we returned home after only a few days.

It had occurred to me the last time I visited I could buy, or build, a resort and settle down into a quiet life. I knew I wasn't there yet. There was still so much to do before I could settle down. But now I was arriving with my triumphant purchase.

The boatyard wasn't a vast enterprise, taking about four years to build a boat, depending on the size purchased. It wasn't a big moneymaking business either. I would need to separate some of my efforts from my consulting to dig into marketing at the boatyard. This was the first business I had ever purchased. Although the excitement still burned new and bright, I would need to ask someone for help. Pops would be no help, but I knew the next best person on the island, and I would pay her a visit soon after my arrival.

I heard a sniffle, turning to see a little boy in the aisle of cars behind me, with tears in his eyes and his index finger in his mouth. He couldn't have been over three years old, looking around with wide, very frightened eyes.

I looked around, hoping to spot someone that I could point in his direction, but was unsuccessful. With a curse under my breath, pushed away from the railing to approach him. He looked up at me, eyes still wide and a string of snot accompanying the finger still stuck in his mouth.

I didn't consider myself the motherly type, but I had the urge to wipe away his tears. The last thing I wanted was to scare him into running away and getting hurt.

"Are you lost?" I asked.

He nodded.

"Should I help you find your mom? Or dad?" After another nod, I straightened. "Do you want to hold my hand, or do you want me to carry you?"

Closing one eye, he considered his choices and looked back up at me. It was oddly enduring, capturing my heart instantly. After a moment, he reached up his arms to me. I couldn't believe this child was trusting me.

I swooped him onto my hip as if nurturing came naturally to me. "Let's go on an adventure, shall we? Maybe we can find you a treat for being such a brave boy."

That at least earned me a smile, but he remained silent as I walked toward the cabin that contained a waiting room out of the wind and the sun, vending machines, snacks and drinks, and the bathrooms.

It was a pleasant day. Most people were sitting on benches or leaning along the railing like I had been, enjoying the warmth of the sun. The boat ride to the island was not a lengthy one, and since it was near the end of summer, there weren't many travelers.

"My name's Regan," I told him. "What's yours?"

I had about given up on him speaking to me at all, even though I had come to his rescue. At his age, I doubted that he even knew what was going on. I pulled open the door and stepped into the waiting area, hoping that someone would notice and recognize their child. There were a few people there, but no one looked up from their phones. I shook my head, walking toward the vending machines. I didn't know how old he was, and I wasn't sure he could have candy. I fed a dollar bill and some change into the machine and secured him a bag of animal crackers.

"Is this what it's like to be a mother?" I asked him, giving him a wink before tearing open the bag with my teeth and handing it to him. He gave me a little laugh before digging into his snack.

I decided it would be more conducive to walk around the deck and walked back to the door just as it swung open to a frantic woman. She looked at me, then the boy, and cried out, reaching her arms out to whisk him out of my grasp.

"Oh, thank God," she said, smoothing her hand down his hair while he was oblivious to anything other than his animal crackers. "I turned around for one second, and the next thing I knew he was gone."

I noted the cell phone clutched in her hand, fervently hoping that she hadn't been on her phone instead of paying attention to him, resulting in him wandering off.

I smiled, holding out my hand. "It was my pleasure."

"Oh, and she bought you some animal crackers," she said to him, taking my hand without paying attention. "You're a very lucky boy, Andrew. Thanks so much for grabbing him."

"I was happy to help."

"Let me at least pay you for the crackers."

"No, no. That's unnecessary."

The woman nodded with a smile and turned out the door, presumably for where they were standing before. I rubbed my hand over my face and followed them out just in time to see him waving to me as his mother carried him away.

I laughed, strolling back to the railing. I had just resumed my lean when a deep voice rumbled behind me.

"Excuse me."

I turned toward the voice.

"I'm sorry. I don't mean to bother you."

I gave him a slight smile. He was a good-looking man with dark hair, ruffled from the wind, and the lightest blue eyes I had ever seen. They were almost translucent.

I had noticed him before. He was that last person to drive aboard in a sleek, silver bullet BMW. When he got out of the driver's seat, he removed a black leather jacket to reveal biceps that strained against the short sleeves of his white t-shirt.

My first thought had been that he must be of Mediterranean heritage to have such deep-colored skin, perhaps Italian or Greek. He had no accent.

"It's fine," I said, casually leaning back until the rails pressed into my back.

"Heading to the island for some time away?"

"You could say that." I held out my hand. "Regan De Luca."

With a smile, he accepted my hand for a firm handshake. "Cameron Moretti. It's nice to meet you, Regan De Luca."

"Cameron," I repeated.

He cocked his head to the side. "Do you know me?"

"I don't." I shrugged, regretting mentioning it. "When I said I was going to the island, someone said they knew a Cameron who was there."

He gave a nod. "I saw what you did for that little boy. That was nice of you."

"I couldn't let him wander around alone. Do you live on the island?"

"I have a house on the beach. It's up the coast. Do you have a house here? I thought I knew just about everyone who lives here."

"I do. On the beach. It's been in my family since I was a little girl. I don't get back here very often, and my dad hasn't been here for years. I haven't been back here since after college."

"That couldn't have been that long ago," he murmured.

I couldn't miss the flirtation, as blatant as it was. I wanted to sigh out loud but refrained from doing so. I had enough on my hands right now. This was just an innocent conversation. Nothing could come of it.

Instead, I smiled and made sure that it reached my eyes. "It was more years ago than I care to admit, but that's a conversation for another day."

"I accept."

Now I laughed. "I'm sure we'll run into each other again. It's not a big island."

"How long do you intend to stay?"

This wasn't a simple answer. It would depend entirely on how long Pops thought there was danger to us both. It could be a couple of weeks, or it could be a few months. I stared into the distance, the island now coming into clear view. I could even see a sliver of my house.

"I'm not sure yet," I murmured.

"Through Labor Day weekend, at least?"

"I'm thinking so."

He grinned. "Great. I look forward to seeing you again, Regan."

I watched him back away from me, returning to the other side of the ferry and giving full admiration to his firm backside in a snug pair of denim jeans. Shaking my head, I turned back to the railing and closed my eyes to the feel of the ocean wind and the warmth of the sun on my face.

The ferry bumped to a stop against the dock at the southwestern tip of the diamond-shaped island. The three-story Palmetto Hotel dominated Main Street. It was the tallest building on the island, looking solemnly out toward the ocean with its swaying implanted palm trees framing the front doors. The top two stories were luxury suites, each having a walkout to view and listen to the ocean.

A half hour later, I pulled up at the black iron gates and dialed in the code. Slowly, the gates opened, and I drove my rented car into the circular drive. Since it wouldn't be long before I would need to leave again, I left the car parked in front of the door.

The two-story home had been my favorite as a child and still was. Green trees and bushes, mixed in with transplanted palm trees and colorful flowers, decorated the backyard with impeccable landscaping while the sparkling ocean and beach were at the front. Above the three-car garage was a private dance studio.

My love of dancing had been the purpose of this design. Even the family house back in California had a dance studio, but this one was special to me. It took up most of the upper level and the windows on the balcony gave it plenty of natural light.

I hauled my bags out of the car's trunk and opened the double doors leading into the spacious foyer. Dropping the bags to the marble floor, I went straight through into the living room, past the open kitchen with a half-wall. Although spacious and an open-concept home, the half-wall gave the appeal of having some type of separation between the living room and kitchen. The house had a modern look with white suede couches and a simple glass dining room table with four cushioned chairs. I rarely ate at the table, preferring to be out on the deck as much as possible.

I threw open the French-style patio doors, inviting the warm breeze to enter the house. Someone had been there to uncover the sparkling in-ground pool and hot tub and to make sure they were both cleaned.

I would soak in the hot tub later. For now, there were things to be done and people to see. Turning, I surveyed the house and found that the cleaning crew had done a very thorough job. I retrieved my bags and brought them into the master suite opposite the kitchen.

My room had a master bathroom with a Jacuzzi tub. It also had a single glass door that led to the deck. I had a feeling that I would be in Cape Haven for longer than I wanted, but at least this room gave me enough peace that I was okay with an extended stay. I would need it for a clear head.

After unpacking, I decided it was time to visit my lair. Passing back through the house and foyer, I bounded up the curving staircase. Behind the staircase was a hallway leading to the other two bedrooms. If I was here long enough, I would let Tatum and Jazz fight over who got the room closest to the ocean when they came to visit. Pops had forbidden me from telling anyone where I would be, but I couldn't keep it from my two best friends.

At the top of the stairs, I walked directly into the spacious room with no furniture. The hardwood floors shined, and the entire back wall was a mirror. Pops had a ballet bar installed at one time during my teenage years, but I hadn't kept up on ballet. I loved to dance. Every kind of dance. But ballet hadn't been one of my favorites.

It had been too long since I had danced. If I had dressed more comfortably, I would have made use of the room immediately. Work had taken over my life so much that I hadn't had time to stop and treat myself to the one thing that provided solitude. I blew the stray hair out of my face and walked right into the middle of the room, twirling around just as my phone vibrated in my pocket.

When I saw who was calling, it tempted me to put it through to my voice mail. I knew this was a conversation that needed to happen. I didn't know if I wanted to have it now. Putting it off would just delay the inevitable.

"Hey, stranger," I answered.

Michael's low laugh caressed my ear through the phone. "I'm thinking that's true. It's been weeks since I've been able to see you. When will you be home?"

I sighed. "I don't know."

There was silence for a minute, as though he was mulling it over. I knew it wasn't what he wanted to hear, and part of me hadn't wanted to say it. That wasn't even the worst part of what I would have to say to him. My heart hurt already.

"Michael," I finally said. "I adore you. You know I do."

"But this isn't going anywhere," he finished for me, a hint of sorrow deep in his voice. "I can't blame you. You're busy. I'm busy. Maybe this isn't the right time for us."

My breath let out in a whoosh. "Our careers are too important to both of us right now. I will always consider you a friend."

He laughed, short and to the point. "Take care of yourself, Regan."

"I will, and I don't have to tell you the same."

"Who knows, you may come in with another ankle sprain and we can pick up where we left off."

Not likely, I thought to myself. But I wouldn't count anything out of my future just yet. I had no ring on my finger yet, and I had yet to meet this man that I was supposedly marrying. But it would never be Michael.

"You never know," I smiled. "I'll see you."

"Bye, Regan."

I ended the call and let out another enormous sigh. I needed hours of dancing to unwind from the stress of the last day. But for now, I needed groceries. I also needed to let Isabel know I was back in town, and what I was up to. Most of all, I needed her shoulder to cry on. Love hadn't been involved, but that didn't mean I didn't care for Michael. I cared about him more than I cared to admit, which was why I felt so awful. He was the best kind of guy. Someday he would meet a woman that he would be happy with. It wouldn't have been with me.

Chapter Three

"Regan! Oh, my word, but look at you!"

Isabel burst through the office doors behind the front desk, hurrying to enfold me in a giant hug with suntanned and   toned arms. A large seashell clip secured her blonde hair, and I noticed that there was not a trace of gray. Her brown eyes were dazzling behind a pair of hot pink-rimmed glasses. She kept my hands in hers, opening my arms wide to look at me.

I laughed.

"How have you been? I've missed you so much!"

"I've been better. As much as I hate to admit that I didn't want to come here, I'm glad I did. I need this."

Isabel removed her glasses, letting them fall around her neck by the matching hot pink keeper. "Honey, I'm so sorry.   Do you wanna talk about it?"

When I was younger, I felt that Pops and Isabel were more than they had let on. I would catch them looking at each other in ways that I didn't understand until later in life. It was longing. It was passion. I knew they had loved each other, or at least had had an affair. It was after Pops met Anne when we stopped coming here. I was fifteen, and I didn't blame him. It wasn't a serious relationship with Anne; I knew that. My mother had been gone for many years, having died when I was too young to remember her in a boating accident. Anne was just there. She didn't try to pretend to be my mother, or even a step-mother. Their relationship was casual. Like my relationship with Michael.

"Did you eat?"

"I was going to grab something at the market, but I wanted to see you first."

"Well, let's go get us some dinner. My treat."

Isabel linked her arm through mine and led me across the hotel foyer, chatting about how it was good to see me and how well she thought I looked. As busy as I was, I tried to take care of myself.

"You're just in time for the Labor Day celebration! You haven't been here for Labor Day weekend since you were a little girl. So much has changed."

"Twelve," I murmured, remembering the carnival set up in front of the town beyond the ferry slip, the games, bands playing in the amphitheater on the beach, and the weekend ending with a spectacular display of fireworks.

It was like being home. I relaxed in the tranquil life of leisure and delightful conversation. I followed Isabel out the front doors and down the sidewalk toward the bistro at the end of the street.

"It is good to see you," Isabel admitted, not releasing my arm until we were standing in front of the host podium in the dimly lit restaurant. It wasn't yet dinnertime, and the restaurant had only a few other guests.

The host grabbed two menus from the slat on the wall behind the podium and led us down the aisle between square tables covered with red and white gingham tablecloths. We sat at a small booth in front of the windows that faced the beach.

Isabel waved over the owner of the restaurant, a short man who was clearly not Italian. He clasped his hands together with a smile, not even allowing Isabel to state her request before announcing he would bring the best bottle of wine for his friend and her guest.

I raised my eyebrows. "No," Isabel firmly said. "Not even close, so don't give me that look. I am happily single, and that isn't about to change with anyone on this island."

"I didn't say a word! But I want to ask you, do you know Cameron Moretti?"

Isabel's eyes widened slightly, and I didn't miss it. "How do you know him?"

"He was on the ferry with me." I watched curiously while Isabel visibly relaxed. "He seems nice. I wouldn't peg him to live on this island. He seems much more worldly. Drives a nice car."

Isabel laughed, but it came out shaky as though she were nervous. "Oh, he must have been returning from some big city. He travels, but he spends a bit of time here on the island." She gave me a look of annoyance. "Why am I telling you about him? He should tell you himself."

"If the opportunity presents itself," I murmured, just as the owner returned with a bottle of red wine.

We lapsed into silence while he uncorked the bottle and poured us each a healthy glass. I picked my glass up, raising it to Isabel, who raised her glass in return.

"To old friends and new friends."

Isabel smiled. "He's quite a looker, isn't he? Cameron?"

I sipped, then nodded. "I'm not jumping into another relationship."

Isabel let out another shaky laugh. "He might be your type."

"I don't have a type." I sat back in the seat, fingers toying with the stem of my glass while I thought about it. Did I have a type?

"You were seeing someone?"

"Michael," I said. "He's an orthopedic surgeon. I met him when I sprained my ankle a couple of years ago when he was doing his residency in the emergency room. It wasn't super serious. I travel a lot. He works a lot. We literally just broke up."

"I'm so sorry!"

"I didn't love him. I wish I could have. It just wasn't there."

"Why?"

I stared at her. I had to be cautious who I talked to about my situation. Although Isabel had been in my life since I was a little girl, I wasn't certain that I wanted this news out in the open. Not yet anyway.

"You don't think ever about settling down?"

I smiled. "It's crossed my mind. I've worked hard to get where I am today, but I've been thinking about it more lately. Maybe that's why Michael and I broke up. I couldn't see it with him."

"You did the right thing, then?" Isabel teased.

"I think so. It still hurts. I hated doing that to him."

"And how's your father?"

Again, I lapsed into silence. I didn't know how much Isabel knew about the family, but there were certain things that I didn't want to divulge. Like the fact that he was on sabbatical, and no one knew where he was. Not even me.

"He's good."

"Is he still with that woman?"

I smiled. I had always sensed that Isabel was jealous. If she and Pops had carried on an affair, it would have been a long time ago. I was sure of it. "Anne. Yes, he's still with her. At least that I know. I haven't been home for a few weeks."

"But he never married her?"

"No."

"Does that bother you?"

"Not at all. She's involved with us as a family, but not so much that I think he would ever consider marrying her. And her daughter, you remember me talking about Amber? She's like a little sister to me. I talk to her sometimes."

"Your dad is a good man."

"Yeah, yeah. He's the best." I smiled. "But I have something positive to tell you. Something that I'm going to need your help with."

Isabel reached her hands toward mine, touching my hands

lightly. "Tell me."

"I bought the boatyard from Mark McCarthy yesterday. Took a lot of convincing, but he finally sold to me." Her face lit up, and I could see the fine wrinkles at the corners of her eyes. "I'm going to need your help on how to run a business."

She clapped her hands together in delight. "This is the best news! That means you'll be here more often now, so I'll be able to see you more! I'm curious why you wanted to buy it? I didn't even know he had it for sale."

"He didn't. I coerced him into selling it to me. You know I've always loved the island. The house. This would be the perfect place to settle down if I ever did. Maybe this is a good start."

"It sounds like you've had some busy days lately."

"It has been. I'm looking forward to opening the house and maybe sitting in the hot tub, listening to the waves washing against the shore."

"It's the perfect night for it." She smiled. "Let's eat, then I'll let you get home so you can relax. It sounds like you'll be around for a while. We'll have plenty of time to catch up."

After a heaping bowl of spaghetti and a large glass of water, Isabel and I parted ways outside the hotel with her, throwing her arms around me in an enormous hug, nearly busting my ribs. For a skinny woman, she was tough. It took me less than ten minutes to drive home, tucking the car into the garage and locking up the house.

I opened myself a bottle of wine and sank into one of the deck chairs to look out at the water washing up against the beach beyond the iron fence that surrounded the house. The sun was going down, casting an orange-red glow across the sky. For now, there wasn't another place I wanted to be.

∞

"Nicco?"

I looked in the rearview mirror for his eyes to shift from the road to look at me. A smile curved my lips when his familiar blue eyes met mine.

"Yes, Twinkle Toes?"

"Do you like picking me up from school every day? I mean, Pops pays you to do it, doesn't he?"

His eyes moved back to the road. "He pays me to do it, yes. But you wanna know a secret?" I eagerly nodded. "I would do it even if he didn't pay me. I like to drive you."

"You do? Why?"

"Because I like to make sure you're safe. And I just so happen to like you. I think you're a delightful girl who deserves to be picked up from school."

I thought about it for a moment. "Why wouldn't I be safe?"

I didn't miss his heavy sigh, and I wondered if I was asking too many questions and was irritating him. I knew Pops had money and had people working for him. But I watched other kids taking a school bus, except those kids who had big, heavy band instruments or after-school activities. Other kids got picked up occasionally, but I was the only one picked up every day without an after-school activity or a large band instrument. After going to private school for primary school, I begged Pops to let me go to public school like a normal kid. He finally relented, and it was the worst possible decision I had made. They shunned me because of my name.

The kids in my school didn't bother with bullying me, they just avoided me like a disease. Very few of my classmates talked to me, and those who talked to me did so sparingly so they wouldn't get caught doing so.

"Your dad just wants to make sure. You're all he has."

I snorted. "He has Gio."

"That's not the same. You are his only kid. He just wants you to be safe."

I looked out my window from the backseat at the enormous mansions tucked behind tall iron gates pass by. I wasn't buying his answer at all. It didn't seem like Pops paid much attention to me. He was always busy. In his office, or at his golf course. With Uncle Gio.

"You aren't telling me the truth."

"There are people who don't like your dad. That might want to hurt him indirectly. But that doesn't mean that they would hurt you. He just likes to know that you're in expert hands, and he knows that I'm the right person for the job."

I smiled. "I like you, Nicco."

He returned my smile. "I like you, too, Twinkle Toes."

I sat up from my beach towel, looking out at the water. The midmorning sun shimmered on the water, casting a glow like millions of sparking lights rippling in the waves. The day promised to be a warm one. Visitors to the island filled up the beach with brightly colored towels, umbrellas, coolers, picnic baskets, and bags of water toys and sports equipment.

I hadn't thought about Nicco for a long time. I missed him. More than I cared to admit. It was so long ago, but he had been my only friend for many years. He had been the only person who I could talk to. Pops didn't have enough time for me; never asked me how my day was, and if anything interesting had happened at school. He didn't know how my classmates gave me sideline glances while whispering to each other. I could tell that they were talking about me. They didn't know me, which made it hurt more.

If they knew me, they would know that I was a person just like they were. There was nothing wrong with me.

I staked out my spot in the sand directly across from where my house was. I could have stayed on my deck and enjoyed the clean water of the pool, but it had been so long since I had felt sand between my toes that the pull of the beach was too much.

I was around ten pages deep into my book about the habits of highly successful people when I noticed a shadow had fallen over me and stayed there. Calmly, I dogeared the page and set it down, squinting my eyes up at the guy standing over me.

"Hey!" he said, plopping down into the sand beside me. "I'm Matt."

All I was interested in was getting a suntan and reading my book. But I wasn't a naturally rude person, and as much as I didn't want to engage in small talk, I also didn't want to be impolite. "Matt, it's nice to meet you."

He had light blond hair, flopping around in the slight breeze of the morning. Tatum would have been all over him. The look of a surfer, but maybe a little more intelligence behind his light green eyes. "Are you staying on the island for the weekend? For the big party?"

I laughed. "Yes. You?"

"Yeah, me and a few of the guys from inland. We're staying at that resort up the road. I forgot the name, but it's got the yellow house on the corner with the front porch. The old people that own it look like hippies. They're cool people."

Lord, was he going to take a breath? I thought. "Sid and Franky," I said.

"Yeah, that's them. You know 'em?"

"Yes. I've been visiting this island for many years." And that was all I was going to tell him. I didn't need someone visiting my doorstep. Especially if he had buddies with him. I was supposed to be on the down low.

I eyed him cautiously. This guy didn't seem like the type that would stalk someone, or have impure motives. Usually, I was an excellent judge of character. Matt looked simple enough.

"Me and the guys are going to play volleyball. Do you wanna join us?"

Aw. "That's very sweet, but I'll pass. I'd like to relax and read for now."

He shrugged and pushed himself up. "It was worth a try. Maybe I'll see you around. I didn't catch your name."

"Regan."

He didn't move, eyes sweeping over me. I was used to getting looks, but I wasn't the only woman clad in a bikini. There were groups of girls, many of whom were much younger than I was, and likely college students.

"I'll see you around, Regan!"

I watched him jog away from me, passing by a familiar face just as I thought I was going to get back to my book. It was just as well. Reading these types of books took intense concentration.

"Beautiful morning."

Cameron strolled over to me, easing down on the sand next to me where Matt had just been. Even sweating, he looked good. The olive complexion of his skin was an interesting contrast to my paler colored skin. I was attempting to change that.

"Am I interrupting you?"

"No." I was being honest. "It's not a very engaging subject."

He picked up the book briefly, looked at it for a moment, and set it right back down. "I've read it. You're right. Why are you even trying?"

I smiled slyly, with a slight shrug. "Boredom?"

That brought a laugh from him, at least. He jerked his chin in the direction where Matt had gone. "Who was that?"

"That was Matt. He was looking for someone to join a volleyball game."

His eyebrows raised. "Are you sure?"

"I'm sure. He was very nice."

He cocked his head to the side and my stomach flip-flopped. "This island is going to be full this weekend. Make sure you're being careful. Lots of college guys."

He was very demanding. I liked it in an odd sort of way. Controlled was not something that I wanted to be, but he said it in such a way it made me feel cared for. It was silly. I had just met him, but it felt like he wanted to protect me. He didn't even know me.

"Did you know where to find me, or was this just a lucky coincidence?"

"Lucky coincidence. I jog in the morning when it's nice out, but this morning I was a little late getting going. I didn't think I'd run into you so soon."

He was getting to me. Athletic, protective, and sinfully good-looking with his dark hair and blue eyes. And that damned little dimple. The bones in his cheeks were high and defined at sharp angles.

It wasn't like me to have a no-strings-attached relationship. It would differ completely from what my relationship had been with Michael. We were together, we just weren't exclusive. Well, I was exclusive because I had too much going on in my life. I was pretty sure that Michael had been exclusive to me as well, even though neither of us had committed to it. To jump into another relationship, after just ending one, would make my life more complicated.

"It was nice of you to warn me, Cameron."

"I can't have an unprotected woman living down the beach from me and not be worried about her."

I placed a hand over my heart with a fluttering laugh. I was positive I wasn't the only single woman living on the island. "Who's going to save me from you?"

"Friends close and enemies closer." He shrugged, the muscles in his arms rippling with the movement. He leaned closer to me. "You should keep me very close."

I wasn't the type of woman to swoon over muscles or a pretty face. It was the intelligence that did me in. If I kept him close, I would have issues later.

"It would complicate a lot of things in my life right now." It was an admittance that I wasn't sure was for him, or for me. "I don't even know you."

"I live for complications. My life is the same way, and I'm not looking for a relationship either," he admitted back. "But you could know me if you tried."

"What do you do for a living, Cameron?"

"I do a little of everything, but in all honesty, I own a few businesses. An entrepreneur. I don't like monotony."

I laughed again, wondering what it was about him that made me laugh so nervously around him. He didn't appear to be trying to be humorous.

"I would be an excellent escort for the weekend festivities." He frowned. "Or maybe companion sounds a little better. I'm not running an escort service here."

"I wouldn't peg you for a male escort. One would think it would be exhausting to entertain at night, then get up so early to go jogging."

"I'm not a heavy sleeper. I'm an early riser no matter what time I get to sleep."

"You sound like me, Cameron."

"What do you do?"

"I'm a strategic consultant." I grinned.

I didn't know if he was trying to be sly, but I caught sight of his fingers inching in the sand toward my hand. His eyes caught mine and held me immobile for a moment. Another time, and another place, and no commitment forthcoming could have made my decisions about him so much different. But I couldn't help but wonder.

"I might need a strategic consultant."

"You wouldn't be able to afford my rates."

"I would love to take you out to dinner."

"No," I laughed. "Thank you for the offer."

"A challenge?"

The charm was coming on again, smoothing over me like a salesperson. And it was working. I knew he owned his own business. Or businesses. He had charmed me. I was interested. I was hooked.

"Not a challenge, no."

"I'll continue to ask until you say yes."

"I'm not looking for a relationship."

"Neither am I."

I pushed myself to my feet along with my book and towel, taking a moment to look out at the great expanse of the ocean before I looked down at him. "I'll think about it."

"Regan!"

I turned to look at Isabel, waving at me from my deck. I waved back at her while Cameron got to his feet. He grabbed my hand, and it surprised me, almost like a jolt of electricity.

"Go out with me, Regan."

"No."

"Go out with me. Once. That's all that I'm asking."

I pulled my hand away. "See you around, Cameron."

I took off in a graceful sprint toward my house, not bothering to look back so he could see my sneaky smile. He hadn't stopped me to press the issue, at least. A moment later, I was giving a quick kiss to Isabel's cheek, ignoring the raised eyebrows in her silent question. I also ignored the glance toward Cameron.

"Is that Cameron Moretti?"

I shrugged, grabbing my water bottle from the table near the pool to take a few gulps. I swiped the back of my hand across my mouth. "He's nice."

"And nice to look at," Isabel said, turning around to watch Cameron continue his jog up the beach toward his house.

"He asked me out."

"And?"

"Not interested. And I just met him yesterday."

"The island isn't big. He's got a house about a mile from here. It's huge and gorgeous with a high iron fence around it. I've never seen him with a woman. He must be lonely."

"Hmm," I murmured noncommittally.

"You might like him. If nothing else, for a pleasant conversation. He's easy to talk to, like you don't have to try."

I merely shrugged. She was right. He was easy to talk to. Isabel watched me pull open the patio door and resigned herself to following me into the house. She sat down on a stool at the kitchen counter and watched me tidy up the kitchen.

"What brings you by, Isabel? Other than my wonderful coffee."

"I would never ask this of you. I truly wouldn't unless I was desperate."

I turned around with a cup of steaming coffee in my hands, leaning against the counter with a smile. "You need my help."

"God, yes."

"You know you can always ask me. What do you need?"

"Two of my housekeepers have called in sick, one out of plain irresponsibility and the other with a sick baby. I need at least two on each floor."

"When do I start?"

Isabel laughed, coming around to hug me. "That's my girl. I truly owe you. Can you be at the hotel in an hour?"

"Can and will."

She grabbed my hands and squeezed with a twinkle in her eyes. "Think about giving Cameron a chance, honey. He's a good man. Sweet. He'll never let you down."

"I'll think about it. In the meantime, I need to take a shower. I'll be at the hotel within a half hour."

Chapter Four

The rhythmic clicks of my high-heel shoes as I walked along the sidewalk threatened to put me in a trance as I walked toward the glass doors of the boatyard office. Today, I was a business owner. Quite the change from yesterday's housekeeper position. Doing the job of two housekeepers exhausted me, but I was happy to have helped Isabel. I felt rotten for turning Cameron down for a date, so helping her might have redeemed me a little. He might have been telling me the truth and was just looking for a conversation rather than a relationship.

The double-glass doors boasted a logo promising a smooth sail. We sold and rented boats. I had noticed the plethora of sailboats in the bay and yachts out even farther. According to Mark's financial reports, business had been steady in the last decade, and I would put up a fight to keep it that way.

Good managers were hard to get, especially on such a small island. The economy had taken a dip in the last few years, and new hires had been even harder to find. The general manager had taken a walk for reasons unknown, leaving me to deal with finding a replacement and reviewing financials more in depth than what I had done in my initial review. They were making a profit, this much I knew.

I stopped at the doors, admiring the bold white lettering of the company name with the outline of a yacht stenciled in gold.

It wasn't exactly a gold mine, but it had brought in enough money to keep afloat. No pun intended.

The lobby was comfortable, with a waiting area with a small couch and two brown leather chairs nestled in a triangle around a low coffee table with several issues of boating magazines. Across from the waiting area was the receptionist's desk with the logo on the wall behind the taller desk.

Behind the desk was a blonde, who looked like she was right out of high school, looking at her cell phone. I slipped my sunglasses off as I approached and raised my eyebrows at her when I stopped. She had yet to even glance up at me. Perhaps a receptionist was an extra expense that wasn't necessary.

I cleared my throat to get her attention, not at all surprised when she raised her eyes slowly and set her phone purposely down on the desk to address me.

"Can I help you?"

With a tight smile, I debated whether I should play the bitch boss part or tamp down my instant flare. I tried not to judge people. Even though she had been on her phone, the office was clean with everything in its place. There could simply not be enough business to keep this role busy.

"I'm Regan De Luca."

Surprise lit her eyes as she leapt to her feet, the chair spinning out from under her and banging against the wall behind her. "Miss De Luca! It's so nice to meet you! Is there anything that I can get for you? Anything you need?"

"No. I don't expect you to be a gopher," I said, looking around and spotting an office in the corner next to the waiting area. "Is there somewhere I can use as an office?"

"Of course. That's the only office we have, but it's not being used anymore."

"How long have you been working here . . . I'm sorry, what's your name?"

"Oh, good gracious, I'm so sorry! Melanie. Melanie Miller. I've only been here for a month. The last manager hired me just before he went to lunch one day and never came back."

"I'd like to meet with you sometime this week to review your duties in the office." The poor girl looked alarmed. "I may want to add some duties so you don't feel the need to be on your phone all day."

"I was just—"

I stopped her by holding up my hand. "Relax. I merely want to make sure that you have enough to do. I don't expect you to be productive a straight eight hours a day. I'm not."

She smiled at me, and I suddenly felt sorry for her. I had been in her shoes at one time. I remembered what it was like   to be intimidated by upper management, owners, and CEOs. Although the desire to reassure her was strong, I waited to do so. I promised Mark that I would not dispatch any staff, but I didn't know whether they knew that.

The office, now mine, took up nearly the entire rear of the office building with a single glass door leading into the warehouse on the same side as the receptionist's desk opposite the office that I walked into. The office had dark brown and mahogany furniture. The massive desk was at the far wall with two tall bookcases on either side.

I set my oversized Coach bag on one of the two chairs in front of the desk and turned to look at the parking lot, the white side of the boat barn, and the lush green shrubbery. It was too bad that we couldn't have the office facing more towards the ocean. I longed for a view of the water, but trees and the boat barn hid it. There was a couch, longer than the one in the lobby, made of the same brown leather with another coffee table—void of any magazines this time—and two more leather chairs with a small table at the center.

I walked around to the large leather chair behind the desk and lowered myself with a longing to kick off my heels. There was an inbox at the corner of the desk filled with mail. I groaned.

Somewhere in that pile of information was a sexual harassment issue that I had yet to deal with, and I had a feeling that the issue might involve the young receptionist.

I set up my laptop before sifting through the pile of invoices, receipts, and mail before I finally came across the manila file marked 'confidential' in bold letters. Leaning back, I flipped it open and scanned through the report. It shouldn't have surprised me that such a thing would happen. I knew from looking at everything about the boatyard from top to bottom, including every single person who worked here, that Melanie was the only woman. My blood boiled.

An hour later, I pressed the intercom button to summon Miss Miller in. I had already removed my jacket, and it wasn't even close to lunchtime yet. A moment later, Melanie opened the door.

"You wanted to see me?"

All sweet and cheerful, naturally innocent. I told her to come in and have a seat in front of the desk and she did so, but not without giving me a nervous smile. No doubt she knew what this was regarding.

"It's my understanding that you are involved in a case of workplace sexual harassment." I laid the folder flat on the desk and clasped my hands together, resting them on the folder. "I don't condone harassment of any kind. I would like to ask you some questions about the incident first."

I watched her cheeks flame with color, and she nodded.

My eyes stayed on her, and I hoped my eyes were sympathetic to her. "This happened two weeks ago?"

She nodded.

"After hours?"

Another nod. "I was here later than usual." She visibly swallowed. "I was behind in getting payroll entered."

"And this is when he touched you inappropriately?"

"He pinned me against the desk here. And kissed me. And touched me."

I stood up, moving toward the window to look outside. This was a tough situation, with very limited options. There was nothing I could do since the manager, who is the accused, had walked out shortly after the incident. It made me wonder if that's why he walked out. This report hadn't come from this office, it had come from Mark's office.

"Thank you for answering my questions, Melanie. I understand how difficult it must be. The manager hasn't been back since he walked out?"

I returned to the desk while Melanie slowly stood up. "No. I'm not in trouble?"

This baffled me. "Why would you be in trouble? He attacked you, right?"

"If you talk to him, he'll deny it. He'll tell you I made it up."

"I'm not even sure I can find him. But if I do, I'll deal with him. Is that what you want me to do?"

"I don't think he's on the island. I haven't seen him since."

I had to remind myself to keep quiet before something slipped out. That would mean trouble for me as the owner. Pop's way of dealing with things was coming out of me. If what she said was the truth, I could pummel him myself.

"I don't doubt it," I said. "If I found him, what do you want me to do? He's not an employee here, but that doesn't mean you can't press charges. I can help you do that if you want me to."

Her face lit up. "You would do that?"

"Are you telling the truth?"

"Yes. I wouldn't lie about this. He's already not here anymore."

"If you're telling me the truth, and he really did this to you, then I would absolutely help you do whatever you need to do to make sure he stays away from you for good."

She smiled, her lips curving into the first confident look on her face I had seen since meeting her. "Thank you, Miss De Luca."

"It's Regan. Please. Now, I would like to have lunch at some point today. Would you like to have lunch with me?"

"I would love to have lunch with you!"

"Great. Why don't you order something for us? Put it on the company account. I am the least picky person you'll ever meet. Just don't order me any fish."

Melanie left the office, and I realized she had a bounce in her step that had not been there before. It made me happy, knowing I might have given her the confidence that she needed to get somewhere in life, other than to be a receptionist. I didn't know her, but I would help her. Woman to woman.

My eyes drifted to the windows in time to see Cameron striding across the lawn, pulling on a white t-shirt while he walked. What a devil, I thought. And why the hell was he here?

Damning myself for being such a girl about it, I couldn't help but admire his long, tanned legs below a pair of tan-colored cargo shorts. The muscles in his torso and arms rippled with the movements to get his shirt on before reaching the office building. I wasn't sure why he didn't just use the adjoining door between the boat barn and the office.

His hair was wind-blown when he walked into my office a moment later. He stopped just inside my door, staring at me and shaking his head with a grin. He probably had young girls falling at his feet daily. The trouble was, I liked him a great deal already, and I didn't even know him.

I crossed to the door, looking at Melanie. Her mouth had fallen open, and a blush had crossed high on her cheeks at the sight of Cameron. The feeling was mutual. I just hid mine better. I winked at her. "Did you order lunch?"

After seeing a nod of her understanding with widened eyes, I closed the door firmly and motioned for him to have a seat while I perched on the corner of the desk. Dear Lord, he was a handsome man. He was still smiling.

"What are you doing here, Cameron?"

He sat down in the chair, but propped his feet up on the desk next to me as though he owed the place, not me. "I might ask you the same thing."

"I'm the owner of this boatyard."

"You clean up nice, Miz De Luca," he drawled. "I like it."

I raised my hand to my hair, still swept up and secured by a clip. I supposed I looked serious in my black suit skirt with a sleeveless white top. Legs bare and in high heels. I caught him staring at my legs.

I stood up, sliding into the chair behind the desk before I could do or say something that I would later regret. My nerves tightened. He was looking at me with piercing blue eyes. It was like he was devouring me, making the situation more difficult.

"You lied to me," he said.

"Not telling you something is not the same as lying."

"You said you were a strategic consultant."

"And you said you were an entrepreneur."

"I am. I also said I said I do a little of everything." He folded his arms in front of his chest, making his biceps threaten to split his shirt sleeves. "I help with supplies."

"I didn't lie. I literally just bought it two days ago. It was a spur-of-the-moment decision while I was consulting for Mark." I shrugged. "I just didn't want you to think I was here permanently."

"Just an inconvenience for us."

"There is no us," I ground out, then sucked in a deep breath.

There was that dimple again as his lips curved into a wide grin. "You think there isn't. I think there is. Why don't we find out?"

"Why don't we just wait to see what happens? If you aren't looking for a relationship, and I'm not looking for one, why rush? I'll be here for a while."

"Fine," he grumbled. "Are we finished?"

"Do you have something else to do?"

"We just got an order for a forty-five foot yacht. They're just getting started on it and they're down two people who left the island and decided not to come back. I need to get the supply order and get going on it."

I groaned. Being a business owner was a bitch. Short-staffed all the way around. This made me uneasy. I didn't want to lose this boatyard.

I smiled at him. "We're finished."

Cameron stood up, but rather than going to the door, he stepped around the desk right up to me and took my hand in his. He kissed my knuckles, his lips soft and barely there. "We're far from finished, Miz De Luca."

I tugged my hand out of his. With a quick laugh, he strode to the door, and with his hand on the door handle and a grin that was full of sin, he turned back to me.

"Regan?"

"Hmmm?"

"You look damn sexy in that skirt."

My eyes snapped up to meet his. He yanked open the door and strode out without another word. I watched him give Melanie a nod, who turned red in the face again and looked down. Damn, there went her confidence again.

"Lunch will be here in a half hour," she told me a minute later.

I looked up to see her in my doorway. "Great, I'm starving. What did you order?"

"There's a sandwich shop downtown that is to die for. I just ordered two Cuban sandwiches. They are so good."

I laughed. "Find something to do, Melanie. We'll review your position tomorrow and see if we can find you some other things to do so you aren't bored all day long."

Melanie went back to her desk, and I looked out the window to see Cameron's long legs eating up the distance between the office and the boat barn. It hadn't taken him long to remove his shirt. I wondered what he was supplying. I'd have to investigate the invoices. Having a little company while I was here wouldn't be so bad. Especially if I could spend it with a man like Cameron.

Chapter Five

The car ride had been long, the two men in the front seat saying nothing during the ride. I tried to watch everything that went by, trying to memorize what I saw so that when I got free, I could find my way back, but it was so long that I had a hard time remembering things.

We pulled up in front of a large house with a circular drive and I could hear the waves of the ocean. We were near the beach. That could be anywhere in California. I looked up at the house when the car stopped before the men took me out. It was a two-story mansion with tall windows on each side. I didn't get a good look at anything else before someone roughly pulled me out of the car.

I worried about Nicco while they dragged in me. I refused to cry out as the man's fingers dug into the tender area under my arm. It wasn't like Nicco to not pick me up and this worried me.

I looked around as we passed under a large archway, heading for what appeared to be a living room of sorts filled with statues and large vases. They propelled me up a staircase, the iron bars of the banister curving up and up to the second level. Soon, the iron bars were behind us and they led me down a hallway and threw me inside a bedroom.

I bit my lip, not crying out when my knee came down hard on the carpeted floor. I rolled just in time to see the door close, hearing the distinct click of the lock. I sat on the carpet for a moment, my knee pulled up while I tried to massage away the hurt.

The room was dimly lit with a large, canopied bed on the far wall. There was a window to the right, and I leapt up and hurried to seek a way out. I could see the ocean, and the beach, but little else. It was a long way down. There were rocks below that would probably break my bones if I tried to jump from the window. I didn't know where I was, and I didn't care. When I got out, I would find my way home.

I tried to open the window, but it wouldn't budge. I went to the window on the other side of the bed, this one facing a courtyard and a shimmering pool. Again, I tried to open it without success. Below was a slab of concrete, so jumping would not help me.

I sat on the floor at the end of the bed, pulling my knees up to rest my cheek on them. "Nicco . . ." I whispered. "Pops . . . someone . . . help me."

I would not cry. I didn't cry when the girls at school looked at me and whispered behind their hands, then laughed. I didn't cry when things would go missing from my school locker somehow. Nope, not going to cry.

I wasn't sure how long I sat there, but soon I heard scratching at the door. At least I think it was the door. I crawled over to the door, unsure of whether someone was on the other side of it trying to get my attention or maybe I was imagining it.

"Hello?" I asked. I felt silly if there was no one there.

"Hi," I heard. It was a boy's voice.

"Are you okay?"

"Yes."

"Are you scared?"

I lifted my chin. "No. I'll get out of here."

"My name's Jake."

"Where am I?"

"My house. I've been trying to sneak around to find out what's

going on, but I can't hear through my dad's office door. What's your name?"

"Regan."

"It's nice to meet you, Regan."

"Why would your dad want me?"

"If I had to guess, I would say he probably wants something from your family, so he took you as ransom. At least that's my theory. How old are you?"

"Twelve, almost thirteen. You?"

"Thirteen."

It was nice to have someone to talk to. I didn't even have anyone at school that I could talk to. Jake must be like me with a dad that did bad things. No one even bothered to talk to me. And here he was, talking to me like we could be friends. I was hopeful, and I smiled at the thought.

Tears prickled my eyes, surprising me. The memories surfacing had me wondering if I was working too hard. The next two days were so exhausting that I barely had time to think about Cameron, let alone my past. After I spent the day in the office, searching for the whereabouts of the runaway manager, and reviewing supply invoices, Isabel had all but begged me to help at the hotel again.

I would help her without hesitation, exhausted or not, which meant I barely grabbed something to eat before donning an apron and helping in the kitchens. I was a one-man band at this point with all the roles that I was filling of late. But I could because someone trained me to be anything anyone wanted me to be. Pops wanted me to know how to handle situations, as much as he wanted to shield me from danger. He wanted me to know how to handle different situations.

I laughed. I had even been an undercover stripper in Las Vegas for about a month trying to get close to one of Pops' "problems." And I had never felt as filthy as I felt after having played such a role. I vowed never to do that type of dancing ever again, and that was about the time I decided exactly what I was going to focus on in college. I distanced myself from any of Pops' errands after that.

I winced at that memory while I sat on a small incline facing the town square pavilion where a band had set up and was playing old songs from Lynyrd Skynyrd. People and children were everywhere. I munched on a bag of freshly roasted peanuts from a food truck that boasted circus foods, complete with a man dressed as a ringmaster.

Teenagers screamed delight on crazy carnival rides, while younger kids begged their parents for just one more dollar to win the bigger stuffed animals at the game booths.

Couples swung their way into dancing like they were once again twenty years old while strings of white sparkling lights   lit their way around the pavilion and trailed through trees leading to the beachfront. Onlookers that weren't interested in dancing, playing carnival games, or riding rides swilled beer while mingling with others.

I found a nice little space on the grass to relax after a tough week and thoroughly enjoyed the music and people-watching until I spotted Melanie, and she spotted me, waving her arms. I pushed myself up and bounded down to the pavilion. I had been perfectly happy watching people and keeping to myself, but it was nice to know someone. Isabel was stuck working. The life of a business owner.

"Hey, Melanie," I said, falling into step next to her while we walked toward the carnival. "Are you here alone?"

"No. I'm here with friends, but we lost each other. You should come and hang out with us. As soon as I find them! Are you alone?"

"I'm used to being alone, but yes. I'm here alone. I'll be heading home soon anyway, but I wanted to enjoy the music for a little while." I dodged basketballs being thrown haphazardly and bouncing off the stand instead of the hoops.

"Have you had any luck locating Kurt?"

Kurt was the manager who bailed. I had followed many leads

and called in some favors from some of Pops' connections with no luck. It was something I wanted to report to Melanie I had success with, to give her some sense of comfort, but I had nothing to give her.

"No. I spent most of yesterday following every lead I could. Apparently, he pulled up his roots in Georgetown, too. Either he doesn't want to be found, or he's running away from more than just this."

Her eyes got big. "He was a creep."

"I understand."

"You know who isn't a creep?" she asked, her voice raising an octave. "Cameron. Oh, he is so dreamy."

I wasn't sure what to respond to that. Melanie reminded me of Tatum about five years ago, when she was a lot more immature. That would be about right. Melanie was only twenty, according to her personnel file. I merely smiled.

"He would never look twice at me. And I would never talk to him."

Melanie continued to babble while we walked the length of the carnival. I could hear the blast of the ferry horn, looking out at the darkness of the water for a minute while Melanie's voice faded away.

"Regan? Are you okay?"

I looked back at her. "I'm fine. I think the last few days have caught up to me."

"I see my friends over there by the rides. Are you sure you don't want to come hang out with us for a little while? Have a few drinks?"

She was sweet. "Thanks, but no. I'm just going to wander home. I'll see you next week. Enjoy yourself this weekend and be safe."

With a wave, Melanie took off like a shot without looking back at me. I sounded like such a mom, telling her to be safe. Ugh, I was getting old without being old. I turned around, heading back toward the pavilion and the couples dancing. After nearly getting bowled over, trying to avoid those dancers, I got to the other side and spotted Cameron just as he spotted me.

His eyes locked with mine, and his stride turned toward me with determination. My stomach flipped in response. Amused, I waited and watched him cut through dancers on his way to me. It made me feel something that I had not felt for a very long time. Desire.

Until a pencil-thin blonde jumped into his path and placed her hands on his chest. For a moment, I just watched. He had stopped for the woman, and I didn't recognize her.

My eyes narrowed when the woman wound her arms around his neck and pressed herself against his body, attempting to move with him to the music. Whatever song they were playing was anything but a slow dance song. Standing by myself at the edge of the makeshift dance floor watching this display gave me a knot in my stomach. I did not want to get involved. I got up quickly and began moving toward the beach on my way home.

The further I walked, the more deserted the beach was. A few bonfires sprinkled the beach, but I wasn't interested in joining in any fun tonight. I only wanted to go home and sulk. Sulk about my exhaustion, sulk about my conundrum with Pops and my contracted marriage, and sulk about Cameron, even though it was innocent and likely not going anywhere other than friendly conversation. I ditched the last of my peanuts in a trash can, then pulled off my shoes to walk in the sand.

The sounds of the waves gently licking the shore helped to calm me down. I hadn't realized that it had been getting so late and I really hadn't realized how upset I was seeing Cameron with a woman. It could have been innocent. And it wasn't my business.

I shoved one hand in the pocket of my shorts while dangling my shoes from my fingers on my other hand, while I scolded myself for jumping to conclusions. He might have known her, but wasn't involved with her. It wasn't his fault that he was so sinfully attractive.

I took out my phone and dialed Jake's number.

"Regan?" he answered after the first ring. "Is everything okay?"

I laughed. "Everything's fine, Jake. Well, as good as it gets, right? I haven't talked to you for so long, I thought I would see what you were up to."

"I'm meeting some friends at a bar. What are you up to?"

I wanted him to know that I was taking a walk on the beach. It was tempting to tell him I was on the island, but I knew revealing too much information to too many people would be dangerous, even though I trusted him. I'd trusted him since I was twelve.

"Do you remember all those times Pops would threaten to marry me off to someone who would take over for him someday?"

Jake was silent for a minute. "Tell me he isn't doing that to you. He can't do that to you. You're a grown woman, Regan."

"He's done waiting. He has someone picked out."

"Who?"

"I don't know, but he's serious this time, Jake."

"So, you're just going to do it?" He was angry. "You're just going to let him dictate your future like that? This is your future, Regan."

Telling him maybe wasn't the right choice. I didn't realize he would be so angry about it. We formed a bond years ago that we never broke, despite Pop's interference. He had been right to threaten it. I wouldn't let anything happen to Jake, and I wouldn't tell Jake about the threat Pops made to him.

"It's not a done deal yet. I just wanted to hear your voice. I miss you."

"I miss you. Keep in touch, okay?"

"Okay," I whispered, waiting for the click on the other end before pulling the phone away from my ear and tucking it back into my pocket.

My thoughts returned to Cameron. I wondered what he would think about this situation I was in. I was so absorbed with my thoughts of Cameron that I didn't hear the man sidle up behind me until I saw the blade of his knife come around, stopping me in my tracks. Cameron's warning rang in my ears about dangerous men on the island this weekend. That stretch of the beach was dark and otherwise uninhabited, leaving me alone and vulnerable.

"Give me your money," he said, his sour breath against my neck. "All of it."

Slowly, I reached into the pocket of my shorts and pulled out my cash. I held it out to him, and he grabbed it quickly. He ordered me to stay where I was while he counted it, swearing when he found it wasn't that much.

"This all you got?"

"Yes," I whispered.

"Where're you goin'?"

Oh no, I thought. This outcome was the furthest from my expectations, and it was the same thing Cameron had cautioned me about. I should have realized it was a bad idea to be walking unaccompanied in the dark on the beach.

"Where are you going?" he repeated, the knife flashing again.

"I'm going home, but . . ."

He pushed me, and I stumbled. "Let's go. I know you have more money at your house. Rich bitches on this island. If you don't have cash, you have jewelry. And don't think about trying to trick me."

The crunch of bone connecting with bone reverberated in my ear, and I stumbled away from the guy and, thankfully, the knife. When I turned, I saw Cameron nail him in the face with another punch, bloodying my assailant's nose and making him fall to the sand. He scrambled to his knees and stopped. My eyes widened when Cameron pulled a gun from the waistband of his jeans, leveling it at the guy.

I wondered why he was carrying a gun. Lots of people carried guns, I knew that. Pops had been all over me when I turned twenty-one to get my concealed carry permit, which I did, but rarely did I carry a handgun with me when I was out. I felt weird to have a firearm I had no desire to fire. It was bad enough I had killed before with one. Then I began traveling and couldn't bring one with me during those times. To appease him, I carried one when I was home in California. To have one on an island that didn't have much crime made me curious.

"Drop the fucking knife," Cameron growled.

I hardly knew him, but something in his voice, raw and merciless, made my skin dance with shivers. He meant business, and I knew why. He wasn't the type of man to allow anyone to get away from mugging someone, especially a woman walking alone. Had the guy not come up behind me with a knife, I might have been able to get away from him.

The knife landed in the sand, followed by the wad of cash he had taken. A whole thirty dollars. The man eyed me, keeping the heel of his hand to his bloodied nose.

Cameron didn't look at me. He kept his eyes trained on the guy, and his hand on the gun while he reached into his pocket and withdrew his cellphone. When he held it out to me, I quickly stepped toward him and grabbed it.

"Look up Sweetheart."

It would have been easy enough, but I looked back up at him. "Do you want to give me your code?'

"10142005."

Obviously, a birthday. Clearly, not his. Once I did as he asked, or ordered, I handed it back to him and he made the call. It impressed me. The gun never wavered or moved from the guy. He was at ease with holding it.

"We should call the sheriff," I suggested.

"Nope. I'm not letting scum like this walk free. Not on this island," he said.

"Aw, come on man," the guy said. "I'm sorry. I won't do it again, I swear. I just need some cash quick."

Cameron kicked him on the leg, but the guy was still kneeling upright, although I noticed his nose was not bleeding as much now.

"Sweetheart, it's Cam. Can you come down to the beach, close to town? Got a guy who tried mugging a woman, and looks to be trying to walk her somewhere. Presumably to her house."

I waited patiently for Cameron to conclude his call, not sure if I should stay to make sure he didn't shoot the guy. His hand seemed steady, his eyes never straying from him as though he had done this before.

"Are you okay?" Cameron asked, not looking at me.

"I'm a little shaken up, but otherwise, I'm fine."

"Mike will be here in a few minutes."

"Sweetheart?"

"Nickname. His girlfriend always calls him that. You'll see why when he gets down here. He's just up at the pavilion. Won't take him long." Cameron nudged the guy with his shoe. "What makes you think you can mug innocent young women?"

The set of his jaw told me he wasn't going to tell Cameron anything. Until Cameron kicked him hard enough to make him fall over this time. "I need the money, man! I wasn't going to hurt her."

"Need money for drugs? Gambling? What do you need it for?" Cameron moved to kick him again.

"Drugs! I need a fix. That's all."

"You will never come to this island for that again. If I see you on this island again, you won't be leaving the island alive. Got it?"

The guy nodded his head viciously just as I heard the hum of a golf cart nearing. Glancing around Cameron, I saw it approaching with three men riding it in and by the looks of it, none of them were small men. They looked like giants in the small, covered golf cart. Like clowns in a clown car, they stopped near us and piled out, the golf cart lifting off the ground a foot when they did.

I pressed my lips together as they approached. Cameron must have felt safe enough to take his eyes away from the guy on the ground when he leaned over to whisper something to one guy.

The guy looked at me and grinned. He had a shock of blond hair that was nearly white, with both ears pierced with small gauges, and when he stepped over to me, I saw that he also had a pierced eyebrow and nose. His hand, three times the size of mine, shot out toward me.

"Mike."

I slid my hand into his, and he shook my hand firmly. "Regan."

"That's Tim." He nodded to one guy with lighter blond hair and no piercings, but tattoos covering his bare arms. "And that's Bret, but we call him Brat." The other guy had brown hair, also with tattoos but not covering his arms.

All three of them had a powerful physique, with wide shoulders and thick legs beneath their shorts. I noticed Tim's tattoos on his legs, too. I watched in fascination as Mike hauled the guy up by the hood of his sweatshirt, half expecting his feet to dangle.

"I wasn't going to hurt her!" the guy cried out. "Please!"

Cameron sheathed his gun and walked over to me, the palm of his hands running over my bare arms before enfolding me into his arms. I hadn't realized that I was shaking until he did that. Danger was something I had faced before, but it had been a long time.

"I'm fine," I said, my voice muffled against his t-shirt.

"You aren't fine, you're shaking."

He released one arm to wave off the guys as they hauled my attacker away, keeping the other arm tucked around me for another minute. It was strange to be standing on the beach, the same beach I had frequented my entire life, in the arms of a man I had met only a few days ago after being mugged. It was just my luck; I suppose.

"You can let me go now," I said with a shaky laugh.

Cameron did, but he was staring at me. "I told you so."

Now, I laughed full on. "I should have listened to you. Please don't be mad that I didn't. I'm used to being on my own, doing my thing. You know."

He reached out, taking my hand in his. He gave it a tug. "Let's get you home."

"Those guys were interesting."

"They're the best. Nobody could find three friends more willing to help anyone. If I'm not here the next time, you should have their phone numbers. It's a good thing I saw you before I got stopped."

I bent down to retrieve my shoes, but Cameron was there and taking them from me. He switched them to his other hand, tangling the fingers of his free hand with mine, and pulled me gently to walk down the beach toward my house.

"Stopped?" I asked, pretending not to know what he was talking about.

"The blonde who stopped me at the pavilion. She's the sheriff's little sister."

"Did you grow up here?"

"No, but I've spent a lot of time here. I love this island." A warm feeling washed through me, and it wasn't from the weather. "But I have other responsibilities, so I return whenever I can."

The lights on my deck turned on automatically when I entered the security code to unlock the gate. Cameron opened the door and walked in with me. He latched the gate and set the alarm behind us.

I led him up to the deck, around the shimmering pool, and to the French patio doors. I flicked on the lights inside, walked into the kitchen and turned on enough lights to illuminate the house.

"Beer? Wine?" I asked.

"Wine would be great."

Cameron rested up against the counter and watched me take out a bottle of wine and two glasses. Pouring two half glasses, I handed him one and then leaned against the back counter, thankful for the space between us. The expression in his eyes unnerved me and I was afraid I would throw myself at him.

"Why didn't you wait for me?"

"Are you playing games with me?" I blurted.

He closed the distance between us, still watching me when he took a sip of his wine and then set it on the counter behind me. The scent of his cologne consumed me, infiltrating my senses and clouding my judgement. It was subtle, with just a hint of spice and the outdoors.

"She's not your type."

Gah! Why couldn't I just stop talking? It wasn't up to me to point out things like this. I didn't even know him! His eyes darkened. Then he grabbed my hand and pulled me closer to him, his wine quickly disregarded.

"What's my type?" he whispered, leaning closer to me. "You?"

I laughed, my voice shaking, while I looked away from him. "No."

His hand slid around my neck, molding his palm against the sensitive skin there while his thumb stroked the line of my jaw. I turned toward him to warn him off with more words when his mouth collided with mine.

Soft lips turned hard, more insistent, until I fell headfirst into the web of his silky-smooth charm. My hand, flattened against the hardness of his chest, found the beat of his heart. My body betrayed me, propelling me toward him and into the demand of his mouth on mine.

I groaned as his tongue swirled against mine. My heart raced, and he pulled me closer, even when there was no space left between us. The taste of him filled me. The crisp, tart wine on his lips and the heat radiating from his body ignited a fire in me. My legs grew weak.

His lips seared against my cheek, my earlobe, the underside of my jaw, before I found the sense to push him away.

"I'm sorry," I whispered, my voice hoarse. "I don't know what I'm doing."

The corner of his lips tilted up slightly when he looked down at me. "I do."

He was going to be my undoing. He relaxed his hold on me, one hand slipping down my side to tangle with mine. His blue eyes sparkled as he pressed my raised hand, studying our conjoined fingers. My breath caught in my throat. I liked it. I hated it. I wanted more of it.

"Look," I said, pulling my hand free. "I don't know you. You don't know me."

"But you will. And I will."

"Can I trust you?" I wanted to look away from him. I was not this person.

"I promise. You can trust me. I would never hurt you."

"I shouldn't ask this of you, but would you stay?" I didn't want to ask it. I didn't know him at all. But Pops knew him, and that made me feel a little better about asking. "I'm worried that the guy will know where I live. We weren't that far, and I don't know if he's seen me before."

"I'll stay." He smiled. He was still too close to me. "I'll sleep on your couch."

Something coiled within my body relaxed, easing the tension in my shoulders. "Thank you. And thank you for coming to my rescue tonight."

"It was entirely my pleasure. I'll lock up."

I smiled, slipping away, and walking across the living room to my bedroom. Once my bedroom door closed behind me, I leaned against it and pressed my hand against my chest. My heart hammered wildly beneath my hand, my head swimming with emotions.

"What the hell am I doing?" I asked myself, grabbing my pajamas and hurrying into them. At least they were modest. A pair of light cotton sleeping pants with a tank top.

My cell phone rang as I emerged from my bedroom with extra pillows and blankets. Quickly, I dumped them on the couch next to Cameron before grabbing my phone from the counter.

It was Gio.

"Is something wrong?"

"No, no. Nothing's wrong. Just checking in. Is this a bad time?"

Cameron brought the wine and our glasses from the kitchen and topped them off. His fingers were long and slender, and his hands were powerful, making me wonder if his hands were as talented as they were attractive. Heat rose to my cheeks, and I turned around to fan myself, trying to be inconspicuous about it.

"I actually just got home."

There was a pause. "With someone?"

I rolled my eyes, turning back to accept the glass of wine from Cameron before I sunk into the couch next to him. But not too close to him. I didn't trust myself that well. "Yes, if you must know."

I mouthed "my uncle" to Cameron, and he nodded but didn't make any move to leave. I didn't mind. I'm not going to say anything that could give insight into my problems.

"You shouldn't stop seeing anyone just because of this contract. You should have a little fun. Please be careful, though."

I laughed lightly. "I'll be careful."

Cameron's eyebrows shot up, but I waved my hand at him to ignore it. He could tease me later about not listening to him in the first place, as I'm sure he undoubtedly would.

"I'll call you in a couple of weeks," Gio promised. "Stay safe."

"Will do."

I ended the call and set my phone down on the table. I smiled at Cameron, suddenly feeling absurd about Gio's words of wisdom and what he wanted to say, but hadn't. Have fun, but you'll be married by this time next year.

"My uncle, Gio. Quite a character."

"Maybe someday I'll get to meet him."

I shrugged. "Maybe."

He reached over and put a hand on my knee. "You aren't seeing anyone, are you?"

I thought about that for a moment. "No, but I just ended a relationship."

"I can't tell you I'm sorry about that. Why did you end it?"

"It wasn't serious. At least for me." I looked at him, deep into his eyes. He deserved to know the person I was up front. "I didn't love him."

"How long were you with him?"

I had the urge to laugh. "Two years."

Cameron whistled. "That's a long time to be with someone you don't love. Friends with benefits?"

"No. It was casual. I think we both maybe wanted more, but it just didn't happen. Maybe we were waiting it out." I shrugged. "Are you seeing anyone?"

There was a beat where he weighed my words with a suggestive eyebrow tilt. "No. I haven't been in a relationship for a while. My last one was vicious." I wanted to hear more. He continued. "Cassandra. She was dark, thin, and incredibly vain. She cared more about her appearance than me. She wanted me by her side for eye candy, nothing more."

I sensed that there was more to his story than he was letting on, but I didn't prompt him for more. There was more to my story than what I was telling him. Fair was fair.

"I travel. More often than I'd like to. Eventually, I'll settle down, get married, and have kids. I just couldn't do that with her. She wasn't exactly motherly material."

It sounded like my situation. I wanted the same thing, but couldn't picture it with Michael. "You want kids?"

"Yes. My sister is sixteen. She'll be seventeen next month. The baby of the family and spoiled rotten. Despite the ten-year gap between us, she became my sidekick."

It clicked. "Your phone code," I murmured.

"Busted."

I sipped my wine, studying him. His lips were full, warm. I could still taste him.

"I don't have any siblings. Pops has a girlfriend with a daughter. She's like a step-sister, I suppose. But Pops never remarried after my mom died. It's like he dedicated himself to my mom."

He took my hand and squeezed it. "I'm sorry to hear about your mom. It made you a strong woman."

"Strong enough."

He pulled me closer, setting down his glass before slipping me into his arms again. He kissed me softly at first. I was still skittish and wouldn't let myself go with it. Instead, he had to test and tease me until my lips finally relented.

"I'd like nothing better than to carry you off, but it wouldn't be gentlemanly of me to do that. Not after tonight. Not like this."

"But it's getting late," I finished for him. "It *is* getting late, and you like your morning jog, or so I heard."

"I could use some company."

"You want me to go jogging with you?" It had been a while since I had been jogging or running. The idea was intriguing. "I suppose I can do that."

"I'll leave first thing in the morning to go home and grab some clothes."

"Are you sure you're okay with staying here tonight? There are two other bedrooms. You don't need to sleep on the couch."

He shook his head. "I'd rather stay on the couch, just in case."

"Just in case?"

"Just in case you want me to ravish you."

"I hardly know you."

"Which is why we're going running tomorrow, and you're going to agree to go out with me. I'll convince you sooner rather than later."

I put my hand against his cheek. "Thank you for tonight."

"Go to bed, Regan. I'll make sure you're safe."

I stood and went to my doorway, turning around just in time to see him take off his shirt to reveal hard, sculpted muscles under a sheen of flawless, tanned skin. Mentally shaking myself, I moistened my lips.

"Goodnight, Cameron."

"Goodnight, Regan. Sleep well."

Chapter Six

Did they not realize that I was just a kid? I had been here for two days. When the door to the bedroom opened, the large man with a small ponytail and thin mustache hauled me up, and I didn't try to bolt. He was not gentle.

"You don't have to pull," I snapped. I didn't care if it made him angrier.

"Mr. Mancini would like a word with you."

That was all that he said, steering me by my arm toward the open door. As we entered the hallway, I looked around. I wanted to catch sight of my friend who had been talking to me through the doorway. I had learned from Jake during my time in captivity that we were in Santa Barbara and that his dad ran in the same circles as Pops did.

Listening to conversations not intended for me at a young age, I had picked up fragments of Pops' business affairs, so this was likely not a good thing. Jake's dad had brought me here for a specific purpose, and I feared I wouldn't make it out until Pops gave him what he wanted.

As we neared the stairway, I dug in my heels. "I can walk myself. I won't try to run," I told the man, biting my lip against the lie. I wasn't sure that I wouldn't run if I had the chance.

It didn't slow the man down and he didn't give me any sign that he would allow me to walk myself. Instead, he continued to steer me down the curving staircase. I felt like a doll being dragged to play with a mean kid.

The living room was large, with a long couch and a few chairs directly in the center of a Mediterranean décor. There were doorways at each side of the back of the area and large, leafy plants that were stuck in huge vases. The ceiling was the height of the entire house, and there were tall windows to the left that went from floor to ceiling. I could see the ocean through those windows.

Jake had given me a lot of information. His dad would be angry if he knew what Jake had been telling me through the door. I didn't want to get Jake in any trouble, but neither did I want to stay here.

We stopped at the edge of the biggest rug I had ever seen, just short of the couch and chairs, and a man emerged from one of the two doors. He looked like Gomez Addams with slicked back dark hair, and beady dark eyes almost black. A long cigar was between his lips. I stepped back, but his henchman held me still, his fingers digging into my arm again. My eyes watered.

"Santino, she's just a little girl. Let her go," he said.

He stopped at the other end of the rug from me and pulled the cigar out of his mouth. He let go, and I quickly rubbed my arm to relieve the pain he had inflicted. I looked at this man, Jake's dad, and I hoped he could see that I was angry about this. If he was anything like Pops, he wouldn't care.

If he did, he gave no sign as he moved to sit in the chair and crossed his leg so his foot rested on his knee. He motioned for me to sit down, but I stood my ground and stayed where I was.

"Regan," he said, his voice sounding like a cat's purr. "Please, sit down so you and I can have a friendly chat. I mean you no harm, truly I don't."

I didn't trust him, but I stepped into the area and slid unceremoniously into the chair on the other side of the coffee table from him without taking my eyes off him. He was lying. He would hurt me if he needed to. I know Pops would hurt someone if he had to.

Santino moved to stand directly behind me, and as he did so, I could see the gun in the waistband of his pants. I looked back at Mr. Mancini, who was leaning forward to place his cigar in an ashtray on the table. When he leaned back, he laced his fingers together.

"Regan, you are in no danger here."

"Unless I try to get away?" I prompted.

"Right. My name is Ludovico Mancini."

I didn't want to hear it. "Let me go."

He gave me a half smile. "I cannot do that. You'll be with us for a little while."

"What do you want?"

He chuckled, and it gave me chills. It wasn't a friendly chuckle, but a sinister one. His dark eyes stared for what felt like several minutes until a slender woman appeared in the same doorway he had come from.

Not Morticia Addams, I thought. She wore a one-piece black swimming suit covered by a gold, sheer cover up that nearly reached the floor. In her long fingers was a cigarette. She gave me the creeps, too. I wondered if she was Jake's mom.

Ludovico glanced up at her, and she sat down on the arm of the chair beside him, crossing her long, slender legs. I watched while her other hand toyed with his hair at the nape of his neck. Gross. They were both gross. I wanted to go back to my room. I didn't want to have any conversations with these people.

"Your father has something of mine," he finally answered.

"So?"

"When I get what I want, he'll get you back."

"Bullshit," I spat. "I don't mean anything to him."

"You do, Regan. He will do anything for you. And he'll give me what I want."

"And that is?"

His eyes were sharp as they met mine, as though I had no business asking. But he had taken me away from my life, hidden me away where no one could find me, and locked me in a room. I deserved to know what I was being bargained for.

"You're just a little girl. These are things you won't understand."

I stuck out my chin, defiant. "I understand more than you think. You took me. I deserve to know what you took me in exchange for."

"Very well. Your father made an agreement with a man with a vast supply of land in Columbia. I want a part in that deal. He cut me out many years ago, and I've never forgiven him for that. He can still make up for it if he lets me in on this."

Pops would never do it. He was the smartest man I knew, aside from Uncle Gio. If he cut out Ludovico Mancini from any deals, there was a reason. I hated grown-ups right now.

Ludovico leaned forward to retrieve his cigar from the ashtray and when he leaned back, he motioned to Santino. Santino hauled me up by the arm and dragged back to the staircase. This was getting tiring, having to be pulled and pushed everywhere when I could walk on my own. When I twisted and tried to pull away, his hand only tightened.

"You're hurting me," I ground out, but he only ignored me and pulled me up the stairs.

I looked back down at Ludovico, who was already in a conversation with the woman. Being a pawn in this game was irritating. The need to find a way out was stronger now than it had been before. Pops needed to be warned.

If I could get my arm away from my guard, I could throw myself down the stairway, hopefully not getting hurt. Then I could try to get to the front door. Not knowing what was outside was risky, but I had to at least try. As much as I tried to pull my arm out of his grasp, he was not relenting.

I eyed the gun at his waist. Dare I try to get his gun? What would I do with it? Shoot him? It scared me, even though I tried to be brave. They had no right to take me and keep me. So yes. I resolved to get his gun and shoot him, except we were already almost to the room and he had the door open even as I tried to swing my other arm toward his waist. He threw me roughly into the room and slammed the door behind me.

I shook in fury, pushing myself up from the floor and clenching my fists at my sides. He wasn't going to get the best of me. The next time he came in to get me, I would stop at nothing to grab that gun. Then he would be sorry.

I felt heavy, like I was under water. Something was around me, so I could hardly move. Had Santino come back for me? Had he killed me instead? I struggled.

"Regan, wake up."

I opened my eyes to a different place. I sat up, heedless of the blankets twisted around my legs, pressing my palms to my eyes. I wasn't twelve. I was in bed. I raised my eyes to stare into pale blue eyes. Cameron had his powerful arms around me, immediately loosening now that I was awake.

His fingers brushed against my jaw, cradling my face in his hand. He sat next to me; his other arm curled around my waist while I shook out my dream. I was in my bedroom in Cape Haven. Cameron Moretti was on my bed. And I was sweating.

Moving away from him, I kicked off the blankets and headed toward the door in my bedroom that opened onto the deck. I opened it, allowing a gust of cool air in, which helped to bring down my body temperature before I looked back to Cameron.

He watched me, reclining on my bed with no shirt on. It only figured he would look so delicious. The smoothness of his skin beckoned me to reach out and touch him. I wanted to taste him. I wanted to feel him. The temperature of my body spiked, and I thought, just for a moment, that it would be nice to run and jump into the pool.

I moved back toward him, picking up a stray hair tie and

wrapping my hair up to clear my neck to the slight breeze that washed in from the doors. He was still watching me, making no move to get me back into bed and not saying anything. It was unnerving me, but I sat back down next to him, dangling my leg over the side of the bed.

Finally, I broke the silence. "What happened?"

"You were talking in your sleep. When I came in, you were shaking." He ran his finger along the skin on my arm, trailing it down toward my wrist absently, as though already familiar with my body. "Are you okay?"

I nodded. "I think so."

"Was it a nightmare?"

I wasn't sure it was a nightmare. It was more like a memory. A memory that I had buried deep while I was growing up. It occurred to me I was having these memories resurface because Pops was unreachable and I had the uncanny sensation that Ludovico Mancini had something to do with this.

I looked at Cameron. I could not tell him any of this without having to tell him the entire sordid story of my life and what a dangerous predicament I was in. I didn't know any more than what Pops and Gio had told me, and that was very little.

"It's hard to explain."

His hand left my arm to curl around my knee. "Do you want to tell me about it?"

A shaky laugh escaped. "Not if I want you to stick around."

I watched a grin curve his lips. Damn him. "You *want* me to stick around? Does that mean you'll let me take you out on a date?"

Even in the dark, I could see his eyes sparkle. It was a mystery why he would want to take me out. I was weird. I didn't know where my place in this world was yet, having been so wrapped up in my career. I had a house in Malibu, but that didn't mean I wanted to stay there. I bought it as soon as I could afford to move out of the De Luca family home.

Removing his hand from my knee, he captured my hand and threaded his fingers through mine. He could sense my hesitation, stopping himself from whatever he was about to do next. I had a feeling he was about to lean over and kiss me.

"Say yes," he whispered.

"It isn't a good idea."

"I get what I want, Regan. I'll keep asking until you say yes. But I promise you to be on my best behavior. It's a date. What can it hurt?"

I shook my head. "I can't. My life is such a mess right now. Getting into a relationship would be a mistake."

"I didn't say anything about a relationship. It's just dinner. Maybe a little dancing. I wouldn't even try to seduce you. I won't even try to kiss you."

"I'll think about it." He looked crushed. I put my hand on his jaw. "Okay?"

"It's better than a no," he said, putting his hand over mine. "Do you want breakfast? I can make a mean omelet if you have the stuff for it."

I turned to glance at the clock on my nightstand. It was nearly sunrise, and an omelet sounded delicious. Protein would be good before a pleasant run on the beach with him. I was already sweaty. Maybe a run was just what I needed to sweat out the toxic memories.

"I have some eggs and some spinach. Maybe a couple of peppers."

As soon as Cameron stood up quickly from the bed and went for the door, my hand fell to the mattress. He turned around to look at me and opened his mouth, but didn't say anything.

I squeezed my eyes to shut out Jake's thirteen-year-old voice from my head. *"I won't let anything happen to you."*

Jake had promised not to let anything happen to me. But it had. And it wasn't his fault. He had done everything he could. I slid off the bed, following Cameron out of the room in time to see him switching on the kitchen light over the sink to start breakfast without flooding the entire house with brightness.

While Cameron rummaged through the refrigerator, I tasked myself with making some coffee. One cup couldn't hurt, and Cameron said he would take one, too. A smoothie from the smoothie shop near my house in Malibu would be better, I thought. I really hoped that Cameron's ability to make a mean omelet was true.

Once I had a pot of coffee set to brew, I slipped into a high-backed chair on the opposite side of the kitchen counter and resigned myself to watching him whip up some eggs and veggies. I admired how deftly he cut the vegetables, staring at his hands. Strong hands that had made me feel more secure than I had felt in my life only moments ago. Even in the silence that had settled between us, I was in big trouble.

∞

There was nothing like the rush of adrenaline when I was dancing. It didn't matter if I was dancing solo or with a partner, so long as I was moving in time with the music. Fast, slow, or meticulously calculated, my body sang. It was like working out or training, except I was in control of my movements and didn't have someone telling me how to move.

Having escaped the monotony of the office earlier, I was doing my best at pouring my soul into my own choreographed routine at the newly remodeled health club just a few blocks inland from the town. Spinning around, I noticed Cameron step into the dance studio, but I continued moving until I bent into a deep knee bend and stopped.

It had been a few days since I had gone jogging in the morning with him after he had stayed the night on my couch. There had been very few words shared between us as we ran the length of the beach from my house to his house and back. Isabel had not been kidding when she had described his house as huge. We stopped to catch our breath, and he pointed at his house. Surrounded by gigantic, lush trees that had to be hundreds of years old and a tall iron fence, the house was barely visible from the beach.

It was a delightful surprise to learn he had his own boat. The Catalina yacht bobbed next to the dock out across the beach from his house. He had a lot of unexpected tricks up his sleeve. It made me wonder what I would learn about him next.

His gaze was on me. He didn't clap, but he was watching my every move while I retrieved my bottle of water and towel from the table. I put an end to the music, leaving us in silence except for my labored breathing.

"I'm surprised to find you here," he said.

"I like to dance, and I thought I'd check out the new studio here."

"Why haven't I seen you around?"

I ignored his question. It was unnerving to know that he was paying attention. "Aren't you supposed to be working on a supply order?"

"I went in early because of the rain. The rest of the supplies should be here next week." He leaned his hip against the door frame and crossed his arms in front of him. "You're a wonderful dancer."

"Thank you."

"Why aren't you making a career of that instead of consulting?"

I shrugged. There were more reasons than I cared to admit. Dancing came easily to me. I liked the challenge of consulting. It was part of the reason I bought the boatyard. It would be something I couldn't fail at. "I guess I don't like it when someone tells me what and how to dance."

"Buy your own dance studio. No one can tell you how to dance."

I mopped my face with the towel and drank more water while considering it. "I live in California. I'm not sure where I want to put down my roots yet."

It was nice to know that he was interested in my future, even though he wouldn't be staying in it. I grew warmer when he stepped closer. He was wearing a muscle shirt, and though he wasn't sweating, the skin on his biceps looked smooth as usual. I wanted to run my palms up and over them just to feel his skin with my hands.

"Go out with me."

"No."

"Dinner."

"Nice try."

"Dancing."

I dropped my towel, leveling a glare at him. "No fair. I told you I would think about it, but you know I can't go out with you."

"You told me you weren't seeing anyone. You're single. I'm single. We both eat. And I can dance."

"Technically, aren't you in my employ, Mr. Moretti?"

"Cameron, and I quit."

Laughter burst forth from my throat. "That's crazy!"

"Technically, I'm not in your employ. I'm a supplier. But I'll stop going to the boatyard this instant and never return."

He wasn't going to let me continue to deny, and I was skirting around the inevitable. Grabbing my hand, he pulled me closer. He was warm. Or maybe that was me.

"Say yes."

He tugged me closer. Sweat trickled down my back.

"I lay awake and think about you at night. You're smart. You're sexy. Your smile stays with me when I'm not with you. Say yes.

Please."

My heart tugged. The look in his eyes told me that the truth had spilled free. If he spoke the truth, I was a goner. The same was happening to me. When I wasn't with him, I felt something was missing. For this reason, I had tried to keep him at bay. If I was feeling it now, the feeling would end in heartache for me. I knew it would.

"I'll go out with you."

He grinned. "Friday. Dinner."

"Whatever this is, may not be more than either of us thinks it will be."

"Maybe it will be." Jesus, he was assertive.

"I'm not expecting anything from you."

"Maybe you should."

"It's not that easy."

"It never is. Above all else, I respect you. I'd never push you into something that you truly don't want." He gave a little more. "Other than this date, of course."

"I want you, Cameron."

He took a surprised step back, and I couldn't believe I'd been so blatant. "I don't know what to say to that. Maybe we should skip the date and go right into-"

"I want to go out with you. To dinner." I groaned. "I'm confused right now."

He pulled me against him with a shush. "Let's see where it goes. No promises."

I nodded.

"Six o'clock on Friday."

When he released me, I felt suddenly cold. I would go out with him. I would forget my impending nuptials and see what happened. When I returned home to California, I would forget him and move on. I fervently hoped that it would turn out that way. I couldn't remember ever feeling this way about anyone in my life. And that was enough to scare me.

"Do you want me to walk you out?" he asked.

"Sure."

Swooping down, I grabbed my gym bag, and we walked out of the dance room together. He didn't make any kind of move to put his arm around me or make any macho claim on me in front of any other men in the club, working out in the open weight area in the middle of the walking track.

"What are you doing later?"

"Cool it," I laughed. "I already said I'd go out with you."

He laughed, too, holding up his hands in surrender. "I was just curious."

"I have some friends coming in." I glanced at my watch. "They should be here within the hour. I need to go meet them. They've never been here before, so I said I would meet them in town."

The look that came over his face made me worried. It was a cross between anxious and dread. Tatum and Jazz being here wouldn't affect our planned date. I hoped he would know that.

"I'll see you Friday, if not before."

We stopped at my car, and he gave me a small wave before heading to his own car. The urge to watch him pulled me, and I stood with my car door open and the open-door ding sounding annoyingly, watching him stride away. I didn't know if I was lucky, or asking for trouble with this. Soon, I would find out.

An hour later, I stepped out of my rented BMW in front of the coffee shop on Main Street, between the Italian bistro and the hotel. A shriek immediately assaulted me as Tatum rushed at me with arms wide and blonde curly hair blowing in the breeze. That she had it pinned up did little good. Hair still escaped every which way. Jazz, who was more reserved than Tatum and had short, dark hair, followed her.

I was so happy to see them, and we all came together in a hug. We fit together perfectly, me and my two best friends. I was so excited that they had come, despite the trepidation that I was supposed to keep my whereabouts unknown. There was no reason to mistrust either of them.

Jazz, a fashion designer, was due in London for fashion week and had pulled strings to have her associates cover for her while she managed a quick getaway. And it would be quick because Milan's fashion week was right after London.

Tatum was the first one to pull away and get a good look at me. She gasped. "There's a man. You met a man!"

I stepped back in surprise at how she could know that. True, we had been friends for over ten years when she had transferred to my school and didn't know any better than to stay away from me. As complete opposites, she and I had hit it off. When she started hearing the rumblings about me, she ignored them. In fact, she put up a fight for me toward others. I was never sure how she had done it, but Tatum had pulled me into a group of friends. People I had known for years, that whispered about me. Once Tate was a part of the group, they were asking me questions and getting to know me as a person. And they liked me.

Tatum moved into my condo on the beach only about a year ago when she secured a job as a salon associate in Thousand Oaks. She had begged and pleaded, knowing she could not pay me a fraction of what I was paying on the mortgage. Having someone there to watch the place while I was away was enough for me to have her move in. In the end, it helped us both out.

"How could you possibly know that, Tate?" I scowled.

She gave me a dazzling smile. "There it is. The sparkle in your eyes. You can't hide anything from me, Reggie. Jazz, look at her. She is positively glowing."

"She's right. You might as well spill it."

Jazz was the total opposite of Tatum. She exhibited reserve, stubbornness, and high intelligence. We met in college in business classes. I liked her immediately because she kept to herself, much like I did. When we began studying together, having multiple classes together, we found we accomplished a lot by not talking. After, we would go get coffee and talk.

I opened my mouth to provide a scathing retort, but even Jazz knew me better than I probably knew myself. We were the unlikeliest bunch of friends there was with Tatum being a social butterfly and obnoxious to boot, Jazz was strait-laced. I was a little in between both. I could be a social butterfly when I wanted to be.

"Does he know that you're seeing someone?" Tatum whispered, linking her arm with mine while we walked into the coffee shop to grab some coffee.

I shot her a look, but she gave me a dazzling smile. I hadn't mentioned to either of them about my breakup with Michael, or the fact I was getting married to a man I didn't know in six months. Getting married was a big thing to keep to myself, one I didn't want to have out. I would tell them soon enough.

Moments later, we settled around a table in front of the coffee shop. Well, I had coffee. Tatum had ordered some type of latte that had about five uncommon requests in the order, and Jazz had a simple chai latte.

"This place is beautiful," Jazz said, leaning back in her wrought-iron chair to look at the ocean with the sun shimmering on the surface like a sea of sparkling gems. "I could get used to this."

Neither of them had been to the family house in Cape Haven. While I had made time to visit now and again, the visits weren't usually lengthy enough. I just hadn't made it back here for a while. I'd been busy.

"I bought a boatyard," I mentioned, as though it was a small thing.

Tatum squealed again, her voice so high-pitched that Jazz and I winced at the same time. "Shut up! You're buying businesses now? Like your dad?"

That was all Tatum knew. Pops owned businesses, and he was wealthy. Neither of them knew about his shady dealings, although I couldn't imagine they didn't hear rumors about him. Neither of them had ever asked me about if Pops ever did anything illegal. Despite this, they knew Pops had constantly threatened me with finding someone to marry me. Being an only child, he had to protect his legacy.

I shook my head. "I bought it for me."

"Why?" Jazz bluntly asked.

"Because I love this island, and after you spend a couple days here, you'll leave here loving it, too." I set my white paper coffee cup down and reached out to grab their hands. "And you are both welcome back. Even if I'm not here."

Tatum gave me a sideway glance. She knew something was going on, knew me well enough to know the signs I was giving. For once, she was waiting for me to spill it instead of rushing at me with it. Except I didn't know how to tell them this.

"Just say it," she whispered. "Something's wrong."

I pulled back, leaning back into my chair and forgetting about my coffee. "I broke it off with Michael. Just after I got here."

Jazz was watching me. I couldn't tell by her reaction if she was judging me or trying to figure out what I was up to. That was the reserve in her. She was waiting for me to be out with the rest of it.

"That explains a new man."

Damn it, Tate. I shot her a warning look, and she held up her hands as though she were promising to keep her mouth closed for now. Folding her arms over her chest, she stuck out her bottom lip in a pout.

"I don't have a new man," I insisted. "I have a date on Friday, but it's not like that. I can't get into another relationship."

There was an enormous lump in my throat. I couldn't get past it to get the words out. They would understand once I said it, but until I could get it out, they would remain clueless. They were giving me no reprieve with their looks.

"Do you remember how Pops always threatened me? To find someone suitable to marry me?"

Tatum's hand came down on the table in a slap that bounced

my coffee cup, nearly tipping it over until I grabbed it. "No. No, no, no. He didn't. He wouldn't."

Tatum kept mumbling, a telltale sign she was upset. I looked at Jazz, who stared back at me. She either didn't believe it, or she didn't believe I would do it. Instead, she shook her head.

"You aren't seriously going to do it, are you?"

I couldn't tell her the truth. Not without giving away what a jackass Pops was. He threatened my career, then he threatened Jake. He was the only one who knew about my relationship with Jake. Tatum and Jazz didn't know who Jake was. They wouldn't believe me if I told them I would do it. As friends, they would know me better than to believe I would bow down to this.

"Please, don't say anything to anyone," I whispered. "I'm going to enjoy myself while I'm here, and hope that this wedding doesn't come to fruition. And please, don't tell anyone where I am."

Never in my life had I seen Jazz look worried, but her eyes had glazed over. "Let me get this straight, because I'm thoroughly confused, Reggie. You broke up with Michael to come to an island. You don't want anyone to know where you are. You're engaged to marry someone your dad picked out for you, God knows why, but you're going out with someone else on Friday. Oh, and you bought a boatyard. Do you know how absurd this all sounds?"

It was absurd. "Try to keep up."

Then we all laughed. We laughed until our ribs ached from laughing so hard. It wouldn't last. Eventually I would need to face the facts, and they were exactly how Jazz had laid it out. I would attend my wedding in March. To someone.

Just the word *wedding* gave me chills. I didn't know anything about the wedding, the exact date, where it was going to be held, who was going to be there–including the groom. My career was at stake, as was Jake, so I had to resign myself to it. I could always divorce later.

"Do you want me to design your dress?" she asked.

"You're too busy, not that I don't appreciate the offer. Pops didn't tell me anything, including who I'm supposed to marry. It's bizarre."

"Could he be lying to you, Reggie?" Tatum asked.

It was always a possibility. I didn't know who I could trust anymore, other than these two right here. "He hasn't given me any reason not to trust what he said. He was serious this time."

Jazz sighed. "You're right. I'll be busy the rest of the year with my design team. But if you need me, Regan, I'd do whatever I can. We need to bring this guy—whomever he is—to his knees."

I nodded silently and sipped my coffee. After finding a gown, I would put the situation out of my head for as long as possible. I would focus on getting the boatyard back on track, have some fun on the island while I was here, and deal with the situation when I returned home, whenever that would be.

Chapter Seven

"He's here!"

I heard Tatum's voice call out even though I was deep within my walk-in closet rummaging through the clothes and shoes. I had always been cool, collected, and confident, and here I was struggling to find something to wear for a simple date. I rested my head against the door frame, willing myself to get it together.

Moments later, I could hear voices in the kitchen and quickly double checked my face in the mirror. Here and prompt. Cameron was serious. It unnerved me how serious he was, but I was getting inside my head. He could have been telling me the truth when he meant this didn't have to mean anything. We could just have fun.

I heard Tatum introduce herself as I turned out the lights in my bedroom and closed the door behind me. He was watching Jazz coming in from the deck in a shocking red bikini with a black sheer coverup, his eyes on her for a second before they swung in my direction. We looked into each other's eyes for a moment before he stepped back and slowly shifted his gaze from my legs to my eyes.

Am I overdressed? I thought. He wore a pair of black dress pants with a simple light blue shirt that brought out the color of his eyes. He watched me as I walked across the living room in my bare feet with my strappy black heels dangling loosely from my fingers. Out of the corner of my eye, I could see Jazz staring at him with an odd look on her face.

"Watch it," I said, teasing. "That's my date."

"I've seen you before," Jazz said, leaning over the back of a chair while sizing him up. She stuck out her hand. "Jazz Marshall."

With a wink, he grasped her hand with a powerful grip. "Fashion designer." She raised her brows in surprise. She wasn't the only one surprised he knew her. "I've been to quite a few fashion weeks, some in New York and some in Paris."

I waited with bated breath for Jazz to bombard him with questions. Instead, she laughed and withdrew her hand. "That would be me. And that's where I've seen you."

"Not for a while. My last relationship with a model was a while ago. She merely wanted me for the eye candy. Or my money. And that stung a little."

They all laughed except for me. I felt as though I was missing something, then I realized he was joking. I leaned down to step into my heels before he stepped closer and put his arm around my waist, looking at me with admiration in his eyes.

"Am I overdressed?"

"No!" Tatum piped up.

Cameron smiled at me and leaned down to brush his lips softly against my cheek like a whisper of a breeze come and gone. "I made her a promise. I'll be on my best behavior, and I won't try to kiss her."

"Oh, Jazz and I sleep on the other side of the house. We wouldn't hear anything." Jazz jabbed her elbow into Tatum, eliciting a grunt. "What I was saying is that you're welcome to ravish her, Cameron. She needs a good ravishing."

"Tatum! Really!"

"Are you from here, Cameron?" Tatum asked, ignoring my gasp at her audacity.

"I grew up outside of Las Vegas. My family lives there. I travel a lot, but I get home from time to time. Not as often as I'd like to."

"Regan travels."

"One more thing we have in common. Except I don't intend to continue. I'd like to settle down soon. Have a family."

I could feel the heat rise to my face with guilt. The last thing I wanted to do was to lead him on. If he was going to settle down soon, I didn't want him to think it would be with me.

As though he sensed my hesitation, he gave my fingers a gentle squeeze. "Ladies, as much as I'd love to continue to get to know you, I'd like to feed my date at some point this evening. I hope to do this again soon."

"Have a good time!" Tatum crooned.

Cameron pulled me possessively toward the door, opening it for me to walk through and closing it behind us. I stopped just past the front door, causing him to bump into me and have another opportunity to put his hands on my waist.

"Is this your car?" I asked.

This was not the same car he had driven onto the ferry when I first saw him. This was a shining silver BMW Z4 sDrive 351is convertible parked behind Jazz's rental car in the driveway. I couldn't help but trail my fingertips along the front quarter panel in awe of such a machine.

I was excruciatingly aware of his eyes following me while I circled the car, my heels clicking on the driveway pavement with a hint of a smile on my lips. I would get to ride in this. I was excited about it, but tried not to seem like I was more excited to ride in this machine than anything else.

"It's beautiful."

I felt his breath on my neck as he whispered, "You're beautiful." He opened the door for me. "Regan, you look stunning."

I accepted his outstretched hand, helping me to slide into the soft leather of the passenger seat. The top was up; the night being a bit on the cool side. While he walked around to the driver's side, I took my time admiring the classy interior.

"Where are we going?"

"Myrtle Beach." He started the engine with a purr, backing the car around the driveway out onto the road a moment later. "We're going to a fabulous beach-side restaurant that has the best authentic Italian food this side of Italy. We'll dine by candlelight with wine, then we're going to a club up the coast so I can dance with you."

The way he said it sent shivers up my spine. I looked down to see if I had goosebumps on my arms. He was commanding and charming at the same time. I was looking forward to spending some time with him away from the island where people gossip.

"What makes you think I'll dance with you?"

"You won't be able to resist."

I turned to look out the window, watching the last of the quaint houses and trees disappear away before reaching town. I could feel him looking at me again, but said nothing as we drove through town to the ferry. The ferry ran several times a day but stopped operating at ten. I was nervous that we wouldn't make it in time, and we would need to spend the night in Myrtle Beach, but I said nothing.

Part of me wanted to. The other part was more scared now than I had been when I was seven and saw one of my Pops' soldiers cut a man's finger off in his office. I wasn't supposed to be there. When he heard my scream, Frank, his right-hand man, had immediately run to me. Without hesitating, he scooped me up into his arms and brought me back to my bedroom. Sitting down with me, he explained that what I had seen was a trick, and it wasn't real. I believed that. For a while.

The ferry was waiting when Cameron drove the car up onto the ramp and parked it on the deck. Only a few cars were on the ferry. Cameron got out of the car and went around to open my door and help me out. Silently, we went to the railing to watch the setting sun on the horizon.

It wasn't long before the ferry ramp lifted and we lurched into motion. Cameron slipped his arm around my waist, resting his chin on my bare shoulder. It was intimate. It made me close my eyes at the feelings that swirled deep within. It reminded me how I had never felt like this before, and I wasn't sure what was happening.

"Tell me more about you," I said.

"I will."

I chuckled. "But not tonight?"

"When the time is right."

I turned to face him, noting that while he moved his chin, his arms still encircled my waist. It felt good. I felt protected and wanted. I also knew that he was charming and had partners previously. I was familiar with the fact that he had gone out with models. I wasn't nearly as beautiful as a model. He was probably like this with every woman he was with. There was something about him that made him protective without trying to be. It was part of what attracted me to him.

"What are you going to do with the boatyard? Expand? Improve it?"

"I'm not sure yet. I hadn't gone in expecting to buy it."

"Why?"

"Because the opportunity presented itself, and I jumped on it. I'm still trying to work on the reason in my head. I think it's because I love the island. I've always loved it. It feels like home."

"I feel the same way. I find myself here a lot. Maybe you'll start finding yourself here more now."

I stared at him. "Please don't make this out to be more than it might be."

"Why are you trying so hard to make it complicated? Let's just enjoy the ride and figure out the rest later. It doesn't have to be complicated. We're both adults. I think we can handle ourselves."

I smiled. "I won't make any promises that I can't keep. If you do the same."

"Agreed."

That really settled my nerves. Until he pressed me gently

against the railing, his hand sliding around to the back of my neck while the other curled around to rest on my lower back, his lips colliding with mine. His mouth captured me in more ways than just a touch. The familiar warmth he induced spread throughout my body until I could feel it in my legs.

His mouth slanted against mine, insistent against my mouth, commanding and possessive like he was. My body responded to his. His heart was pounding faster, and I could feel it through my fingers, pressed against his muscular chest. This wasn't the time or the place and I was positive that people were looking at us, yet I couldn't bring myself to pull away from him. He was consuming me and I was letting him.

"You promised," I murmured into his mouth as soon as he eased his mouth from mine for a second. "You said you would be on your best behavior."

He tipped his head up and laughed. "I said that, didn't I? I'm sorry. I just don't know what happens to me when I'm around you. I just want to . . ."

I put my fingers to his lips. "If there is anything at all between us, it would be that. And I don't mind. There is no need to apologize for it."

"Oh, I'm not sorry about kissing you."

"Of course not," I said, wryly.

"You scare me, Regan."

"I scare you?"

"I can't get you out of my head when I'm not with you. And when I'm with you, I just want to look at you and touch you. I want you more than I've ever wanted anyone else, and I don't want anyone else to have you."

His candor surprised me. And it scared me more to hear it. If Cameron was truthful, and I think he was, we were in far deeper than either of us knew because I felt the same way. And I had never felt this way before, which made me even more scared. I couldn't let this get out of hand, knowing that I could never be his. He could never be mine. I couldn't share my life with him outside of the island. That scared me worse than my feelings.

"Let's just enjoy the ride. No promises," I reminded him.

He lowered his forehead to mine, his eyes still locked with mine.

It was about forty-five minutes later when we were back in his car, pulling up to the restaurant. It was a white beach house at the far southern end of the beach that looked like they had turned it into an Italian bistro. The valet opened the door for me, but Cameron motioned him away while he helped me out.

The foyer was dimly lit, and the host, in a formal tuxedo, gave them a curt bow. "Good evening, Mr. Moretti. It's good to see you again, sir."

Cameron's hand pressed against my lower back and we followed the host through the restaurant. Everyone was staring at us, including those that were dining. I could tell that people recognized Cameron. More than he was admitting to, but I would wait for him to explain it.

We stepped into a private room in the back of the restaurant that was filled with more tables covered in white linen tablecloths, but where no one was dining. Instead of taking one of the vacant tables, he led us out to an enclosed balcony overlooking the beach and ocean.

There was another enclosed balcony on the same side of the building, but it wasn't connected to our balcony. Cameron pulled out my chair, and I sat down, purposely with my back to the people watching us. It was making me feel weirded out. I wondered for the second time that night if I had overdressed, but I had seen some of the other diners, and they had dressed nicely.

I opened my menu while a server approached and poured us each a glass of wine. I could feel his eyes on me, and lowered my menu. "You aren't one of those men who are going to order for me, are you?"

"No. I always order the same thing, but I can recommend."

My smile was tight. "What kind of supplier are you?"

"What do you mean?"

"You own this restaurant, don't you?" I tapped my fingers absently on the table, setting down my menu, and wondered where to begin.

"Why would you think that?"

"You don't have the type of car I would expect a supplier of a boatyard would own. You also told me you're an entrepreneur."

"Who said I own the car?"

I laughed. "What are you afraid I'll find out?" I leaned back.

He grinned. "I own a vineyard in Italy."

"Don't change the subject, damn it." He chuckled at my frustration, but reached over the table to hold my hand. "Like you, I travel. I went to college in New York. New York University, a private school. After I got my Master's, I went to Italy and spent time there with my uncles."

"And you live in Las Vegas. With your family."

"The only place I 'live' is here. I don't have a house anywhere else. I spend most of my time on the island when I'm not traveling, but I get back to Vegas to see my family, or my sister, as often as I can."

"I went to Vegas once." And that was all I was going to tell him. There was no need to tell him what I was doing there. "It's an interesting town. You told me you have a sister. Do you have other siblings?"

"Two younger brothers. And Zoey."

"Does she stay out of trouble?"

He clenched his jaw. "She damn well better be, or she'll answer to me. You?"

"I'm the only," I said. "Pops never remarried after my mother died."

"Again, I'm sorry to hear about your mother."

My eyes drifted up to meet his. "Thank you. I never knew her. I was too young to remember her. I wish I did, though."

He rubbed the pad of his thumb over my hand as the server approached cautiously. A heavy sigh escaped from Cameron, and I couldn't help but to smile. He was going to have to tell me his flaws, eventually.

The server approached cautiously. "You would order, yes?"

"Regan?"

"Roasted chicken with a side salad, vinaigrette."

"And for you, sir? The usual?"

Cameron nodded. He bowed shortly, clicking his heels together before turning with a clap of his hands at the staff to get moving on their food preparation. I sipped my wine while he took the silence to study me in the candlelight.

"See something you like?"

"What are you doing to me?"

"Can't focus?" I asked. "Sleepless at night? Heart palpitations when I come near you?"

"Yes."

"I get the same way around you," I whispered. "Look, I like you, Cameron. I wasn't ready for you, or anything like this. I'm still not ready."

"But it happened."

"Yes, but I have plans. I can't promise that I'll be there in the morning." I closed my eyes briefly. "Just promise me you won't hold it against me."

He smiled. "I couldn't hold anything against you. Who knows, your plans may change and you may be there in the morning."

Conversation came so easily for us that even as we continued with our dinner, we chatted smoothly. He told me about Italy, and his two mischievous uncles that live there. When he described his sister, she sounded like someone I would want to meet. His younger brothers seemed like they were several years younger than he, and he wasn't close to either of them.

"I wasn't a good kid," he admitted, finally. "I was a rebel."

I wanted to laugh. We were all rebels when we were kids. I

wondered what he could have done as a kid to be rebellious. A tattoo somewhere, maybe? There were no piercings I had noticed.

By the time the server cleared away our dishes, most of the main dining room was empty. Even after learning about my life, Cameron still refused to bring me home until we had danced at least once. It was getting close to ten, but I kept my mouth closed.

A half hour later, I could hear the heavy beat of the music when we stepped from the car in front of the two-story club, also on the beach with a large balcony on the second level that overlooked the ocean.

"This is a club?"

Cameron tucked the keys into his pocket. "That's what I heard."

There was no mistaking that it was a club as soon as we stepped onto the crowded first floor. The size of the dance floor was twice the size of my private dance room at home. It had been several years since I had been to a dance club.

We passed a bar, pushing through people until I had my high-heel-clad feet on the shining wood of the dance floor. The disc jockey looked at Cameron and winked at him.

I laughed while I moved with the music. As crowded as it was, people moved away from us to give us space. Catching me around the waist, Cameron tried to catch up with my moves and I laughed, wrapping my arms around his neck. He nipped my lips.

"You wouldn't change your mind and spend the night in Myrtle Beach with me tonight, would you?"

"Maybe another time," I answered, knowing that we missed the ferry already.

He grinned. "A next time?"

"Oh absolutely. I love a man that can move with me. There aren't many who can."

Cameron stopped moving. His eyes were so intense I wondered what I'd said. I shook my head, willing him not to say anything that he would regret later.

"Let's get a drink," he said instead, sliding his hand down my arm to grab my hand and pull me away from the dance floor. People wasted no time filling the space while the disc jockey spun another song.

I glanced down at the slender watch on my wrist and Cameron caught me. "Missed the ferry, didn't we?" His smile held guilt.

"Guess so."

He raised his brows. "You would spend the night with me?"

"Do I have a choice? We missed the ferry."

Tapping his card on the bar top while we waited for the bartender to come by and take our drink order, Cameron glanced up at the ceiling for a moment before looking back at me.

"We didn't miss it."

"We didn't?"

He shook his head. "I know the owner of the ferry. He said he would bring us back no matter how late it is. I gave him a little padding in his wallet, of course."

Disappointment settled in my gut and I hoped the look on my face didn't betray me. He didn't know how much I wanted to spend the night with him, even though I had only met him a little less than a month ago. We had spent a few different times in each other's company and conversation came easy, but that didn't mean I knew him. I was certain that I could walk away from him when I needed to. I wasn't given a choice. I had to.

"Hey," he whispered, searching my eyes. "You wanted to spend the night here?"

"No, no." I put my hands up. "I would rather not shack up in a seedy hotel with a guy that I just met. Unless you haven't told me the entire truth and own a hotel in Myrtle Beach, too."

"What if I do? Is that a bad thing?"

"Do you?"

"No, but that is a great idea, and I'll look into it."

The bartender finally came over and grabbed Cameron's card,

along with our order for a couple of glasses of wine. Cameron had assured me he was perfectly fine to drive when   it was time to leave, and I believed him undoubtedly.

∞

My first thought when I woke up the next morning was of Cameron. Damn him, but it was the perfect date. It occurred to me this spark between us would turn into something more, but I hadn't thought about my heart. I would be in trouble of losing it to him if I was not careful.

It was his eyes that made my stomach flutter. He looked at me like no other man before, as though I were the sole object of his attention. It was in the way he had shaved before our date but had a faint stubble when he kissed me at the front door at the end of the night. Not just a first date kiss. He had pushed me against the door, molding his body perfectly against mine, sucking and tasting the raw emotions right out of my mouth.

And it was in the way he had danced with me. I had had dance partners through the years, but they were stiff with years of strict dance lessons. He had matched me, move for move. Damn him, I swore inwardly while I stretched out like a cat, wondering when he would be next to me when I awoke, molding his naked, muscular body against mine. Touching me.

My second thought was that I hadn't had any dreams that night, no memories that had taken over or nightmares of my past. I had slept deep, and dreamlessly. No resurfacing recollections.

"Good morning, sleepyhead!" Tatum waltzed into my room with two steaming mugs of coffee. I pushed my face into my pillow and groaned while Tatum set the coffee down, perched on the edge of my bed with a bounce.

"That good, huh?"

I sat up sluggishly and took my coffee. "Yes," I growled.

Tatum peered around me at the empty side of the bed. "If it was that good, why isn't he here? Or better yet, why are you here?"

"Tatum." I signed wistfully, running my hand over my face. "What am I doing?"

"You're having fun."

"At what price?" I took a tentative sip and set the mug back down, pulling my knees up to my chest. I laid my head on my knees thoughtfully. "I like him, Tate. I like him a lot."

Tatum rubbed my back. "Then have fun, Reggie. Worry about leaving later."

I sighed as Tatum stood up to leave me. She stopped in my doorway and turned to look at me, her lips pursed.

"Speaking of leaving, Jazz leaves for Milan on Sunday. I'll be going on Thursday. You'll be alone."

"And I'll miss you."

"You won't. You'll have Cameron." She grinned. "Get up, lazy, and come outside. It's a beautiful day."

A half hour later, I walked over to the door that led out to the deck. It obscured part of the beach from view from the lush trees on that side of the house, but I could still see it. I could hear the waves spilling against the shore and pulling away, smell the poignant sweet fragrance of the flowers in bloom. I could tell that the beach was crowding quickly with people left over from summer who were waiting for the Indian summer, but there was no sign of Cameron. Just as well, I was suddenly not sure what I would say to him.

I could see Jazz in the crystal-clear water of the pool, and Tatum lounging in a chair with her coffee and tabloid magazine. With a deep breath, I opened the door and walked out into the brilliant sunshine. It was warm outside still. I didn't foresee a change in the weather for another month.

Jazz swam over to me with a wide grin.

"I know, I know," I said.

"Did he ravish you?"

"No."

"What is *wrong* with him?"

"Maybe he's waiting until he knows Reggie is ready," Tatum chimed in. "A man like Cam knows exactly what he's doing. Should be against the law, looking like he does all handsome and charming."

I raised an eyebrow. "Cam now?"

"Hello, ladies!"

At the sound of the deep voice at the gate, Tatum tore off her sunglasses and tossed the magazine aside while Jazz stepped out of the pool. I looked between them, then at the two guys standing at the gate. Tatum shrugged, waving them in. Both were tall, one with brown hair darker than Cameron's and the other dark blond. They were both well-muscled, but not nearly as muscular as Cameron. Muscular, but not bulky. I groaned, not believing that I was comparing other men to him.

The dark-haired one walked right to me; his hand extended. "Bryce."

The dark blond one walked over, giving Bryce a hip bump to get him out of the way. He offered me his hand next. "Alex."

"Regan."

"Jazz and Tate told us this was your house when we met up with them last night. Thanks for letting us come in and hang out."

"Let her go if you know what's good for you."

The growl belonged to Cameron, who was walking through my gate and looking dangerous with his scowl. Alex dropped my hand immediately. My mouth went dry at the sight of him, bare-chested with a pair of loose athletic shorts resting lightly around his lean waist.

He leaned down, kissing my cheek before he pulled me up tight against him. I gasped, and he claimed my mouth with his, leaving me weak in the knees. After thoroughly kissing me, he loosened his hold but didn't release me. Thankfully, he kept me in his arms, otherwise I may have stumbled.

"I couldn't stop them when they told me they met these two girls, one of whom has beautiful curly blond hair," he murmured, resting his forehead against mine. "I missed you."

I smiled. "You saw me not even eight hours ago. And I have a feeling that those two girls, especially the blonde, are not so innocent."

He was so close to me. My heart was beating hard in my chest, threatening to beat all the way out. He was looking down at me, and I was afraid to look into his eyes.

"Regan," he whispered.

Slowly, I met his eyes, mesmerized. I had been right. He was so perfect for me. I wanted so badly to say the hell with everything and just stay here, see where things went. To hell with everything for as long as it mattered. Damn Pops, I said silently. I loved Pops, but he hadn't exactly made my life easy. He was demanding, even when he wasn't around.

"The foursome here would like to go to the club tonight. Would you go with me?"

"Yes."

"Yes!" Tatum shouted, having been close enough to hear me.

"Cameron."

He leaned his head to the side, a smile on his lips. "You know you can call me Cam, right?"

"This thing that's happening between us . . . it just can't."

"It won't stop me from trying."

Chapter Eight

"Come out of there, Regan."

I stuck my head slowly out of the private bathroom as the bedroom door opened to see Ludovico standing in the doorway. He wore a snappy pair of tan dress pants with a loose button-up short-sleeve shirt that was a dark gray color. No cigar this time. He stood at the threshold and stared at me, not making any move to come into the room.

"I trust your stay with us has been decent."

"Fuck you," I said, jumping across the carpeted floor to sit cross-legged on the bed.

He blanched at my choice of words. You didn't live with a man like my Pops without learning the very best of nasty language. And I wasn't about to let these people know I was cornered, caught up in a web of games as a pawn. I was angry, and he needed to know it.

"Regan, please refrain from that language. It's unnecessary, and it's not becoming of a young lady," he said smoothly, stepping into the room but stopping just inside. "I would like to invite you to our dinner table. But I will warn you if you try to escape or run away, you won't get far. Even if you get outside, you won't be able to leave."

I said nothing. There was hope. He could be lying to me just to make sure I didn't try to do anything impulsive, but he didn't know me. He didn't know if I was smart or stupid. I may be young, but I wasn't stupid. Hearing things through doors and witnessing activities that Pops didn't know I had observed gave me the street smarts to survive.

"Will you come to dinner?"

I lifted my chin, thinking maybe I would meet Jake face to face. "Fine."

"I have two conditions, Regan." He held up two fingers. "You will shower and change your clothes. My wife, Victoria, has gone shopping and left you with everything that you need. And you have yet to bathe yourself."

I knew it. I could barely stand the stink of myself, but this was about the only stand that I could take. They had locked me in this room for almost a week now, like a prison cell with nothing to do and no one to talk to. They didn't know that I had been talking to Jake, and I wasn't about to tell him.

"Will you do that, Regan?"

Slowly, I nodded my head. They had given me regular meals and snacks so I wouldn't die from starvation, but it would be nice to sit and dine with people even though they were enemies. And bad people. They didn't know me. They didn't know what I was capable of. Dining with them and listening to their conversations might give me more to work with.

"I will have Santino come to retrieve you in an hour's time."

Ludovico turned to leave the room, but I stopped him, and he turned back to me. "He isn't going to grab me and drag me down again, is he? He's bruising my arm and I can walk myself."

He shook his head almost sadly. "I'm sorry about that. Santino is used to having to manage bigger people. I will talk with him and make sure that he does not do that again."

"I don't want him to touch me at all."

He nodded. "Understood."

I watched him walk out of the room, closing the door behind and leaving me alone again. He hadn't been lying. Victoria had purchased clothes for me, along with necessities to bathe and wash my hair with and other girl stuff, like deodorant, lotion, and feminine products. The clothes were nothing fancy, some jeans and t-shirts, socks, and underwear. I would survive wearing clothing that someone else had picked out for me, even if they weren't exactly my style. I would survive wearing jeans, even though I preferred leggings.

True to his word, Santino showed up at my door an hour later. True to my word, I had showered and dressed in a pair of loose-fitting blue jeans and a simple t-shirt the color of a clear blue sky. The jeans and the shirt were a size too big. Did his wife think I was overweight? When the door opened, the man looked at me with hard eyes. He didn't seem happy. Ever.

I stepped cautiously forward, skirting around him to get into the hallway and make sure that he didn't grab me again. He didn't touch me or attempt to grab me by the arm, but swept out his arm for me to go ahead of him toward the stairs. I did so, a little disappointed that I had had no chance of grabbing his gun. I just wanted to go home. I didn't care how I got there.

The only words that Santino spoke were directions, leading me to the family dining room that was to the right of the living room. I entered the long room, my eyes taking in the family that was already seated at the long table, with Ludovico himself at the head of the table. Victoria was to his left and a young boy, looking to be about my age, was to his right.

All eyes landed on me when Santino pressed his hand lightly into my shoulder, careful not to 'hurt' me. I stepped in, suddenly self-conscious of the attention that was on me. My eyes met the boys' and I knew instantly that this was Jake. My only friend. He had dark hair like his father, but his eyes must have been like his mom's because they were an interesting shade of green instead of dark brown. His eyes stayed on me as I walked into the room toward the seat next to Victoria, where there was a place setting waiting.

"Regan," Ludovico said, his voice filling the room. "I'm pleased that you could join us. This is my wife, Victoria. And this is my son, Jake. Our daughter is too small yet to join us for dinner."

Victoria didn't look at me, but I could sense Jake's eyes following me to the seat where I slid into, waiting for Santino to push my chair in. I was blushing even while I looked down at the white plate and sterling silverware in front of me. I was afraid to raise my eyes, sensing Jake was still staring at me.

"Jake's about your age, Regan," Ludovico continued. "Jake, maybe you can spend some time with Regan out of her bedroom and show her around. I don't want you to feel like a prisoner."

But that was what I had been, I thought. Although my conversations with Ludovico had been full of anger, I was suddenly unwilling to be such a brat in front of Jake. I hadn't known him long enough for it to matter, but somehow having someone other than Nicco had meant something to me.

"I'll advise you again, Regan, that there is no way to escape here. Jake knows this as well. Please do not try. I'd hate to continue to lock you in your room."

My eyes lifted to meet Ludovico's eyes. I was so mad I clenched my fists under the table where no one could see. I wanted to shake. I was spitting mad. But I didn't say anything, and suddenly I wanted to cry. I couldn't remember ever being so mad. Ludovico was looking at me as though I was nothing. I had done nothing, but here I was having to pay the price for it.

I wanted to stand up and stomp my feet, throw a hissy fit if I had to, and yell at him to just let me go home. But I sat there with my eyes cast down, slowly releasing my fists while tears burned the back of my eyes, threatening to break free. I took a deep breath. The last thing I wanted was to cry in front of this family. Shedding tears in front of Jake, who had become my friend. I was stronger than that. I was better than that.

Slowly, I raised my eyes, focusing on the vase of beautiful tiger lilies in the center of the table. Then I met Jake's gaze. His eyes were sympathetic. But then his lips curled up into a smile and I knew I would be okay. I returned his smile. I had a friend.

While dinner went on, I paid very little attention to the conversations and made sure I stayed quiet. Ludovico would ask me a question every so often to engage me in the conversation, and I would answer briefly. It was the longest meal I had ever had to sit through.

"I hope you don't think that I'm bad," Jake said while we walked together after dinner. "I'm not bad like my dad is."

We were like awkward kids, walking out of the dining room and into the living room. His voice was smooth, but seemed like it was changing. When I looked over at him, he looked back at me with a tilt of his lips in a reassuring smile. Ludovico had told him to show me around the rest of the house and outside. I think it was a ruse to show me how many people he had outside, standing guard. I wondered what they were guarding. It couldn't be me. I was a weaponless, twelve-year-old girl. These were big men with powerful guns. I wouldn't stand a chance.

"I don't think you're bad," I said.

"Because I talk to you through your door?"

"Yes."

He shrugged. "Figured you could use a friend."

He was right, but I didn't say it. I didn't want to seem like a needy girl or anything. There were girls in my school with boyfriends, and they were annoying about it. Everyone in school ignored me, but I wasn't blind to what went on. I would never be a girl like that. It was embarrassing to watch.

"Thank you," I whispered.

I had learned that Jake had grown up in Santa Barbara and had attended a private Catholic school all his life. He hated it; he had told me. His sister, Hailey, was only five years old and had a nanny that looked after her and helped her with preschool stuff. Victoria—Vicky, he called her—was not his real mom but was his sister, Hailey's mom. I had told him about Anne. Vicky and

Anne were like the same person, sitting around having people bring their things, going shopping, and getting their hair and nails done. Real rich bitches, I thought. Except I didn't mind Anne so much. She talked to me. Jake said that Vicky didn't talk to him much.

Jake was like me and didn't have many friends. He at least had one or two that he talked to at school, but he didn't do much outside of school. Ludovico made him do some extracurricular learning, but he was bad at sports, so he was in the chess club. Like a nerd, we laughed. He didn't mind being a nerd, and I didn't mind that he was.

"This is the backyard."

The sun was bright outside, lighting up the backyard and bouncing off the water on the pool that was as still as glass. A small building was on the opposite side Jake said was the beach house.

I looked up at the back of the house. It was a big house, just like the one I lived in with Pops. Sometimes Anne and Amber were there, too.

"Do you want to go swimming?" Jake asked, looking over at me.

"I don't have a swimming suit."

"I thought Vicky bought you some clothes."

"Not a swimming suit." I looked back at the pool, longing to do something other than sit in my room. "Is there anything else that we can do?"

While he thought about it, I scanned the backyard for an escape route. Ludovico had been telling the truth. The fence around the perimeter was tall and there was no way I could scale it. I sighed heavily, hope dwindling with every possibility I could think of. I didn't want to ask Jake for his help and get him into trouble.

We settled for rolling up our pants to dangle our legs in the water while sitting on the edge of the pool. Sitting side by side in silence, swinging our legs back and forth and sending ripples *across the surface, it was peaceful and nice. My hand was just inches from his and I didn't even realize that he was moving his hand closer until I felt his fingers brush mine. Then our hands locked together.*

"I like you," he whispered.

A warm fuzzy feeling came over me. I liked Jake, too. He was my savior in this situation and we had a lot in common, having parents that were not necessarily good people. I wasn't sure what my Pops would do to get me out of this situation, but part of me wasn't hopeful.

"I like you, too. Thanks for being my friend."

"I'm going to get you out of here."

We kept our voices low, never knowing who was listening. He would get into a lot of trouble if he were to get me out. I didn't want him to get in trouble, or worse, hurt.

"My dad told me to think of you as a friend. I think he means sister."

I scrunched up my face. "I don't think of you like a brother."

Without warning, he leaned over and pressed his lips to my cheek. I was so surprised that I turned my face toward him and our lips collided. My eyes opened wide. His eyes opened wider. Then we pulled away, both of us still with our eyes wide. Heat flooded my cheeks, and I saw the heat rise to his face, too.

A guilty smile lifted the corner of his lips. "Whoops," he said sheepishly.

I laughed. Then he laughed and together we laughed so hard we were nearly crying. I really did like him. I was glad that he was my first kiss.

"Please don't try to get me out of here. I'd rather get myself out or wait for Pops."

"That could be a long time."

I shrugged. School would end in the next couple of months, and I wasn't being mistreated here, other than the beast Santino. I missed home. I missed Pops. Even though she was younger than me, I missed Amber.

"As long as I'm not locked in that room anymore."

"I'm still gonna try."

"Don't. I wouldn't forgive myself if something happened to you."

"It's not going to. I know how to handle my dad. He won't punish me."

"Have you done anything like this before?" I teased. "Like bust anyone out your dad has kidnapped?"

We laughed again. I would miss him when I left. If I left, I wouldn't see him again, maybe even ever again. I didn't think Santa Barbara was too far up the coast from where I lived, but it was far enough.

"I won't ever forget you."

"Don't talk like that. We'll see each other again sometime after you get outta here." He pulled my hand into his hand again. "I promise you."

Jake. He had stayed true to his word and found me about a year later on social media. I was fourteen by then and still missed him all the time. I still didn't have any friends when I returned to school the next school year, the taunting and whispering more frequent than they had been before, especially since I had up and disappeared at the tail end of the previous school year. I was the anomaly, the weird one in school.

"Regan?"

I turned to look at Cameron, fully aware of him beside me in the Uber from Myrtle Beach Ferry to the club. The Uber was big enough to fit all six of us and Cameron had once again paid his friend extra to bring us back to the island that night. It would have been nice to stay the night on the beach and wake up to the sunrise. I was a big fan of sunrises and sunsets. It reminded me I was alive.

"Sorry, I zoned out."

I didn't have an excuse for zoning out. I did, however, wonder why these memories were flooding back to me now after almost fifteen years. Jake and I had always stayed in touch, even now, and I saw him after we had gotten our licenses to drive—him before me, of course. It had taken me a while after turning sixteen to convince my dad that I could drive myself to school.

Nicco, as much as it pained me to think about him, had disappeared after I returned home after the kidnapping. I had a new driver after that who never spoke to me before or after school until I got my license and Pops even bought me my first car. I begged him for a normal car, nothing flashy. Even an old junker was good enough for me, but he insisted I drive in a safe car and bought me a brand new Audi A6.

"You're deep in thought." Cameron squeezed my hand as the van pulled up to the doors of the club, keeping my hand safely tucked in his while he reached over and slid open the door with his free hand.

As soon as he stepped out, he pulled me out and kept my hand in his even after everyone had piled out after us. Tatum elbowed me in the ribs lightly and when I glanced at her, she had an ear-to-ear grin on her face and wiggled her eyebrows up and down.

I was about to tell her to shut up when Cameron pulled me into the club. It was just as crowded as it had been the night before, wall to wall and butts to nuts, people from the dance floor to the several bars. Every single table was full, and I had nearly given up hope of finding one when Cameron led us up the stairs to the second level, where there was an open, very private table just for us. I knew it. I couldn't believe that I had missed it last night. Cameron owned this club.

Tatum and Alex ran off to the dance floor before I could take it over while Jazz and Bryce slid into a simple conversation. I wasn't sure if Bryce was trying to get with Jazz as Alex clearly was with Tatum, but I also wasn't sure if he knew Jazz had a girlfriend. It would be fun to see it play out.

Cameron pulled me over to the bar, ordering a round of drinks for everyone. He cradled my hand, but possessively, turning back to me for a soft kiss on the line of my jaw while the bartender mixed up drinks.

"Let's dance," he murmured in my ear.

I shook my head. "I always let Tatum get a head start. Let's just sit and enjoy the music for a bit."

The bartender handed us our drinks and waved a server over to bring the rest of the drinks to the table. I wrinkled my nose at the pink pastel-colored drink with a little umbrella and cherry, but sipped it.

"I'm not a big mixed-drink drinker," I confessed to Cameron as we stood next to the railing sipping our cocktails. "I may regret this."

But I laughed, feeling the effects of the drink mingled with the heavy beat of the music. It was like being drawn into a paradise, and I burned with the need to dance. I stole a look over the railing trying to spot Tatum's crazy blonde hair on the dance floor and smiled when I saw her dancing with Alex. The two of them looked great together.

I set what I left of my drink down on the table and held out my hand to Cameron to take, beckoning him to follow me. I led him down the lower level to the crowded dance floor. Tatum saw me coming and moved out of the way to make room.

His confidence in me made me giddy as I moved, quick snappy moves. If he thought I was graceful before, this dance routine made me into a siren and I took full advantage of each hip grind and every well-placed hip roll. Dancing to the edge of the floor, I turned around and around, circling around Cameron. If I thought he wouldn't catch me, I was mistaken when his firm hands connected with my hips so powerfully that I gasped.

He moved with me, putting his hands on parts of me I had only up to now fantasized about. I heard gasps from the other dancers while they moved, like one rather than two. And I reveled in the feel of his hands. I craved more. I wasn't sure I could wait for him anymore.

When his mouth caught mine, it nearly drained me of all feeling in my legs. I clung to him, dizzy from the lights. They were blurry. Something was wrong.

"I need to sit down," I whispered, trying not to alarm him.

Cameron immediately sensed my distress and helped me away from the dance floor and back to the second level without causing a scene. With a firm arm around me, he helped me back to the table, with Tatum and Alex right behind us.

I sat down, trying to get the room to stop spinning, but it was becoming worse, getting darker as though someone was slowly turning down the lights. My breathing was slowing, and I was trying to swallow more air. Why couldn't I get more air? I could hear my heart beating erratically in my ears, and I heard Tatum say that something was wrong.

"Reggie?" Tatum shouted. "Regan! Can you hear me?"

I was slipping away, falling into dark oblivion, but strangely, I could still feel Cameron's hands as he tried to stop me from slumping over. I felt water on my lips while they tried to get some into my mouth and throat, but it trickled down my jaw and throat.

"Regan. Can you hear me?"

"Air," I gasped.

I felt myself being carried, but it was too dark for me to make out anything else. Not even a blur. Suddenly, cool air rushed against my face. I was limp, feeling in my body quickly going from pinpricks to nothing, but I felt something against my back and looked up at the dark night sky, or what I thought was the dark night sky. It wasn't the night sky, there were no stars. I was blacking out.

I was going to puke. I wasn't sure how I did it, but I rolled over and crawled to the edge of the deck with only the feel of my hands, and threw up over the side. I didn't even care what was below. I just had to get whatever was inside out.

My throat was burning like it was being cut open with tiny

knives, but my hearing was returning, and my vision was returning slowly. The beat of my heart was still a heavy thud in my ears, and I was still dry heaving, but I could feel Cameron's hand on my back and his other hand wrapped around in my hair. God bless him, I thought, and I would have smiled if I wasn't still hanging my head over while trying to get everything out of my stomach.

"Tatum!" Cameron yelled. "Go back to the table and grab her drink. I think someone put something in it."

After a moment of resting my forehead against the deck, I pushed away from the edge of the deck, satisfied that I wasn't going to heave anymore. Cameron helped me up and into a chair on the deck, trying to get a little water into me while pushing my hair back behind my ears. If he hadn't been holding my hair back, I would have puked in it. What a sexy view that would have been for the evening, I thought with a silent laugh. My heartbeat had slowed back down and my vision was clearer now. Of all the mortifying things to do on a date, this was about the worst. My breathing was still labored, but I was managing it.

Cameron knelt in front of me, pulling my hands into his while he looked into my eyes. "You don't think I would drug you, do you?"

"No," I whispered, then with a laugh I added: "You don't have to drug me to get me into your bed."

"I would never sink so low," he growled.

I looked around. People were watching me. "Am I dying?"

He stroked my cheek with his fingertips. I could see the anguish in his eyes. "No. And don't. Please."

Tatum returned, pushing her way through the crowd but without good news. The server had already cleared their table, which was strange since we hadn't been done with them. He ordered Bryce to go find the server.

"Tatum, I need you to call for an ambulance."

"No!" I grabbed his hand. "No ambulance."

"Reggie, please," Tatum said, the softest I had ever heard her voice. "It doesn't mean they'll take you to the hospital. We just want to make sure that you're okay. They might know what made you sick."

"I don't care. I don't want an ambulance. I'm better now."

I sounded like a petulant child. Cameron continued to caress my cheek absently, and I knew he was trying to keep me calm, but as soon as Bryce brought the server, he was the one who tensed up. He changed positions, rising while Tatum remained kneeling beside me. I felt Tatum's hand on my back where his had just been.

"Who made the fucking drink?"

I had never heard Cameron so angry before. When he had saved me on the beach, his voice hadn't been as furious as it was now. I caught the server in her short little skirt, looking at Cameron like she could wrap him around her little finger.

"Bitch," I said, barely audible.

Tatum smoothed the hair away from my forehead. "Cameron will handle it."

I watched the server walk away with a sway in her hips. Just before she went back in, she met my eyes with a twinkle. She knew. She was as aware as she could be of who had added something to my drink, almost as if it had been she herself.

Cameron knelt in front of me again. "I'm taking you home."

"Is that okay, Reggie?" Tatum asked.

He didn't wait for my answer. "We should stop at the hospital. Like Tatum said, maybe they can pinpoint what it was."

"I don't need to go to the hospital," I grumbled. "I don't give a shit what it was. Throwing up probably saved my life."

Cameron helped me stand, holding me close to him when I swayed on my feet. "Should I carry you?"

How humiliating. Being taken out of a club by ambulance was bad. Being carried out would be even worse. "No! I'll be fine. Just walk slowly. My legs feel like spaghetti."

"Bryce," he called out, whispering something to him.

Picking up on my discomfort, Cameron was intuitive enough to take me away from the club, using the stairs on the deck that went to the beach. I could avoid walking through the club, which would have probably caused quite a stir. I was already feeling overwhelmed, and I didn't want any more of it.

I wished I knew what he had said to Bryce. He stayed beside me, helping me down the stairs to the front of the club. There were a few people coming and going, but they didn't pay attention to us. Likely, they thought he just had his arm around me. He guided me to a parking barricade, and we sat down to wait for an Uber.

"Who would want to hurt you?" he asked.

I shrugged. There were lots of people that would want to hurt me, but I didn't need him to know that. Lots of people that would hurt me to get to Pops. "It might have been a freak accident. Maybe something I just didn't agree with."

By the narrowing of his eyes, I knew he wasn't buying it. He knew there was more to it than that. All he had to do was talk to Tatum. Tatum knew the whispers from high school, even though she had never confirmed with me whether they were true.

Cameron dropped it when the car showed up. After tucking me safely into the backseat, he slid in next to me and pulled me close so I could lay my head against him and rest on the ride to the ferry.

"Is she okay?" the driver asked.

There was a flash in Cameron's eyes, and I felt his heart beat kick up a notch. "She's fine," he bit out. "Mind your business."

The sensation of his fingertips drawing circles on my arm along with the steady beating of his heart under my cheek put me into a deeply sated sleep, and I didn't wake until the bump from the car driving over the ferry when we arrived back on the island.

The car pulled into my driveway and Cameron moved quickly to get me out of the car, carrying me into the house and straight into my bedroom, where he set me down on the end of the bed.

The car ride nap had made me feel much better, but I was not nearly back to normal.

"Where're your pajamas?"

I gave a quiet laugh. "I don't care. Just put me into bed naked for all I care."

His eyebrows kicked up. "This won't end well if I do that."

I think he had meant to whisper it to himself, but I heard it. I couldn't help but smile, which he didn't see because he was busy opening drawers in my dresser in search of something for me to wear.

When he walked back over to me, I saw he had a pair of sleep pants and a tank top in his hand. I studied his top of dark hair as he bent down to pull my shoes from my feet before pulling me up. He misjudged my weight, and I smacked against him, causing us both to stumble back a little with laughter.

I loved his laugh. It was deep and melodic, but smooth. It washed over me, allowing me to appreciate it. I would miss his laugh. And his smile. How on earth was he single?

"God, I wish this hadn't happened tonight," he whispered, running his hands up my arms and pulling them both up over my head before proceeding to peel my dress up and flinging it across the room heedless to the fact that I had nothing on beneath except panties. A girl could always hope that an evening to turn out to be more than just a date. Especially when Cameron was the one at the center.

His arms came around me, strong and possessive, the feeling of our skin meeting making me hyperaware of the pulse at the center of my body, yearning for him to touch me. It had been a long time. I wasn't sure about him, and I didn't care. I just needed him to touch me.

His eyes caught mine as I draped my arms over his broad shoulders, but I turned my head. The last thing I wanted him to do was kiss me before I brushed my teeth and rinse heavily with mouthwash to get the reek out of my mouth.

"Why?" I whispered, looking at his rounded shoulder and wanting to taste his skin there. "I know why I wished that this hadn't happened tonight. Why do you?"

His hands slid down my waist, cupping me just above the backs of my thighs, raising me until my legs wrapped around him. I could feel him. He was just as aroused as I was. All he had to do was move my underwear out of the way and slip inside, granting us both the reprieve that we needed. I ached for it.

"Because I would worship your body like you deserve to be worshipped," he whispered. His breath hitched when I pressed myself further against him.

"Do it anyway."

He shook his head. "Not after this. No." Gently, he sat me down on the edge of the bed again and slid the sleep pants up my legs. "I want our first time to be untainted by the bullshit that happened tonight."

Goosebumps raced over my skin. As much as my body was throbbing for his touch, he was right. I lifted my hips for him to finish pulling them up. He was staring at my breasts as I raised my arms over my head. I heard his heavy sigh, and he pulled the tank top on to cover me.

He left me to pull the bedding down, helping me to scoot back and bringing them over me when I settled down with my head against my pillows. Cameron leaned down to place a kiss on the center of my forehead and reached over to turn out the lamp. He moved to leave, but I caught his hand.

"Stay," I whispered. "Please."

I saw his smile in the dark. "Oh, you can count on that."

Embarrassed, I released his hand and watched him move over to the bench at the wall across from the bed, not able to tear my eyes away from him while I watched him peel off his own clothing. First came his shirt, revealing his marble-like chest, then kicking off his shoes and unbuttoning his pants. My mouth went dry, watching him slide the pants down his long legs, revealing a simple pair of black boxer briefs.

I closed my eyes, licking my dry lips. How one man could make me feel like I was a lovestruck teenager again was crazy. The bed shifted under his weight on the other side, then his arm slid around me, pulling me back against him and I had never felt so safe, so secure, as I had at that moment.

Chapter Nine

"Do you think one of them put something in your drink last night?"

Without raising my head from my chaise lounge beside the pool, I turned my head to look at Tatum wearing my dark sunglasses. I didn't want to lift my head. I woke up that morning with a pounding headache, a scratchy throat, and ridiculously sore abdominal muscles.

When I had woken up, Cameron was sleeping deeply beside me. Our arms and legs tangled were together, and I couldn't tell where I ended and he began. The feeling had been euphoric. I had studied the features of his face while I could, my gaze sweeping from his long, inky-black eyelashes to the high and bold cheekbones to his full lips. There was a dot on his earlobe, where an earring had once been. I smiled at the thought that he was probably a bad boy when he was younger. Rebel, indeed.

"Cameron wouldn't have hurt me."

"I didn't think so either. Bryce closed the bar and combed it. There was nothing. The bartender and that little bitch of a server ditched, which means one, or both, of them, had something to do with this."

"Cameron owns the bar," I said, suddenly.

"Does it even matter?"

"No, it doesn't. I'm too far gone to care."

Tatum opened her mouth. "You're falling in love with him."

"Too late, already fallen."

"Did you sleep with him last night?"

She knew Cameron had spent the night. I don't know how she knew, unless she figured he wouldn't have left me alone after what had happened. Jazz had left early for the airport, having to catch her flight to Milan. She came in to say goodbye, urging me to be careful. She had an ominous feeling about the events of last night.

"Sleeping in the bed with him, yes. Having sex with him, no. He's not the type of guy to take advantage of a woman that was drunk, or in my case last night, drugged. Poisoned? I don't even know."

"You should have gone to the hospital, you nut."

"No. It doesn't matter what it was. I'm fine now."

Tatum continued to stare at me. "I find it really strange that someone would have put something into your drink, Regan. Are you in some kind of trouble?"

I looked away from her.

"Is it your dad?"

And there it was. Never had she asked me about him. Until now. "Tatum," I whispered. I wanted so badly to spill every dirty secret I had. "He doesn't do good things. And that's all you need to know, and you cannot tell another soul."

Her face went pale. "Someone is trying to get to him through you. Someone is trying to kill you because of him!"

Her voice was getting higher with each word, and I didn't need her screeching to raise an alarm. Cameron did not need to know any of this. No one needed to know any of this. If someone knew where I was, and someone was trying to get to Pops through me, I was in trouble. I would need to leave sooner than expected. Except, if I wasn't safe here, where would I be?

"Tatum, shush. You're jumping to conclusions. It could have been for someone else." She gave me a look that told me that was a stupid thing to say. "It could have been anything. I'm fine now, and Cameron took care of me."

Cameron had taken wonderful care of me last night, although I had woken up with an ache in my heart when I was looking at him and even more when he opened his eyes. I could get used to waking up next to him, scaring me even more. It was too soon to be falling for him, besides the fact that Pops had given me to another.

"What about you and Alex?"

"Averting the subject isn't going to help you," she accused, then her eyes glazed over wistfully. "He's a great kisser. I like him a lot. You know I haven't had a lot of luck with men. Usually, I scare them away."

"You didn't sleep with him?"

"No, and I'd rather not rush it, either. I know we just met, but I really do like him."

"He seems nice."

"If I was in your situation, I'd be hooking up with anyone I could." She grinned. "Lucky you. You get one while you're here and he's head over heels for you."

"How do you know that?"

"Come on, Reg! He would not leave your side and he was about to turn that place upside down to find out who did it. It wouldn't surprise me if he went go back there to search the place himself."

Other than Tatum, Jazz and Gio, no one knew where I was. That would mean that someone very close to me had either done it or hired someone to do it. The server had looked me in the eye before going back into the club, almost as though telling me she was responsible. I had lied to Tatum when I said it could have been for someone else. I had no doubts that someone had meant the drug for me. Whatever it was in my drink would have killed me had I not thrown up.

The doorbell rang, and Tatum sprang up from her chair to run and answer it, eager to take care of me. I envied her good health this morning while I felt like horseshit. A shadow blocked out the sun.

"I forgot to thank you this morning for a wonderful night last night."

"I'm sorry, Cameron. You shouldn't have had to stay." I eyed him. "Or remove my clothing, although it was interesting."

"Next time . . ."

"Oh!" Tatum stepped out with a gigantic bouquet of red roses. "Hi, Cam!"

"Good morning, Tatum. I was just coming back to make sure Regan's okay."

"Did you sleep at all?" I asked.

"I slept better last night with you in my arms than I do in my own cold bed." He looked pointedly at me.

"Someone sent you roses! I wonder who it could be from?"

Cameron threw up his hands. "Guilty. They were supposed to be delivered this morning *before* I came back."

"Thank you."

"I was hoping for more than a thank you, but I understand if you still aren't feeling well. It could have been a lot worse."

"Come here," I commanded, even though my pounding head was warning me against any movement.

Tatum turned, using the excuse to put the roses in the water so she could leave us alone while he sat down in Tatum's vacant chair. I looked into his eyes, running my hand up his naked biceps and along his neck before tangling in his short hair. He let me pull him toward me until I pressed my mouth against his. Our tongues tangled, tasted, and warred while he pulled me gently up to meet him and held me prisoner. Despite the throbbing in my head, I let him ravage my lips without mercy.

After a moment, I pulled away.

"What do you do to me?" I whispered.

"What do you do to me?" he countered. "I would've committed murder last night had I found out who poisoned you. I was so angry. I was so scared."

"Thankfully, I didn't like it." I put my hand on his knee. "Tatum said you went back this morning. Did you find anything?"

His jaw clenched, the muscle tick in his cheek attractive even when he shook his head. "Who would try to kill you?"

I couldn't answer him.

"Why you?"

I shrugged, the same answer I had given him last night. I would tell him the truth about me in a heartbeat if I thought it would do any good. But it would only rip him out of my life sooner. Selfishly, I wasn't ready to relinquish him. Not before I really knew him. There was so much more to know. And there was more of me to know, except the truth. The truth would have to stay buried deep and maybe never come to light.

I hoped it would be clean. One minute I would be here, and the next gone. He didn't know how to reach me; we hadn't so much as exchanged phone numbers or addresses. There hadn't been a need to. He wouldn't know where to find me.

"I'm keeping my eye out for you, and on you. I won't let anything happen to you."

If only that were true . . .

∞

I could not believe my luck. Of all the things to go wrong, I didn't know who to call in this situation, and I didn't have Cameron's number. Tatum was out with Alex for the evening, and I didn't want to ruin their date.

Alone, with a leaking pipe under my kitchen sink. While in the kitchen, I heard water spraying. I opened the cupboards below the sink and water sprayed at me from a pipe. And it was getting more forceful.

I tried to hold the water spray back with my hands to keep it from soaking everything within sight, including me. This was not good. I would need to let it go to get to the water shut-off valve.

"No!" I cried. "Please!"

The floor was getting wet enough to be slippery, and it wasn't long before my feet slipped out from under me. I cried out when I fell on my hip. I started to cry and laugh at the same time.

"What the hell?"

I looked up as Cameron came into the house, eyes wide, when he saw what was going on in my kitchen. He hurried over to help me. The tears stopped and laughter took over while I stretched out on the floor, shaking at the absurdity of it. He nudged me over, getting himself wet. He reached in and turned a knob, and the water stopped. I felt stupid. I should have just shut off the water. Everything was going to get wet, anyway. It was as easy as just twisting a knob.

"How long were you going to sit here for?"

I smoothed the wet hair away from my face. "I don't know."

Cameron stared at me. It hadn't occurred to me he could see right through my tank top. The leggings were stuck to my legs like glue. It soaked me through, as though I had just jumped into the pool fully clothed.

I tried to laugh again, but it came out sounding ridiculous. Instead, I struggled to my feet amidst the mess in the kitchen. He followed me up, putting his hands on my waist. My gaze found his and collided. I rested my hands on his biceps.

"Regan."

His rough voice sent shivers rippling down my spine, his mouth catching mine before I could stop and think about it. I didn't want to think about it. I just wanted it to happen. For a long time, I wanted this to happen.

"Put your hands on me," he demanded, tearing his mouth from mine to taste the skin along the slender column of my neck.

His hands moved up my waist, coming around to cup my breasts. With a gasp, I dropped my head back while he continued with his lips and tongue along my skin until he grabbed me around the waist again and lifted me until I sat on the edge of the counter with him wedged between my legs.

"Regan," he said again, his voice hoarse.

My hands pulled at his shirt, frantic with the need to feel his bare skin beneath my hands. He lifted his arms, and I tugged his shirt off, revealing his finely sculpted chest. I placed my hands on each side of his waist, drinking in the sight of his chest. It drew me in, held me captive. Who knew that a man could have such a sexy bellybutton. He grasped the front of my tank top and ripped it right down the middle, peeling it away from me and dropping it to the floor in a wet thwack.

Knuckles skimmed over the tops of my breasts above the black lace cups. My head fell back again as he leaned over to kiss me there, all the while working to unhook my simple bra. Freed of the constraint, he caught them both and drew his thumbs over my nipples before pressing his greedy lips to each of them.

"Tell me to stop," he said, desperation and need raw in his voice. "Or I won't be able to."

"Don't," I whispered.

He wasted no time after that, picking me up with one arm from the counter and carrying me, legs wrapped around him, across the living room to my bedroom. He kicked the door shut with a thud and placed me down next to the bed.

"Last chance," he warned.

I said nothing, even when he gave me a little push until I fell back on the bed and let him pull the wet leggings from my legs. My panties followed swiftly behind. He stared down at me, splendidly naked before him. The desire hooding his eyes caused my breath to hitch in my throat. He leaned down, his knuckles brushing against my cheekbone.

It didn't seem like his hands left me for a single moment after that, yet suddenly his jeans were gone and he was pressing me back onto the bed. His jaw clenched, pressing his hardness against my softness before his lips continued their exploration of my body.

My hands smoothed along his muscular arms, up to his neck. My legs felt languid when his hand slid up between my legs, a gasp falling from my lips when his fingers sought entrance. "Tell me you want me."

His finger created a rhythm that made it hard for me to say any words. I didn't know for certain I could find my voice. I was riding a wave that was about ready to crest, bringing me higher while my heart was threatening to beat its way out of my chest. Heat washed over me, like the flush of a fever.

When I whispered the words he wanted to hear, he crushed his mouth to mine, while one swift movement drove into me, and pressed against me until I thought he would push me all the way to the headboard. He pulled my legs up higher to ease in deeper, running his palms along the back of my thighs, coming to rest just under where the backs of my legs met the gentle swell below my ass.

"Christ..."

I still couldn't find my voice, a squeak coming out instead of any resemblance to a word. I wasn't sure how he could form words right now. It sucked the breath out of my lungs, and he pulled me up to his chest and stopped. We were both still. Holding our breath as though we were both afraid to move, my legs wrapped tightly around his waist while he was deep within me.

"Cameron," I whispered.

"Say it again." His voice was raw, lower than I had ever heard his tone before. His fingers dragged up to the base of my neck, tangled in my hair, and tugged until it exposed my neck to him like a vampire. His lips pressed a fiery trail to just under my ear. "Say my name again."

"Cameron."

He moved sensuously, as though he was taking great care, while his lips pressed to my skin wherever he could, without losing his groove. The sensations grew in my lower extremities, threatening to burst into a million pieces. Stars swam before my eyes while his mouth caught mine, working in tandem to bring me to heights I had never reached before.

"Regan," he said, never once losing his rhythm.

I thought for a moment he was going to make the dreaded confession of love during sex, but he dropped his forehead to mine and stopped talking. His arms tightened around me while he picked up speed, pushing faster until I couldn't contain myself anymore and shouted my release. My legs, still hooked around his waist, shook from the force and it wasn't a second later he was growling out his own release.

His arms stayed, keeping me close to him, and neither of us moved. The only sound was our heavy breathing. I didn't want to pull out of his embrace, and it didn't seem like he wanted to move away from me, either. So, we stayed as we were. It was secure. It was almost possessive, but it didn't scare me. I knew beyond a doubt that he wouldn't hurt me.

Chapter Ten

Since the beginning of September, visitors to the island had tapered off, leaving those that lived here to sweep up after the busy season and hunker down for the slow season. Isabel had been busy, but not too busy to check in occasionally. She hadn't needed my help since I had first arrived, thankfully. The boatyard had me busy enough.

I had just seen Tatum off on the ferry, sad to see her go, and I wondered if a part of me was sad that I wasn't going with her. I missed home, weirdly. She had gone with me to the boutique in Myrtle Beach to look at wedding dresses. Gio made me promise I would look, and I looked. I followed through with it. The boutique owner was a lovely woman who explained to me her process of hand creating each gown.

It had felt strange sifting through the gowns on racks like the pages of a book. Every gown I saw made me think about Cameron, and how he wasn't my person. Maybe he was my person and fate was doing me dirty. Pops was doing me dirty. I loved Pops, but I was so mad at him for this. Damn him. When I thought about it, I had to leave the boutique. I couldn't look at the dresses anymore. I couldn't settle on one. I didn't want to think about any of it.

Gio had called last night, satisfied that I had looked at wedding gowns but not pleased that I had given up so easily. Pops was still on sabbatical. I should call Jake again and see if he knew anything about why Pops had felt the need to take an extended vacation. He and I had been very careful to stay under the radar, not wanting issues. We were both toeing the lines in the sand carefully. I tried not to outright call him. Sometimes I even took to social media to send him messages just so no one accidentally saw a text, even though Jake had assured me he had me listed on his phone by a different name. I, too, had him listed under a pseudo-name.

"Well, look what the cat dragged in," Isabel said, coming around the front desk to give me a long, drawn-out hug. "Honey, you look blissfully happy. I would say this island air has got you turned in the direction you needed."

I smiled, remembering waking up next to Cameron that morning. Since the night of the kitchen incident, we had rarely been apart, and he had been sleeping at my house instead of his own. Isabel wasn't wrong. I was happy, maybe blissfully so. The sadness was ebbing after seeing Tatum leave. The happiness was seeping back through knowing I would see Cameron later.

"Spill it. I can tell by your smile that you've been with a certain someone. Don't tell me you haven't been."

Together, we headed for the coffee shop on the corner and I filled Isabel in on what had transpired with Cameron. I made Isabel happy with the information I was feeding her, but I had yet to tell her I was otherwise engaged to someone else. I didn't tell her anything about what was going on. I had known Isabel since I was a little girl. She was someone that was as transparent as they came and I could trust her.

The fact remained that there had already been an attempt on my life at the club and that left me chilled. There were a few people who knew where I was. Of those that knew where I was, I trusted them implicitly. None of those within my circle would hurt me.

Isabel clucked, bringing me out of my thoughts. "I knew he would convince you. Charming, and the devil to look at. But he's a good man."

I gave her a brilliant smile before taking a sip of my coffee and looking out at the ocean. The days were cooling now that it was October, but the waves still caressed the beach. "Has he ever stayed at the hotel?"

"Yes," she said, quickly adding: "But alone. It was just before he bought his house on the beach. Regan, I've known you since you were . . . Oh, I've known you for a long time."

I nodded. "You're like a mother to me."

Isabel looked at me, eyes widening slightly. I knew she didn't have children and hoped that I hadn't struck a nerve. She gave me a gentle smile. "Do you know what you're doing?"

My laugh was nervous. "No. I don't know what I'm doing. I told him up front that whatever it is, it won't last. It can't last."

"Why not?"

I wasn't ready for this conversation. Guilt at not telling her what was happening in my life was eating me up. She was waiting patiently for an answer and not pressing me to say more than I needed to say. Like Tatum, there was a time and a place. Maybe it was time to let Isabel in.

"What's going on?" she gently asked.

"I don't even know where to start. The entire situation is asinine. It makes me think this is all a nightmare that I'll wake up from. It's bringing out all kinds of things from the past."

Isabel leaned back in her chair. "Your father?"

I nodded. "He's taking a sabbatical. He called the night before I arrived here to tell me." I watched the worry appear on her face. She had known him for many years. It wasn't crazy to think she might still have feelings for him, even though she never confirmed that they had been together at one time.

"What else?"

I thought she wasn't going to press, but she knew my family well enough to know that Pops was into some dangerous things with some dangerous people. As long as he was carefully on sabbatical somewhere, he wouldn't end up dead, dumped into some lake or river, or stuffed in a barrel or someone's freezer. I shuddered.

"Pops been threatening me for years that he'll find someone for me to marry if I don't find someone suitable to take over. He told me he made a contract. For me to marry some family friend's son." I looked at Isabel, but she didn't flinch. She didn't look surprised. "Apparently, Pop's in danger and because he's in danger, I'm in danger and he told me to go somewhere to lie low. I'm just confused about why I would be in danger. Then I was at a club with Cameron, and some friends last week, and someone poisoned my drink."

Her face was now showing alarm. Bolting upright in her chair, she reached across the table to grab my hand so fast that she nearly dumped her cup of coffee. She didn't say anything, she just held my hands.

"Did your father tell you who this family friend is?"

I shook my head. "I don't even know when. I only know that when I went wedding dress shopping with Tatum, the guilt of stringing Cameron along was eating me alive. I have no right to have a relationship that will go nowhere. I told Cameron from the start that this couldn't really go anywhere, but he didn't believe me. He thinks things can change. God, I wish that were true."

"You love him."

I closed my eyes. "I shouldn't."

When I opened them, Isabel was smiling over the rim of her coffee cup. It wasn't a matter-of-fact smile, but more a smile that told me she was happy for me, regardless of the outcome.

"I love the one man I can't have."

"Regan, you're not leaving this island yet. Things can change. Just go with it. Worry about it later." Isabel released my hands with a gentle, motherly pat. "It will all work out."

An hour later, I was walking into the boatyard office feeling better after my talk with Isabel. It eased a bit of a burden to talk about my situation with her, even if Isabel was as optimistic as Cameron was for a situation that wasn't ideal. This man that I was supposed to marry was probably involved in the same shit as Pops was and I was going to have to marry into it and I would never get away from it. Not that I had thought my future would be any different. I guess I had hoped someday my life would be mine to do something with. I never thought for a moment Pops would make good on his threat. On the flip side, perhaps if something happened to my unknown future husband, this entire contract would be void. But that wasn't me. I wasn't a person to wish harm to someone I didn't even know.

Melanie was filing her nails when I walked into the office an hour later. I shook my head. We had formed a good relationship. We talked about adding duties to her job description to avoid boredom, and she seemed excited to have more responsibilities.

"Good morning, Melanie."

"Good morning," she said, without looking up from her nails.

I walked into my office and closed the door with a definitive click. Weeks ago, I took out an advertisement for a manager and received one application, much to my surprise. The man was due to come in today for an interview. I was in the middle of getting my laptop started when Melanie opened my door and leaned against the frame.

"So . . ." she said. "You and Cameron."

I wasn't sure what to say about that. I had tried every which way to avoid it, but it wasn't against the law to date someone, or even sleep with someone. Cameron wasn't employed directly by me. It wasn't something I felt the need to talk with Melanie about.

"I am so jealous."

"Don't be," I laughed. "There are plenty of good guys around."

"My ex-boyfriend wasn't one. He got into drugs," she said. "I still see him come to the island sometimes, and it scares me. I swear I saw him that night we were hanging out Labor Day weekend at the festival."

My smile slipped away.

"Is that why you've been stealing from the company?"

Her guilt was clear when I watched her face grow pale, her hands tremble and her refusal to look me in the eye. This was not the young woman I knew during the last month. Melanie Miller was not a dishonest person.

"Melanie," I said, standing and coming around to the front of the desk, where I leaned against it and crossed my ankles. "Tell me why you're stealing from me."

She winced.

"I could have you arrested," I pointed out, gently. "Are you ready to go to jail or are you going to tell me what this is really about?"

"I needed the money," she whispered.

"For what? And why this way?"

I saw a tear slip from the corner of her eye. "I moved here with him only six months ago. It was going to be great. Then he bailed, leaving me with the rent and all the bills. Plus, he convinced me to buy him a car, which he took and I have to pay for it." She sniffled. "I can't afford all of this. Not on a receptionist's salary."

"Melanie," I said, my heart aching for her. "Why didn't you come to me? Why didn't you tell me this? We could have figured something out. There's always another way other than stealing."

She nodded. "Are you going to have me arrested?"

"No," I announced, standing up and going back around the desk.

I sat back down behind the desk and handed her a tissue before I unlocked the top drawer. I withdrew a plain white envelope and handed it to her, waiting patiently for her to open it. She blew her nose before opening the envelope.

"What is this?" she asked as she pulled out the check.

"A check."

She looked up, surprise in her eyes. "You're giving me money?

After I stole? Why would you do that?"

"You must have had a reason to do it. I knew as soon as I saw the signs, there had to be a reason. I'm hoping this can get you out of your struggles."

I waited for her to agree or disagree. The check was for a substantial amount of money. If she had been in her lease for six months, this would pay for the rest of her lease plus her utilities, plus some of her car loan.

"This will pay for everything," she breathed.

I tilted my head to the side. "Does this ex-boyfriend of yours wear hoodies?"

She nodded. "I always see him in a black zip-up hoodie. Why?"

"The night of the festival, I think he was the one who mugged me."

A gasp ripped from her throat. "I knew I saw him! Did he take your money?"

"He took all thirty dollars. Cameron got it back and had some friends take care of the mugger. I'll find out what they did with him. Did you report your car stolen?"

She nodded. "The sheriff said because both our names were on the title and loan, he had a right to take it. If I don't make the payments, my credit will drop and I'll need my credit to get a cheaper place when my lease is up. Ms. De Luca . . ." I eyed her. "Regan. He's not a good guy. Please don't try to go after him."

"You're sweet." I leaned forward on the desk. "The only reason he got away with mugging me was because he came up behind me with a knife in the dark. Trust me when I say next time he won't be lucky."

Cameron would need to find out from Sweetheart what they did with the guy. And if they let him get away, I would need to make some calls. He wouldn't get away with this. I looked back at Melanie. She didn't need to know it.

I checked my watch. My interview was due at any moment.

"Promise me you'll come to me if you need anything else." She nodded. "Anything, Melanie."

She stood up and went to the door, turning back around. "Why are you so nice to me? People aren't always so nice."

"I am. Now, get back to work," I said with a smile. I hadn't told her I had located the old manager two weeks ago, and she hadn't asked me again about it. I hoped she thought he was long gone. And he was. He wasn't going to bother her again. Gio and Frank made sure of it.

I heard the bell on the front door and snapped my laptop closed before going to greet the person. The man looked casual in a pair of blue jeans and a sports jacket over a simple button-up shirt. At first glance, I wondered if he should model for a career instead. He had dark blond hair that was windblown and light green eyes.

I extended my hand. "Justin Roberts?"

He smiled, straight white teeth flashing at me as he gripped my hand. "Regan De Luca, I presume?"

"Yes." I withdrew my hand and swept out my arm, motioning him into my office. "I appreciate your interest in this position. You don't live on the island?"

He shook his head. "I'm from Charleston. I'm looking to settle down here."

Curious. Personal questions burned in my head, wanting to ask him why, but I had to remind myself to remain professional. His personal life was not my concern. He unbuttoned his jacket and sat down in a chair in front of the desk, setting his portfolio on the vacant chair while I settled into my chair. I had the strangest feeling that I had seen him before, but I would have remembered a man with his good looks. But he wasn't Cameron.

"What is your interest in this position, Mr. Roberts?"

"Justin, please." I nodded. "Being from Charleston, my brothers and I have built boats for most of our lives. I got my bachelor's degree in business administration and have been managing boat businesses since."

I sifted through his resume, even though I had already read through the three-page report on his background in management and his education. He was qualified enough for the job. I hoped this boatyard business would be enough to keep him busy.

"This isn't a big boatyard. Business has been slim lately, but is on the rise now. I lost the manager and two of the boat builders." I set the papers down. "I'm in a bit of a bind."

He smiled and again I noticed how his smile was lovely. It threw me off how good-looking he was. I hoped he would leave Melanie alone. I didn't need another sexual harassment issue.

"Down that many people, huh? Well, Miss De Luca, I would be more than happy to help you out. When can I start?"

I was just about to respond when my cell phone buzzed. I had meant to shut it off during this meeting. I thought it was highly inappropriate to be interrupted during an interview process.

"You can take that if you need to."

I looked down at my phone. Gio. I hit ignore. "No, no. I should have turned it off before we began. I can call him back."

"Him?"

I didn't like that question, although I liked him so far. It sounded like it had a bite to it and my personal life was separate from my business life. It always was, and it always would be. I ignored the question. "Please, call me Regan. I need to ask: Are you sure?"

"Absolutely. It sounds like you could use me, and I don't mind digging in and getting down to business."

"The pay isn't great. Once business gets back to full swing, I don't mind bumping it up, but for now, we're at a bare minimum."

"Sounds perfect."

I raised my brow. He stared back at me, unfazed. He was certainly eager to get started and at a minimal salary. It made me wonder what he saw at this opportunity. He seemed too good to be true.

"Can I start right away?"

Seriously. Way too good to be true, I thought. "Yes. Absolutely. We just need to get the paperwork set up. Can I email it over to you later tonight?"

"That works. I'm staying at the hotel in town, so if anything comes up, you can reach me there, or on my cell phone. My number is on my resume."

"Yes, I have that." I studied him for a moment. "May I ask you a personal question?"

"Ask away."

I glanced down at his application before looking up at him. He was only thirty. "Why would you want to settle down on this island? It's so small and, to be honest, very inactive during fall and winter until the spring and summer crowds start spilling in. It's quiet, remote and everyone knows everyone."

He shrugged. "I guess you could say I didn't feel like I had a choice. This was just too good to be true for me to pass up."

I got the feeling that what he told me wasn't the entire truth. If he thought this opportunity was too good to be true, I most definitely felt that way. If he had been honest in his application and resume, it was a good hire for me. He might regret it later.

I stood up just as my cell phone buzzed again.

"Mind if I look around before I leave?" he asked. "That way you can take your call and I can ask you questions when you're finished."

"Yes, that would be fine."

I accepted the call as Justin stood and walked out of my office. He turned and winked at me at the doorway and left, keeping the door open.

"Gio," I said. "I'm in the middle of something. What is so urgent that you couldn't send me a text or leave a message? I would have gotten back to you soon."

"Regan, someone knows where you are."

"I'm not leaving yet. I still have a lot of stuff I need to get done before I leave. What makes you think someone knows where I am?"

Maybe Gio would say something that would give me an idea of who might know. "I think Mancini is behind your father's decision to take an extended, very private vacation from his life lately."

"Are you sure it's not some other deal gone bad?" I asked. "Mancini failed the last time. He'd be stupid to try again."

"I think this thing with Mancini is far from over. Don't underestimate him."

"I'll never underestimate Ludovico Mancini again." I walked over to the window and back nonchalantly to see if I could see Justin.

"Regan . . ."

"Don't 'Regan' me, Gio!" My voice was louder, then I dropped it down to avoid possible eavesdropping. "I can't leave yet. I'll be careful. I promise. But I can't leave right now."

It was because I couldn't leave Cameron yet, not so much at the boatyard and my safety. Cameron would keep me safe like he had the night of the poisoning. Even if he didn't know my full background, he wouldn't let anything happen to me.

I pinched the bridge of my nose, pacing around the office like a tiger trapped in a cage prowling for something to do or eat. I was under too much stress right now to be thinking straight.

"Regan, calm down. I'm worried about you. Maybe that's not the best place for you right now."

I sighed. "Someone knows I'm here. Someone tried to kill me by poisoning my drink when I went to Myrtle Beach with some friends a week ago."

"And you didn't think to tell me this?"

"Please. I handled it."

"You caught who did it?"

"Well, no. But nothing has happened since and I'm being careful. I'll come home when I can. In the meantime, please let me know if you hear from Pops."

"I will," he whispered. "I'm sure it won't be much longer. Anne is beside herself with worry."

"I don't blame her. How is she?"

He chuckled. "She's busy planning your wedding. I didn't think that you would mind if she stepped in to plan it, being that you don't really have a choice in it."

I was quiet for a minute. I hated thinking about it, and I hated talking about it even more. "Is there a date, then?"

"March eighteenth."

My heartbeat rose, my palms began sweating. I wiped them on my skirt. I wasn't ready for this. Justin ducked his head back through the door.

"I have to go."

"I'll call you soon."

I ended the call, praying that if Justin had overheard anything of what I was saying, he wouldn't be able to make sense of it. The last thing that I wanted was for him to back out of the hiring process because I might not be sticking around much longer. That might be a good thing too. Some people didn't like someone watching over their shoulders and I didn't like to do that either.

"I'm sorry about that. Did you look around?"

"I did. Very impressive place you have here. When can I start?"

"Can you start on Monday?"

"Yes. I planned on maybe staying the weekend to familiarize myself with the island life in hopes I got the position. Looks like that was a good idea!" He grinned. "Maybe we can grab some coffee this weekend, sort of pre-meeting before Monday?"

I stared at him. Hitting on me? Not a good sign. "I don't think that's a good idea, but thank you. I would be happy to sit down with you on Monday to review things."

He didn't press it, and I was glad about that. I didn't want this to be awkward for either of us, as odd as it was to ask your boss out for coffee immediately after being hired. He was just being nice; I was sure.

"It was a pleasure to meet you, Justin." I held out my hand. "I look forward to Monday, and I'll have all the paperwork emailed to you this evening. If you need to print anything, please ask the hotel front desk and they'll help you, otherwise don't worry about scanning and returning. Just bring everything with you on Monday. I'll have my belongings out of your office."

"I don't want to put you out. I can work elsewhere."

"Nonsense. This is the manager's office, not mine. I won't be here much longer, I don't think."

"You won't?" he asked, following me out of the office. "You don't live here?"

I laughed nervously, getting rattled by these questions about me. I did not want to have to start back at the beginning of this process now that he had accepted this position, but the personal questions were discomforting. "No, but I visit from time to time."

He nodded in understanding. "I'll see you on Monday then."

"Yes, looking forward to it."

I watched him leave out the front door, a little perplexed. He was being friendly; I assured myself. No one would be that bold after just being hired, asking such personal questions. And I had asked him personal questions about wanting to live here.

I couldn't help but think about Gio's warning on my way home. If someone knew where I was, I would have a lot more to worry about than just one random poisoning at a club. I would need to keep vigilant. It didn't seem like Cameron was going anywhere and since he spent every night at my house and made sure that the security system was on, made me feel more at ease.

The knot in the pit of my stomach that Cameron would get hurt in this mess didn't diminish when I pulled into my driveway and turned off the car. I sat for a few minutes, wondering if he was home. I needed to see him. The need to feel his arms around me was endless.

I unlocked the door and walked around, checking the deck,

only to find that no one was home. Disappointment was heavy in my heart, but I settled for a soak in the hot tub to ease my stress. It had been a good day and a bad day. Good, that I hired someone for at least something, but bad that Gio had to mention the wedding.

"Please, Regan. Get out of here."

I smiled over at Jake. We had made a habit of sitting poolside after dinner in the evening to talk until we were both called in to go to bed. Victoria had flat out refused to go out and buy me a swimming suit, even though Ludovico had argued with her over it. She had bought enough for 'the brat.' I didn't pretend to be hurt by her words. I didn't like her either.

"You don't like me here anymore?" I teased.

"You know that's not it. It's been weeks now. Don't you miss home? Your family? I bet they miss you."

I leaned into him, resting my head on his shoulder. Jake was not only my friend; he was the closest thing I had to a boyfriend even though we had only kissed the one time. We held hands a lot. He had repeatedly told me he liked me and I reciprocated. I did like him. More than I liked anyone else in this world, even my family. Jake listened to me. He told me about himself. He was the easiest person to get along with, and he was all I had.

"I don't think they know that I'm gone," I whispered.

I meant it. It had been almost three weeks. Pops should have found me by now, or something should have happened. But nothing. Nothing had happened. I was still here, living, but not really living. "But I know I have to leave. Eventually."

"I wish you didn't have to, but you do. For yourself."

How did he get so mature? I wondered. "There is no way I can leave here with the gates always closed. That fence is too high for me to climb, and that's assuming I wouldn't get impaled by the spikes on top of it."

Between the two of us, we tried to come up with several plans. Even tying my sheets and escaping out of my window. That wasn't the problem, I could do that. What I couldn't do was get out of the gates. The gates were the problem!

"Too bad you don't have a dog that likes to dig. The dog could dig a hole for me to crawl under the fence to get out."

"Yeah . . ." he said. "Vicky's allergic to dogs and cats."

I rolled my eyes. As if my opinion of her could get any better. If anything, she was nonexistent in my world, a very menial thing to think about it. It was Jake who I worried about having to live with her and her only caring about her daughter and not him. It wasn't fair. He didn't ask for a stepmom like her.

I heard the patio doors slide open and immediately pulled my body away from Jake as though lightning had struck between us. I still did not want his dad to be suspicious that Jake would help me escape. Santino came out and toward us, and I groaned. What did he want now? It was usually Vicky who came to tell us we needed to go in.

He stopped just behind us, looking down at us with a sneer. Looking directly at me with a sneer. Jake wasn't the intruder in this home. I was. He motioned me up with his fingers, but I stayed where I was. It was stupid; I know. I didn't want to anger the very man who had manhandled me since snatching me from my school.

"We're going for a drive," he said.

I didn't move. What did that mean? Were they bringing me home? Not liking the fact that I was not moving, he reached down and grabbed my arm, pulling me roughly to my feet despite my cries of pain at his fingers in my small arm.

"Santino!" Jake scrambled to his feet. "Dad said you couldn't hurt her like that. Let her go or I'm going to go get him. He'll put a bullet through your head."

My eyes widened. I had never heard Jake so angry before. I agreed with him, though. This maniac that held me by the arm so tight that my feet were nearly dangling shouldn't be alive. I wasn't sure if I was a bad person or just so angry at this *situation.*

Santino ignored Jake, pulling me along with him back toward the house without a response. If we were leaving, it could give me the chance that I needed to escape! I looked at the gun at his waist, on the other side from where he held me, of course. If I reached out, I could grab it, but he was walking so fast across the living room. Dare I try to punch him?

I didn't get the chance.

Chapter Eleven

Santino opened the front door, and I glanced at Jake, who had a scared expression as he was running after us. With a loud bang, the door shut and Jake disappeared from my view. I took that moment to look around at my surroundings, just in case I was coming back. The black car they had kidnapped me in weeks ago was waiting in plain sight just beyond the front doors. Santino hauled me over to the car, opened the door, and threw me in. I waited, rubbing my sore arm. I would kill him if I had the chance, I thought, and I didn't even care if it was something that a horrible person would think and a twelve-year-old girl shouldn't think. I would do it in a heartbeat for hurting me.

The door slammed behind me and a moment later the other back door opened and Santino slid in next to me. The gun was all the way on the other side and that was considering the gap between us. I would have to attack him somehow, but I wasn't sure how. He was at least three times, if not four times, my size. Even as mad as I was, I wouldn't overtake him.

I drew away my attention from the gun when the front door opened and the same man got in that had been driving before. I wondered if we were going for a drive without Ludovico. Why would we be leaving without him if he was the one that ordered me to be taken in the first place? I had seen enough movies to know that if he had taken me for something, an exchange would have to happen. Was he going to kill Pops?

My head spun with unanswered questions. I know I was young and unexperienced, but everything happened for a reason. At least, that was what Uncle Giovanni always told me. I missed Gio. He talked to me more than Pops did, but I missed Nicco the most. I couldn't wait to get back and see him. I couldn't wait to tell him about Jake.

The car lurched into motion and pulled out of the driveway. I turned my attention out the window to watch where we were, even though my mind was racing on how to get that gun away from Santino. When I looked back at him, he was staring at me as though I was up to something. I am up to something; I thought. I'm going to wipe that smirk off your ugly face.

We had to be far enough away from the Mancini house for me to make any kind of move, but not so far away as we got to where we were going. And there was the fact that they were taking me to Pops. I didn't want Pops to die. Maybe I had watched too many crime shows on television.

I sat quietly, biding my time while watching things pass by. Houses on one side, ocean on the other. I didn't know where I was. I was so lost that even if I found a way out of this situation, I would be alone. Then again, if I killed this man, the police would come. It would be impossible for me to go to prison at this age. It would be self-defense. Right?

I was getting tired now that darkness had fallen; I didn't know what time it was, but I had to fight to keep my eyes open. The blur of things going by as we drove was hypnotic. We were still going south because I could see the ocean out my window. I was suddenly optimistic that I was being taken home.

I wasn't sure if I was running out of time or not, but I didn't want to fall asleep and then something to happen. There were too many what-ifs and if I was going to take matters into my own hands, I needed to get out of this situation no matter where we were going.

Biting my lip, I let out a bloodcurdling scream and leaned down to grab my leg, which startled Santino enough to crouch close to me to see what was wrong. I took that moment to push against him while reaching out to grab his gun, but he pushed me back.

At that moment, I felt like a hellcat that wasn't going to back down. My fingers brushed the handle of the gun. I was so close! Just a little more. He pushed me back into the seat and I bit down as hard as I could on his forearm, causing him to howl and move away enough for me to grab the gun and yank it out of the holster. My fingers curled around the handle and I pulled the trigger.

My eyes popped open at the most vivid detail of my memory. My muscles had relaxed, the pulsating jets of the hot tub massaging my tired body. If only the stress in my life would stay away permanently. It was only going to get worse.

I wasn't surprised when I heard footsteps across the deck and moments later, another person sinking down into my hot tub. My lips curved when Cameron's arms came around me possessively, pulling me into his arms and not wasting any more time before he pressing his mouth to mine.

The release of harmful toxins gathering in my body melted away while I let him move his lips against mine. All I could do was moan in return, my legs wrapping around his waist, and he pulled me from the edge of the hot tub. He intertwined my fingers with his and began leaving a blazing a trail with his mouth along my neck. I was getting far too used to this, but I didn't care.

That memory had shaken me to my core. It was only the start of the horrors that I would face, not only from the fact that someone was dead because I had a hand in it, but it started the motions of what my life was today.

"I've been waiting for this all day . . ." he murmured against my mouth. "Tell me about your day."

"Not when you're doing that," I growled.

He stopped his assault on my neck, but kept his arms firmly around me. "Tell me. Let me carry your problems for you for a while."

"I had a minor issue at the office."

"Minor?"

"Melanie's been stealing from me."

"Are you kidding me?"

"No, she was padding her paychecks. But that was only because her boyfriend up and dumped her with an apartment lease, bills, and a car loan with a car that he stole." He shook his head, but I continued. "That's not all. Her ex-boyfriend got into some drugs. An ex-boyfriend that she said comes back to the island from time to time, and thought she saw the night someone mugged me."

He pulled away from me a fraction, surprise lighting his eyes. "Not the same."

I pulled away from him to sip my wine before continuing my tale. "Wears a black zip-up hoodie. Could you find out from Sweetheart what they did with him? He stole her car, leaving her with the loan."

His throat vibrated with the anticipation of a thrilling adventure. "This ought to be fun. I'll call him later." He moved back in to kiss me, but pulled back at the last second. "What did you do about Melanie?"

"I gave her more money."

"Why would you give her more money?"

"Because I feel bad for her. She got taken in by some asshole that left her high and dry. I told her to come to me next time, and I trust she will."

He laughed, his lips at my neck without pause this time. I left out the part that I had hired a replacement for the manager with a man that had given me vibes that he would pursue a relationship with me outside of work if given the chance. Cameron would not take that well, although it would never happen. Even if things took a different turn, I was too involved with Cameron to look twice at another man right now.

Cameron shook his head. "Are you monitoring her?"

I shrugged. "I'll need to. It might delay my departure."

"No complaints from me. I think I can handle you being around for a while longer."

I didn't figure there would be any protests from him, silently smiling when he pulled the string on my bikini top and watched it float to the surface. A moment later, he had pushed me against the edge of the tub while I toyed with the end of his hair next to his ear. His hand disappeared under the rolling water, the bottoms of my bikini floating up next to the top.

I gasped loudly when he pushed into me and stopped, holding me like I was a captive in his arms while he continued pressing his mouth against the skin on my neck. His lips were strong, possessive. It made me feel like he would never let me go. And at that moment, I didn't want him to let me go. Heeding his advice to let him carry my problems, I let my worries slip away.

"I could get used to this," he said.

I said nothing and hoped that he received the message loud and clear before he brought me to the brink of sparks flying throughout my body. He wanted to keep me here for a long time.

It was several moments later when he pulled me into his lap in the tub, nuzzling my neck. I was content where I was now, not bothering to reclaim my bikini bottom from across the tub.

"Tell me why someone is trying to hurt you," he whispered.

Caution edged his voice, and I looked into his eyes. He had the most breathtaking eyes I had ever seen. Eyes that were only on me, intense and caring. It would be so easy just to tell him my whole sordid life, in hopes he would shrug and not give a damn. Maybe he wouldn't care. Selfishly, I think he would care. He would be angry and leave. I wasn't ready to give him up yet.

"I can't," I whispered. "I don't know why."

"I can help you." He toyed with my earring. "But I need to know. I need to know why someone would try to drug you."

I pressed my wet palm against his roughened cheek but didn't say anything. What would I say? We will never truly be together. I will be married to someone else within six months? It sounded absurd, even in my head. I opened my mouth to deny it again, only to choke on an outgoing sob. How was I going to leave him?

"You're safe with me."

"I know."

"I like your house."

"Good."

"I can see me in it on a more permanent basis."

I shook my head. "Stop it. Trying to win me over is pointless."

"Because you'll eventually give in, or you're scared that you might love me more than you think you do."

"I never said I loved you."

He looked at me as though he was going to counter it, but didn't want to appear cocky. I said nothing, knowing that he was right. My heart beat faster.

The love that I had felt for him had only grown stronger since the night someone drugged me. It felt like nothing I had experienced before. Now, it was only heightened and marriage or not; I knew I would never get over him. I would never love like this again.

"You want me to visit you in California for an occasional, maybe frequent, hookup and nothing else?" He shook his head. "I'm done with those types of relationships."

I stared at him. "It might be all I have to give."

"You mean more to me than that. I don't know why, or how, but you fit into my life. Unless you show me some flaws, I'm going to say-"

I sat up straighter, alarmed, shaking my head. "Don't. Don't say it."

"I agreed I wouldn't push you. And I've kept my word. We have something here. Something is going on that neither of us expected. We have to face it."

Giving in would mean giving him more than I could. There was too much at stake. Too much to lose. I tried not to imagine what it would be like to marry someone else. I had put it from my mind as much as I could, but it was always there.

Every conversation with Gio, or when I had to go look for a wedding dress, was like a punch to my stomach. Every time I glanced at Cameron sleeping near me, it filled my heart with an emotion so strong I was sure it would burst in my chest. He would never be permanent in my life. I knew I would never open completely to him. Having only known him for a little more than a month, I knew exactly where this was leading. And it would be a disaster when it ended.

"Marry me."

Damn it all to hell, he'd said it. I sighed, lowering my forehead to his. I wanted so badly to say yes. We would break up later, anyway, if I said yes. I knew my heart would break in this process. I was strong. I could handle it. The thought of him hating me in the end was unbearable. If he were to find out, I'm sure he would despise me.

"You know that isn't something that can happen," I whispered.

He searched my eyes. "Is there someone else?"

My heart lurched. "No. I told you when this all started, there was no one else."

"Then tell me why."

"Can't we just stay like this while we can?"

He wouldn't release my gaze, even though he was quiet. I could almost see his mind working, and I wished there was some way I could convince him that marriage wasn't an option for us without telling him the truth.

"For now," he whispered.

Cameron wouldn't back down now. He didn't quit when he wanted something. That wasn't the problem. The problem wasn't that I didn't want to marry him. It was that he didn't know that I couldn't marry him.

Chapter Twelve

"I don't know much about your family," Cameron commented while I watched him trim the mainsail from my seat at the back of the boat where the wheel was. He laughed. "I don't know anything about your family, other than you have an uncle named Gio."

Satisfied with the position, he jumped over and took the wheel, sending the boat careening toward the open water of the Atlantic. He hadn't mentioned our conversation from almost a week ago or pressed me about saying yes to his impromptu proposal. We had slipped back into the same routine and the boatyard was running well enough to have told Justin just yesterday that I was not coming in daily anymore. He had it under control and could always call if he had questions.

I tried not to be alarmed that the end of October was closing in quickly. For two months, I had been here, and I had known Cameron for as long. I knew my time here was ending, even if Gio hadn't come right out and told me. I couldn't stay here forever as much as I would have liked to just fade out. Pops was still on hiatus. Neither Gio nor I had heard from him.

"You're very good at this," I said, pulling up my knee and resting my cheek on it while I watched him handle the wheel. He wore a pair of blue jeans and a white t-shirt. The day had turned out to be cold, and I had opted to wear a bulky sweater I could remove later. The sun was warm. It wouldn't get colder until the next month or two. Being away from the mainland, the island was cooler during the winter months.

"You're avoiding it."

"I'm avoiding what?"

"Tell me about your family," he urged.

I sighed. "I'm an only child. What is there to tell?" He gave me a face. "You know my mom died when I was young. Too young to remember her. It was just me and Pops for a while until he met Anne."

"Your stepmom?"

I shrugged. "Not legally. I don't have much of a relationship with her. Her daughter, Amber, is six years younger than me and in college. I never really had much of a relationship with Pops, either. He's family, but he never really got involved when I was growing up. He' still my Pops though."

"That must have been lonely."

It wasn't. I had Nicco to talk to, except during the summer. Nicco was still around to drive me wherever I needed to go, but he wasn't there every day like during the school year. I guess it had been lonely. I had my dancing. I refused to stay stuck in the past, dwelling on all the hardships I faced in my childhood and what Pops did or didn't do for me.

"Regan?"

I smiled. "You told me about Zoey. Tell me about your brothers."

"Stefan and Peter. Stefan is five years younger than me."

"Twenty-four?"

"Yes. Peter is twenty-two, and he knocked up his girlfriend when he was eighteen, so he's married and has a three-year- old."

My mouth shot open. "Shut up! You're an uncle?"

He laughed. "That's what they told me when Caleb was born."

"So, what happened when Peter knocked her up?"

"Emma. My father made Peter marry her. There is no shirking

a duty like that in our family. Peter messed up, and he needed to make it right. My father made sure that Peter took care of Emma."

"How old was Emma when she got pregnant?"

"She was eighteen. Poor girl was so scared. Her parents put up one hell of a fight not to marry Peter, but my father was   not having it. They were getting married, and that was all there was to it. Peter would take care of her and the baby."

"Now where are they?"

"They live in Henderson. Close to my parents."

"What does Peter do?"

When Cameron looked in my direction, the look on his face was strange, like he didn't want me to discover Peter's job. Now, I was curious. "He's a banker."

Nothing wrong with a banker.

"And you grew up in Vegas?"

"I grew up in Lake Las Vegas so technically the area. It's a desert. Dry and hot except in January and February, then it's just dry and not as hot. It gets cold sometimes." I laughed. "My parents are still alive, still married, and still live in the same house."

Sounded delightfully boring, I thought to myself. I had imagined a life like that in California with my mom still alive. Having my mother around would have changed my life. "Did you always think that maybe you would settle down in Vegas? Or somewhere else?"

I could feel his eyes on me and I sincerely hoped that he didn't think that I was asking him that to gauge where his future was going. "No. I don't want to raise a family in Vegas."

"Seems like you turned out fine."

"Okay, let me rephrase that. That's not a place I want to raise *my* kids."

"You want kids?"

He shrugged. "Yes. Even though Zoey can be a pain in the ass. You?"

I'd been so busy in my life that I hadn't given much thought to kids. My mind wandered to the little boy that was lost on the ferry and how I had scooped him up into my arms to find his mom without thinking about it.

"Yeah, I guess so."

He laughed. "You guess? Seems like something that you should want to be certain about. It's not a commitment for a short time. It's a lifetime commitment."

"I want kids. I just don't want them growing up with a mom who's always gone. With my career, I don't know how I'd do that."

I knew precisely what I would do. I wouldn't be working the career I'm in. I kept that from him. If I were a mom, I would devote myself fully. I would be all in for my children. I would sacrifice for my family. Not like Pops was my whole life. But I was nowhere ready for that.

"I think you'd make a great mom."

I smiled and gave him a wink. "Thanks."

"I found Melanie's ex-boyfriend. Lives in a seedy part of Myrtle Beach. Didn't have a car. I'm not sure what he did with it. What do you want me to do with him?"

"Do you think he'll come back to the island?"

"Not after Sweetheart and the boys roughed him up some."

"I'll take care of her car loan for her," I said.

He held out his hand to me, motioning me over. I jumped to my feet and went over to him. He moved away from the wheel and pulled me in front of it, caging me in with his arms. I had no choice but to be between him and the wheel.

"Ever sailed a boat before?"

"No, but it doesn't appear to be too difficult. How far are we going out?" I asked, glancing over to see the shore getting farther away. In time, it would become a small dot on the horizon.

"Not too much farther. Just far in enough to weigh anchor and enjoy the sun for a while. I could use a little quiet away from the island."

I was in full agreement. I could sail away and never return home. Never face my responsibilities or the fact that, in doing so, I would put not only my own life at risk, but Jake's too. I wasn't that selfish, though. We could live in this boat. It was spacious enough for a cabin that included a bedroom, bathroom, and kitchenette. Not enormous, but still reasonably large.

We stopped and dropped the anchor not too long after that, lapsing into a comfortable quiet as we both sank deep into our own thoughts. Cameron went below and brought up some blankets and pillows to put on the deck so we could relax. He held up a bottle of white wine and two glasses with a grin.

We settled down on the blanket and he pulled me to recline against him between his legs while he poured us each a glass of wine. I draped my legs over one of his and accepted some wine.

"Did you bring your swimming suit?"

I shook my head. "I wasn't sure if it would be warm enough."

"No matter. We can always skinny dip." I punched his arm playfully. "I wasn't kidding. I always wondered what it would be like to make love in the ocean."

"You've never?"

"No. You're the only woman I've had on this boat. And I've never had sex with anyone in the ocean. You'd be a first for that, too." I looked into his eyes to check if he was being honest.

I thought he had led a rather worldly life, but it turns out he was just as reserved as I was. I never took risks in my relationships, the very few there had been. Other than Michael, which had carried on for only a couple of years, and the short relationship I had at the end of my high school year, I had only two other relationships. Both were in college and weren't serious. If they had lasted longer, they might have been, but they didn't.

"How are you even single?" I teased.

"I'm not single. I'm with you."

I bit down on the inside of my cheek as a warning to myself to keep my mouth closed. I didn't want to rehash this argument with him. I was stealing away these moments, and I was fortunate to spend them with him. I wouldn't take them lightly.

It occurred to me that maybe I should have returned home a while ago and avoided falling into such an easy routine with him. We truly hadn't spent a night without each other.

"Regan . . ."

I shook my head. "I'm not talking about this again, Cameron."

He didn't say anything else or start an argument that might ruin our nice day and that I was grateful for. We sipped our wine, basking in the sun and each other's company.

We had been so engrossed in our conversation that we didn't hear the boat pulling up behind us until we heard an 'ahoy' from starboard. I sat up, trying to see who would disturb us. I had never been on a sailboat before, but I was sure that people just didn't swing by to say hello while out at sea.

Cameron was the first to stand up, followed by me, and that was when I saw Justin. What in the world . . . He was looking at Cameron, sizing him up, and I was getting angry. This was highly unusual that he just happened by.

"Justin?" I said, walking over to the side of the boat. "What are you doing here?"

He spread his arms wide. "Exactly what you're doing. Enjoying the day." He looked pointedly at Cameron. "I'm Justin. Regan hired me for the manager position at the boatyard."

"She mentioned that," Cameron said, the words coming out slowly and calculated. This was a side of him I hadn't seen. He was jealous. "I'm Cameron. Regan's boyfriend."

That had yet to be declared. I guess he was, but we had never stated it outright and it didn't give him the right to introduce himself like that. Then again, he declared it because Justin was young and he felt threatened by him.

Cameron moved his hand toward the waistband of his jeans, a clear sign to me he was reaching for his gun. I slipped my arm around him in alarm, my breath releasing when he abandoned the action. My mind was racing, trying to figure out why he was going for his gun.

"Is everything okay?" I asked Justin.

"It is. I'm just out enjoying my day off. It seemed like a good day for a sail. Light breeze, warm sun. I'm not fortunate enough as Cameron to have the company of a beautiful woman, though." I felt Cameron tense beside me. "I just wanted to say hello as I passed. I'll be going now. Enjoy the rest of your day."

Cameron and I watched Justin sail on without a word to each other. I tightened my arm around him, feeling the muscles in his arm stiffen. He wasn't happy. I wasn't sure if he wasn't happy that Justin had said what he had, or that I failed to tell him I hired someone for the manager position. Not that it mattered. Justin was an employee.

"Cameron," I whispered.

"Why didn't you tell me?" His voice was flat.

"Tell you what? I hired someone for the boatyard and now I don't have to go into the office anymore. Justin has it under control." I slipped my arm away from him, turning to go back to our blankets.

Cameron grabbed my upper arm to stop me. My breath caught in my throat, and my eyes widened while my heartbeat picked up speed. I tried to focus, tried to pay attention to my breathing, so I didn't completely freak out. No one had dared to touch me this way since . . .

"Let go of my arm," I whispered.

He didn't move.

"Cameron," I said, urgency laced in my voice. "Please let go of my arm."

Panic was setting in until he slowly released my arm and dropped his hand away. I almost dove right over the side of the boat and started swimming for shore. I didn't want these memories to flood me today. I didn't want to think about that time. It was long ago, deeply buried. The memories that were coming up now had no reason to come up.

I sat back down on the blanket, drawing my knees up to my chest as tears spilled out of my eyes, burning trails down my face. I felt Cameron sit behind me, but he didn't reach out to touch me.

I was confused. When was the last time I had cried? I don't think I had shed a single tear following the incident. I never cried about it. Just like Pops did, I buried it deep. I could sense Cameron wanting to reach out.

"Don't," I said, my voice raw and terse.

"I didn't mean to grab you. I would never hurt you."

"It isn't that. Please. I just need a moment."

I closed my eyes tight.

There was a pop. I squeezed my eyes shut, knowing that the gun had gone off. I didn't want to see what I hit, or I didn't want to see Santino's eyes. My ears were ringing from the shot, but I didn't care. He went limp, and I knew I had hit him. I didn't know if he was dead and I didn't want to see. The disbelief at what I had done rushed me. It gutted me.

Then I thought I felt him move and someone suddenly threw me away, but I still had the gun in my hand, so I pulled the trigger again. There was another pop. It threw me against the front seats while the car veered. The sound of tires screeching echoed through the car. My hands fumbled, and the gun slipped out of my grasp.

What was happening? Why was the car driving like this? I thought, and then I thought maybe I was going to die for what I had done. The impact of hitting something bounced me around in the backseat and I closed my eyes. A body slammed into mine and I thought it was Santino grabbing me again. I screamed and didn't stop screaming even when everything around me stopped.

I felt hands come around me and I kicked my arms and legs, still screaming as hard as I could. Santino wouldn't get me this time. Arms came around me, a warm voice washing over me.

"Regan . . . ssshhhh . . . you're safe."

I stopped screaming, but my ears were still ringing. I stopped struggling and opened my eyes to see the familiar dark mustache and goatee that belonged to Pops. I blinked. Was I dreaming? Was I dead, and I was seeing him before hell opened and swallowed me whole?

"Regan, you're fine," he said, smoothing down my hair. "You're safe now."

"Did I kill him?" I whispered.

There was a soft chuckle. "You killed them both, my brave girl." He pressed a kiss to the top of my head. "You killed those bastards that took you."

They had taken me, yes. But it was Ludovico. Somehow, I couldn't bring myself to tell him about Ludovico and Vicky, about Jake. I didn't want anything bad to happen to Jake. I kept quiet, and I said nothing. I never did. But Pops knew. He knew who had taken me.

A blanket came around me, and I looked around. We were in a parking lot and it was dark outside, but I could see the crumpled black car wrapped around a pole. I wasn't stunned. I didn't feel bad. I should feel bad. What was wrong with me? Pops said I killed them both. But I was safe now, and I was going to go home. That was all that mattered to me.

Pops set me down to sit on a concrete parking blockade and moved away to talk with Frank. Pops didn't go anywhere without Frank. He was his sidekick. I could see that Pops' lawyer Ezekiel was there too and several others who I knew worked for Pops. I wondered what we were all doing there.

"She shot them both?" Frank leaned toward Pops to ask.

"She did. She shot the one in the backseat right through the heart. I think it severed his spine because he looks like it killed him instantly. The other bullet went right through the driver's head, and the car lost control."

Frank laughed then. "She's your daughter. No doubt about that."

"No doubt," Pops agreed.

Ezekiel stepped over to them. "We need to get out of there. There could be witnesses who saw them pulling in here."

"How did she know they were almost here?" Frank asked.

I couldn't hear the reply from Pops. I wondered that same thing. How did I know we had been close? It was then I heard a couple more pops that sounded like gunshots. Frank tackled me, and I was going backward with my legs flying up in the air.

I winced when the ground scraped my arm, but I didn't say anything or cry out. We were under attack. I lifted my head and saw Ezekiel and Pops crouching down behind a dumpster. There were more pops, and I clamped my hands over my ears, watching as Ezekiel pulled out a gun and fired a couple of shots. I looked across the parking lot and saw a person laying there, his eyes open and staring blankly back at me. He was dead. That was a man that worked for Pops. I had seen him before. I gasped.

"Close your eyes, Regan," Frank whispered to me. "Close your eyes and keep your hands over your ears."

I did what he said, not wanting to watch this. I squeezed my eyes shut as hard as I could, keeping my hands over my ears until my arms ached. After a while, I felt a tug at my arm, but I kept them clapped over my ears with my eyes closed.

"Regan," Frank whispered. "It's over, baby girl. I'm going to pick you up and put you in the car. Keep your eyes closed while I do that, okay?"

I nodded. "Is Pops okay?"

"Your Pops is fine."

"Ezekiel?"

"He's fine too."

He lifted me up like I weighed nothing at all, cradling me in his arms while he walked across the parking lot. I did what he had said and kept my eyes squeezed shut until he put me in the backseat and told me to lie down and try to sleep.

The door shut, leaving me in darkness and silence.

"We need to get out of here," Ezekiel said. He had a scratchy voice. For as long as I had known him, his voice had been that way. He must be standing near the car, unaware that I could hear him. "The cops will be here soon after those gunshots. No doubt someone would have called that in."

"Ludovico?"

My ears perked up.

"He got away."

I heard Pops say the 'F' word, and I smiled. Ludovico had those two thugs bring me back to Pops, but Ludovico had been following behind. This was the exchange. Ludovico was trading me back to Pops for whatever he wanted. The drug deal he wanted in on. Except I screwed it up when I killed his men. He may have been planning to kill my Pops, or Frank and Ezekiel. By killing Santino and the driver, I might have saved them.

I wanted to sit up and ask them questions, but Pops wouldn't be happy if I started asking questions. Or maybe he would. I still didn't want to get Jake in trouble. Pops knew it had been Ludovico that took me.

The door opened, and I sat up to see Pops. I gave him a smile. Not a cheerful smile, but a smile that would tell him I was okay. He reached out to pat my leg, frowning at the pair of jeans that I was wearing. I shrugged.

"Did they hurt you?"

I shook my head.

"Are you telling me the truth?"

I didn't nod or shake my head. It didn't matter anymore. The one who hurt me was dead. I did that. "Am I going to jail?"

"No. No one will ever find out you killed anyone. It shall remain our little secret." He paused for a minute, still looking at me. "What did it feel like to kill them?"

I shrugged. "Santino hurt me. The other one was an accident."

A darkness passed over his face. "Hurt you how?"

"He was always grabbing my arm. Right here." I pointed at

my left upper arm. "Always pulling me. But then he came and got me, and did it again and said we were going for a drive. After that, I wanted to kill him. Ludovico told him. He told him not to hurt me anymore."

He patted my leg. "And he won't, baby. He won't hurt you anymore."

And no one did.

I took a deep breath, looking out at the ripples in the water. I had killed two men. I hadn't cried about it. I hadn't felt remorse. After Pops put me into martial arts training, I thought I was a machine. In high school, I had even felt like a machine. No one would hurt me again. I would make sure of that.

"Regan?"

I looked up at Cameron, wiping my hands across my face to clear away any remaining tear streaks. I wasn't embarrassed this time. I hadn't cried at all. Ever. Not in my life, even after I killed Santino and the other man. I had taken two lives, and I hadn't been remorseful for it, no matter if they were bad or not. That was my burden to carry.

Cameron lowered himself down next to me. "I'm so sorry for grabbing you like that. I swear, I didn't know it was a trigger."

I looked at him. "I didn't know either. I'm fine though. Why were you reaching for your gun when he pulled up?"

I saw his jaw clench. "I saw him. The night someone poisoned you at the bar."

Chills skimmed across my skin. It made sense why he was asking so many questions about my life, where I lived, about the phone call. Suddenly, I was nervous that he had been listening to my conversation with Gio and tried to recall if I had said anything he would have picked up on. Panic was settling in. Had I accepted his invitation to coffee, I might have been putting myself in the line of danger.

I could be jumping to conclusions. Justin could have just been in town that night, and Cameron recognized him. In all the people that were at the club that night, he remembered seeing Justin, of all people.

"Are you sure?"

"Positive. He was at the bar, and he looked right at me. He looked at me like he was challenging me. Regan, you need to . . ." He shook his head. "No. I'll take care of it."

I laid my hand on his arm. "Cameron, don't get wrapped up in this."

"I'm not going to let you go to office and fire him. If he is the one that dropped something in your drink that night, I'm not letting you go anywhere you'd be alone with him." His jaw remained clenched. My hand slipped away from him. "I will take care of it."

Having no desire to see Justin again, if this was the truth, it was best to let Cameron handle it. I didn't want Melanie alone with him, either. I nodded, too numb to speak. I had let my guard down, and it could have been my undoing.

"Do you want to tell me about your trigger?"

I thought about it. I could tell him about this and not incriminate anything else about my life or my future. If he asked questions, I could always not answer them. This story was mine, and it was unique. But I didn't want him to think of me as a killer. I didn't want him to look at me any differently. Not yet.

"They kidnapped me when I was twelve," I whispered. "The man who took me used to grab my arm like that and pull me. I was twelve. I killed him."

Cameron stared at me. I waited for the onslaught of questions. But none came. He slipped his arm around my shoulders and pulled me into him and just held me. He didn't say anything. Cameron just held me. Like he understood.

Chapter Thirteen

I looked down at the glittering gems covering the front of the wedding gown. The gown was nothing short of amazing, tight in the bodice and flowing in the skirt with tiny off-the-arm sleeves that were not much of sleeves, more of just an ivory slip of fabric on each side. The skirt and train weren't extra thick with material, like some gowns were. It hugged me in all the right places and trailed behind me by only a few feet.

"This is silk-faced material," Jane said, tucking and pinning while she circled me. "How does it feel?"

Mirrors covered every wall in the dressing room where I stood on a platform. When I looked at myself, all I could see was Cameron. Here I was, getting a handmade wedding gown for a marriage that I didn't want. My wedding day was something I should be excited about. All I wanted to do was throw up. This was wrong in every way I could think of, and I hated it. Desperately, I wanted to talk to Pops and see if he would change his mind.

I was only here because Cameron had to fly home to manage some family business, which was oddly good. Before I had gone to the office on Monday, he assured me that Justin was not there. He wasn't on the island, and wouldn't be on the island again. I was safe. The question was right there to ask him what he had done, but I hadn't asked. I didn't want to know that Cameron was maybe just like I was. He would do anything to protect what was his.

October had ended swiftly, and November had taken over even faster. I didn't question Cameron's need to go home so suddenly, and he didn't even ask if I wanted to join him. I was astounded he didn't, but I was appreciative to not have to decline. He would start thinking there really was someone else in my life. But I wasn't lying to him. There wasn't someone else in my life. There would be. But there wasn't now. I was treading a very thin line.

"It's exquisite. You really should move your boutique to California. You would make a killing with these dresses."

She laughed, a pin between her teeth, but didn't say anything.

"People will ask who made this gown."

"I import the lace from Venice, and I hand sew the gems on myself. All my dresses, including the bridesmaid dresses, I've handmade."

"You've quite a talent."

"Years of sewing that morphed into wedding gowns. I like it, and it keeps me busy enough even in this location. There are people willing to pay for good work for their special day."

"I don't doubt that."

"When is your special day?"

Special day, I scoffed silently. "March."

"And we're doing your last fitting now? It's way too soon, Miss De Luca."

"Please call me Regan. And I need to do the last fitting now because I'll be going back to California soon and I'm not sure I'll be able to return."

The front bell jingled, but Jane kept pinning without hesitating that she might have more customers to greet or attend to. The boutique was small, but spring weddings were not too far off in the future.

"Do you have another customer to tend to?"

"Oh, that's just my niece. She lives on the island over there,

Cape Haven, but she visits me sometimes."

I froze, the smile on my face sliding away. Jane stopped and looked up at me just as Melanie stepped into the room. Melanie stopped, seeing me standing there, her eyes growing wide.

It must be shocking to see me standing in a wedding dress, assuming that Cameron and I were engaged after knowing each other for less than three months. It's what I would assume if I were in her situation.

"Melanie, this is Regan."

"Yes, I know her. She's my boss," she said. "Hi Regan!"

Shit, shit, shit! I thought. I needed a way out of this, but I was not adept at telling lies. "Melanie, this is not what it looks like. I'm doing this for a friend. Cameron and I are not getting married, despite how crazy this looks."

Jane looked at me, now confused. I felt nauseous. I was lying to everyone in my life right now, even those I wasn't close to. I didn't recognize the person I was becoming.

"That's crazy," she said. "Why isn't your friend here? Isn't getting a wedding dress part of the total experience? It's weird."

"It is," I said, trying to make it seem like a plausible explanation. "I'm glad you're here. I need to talk to you about something. Jane, can I step down for a minute? I feel silly up here."

"Of course. I'll just be in the back room for a moment."

Melanie eyed me cautiously while Jane left us, like she was preparing to be in trouble. I stepped down from the pedestal, still feeling awkward, adorned in a bridal gown, and trying to act like it wasn't mine.

"Melanie, you know how Justin left and never came back?"

"Right, that was so weird," she said. "He works for a while and then all of a sudden stop showing up?"

"I suppose he changed his mind, and rather than giving me a head's up about it, he just left and found something else. But that leaves us without a manager still. I need to go home. Soon."

"To California?"

"Yes. I can put out another ad for a manager, but it took so long to get one applicant this time. I'm wondering if you would be interested in doing it. It would be like a dual position since the receptionist position would be open, but . . ."

With a squeak, she launched herself at me and knocked me to my ass on the pedestal. Her arms hooked around my neck and she didn't seem to care about the pins that were in the gown, but I did. They were poking sharply into me.

"Melanie!" Jane shouted, hurrying over to pull her off me. "What on earth are you doing? You can't attack people like that. Excuse us." Jane took Melanie by the hand and pulled her out of the room.

"Before you go, I need an answer." I pushed myself up, trying not to wince.

A grin lit Melanie's face. "Are you serious? You want me?"

"You're a smart woman. I'll increase your salary, of course. I expect you to handle the incoming calls and visitors still, but you probably won't have time to file your nails."

She looked down with a blush, but looked back up after a moment as though her confidence was finally building. I knew she was smart. A push was all she needed and she could find success.

"I'll take it!"

"Oh, and I couldn't find your car, but I'll be taking care of your car loan. You shouldn't have to pay for something that was stolen from you. I'll get you a check this week if you can get me the payoff amount."

She was going to launch herself at me again, but Jane caught her and pulled her out of the room before she could do more damage. They left me standing alone, and although I was pleased that she was accepting the role as manager; I was thinking she would say something to Cameron about this if she saw him. All it would take is congratulations, and he would be confused. It would completely throw him off base, and I would have no choice but to give him the entire sordid story. I knew it was coming sooner rather than later, but I always thought that we would just stop. He would never need to know about this stupid situation.

Jane returned, looking highly upset. "I am so sorry, Regan."

"Jane, please. Don't be sorry. This is a rather odd situation. I would rather no one else knows about it, regardless of why I'm here. In fact, I would prefer if no one knew I was here."

"There will be discretion."

I closed my eyes, the sourness in my stomach rolling. "I would certainly be willing to pay you extra. For your discretion."

"That is unnecessary. Melanie will be discreet."

"I think she will, but thank you."

"That was awfully nice of you to offer her a better position at your company."

"I've been considering her for a while, even before the application came in. I think she's bright and can handle it. She knows where to reach me if she has issues. I can always fly back."

"You're a wonderful person."

If she only knew, I thought. She probably wouldn't think that of me. "You'll have the gown finished and delivered to the address I left with you before March?"

Jane stood up, letting the rest of the pins drop from her mouth to her open hand. She took my hand in hers as though we had known each other for many years. "Yes, and I wish you the best of luck, my dear."

"Thank you."

I didn't see Melanie again before I left, and I wasn't sure how I felt about it. I would have preferred a conversation directly with her about what she saw. With this, I couldn't trust what Jane had said to her. I needed her to know I would pay her more for additional discretion, if only for another few months.

I pulled my car into the driveway a couple of hours later while the sun was setting, closing the gate behind me, and enabling the security system as soon as I got into the house and closed the door.

The house was too quiet. The island was too vacant. It gave me an uneasy feeling not having Cameron here. I berated myself for being such a softy. He hadn't even been gone one day, having only left yesterday. Still, the house was empty without him.

I didn't even feel like sitting in the hot tub. I poured a glass of wine and sat down on the couch with my phone to review my messages. After I reviewed my emails, I made myself a quick dinner and resumed my position on the couch in hopes Cameron would at least call like he had last night after he arrived in Vegas.

But instead of Cameron calling, Jake called. Frowning, I answered the call and pulled my knees up to hug myself.

"I didn't expect to hear from you," I said.

"I missed your voice," he laughed. "Are you still 'away'?"

"Yes. Still away."

"Still expecting to marry someone you don't know?"

I didn't know otherwise, not having talked to Pops for almost three months. "I think he was serious this time, but I haven't spoken with him. My uncle says it's still being planned."

The breath Jake blew out was audible through the phone. I knew how I felt about it, but his anger surprised me. I wondered if he thought there would ever be anything between us. That would be impossible, and we both knew it. He still didn't know that Pops had threatened him if I didn't go through with this, and I wasn't planning on telling him.

"Is everything okay there?"

I perked up. "Yes. Why do you ask?"

"Regan, of all the people you can trust, you can trust me the most. I promise you. I would never be the one to betray anything. I hope that you're somewhere safe, and that you stay safe."

"You know me. I'll take someone out if I need to."

He laughed again, a deep, rumbling sound. "I know you would. Will you call me when you get back? I'd love to see you when you get back. If you can."

"I'll call you when I get back."

"Bye, Reggie."

After hanging up, I got up from the couch to look out the window at the deck. Rain slashed against the windowpanes and was spraying across the deck, the sky impossibly dark. Lightning zipped across the dark sky and I jumped when the lights went out. This was all that I needed right now.

I turned the flashlight on my phone on and went into my bedroom to see if the neighbor's house was also dark and to light candles. At the very least, I had my phone. I pulled back the curtains to see that their deck lights were on.

They had power. I didn't. That would mean that my power was out for a purpose. I was on full alert, moving quietly to leave my room until I saw the shape of a figure near the front door when lightning illuminated the house. This was not good. Of all the times I wished I had a gun, now was one. I would have to use good old-fashioned fist-fighting with anyone who dared to attack me.

I had a baseball bat. And I had a way out from my bedroom, except I would have to cross the deck and get down to the gate. I had no way of knowing whether I could get the gate open with the security system out. But there had to be a way, and I would try it.

I slid along the wall toward the door to the deck. Unfortunately, the bat was under the bed and I didn't dare try to find it when someone could enter my bedroom. Slowly, I reached for the handle of the door, but I couldn't unlock it one-handed.

Quickly, I moved so both my hands were on it and I heard the click just as I saw a shadow behind me. Someone grabbed me around both arms to immobilize me. Nice try, I thought, and threw my head back into his. I connected with his nose and heard him yell and cuss. He threw me across the floor, and I landed near my door in a tangle of limbs. I recovered as quickly as I could, running into the living room, intending to run to the patio doors there.

There were two of them. Someone grabbed me with enough

force to spin me around. I bent quickly, using my body weight to throw him over my shoulder, right onto the coffee table, shattering it. I took a punch to my shoulder, momentarily stunning me and another one just below my eye. These were powerful men. It had been a long time since I had been to martial arts training, trying to recall moves that would save my life. They were here for one reason. To kill me.

I took another punch to the gut, the breath expelling from my lungs in a whoosh, and dropped to my knees. He was cocky, though, pausing as though he had me this time. I saw the flash of a gun when lightning illuminated the room.

I pushed myself to the side and swung out my leg, catching him off-guard and taking out his legs from beneath him. Lightning was on my side, lightening up the room again so I could see the gun in his hand and I kicked as I jumped and the gun flew out of his hand. There was no doubt the other man had a gun, too, and I ran for my room.

I slammed the bedroom behind me and dashed across my room toward the door, throwing it open, and sprinted across the deck. My bare feet had me sliding on the deck boards from the rain as I ran. I scrambled down to the gate and threw the latch open. Thankfully, it opened, and I took off in a hard run down the beach, regardless of the rain pelting me. It wasn't the rain I was worried about; it was the lightning. As I ran, I tried to look behind me, and at least one of them was coming after me, quickly.

I would make it to town before him or die trying. I'd fought my way out of situations before. He would not get me. I would get to the police station and hope that someone was there. If not, I hoped I would make it to the hotel, although I had no desire to put Isabel or her staff in danger.

The wet sand made it difficult to run in, but at least I didn't have shoes. My lungs burned with the exertion that I was having to maintain to keep a distance between us. My stomach hurt, my shoulder hurt, and my face hurt, but he would not catch me.

I swiped the hair out of my face. If only it wasn't raining. This was making it much harder than it needed to be. At least it would make it hard for whoever was following behind me. I risked another look back to see that he was gaining on me. Damn it, I thought.

I was nearing the end of the row of houses, and just around the corner was the town pavilion. I was almost there. Just a little more and I would be on pavement. I was out of breath, my lungs were screaming in agony, and my heart was beating so hard that I could feel it in my ears.

Lightning streaked across the sky. My bare feet hit the pavement as I darted to my right. The buildings along the main street were lit up. I doubled my effort to get there faster.

I tried to zigzag across the town square, the police station within my sights. The rain was coming down so hard that a car nearly hit me when I ran across the street between the start of the town square and the police station. I rolled off the hood and ran smack into the door of the police station. I looked across the street, and the man chasing me was still there.

I yanked open the door. Ryan, the deputy, sat behind the tall front desk and looked up at me when I ran in. He noticed my state of fear; the red mark on my cheek, and stood up just as the door opened behind me. A gunshot went off, my ears ringing from the familiar sound.

I screamed at the blood that suddenly appeared on the front of Ryan's uniform, but he had had his gun out too and I looked back to see the guy fall to the floor just as another man dressed in black stepped through the door, holding a gun aimed at me as he stepped more fully into the station. This was it. This was how I was going to die. And I hadn't even been able to tell Cameron that I loved him, that I would always love him. No matter what happened.

The man pulled his hood down with his free hand, and my eyes widened. Justin. Cameron told me he took care of him. The look in his eyes was that of triumph, and I could hear his deep chuckle.

"Couldn't have just let things happen the way they should've. Your boyfriend should've made sure I was dead. Now I can finish the job."

My eyes narrowed. "Who sent you?"

He laughed, then shook his head. That wasn't information I would get so easily. The gun raised a fraction. I closed my eyes, waiting for my lights to go out. The sound of a gun discharge was familiar to me, the second buzz in my ears without ear protection a known sensation, but I didn't feel anything. I slowly opened my eyes. The gun dangled in his hand, blood trickling down the side of his head out of his temple. He fell to the floor sideways.

Isabel stood holding a gun in front of her. Her gaze was solemn and her hands were steady. It was as though she had held a gun, used a gun, before. She knew what she was doing.

"Oh my god," I whispered. "How did you . . . my god . . . Ryan!"

I ran around the desk to the deputy. He had his hand, blood oozing between his fingers, at his shoulder. I pulled my thin cardigan off and wadded it up. I pulled his hand away from the gunshot wound, unbuttoned his brown uniform shirt and pressed it inside against the wound, placing his hand back over it. He was damn lucky it wasn't a fatal shot. Judging by how close it was, if it had been nearer, it would have gone right to his heart.

"Pressure," I told him. "You're a cop. You should know that."

He gave me a weak smile as Isabel came around the desk and knelt next to him. "What was that all about?" he asked.

I didn't even know where to start. Ryan wasn't used to something like this occurring on the island, typically he only had to take care of rambunctious parties. There had never been a murder on this island. Now there were two.

I looked over at her. Questions raced through my head. "How in the hell did you know what was going on?"

"I have a lot to tell you," she whispered. "Let's get an

ambulance for Ryan first. Then we'll call the sheriff and we can go over to the hotel so we can talk. As it is, I have several available rooms right now."

I nodded, slumping down to the floor. My everything hurt. I left Ryan and Isabel to keep pressure on his wound while I tried to run my fingers through my tangled hair. How would I explain this mess to Cameron? I didn't even have my phone. I had dropped it somewhere during my impromptu run. It was gone and I would probably never find it again. I'd have to get a new one, and soon.

It was only a matter of minutes before the ambulance showed up, followed by Sheriff Deidrick. He took one look at the two bodies in the lobby and shook his head.

They loaded Ryan up onto a stretcher. The paramedics assured us that Ryan would be fine. I was right. If it had been closer, he would've been carried away in a body bag, but luckily, it missed his vitals. I wasn't sure where to begin.

"Sheriff, can we give you the sordid details tomorrow? I would really like to get Regan over to the hotel to clean up. As you can see, she's in rough shape."

"Now wait just a minute, Isabel. I've got two dead bodies in my lobby, and a deputy on his way to the hospital with a bullet hole in his chest. Someone better tell me what's what now before anyone leaves here."

"These two men attacked her!"

"I'm not skipping town," I said.

He shook his head. "I've known you both for a very long time. This needs to get on record before I document the crime scene and call the morgue to come to retrieve these two bodies."

I nodded and leaned up against the desk. Isabel suggested she get me a cup of coffee so I could explain my perspective before she shared hers. I couldn't wait to hear her side.

"I was looking outside at the rain when my power went out," I started.

The sheriff wrote in his notepad everything I told him. If I had been the one to pull the trigger, I was old enough to do jail time, but I hadn't. Ryan shot one, and Isabel shot Justin. I would be damned if Isabel would go to jail for me, though. Isabel pressed a hot cup of coffee into my hands and leaned   up against the desk beside me.

"Why would someone target you and your house?"

I shrugged. "I'm not very popular, I guess."

"Right," he said, meeting my gaze. He didn't bother to hide his skepticism. "Isabel? Have anything to add to this?"

"I do. I went to Regan's house, knowing that Cameron wasn't there. When I was pulling up to her gate, I saw the house go dark. No other house had gone dark, so I knew that something was wrong. I drove up the street a little so I could do a U-turn to head back into town and get Ryan when I saw another car pull right out in front of me. A storm like this . . . people just aren't out and about, so I was a worried."

The car that had nearly hit me, I thought. That was Justin. Damn it, vehicular homicide had almost taken me out. The rest of what Isabel said made complete sense. She saw me run across the street and almost get hit by the car that she had been following, then she saw another man run across the street after me. She parked her car just after the other one and had just gotten through the door to kill Justin before he could kill me.

I watched the sheriff set his notebook and pen down on the desk and run his hand over his face. This was going to be a hell of a report. He looked back over at the two dead guys in the lobby and then back at me.

"I guess it's not unheard of for someone to be watching someone's property and make a target out of them. I'm just not sure why they followed you here and tried to kill you. That makes no sense."

"We don't get it either, Sheriff. Now, can I get my girl out of here?"

Isabel put her arm around me, the other one pressed against my forearm like an affectionate gesture. I was in trouble and yet she had come to my rescue. I owed her an enormous debt.

"Don't leave the island. I may have more questions."

Isabel guided me carefully out of the lobby, keeping me shielded from the two bodies as if I hadn't already been tainted by violence in my life. She didn't know that, though. From what I knew, Pops had never told her about the kidnapping. Or that I had killed two men.

Isabel brought me to the hotel, telling the concierge at the front desk to give her the key to the top corner room and to send up a bottle of wine. It was the very best room she had, and most of the rooms on the top floor were the best. We rode in the elevator in silence.

"You'll be safe here, Regan," she said, unlocking the door and switching on the lights as we entered. "I promise you."

The room was spacious, with a small kitchenette to the left before going into a sunken-in living room with a large balcony beyond. The bedroom and bathroom were directly across the living room through a doorway next to the kitchenette and boasted of a large king-size bed at the far wall and a long dresser with a hidden television.

"I'm going to send someone to your house to check on things and grab you a change of clothes. And shoes." I shook my head. "Regan, I can even send the Sheriff if you would feel better."

"No," I said. "No one goes back there tonight."

She frowned. Knowing Isabel, she was trying to figure out a way to make me comfortable, even though I was fine just to be in a room with a bed and soft carpeting for my aching feet.

"Well, I'm not putting shit from the lost and found on you," she grumbled.

I went over to the couch, flopping down in the comfort of the cushions and easing my feet up onto the coffee table. The soles of my feet were angry red. I chipped my pretty red nail polish and some of my toenails. My feet looked bad. I wanted nothing more than to slide them into a pair of fuzzy socks. I caught Isabel's pained look when she looked at my feet.

"I probably shouldn't be sitting on this nice couch. I'm still wet."

Isabel sat down next to me, brushing a strand of hair out of my face, and tucking it neatly behind my ear. "How about I run you a nice warm bath so you can soak your feet and warm up? You can wrap up in a bathroom robe until we can figure out how to get you some clothes."

"How about you tell me what the hell is going on?" I asked. I was nice about it. My voice had no edge to it. It was just a simple question.

She opened her mouth just as a knock sounded at the door, saving her from having to tell me anything. I hoped beyond all hope that it was wine. I needed a very tall glass of heady wine to calm my frayed nerves. But I needed answers as much.

She returned with the wine and two glasses, setting them on the coffee table and getting to work pouring us some. She handed me a glass, and I downed the entire thing, holding it out for another. When she filled it again, I simply took a sip of this time and set it back down.

"You know you're supposed to sip wine."

"Out with it."

She closed her eyes, taking a couple of gulps from her own glass despite her statement. I watched her look down, running the tip of her finger around the rim of her glass in a hypnotic motion.

"Let me ask this," I whispered. "How much do you know about Pops?"

She raised her eyes to meet mine, the wrinkles at each corner of her eyes not in their usual smiling form. This was serious. I was serious. She gripped the gun as confidently as she did her glass of wine. She hadn't faltered.

"Before I tell you this, hear me out before you ask questions."

"This is not the first time that I've been attacked. Someone is trying to kill me, Isabel. I need to know what you know. No one is supposed to know I'm here, but someone does."

A deep breath rattled its way out of her lungs. "Promise me you'll hear me out before you ask questions, Regan. Promise me."

"You have my word."

Her eyes met mine, and I could see the glimmer of tears threatening. Whatever was about to come out, she had never intended to come out. That made it more necessary for me to know all of it.

"I'm your mother," she whispered, her eyes never wavering from mine.

Chapter Fourteen

"You're my . . . mother? My mother died when I was little."

She held up her hand. "You promised."

I nodded, even though my brain was screaming. Of all the things I thought she was going to say, prepared for her to say, admitting to being my mother was not one of them. My mother had died in a boating accident when I was not much bigger than a toddler. They never found her body.

"I'm not sure now is the time to start this conversation. You must be exhausted. Perhaps tomorrow after you've had time to rest . . ." I stared at her, not about to let her stop now. "I met your father in the summer of 1993. I had been seeing someone else, but it was very new. When I met your father, everything changed. We married the following year, and you were born the next year."

She smiled, nostalgia overcoming her, but she continued. "We realized after you were born that we needed to make sure your future was secure. I experienced complications during my pregnancy with you. I couldn't have any more children. Everything that we had built together would someday fall to you, and we wanted to make sure that you had another powerful family to support you."

"So, you put me up for bait to another family?" I couldn't help the sourness in my voice or how vehement I felt. I knew it was because I couldn't confront Pops about it right now. Isabel was the only one that I could vent to.

"Not bait. We were best friends with the other family. It was a perfect fit between our two families. They would always protect you."

"Because I'm a woman and can't handle things for myself."

"Good gracious, no. We wanted the support to continue, and one night, after having some drinks, we thought our children should be together. You were little, but their son was a little older."

She put her hand on my knee. "Regan, knowing you—even from far away—and knowing them and their son, it is a perfect match. You are perfect for each other."

"But you won't tell me who he is, or who this family is."

She shook her head. "Not until we know it's time. Especially now, after you have had two attempts on your life."

"Why were you pushing me to get into a relationship with Cameron?"

"Good gracious, I hope you don't think I was pushing you. Maybe I was thinking you should have fun while you're stuck here." She took a sip of her wine. "I don't know what your father is up to right now, but I know he wouldn't tell you to lie low without a reason. I think part of me thought Cameron would be an excellent protector for you in the meantime."

I know I gave my promise that I wouldn't ask questions, and I was sure that she was probably getting to it, but I couldn't help myself. "But you know why I'm always in danger."

It wasn't a question. I knew she knew. She nodded confirmation.

"You know Pops is not good. He's killed people."

"Of course, I do. He'll need to tell you more than I can. It was his deal, not mine. I never thought his old friend would have tried to kill me years later for it, though. His old friend has never forgiven him for putting a deal in motion that excluded him."

"Not the family friend that I'm supposedly marrying into?"

"No, but he was a part of it, too. Your father and I thought it would be best if I went into hiding for a time, faked my death, and I came to stay here permanently. We would communicate with fake names, and he would bring you here as often as he could."

"Until he met Anne."

She nodded. "Another plot to make sure that no one questioned my death. He started a relationship with her and eventually stopped bringing you here. But you still came, and I still have a relationship with your father. It's just been more long distance, and not physical."

I felt bad for her then. She had missed out on my entire life in order to save her own. She had missed out on spending time with Pops, and even had to step aside for another woman to enter his life. I closed my eyes, wondering how my life may have been different had none of it happened. If she had been in my life.

"Say something."

I opened my eyes, searching. I had always liked her. She had always been there for me when I came to the island, and I never hesitated in helping her any time she needed it. We were friends when it was really a mother-daughter relationship. She couldn't have told me without blowing her cover.

A tear slipped out of the corner of my eye and her arms immediately came around me, holding me close in a comforting hug that only a mother could give. It released more tears until it was a hailstorm of emotions. Everything that had been building from earlier that day and the confrontation to now spilled free, and I cried in her arms. And she let me. "

"You don't know how many times I wanted to tell you," she whispered. "There never was a good time to say something like this. Until now."

I looked up at her, swiping at my eyes. "Why now?"

"It's time that you knew. You saw me kill that guy. You know I'm comfortable with a gun, even knowing me and my quiet life on the island. I was almost sure that you'd question it. And you did."

"But this changes nothing. This old friend of Pops is still out there."

She nodded. "And he'll stop at nothing to stop this wedding. I'm almost certain of it. The merging of the two families that shut him out to begin with? Oh no, he's cunning, deliberate in his actions, and extremely intelligent."

"What's his name?"

I wasn't sure why I asked. I had a feeling about who the person was. It didn't make a difference who it was. I still wasn't convinced that making me marry someone that I didn't know, that I didn't choose, was the answer to anything.

"Ludovico Mancini."

Chapter Fifteen

"Ludovico Mancini," I repeated softly. That bastard would always show until someone put a stop to him. He kept on coming back, like a bad omen.

"I know what he did when you were younger, Regan. I know he kidnapped you, and I know you killed two of his men trying to get away." She had tears in her eyes. "I was never so proud of you then I was at that moment. I knew you were a true De Luca. You did what you had to in order to protect yourself."

"Like you did. You sacrificed your life with Pops and me. You sacrificed so much, Isabel . . . Mom." A shaky laugh tore from my throat. "Mom . . ."

She pressed a hand to her heart. "You don't know how long I've waited to hear you say that to me. I knew it would eventually happen, but I was so scared that you would be angry. Angry with me for running away."

"You didn't run away! You saved yourself!"

"I deprived you of a mother."

I shook my head. "But you were there. You were always there."

"I really would love to keep talking, but I need to be your mom first and tell you that you need a good soak in the bath followed by rest. You've been through enough today already. We can talk more tomorrow over breakfast." She pressed her hand lightly to my jaw. "Look at what those bastards did to your face . . ."

My stomach and my shoulder didn't feel much better, but they were out of sight. I was sure this was going to bruise. But I knew she was right. I needed a bath and some rest. She helped me to my feet and into the bathroom, where she sat me on the toilet and started the water in the deep Jacuzzi tub. She grabbed a small bottle from the vanity where the complimentary shampoo, conditioner, soap, and lotion displayed on a square mirror and opened it, squeezing a couple of drops into the bath water as it filled.

Lavender permeated the air in the bathroom and I breathed in deeply. I didn't think I would have any problems getting sleep tonight, and this would ensure I did. Suddenly, I couldn't wait to slip into bed. I knew the hotel had the best accommodations. The beds were the most comfortable beds and made with the finest bedding.

"You have a nice, long soak. I'll be out in the living room."

I nodded, removing my shirt before she left the room, followed by my leggings. I dropped them both on the tile floor, shimmying out of my underwear and letting it fall heedlessly on top. For a moment, I stared in the mirror at the angry red welt on my cheekbone and the bruising on my chest. It could have been worse.

When I stepped into the tub, I winced at the temperature, but I forced myself the rest of the way in and sunk down until my head nestled against the edge. The water began repairing my body, even though my feet felt like they were on fire. But I was alive. I had survived. Again. How many chances would I get before I didn't survive? Eventually, I would run out of chances.

I turned off the water when it was deep enough for me to plunge my head under and when I came up, I could hear Isabel talking with someone in the living room. I assumed it was someone on the phone, but it piqued my interest. The one person I would think she would call would be Pops. It hadn't occurred to me to ask her if she knew where he was. I wish he had trusted me enough to tell me where he would be.

I tried not to move, trying to hear her conversation clearly enough to guess who she was speaking to, but she was walking from one end of the room to the other, pacing, and I couldn't speculate.

As the heat consumed me, I closed my eyes, careful not to fall asleep, and slid underwater. After everything I had been through today, I wasn't about to lose it all by doing something so stupid as to drown.

Isabel popped her head in later on to check up on me. The water was cooling, and I was ready to get out. She handed me a towel as I pulled the plug. I dried myself off and slipped into the luxurious white bathrobe, the fabric whispering over my skin.

I sighed, and Isabel gave a quiet laugh. "That's why I have these robes. And the complimentary bath oil. Nothing but the best for my guests."

"Do you think Ludovico is after Pops, too?"

"I wouldn't put it past him, but I think this is a separate deal that possibly went bad. Ludovico is deliberate in his actions, and he's good, as you probably know, at biding his time."

"Who were you talking to?" I asked, and she looked at me sharply. "I thought I heard you talking to someone."

She smiled, ushering me out of the bathroom. "Just a friend."

Instead of guiding me into the living room, she took me into the bedroom and turned on the lamp next to the bed. I didn't have the energy to argue with her. I wanted to talk more and not sleep, but the bed looked inviting. The bedding looked as luxurious as the bathrobe was, if not more so. The pillows, eight of them, were fluffy and the purest of white.

Isabel pulled back the duvet, and I sat down, then stretched out as the mattress nearly swallowed me up. She smiled down at me, pulling the blankets over me. I was so tired that I didn't even care about my hair still being wet. I didn't even have a brush. No toothbrush or toothpaste, no clean clothes. No phone.

She sat on the edge of the bed, brushing the hair over my forehead back gently and very much as a mother would. I smiled, sinking in under the blankets. It didn't matter what I didn't have. I had my mother.

"Sleep, Regan. I'll make sure you have everything you need by morning."

"You aren't staying?"

"I'll stay long enough for you to fall asleep. You're safe here."

I didn't doubt that I wasn't safe. She wouldn't need to wait long for me to fall asleep. I could feel my eyes growing heavier and heavier, closing, then opening like I was a child fighting sleep.

The feel of her fingers brushing against my hair lulled me even faster until my eyes closed and didn't reopen again, pulling me into a state of dreamless, unfettered sleep.

Sleep held no memories, no dreams of my past, no nightmares. Nothing that would have interrupted my much-needed rest. My mind needed it, and my body needed it after what I had been through.

It didn't seem like long enough before I woke when the bed moved, or something was on the bed. The room was dark, only a dim light coming from the window from an outside streetlamp where the windows weren't covered by the curtains. Someone was in my room.

I sat up, a scream starting low in my throat but cut off swiftly by a large hand clamping over my mouth. My hands immediately went to my intruder's arm, trying to pull the hand away from my mouth. I struggled to take in a breath, and my heart beat faster.

"Sshhh . . . Regan. It's me, Cameron."

I stopped struggling against him and he moved his hand away from my mouth to reach over and turn on the lamp, proving to me he wasn't lying. He was here. I launched myself at him, throwing my arms around his neck and burying my head against his chest, my eyes erupting into tears and sobs ripping from my throat.

His powerful arms came around me, folding me in safely. What was I going to do without him in my life? Never had I ever had to rely on someone to be there for me. There had been no one there for me to rely on. Not even Pops, even though he was there. He never dried my tears or hugged me when I got scared.

How was Cameron here? He would have had to have flown all night to get here, but how did he know? I closed my eyes. Isabel. She had called him.

"No one is going to hurt you again. I promise." He pulled me away from him, tipping my head back so my eyes met his. His eyes darkened when he saw the bruise forming on my cheek. His thumb traced just below the mark, and he leaned in to press his lips to my hurt. "No one."

The vehemence of his words, the intensity behind his eyes, gave me no doubt he wouldn't uphold it. If he could. The last thing I wanted him to feel was guilt. Guilt for leaving me, for not taking me with him. If it hadn't happened this time, it would have happened another time.

"Isabel?"

He nodded. "A friend of mine has a private jet. I got here as quickly as I could. I'm so sorry I left. I should've brought you with me."

I slid my hands behind his neck and pulled his mouth down to mine. My lips frantically moving against his, and he held nothing back as he let me. His tongue swept against mine, teeth clashing and sighs swallowed whole. I didn't want to be apart from him again. This was the reason my heart beat so erratically.

He tugged the robe from my shoulders, his warm hands curving over my shoulders, sweeping down my back until they were at my waist, locked at my hips. Our mouths warred, as though there was an unknown hunger that we couldn't quench. My hands trying to rip away his clothing.

"Slow," he whispered against my mouth.

I lifted the shirt, and he reluctantly moved his hands until it was clear of him, leaving his chest bare to my searching hands.

With little effort, he curled his arm around me and lifted me until my back pressed against the mattress. Leaving only briefly, he divested himself of his jeans and boxers before I could feel the glorious, very naked muscles of his body cover mine.

He knelt between my legs, then pulled me until I was sitting on him before resuming his assault on my mouth. His hand fisted in my hair, fingers intertwined with the hanks of hair that had dried without being brushed, while his lips slanted against mine until it left me breathless.

"Please," I whispered against his mouth.

"What do you want?" he asked, his voice rough with desire. "Say it."

"You," I gasped. "I want you."

He moved only slightly and I could feel the length of him push into me, slowly at first, then with a sudden jerk of his hips fully into me until my pelvis met his. His hand was still tangled in my hair and my head fell back, his lips at my neck and burning his brand into my skin there.

"God," I muttered, never having felt so fulfilled in my life.

He moved, slowly at first, then picking up speed until he moved my legs around his waist, making it seem like he was even deeper while he crashed against me until I was crying out with release. Fireworks exploded within my body while he pushed me into the plush headboard, his body rocking against mine with a ferociousness that I responded with by tightening my legs around him.

Hadn't he just told me to slow down? My fingers drove up into the hair at the base of his neck, my lips finding his mouth again as he let out a growl that I swore shook the bed and he continued his clutch to my soul. I would never have this again.

My skin burned everywhere his hands and mouth touched, his hands grasped my wrists and pinned them to the headboard, no escape to be had from his grip and I marveled at the power of him while he kept me up from the sheer control of his body. A guttural scream ripped from deep in my throat. He caught it with his open mouth while a growl soon crawled from his throat and he slowed to a stop, releasing my wrists to slide around my torso.

Cameron held me firmly in his arms, not allowing me to go anywhere while he regained his breath. His forehead, decorated with sweat, rested against my collarbone while I trailed my fingers down his neck to his back.

"I love you," he whispered.

The words stuck in my throat. I loved him. I knew that my heart was long ago lost to him, the recent events only solidifying the fact that I was too far gone to get it back from him. Saying it in return could mean there was no going back.

"I . . ."

He lifted his head, looking deep into my eyes as though he were waiting for me to say it. All I needed to do was say it. Three simple words. Anyone could say those words. Some meant it, and some didn't mean it. I would mean it, though.

He pulled away, but I stopped him. My legs stayed firmly wrapped around his waist as my hands cupped his jaw, making it impossible for him to look away.

"I love you."

For the briefest of moments, he stared into my eyes until his mouth was back on mine, pulling free the last fragments of my heart that were still mine to give. They were all explicitly his. No one would ever have my heart again, or even a small part of it. It was all, completely all, his.

He made love to me after that, slowly and completely at his leisure. He took his time, running his hands over my entire body as though worshipping me. And I let him. I let him have this time, my head full of thoughts of only him for the time being. I would worry about the rest tomorrow.

Except it was tomorrow. Afterward, he lovingly pulled me against him while we buried ourselves under the blankets, his arm curling possessively around my waist while his leg stole between mine. I was in trouble.

"What time is it?" I whispered.

"Almost morning. Let's get what little sleep we can. Isabel won't be far behind this morning, I'm sure. She was extremely worried about you last night. As was I."

"I'm okay."

"Never in my life have I experienced such fear as when she called." I felt his lips press against my bare shoulder, the skin tingling there until I could feel the warmth of his breath scatter across my back. "I never want to feel that way again."

I closed my eyes. Tears spilled free from my eyes, absorbed into the pillow silently. I was in trouble. Tomorrow. I would deal with it tomorrow. For now, I could only keep the feelings that I had with his body wrapped around mine like a security blanket.

I finally found solace in sleep, but not for long before I heard Isabel's singsong voice as she let herself into the hotel room with an announcement of breakfast. I didn't want to leave the safe cocoon of Cameron's embrace. If I could stay forever, I would.

"Don't come in here," I called out, turning until I was facing Cameron.

His finger trailed lightly over my jaw before he pressed a kiss to my lips and swept the blanket from him, leaving me alone in the enormous bed while he got dressed. I picked up the robe from the floor where it had heedlessly landed not so many hours ago, stretching before I slid my arms in and pulled it around me.

He finished dressing and pulled my hand into his, his fingers threading with mine before pulling me out of the room to face Isabel. My mother. Mom. She looked refreshed, as though nothing had even happened the night before while she laid out a feast on the coffee table. Fluffy scrambled eggs, fresh fruit, bacon, orange juice, croissants, coffee, and scones.

I shrugged off Cameron's hand, almost diving for a croissant and groaning, when the buttery flakes hit my tongue. I would have told Isabel how much I loved her if my mouth hadn't been full.

Cameron smiled at Isabel, who pretended it surprised her he was there. I wasn't daft. She called him and gave him a key to my room. I was happy she had, even though it had scared the daylight out of me.

"I brought you some stuff," she said, setting a brown bag with handles down next to the coffee table.

One hand on a cup of coffee, I rummaged through the bag with my other hand. Cameron sat down on the couch next to me while Isabel sat in the chair across from us. I set down the coffee to use both hands to retrieve a pair of leggings, tank top, baggy sweater, pair of socks, a pair of underwear, a bra, and a pair of tall boots. She also provided me with basic toiletries.

"You've been shopping already today," I said with a smile. "Thank you. I wouldn't be alive today if it wasn't for you."

"And I thank you for that," Cameron said, his voice thick with emotion.

Isabel shook her head. "Let's not rehash that. I'd do anything for you, Regan. You're my daughter and I love you more than anyone can love another person."

Cameron smiled, even when I looked over at him. He had known. He had known this whole time she was my mother. I suppose he had felt that it was not his to tell, and he would be correct.

"Will you return to California now that I know?" I asked, already knowing the answer to my question.

"No. There'd be no point in me returning now. Your father is still gone, and putting me back into the mix would just make things more complicated."

Cameron perked up. "Your father is gone?"

I hadn't told him that. I still hadn't told him hardly anything about my family. "Yes. He's taking an extended vacation. From everyone, including me."

"Did he do something?"

I shook my head, more so to put him off from asking any more questions about it. "He probably did. My uncle has it under control, though. Pops will show back up when he wants to."

"I hope so," he said.

"Don't you think coming back might help?" I asked, hoping Isabel didn't betray my situation to Cameron.

"I don't think so. Not right yet, anyway. We'll have to see."

Cameron didn't ask questions after that and we ate our breakfast with gusto, both having been starving after such a long night. I escaped to the bathroom shortly after to change into fresh clothing and brush my hair and teeth. My old clothing, I tucked into a plastic bag and threw into the brown bag.

I wouldn't admit it, but I couldn't be more grateful that Cameron would be with me when we returned to my house. That was something that I was not looking forward to doing today, but having him here put me at such ease.

I hugged Isabel goodbye, kissing her cheek and telling her I loved her. I had loved her before as a friend, and now I could love her like my mom. She waved us off and out of the hotel into the bright, but cool, morning sunshine.

Cameron didn't say a word as he walked me to his car and made sure I was comfortable in the passenger seat before he closed the door and got in on his side.

It didn't take long to get back to my house. When we pulled into the driveway, I shuddered at the memories that would haunt me now. I didn't need anything else to have nightmares about. The security system was useless if someone cut the power.

"We can go to my house instead," he said, before getting out of the car.

He was right. We could go to his house. Maybe I should have been at his house while he was gone. No one would have thought to find me there. I didn't have to go into my house until I was good and ready. But I was never one to back down from terrible memories.

I shook my head. "No. I won't let those bastards drive me out of my house."

The power was back on when we stepped inside, and I had Isabel to thank for that. She took care of everything, so I wouldn't have to. Cameron entered the house first, walking around the kitchen, living room, and making sure that no one lingered inside while I peeked around the front door. He waved me in.

"I'm going to check your bedroom and make sure the door doesn't need to be repaired," he said. "I'll clean up the glass in the living room after that." I watched the corner of his mouth lift. "Put up a fight, did you?"

I stepped into the house, but stopped and stared at him. "How did you know I escaped out that door?" Goosebumps scattered across my arms and a chill stole up my spine.

Cameron stared back at me, his eyes void of surprise or even guilt. He just stared at me. "Isabel told me the story."

I continued to look at him. I had trusted him explicitly from the start. He had been the one to raise hell after someone had drugged me at the club. He had flown from Vegas to South Carolina overnight to get to me, so he hadn't even been here. Was it all too easy?

He came over to me, running his hand down my arms. "Do you think I would do this to you? Do you think that I'm the one trying to hurt you?"

I couldn't mistake the thickness of the hurt in his voice that I would suggest such a thing, and I closed my eyes. I didn't know what to believe anymore. I wasn't even sure that I would be safe here on the island now. I wasn't safe here. Soon, I would leave.

I shook my head. "No. I don't think that."

He gave my arms a pull until I was up against him, his arms coming around me while he rested his chin on the top of my head. "I understand your need to question everything right now. I did not do this. And I didn't drug you."

"I'm sorry to have questioned it," I whispered. "You should know that Justin was one of them."

I felt his muscles tighten. "I took care of him."

"He came back. Isabel killed him."

He frowned. "He should be dead."

I shrugged. Things happened. Whatever it was Cameron had done to make sure he didn't get back here was a mistake that wouldn't happen again. Justin was dead now, as was his companion. They wouldn't be reporting back to who had hired them.

"All the signs were there, Cameron. When he came in for the interview, he asked me questions about myself that were weird. If I lived here, when Gio called, he questioned it was a man calling me. He asked me to have coffee with him. I just had a weird feeling, but I didn't want to start all over again, so I ignored it." I questioned my own convictions. "I was stupid. I put myself and Melanie at risk."

"I wish you would have told me you hired someone. I could have looked in."

"You can't always be there to protect me."

"You'll tell me if you hire someone else?"

"I'm not sure I'll hire someone else."

When he pulled away from me and looked down at me, there was a light in his eyes. "Does that mean you're staying here?"

"No. I'm not sure I'll be able to get someone to fill the position. I might have to go without it for a while."

He pressed his lips to my cheek, careful of my bruise, before he moved away to go check the bedroom. I set the brown bag down next to the couch and went to the patio doors, looking out at the water. I needed to talk to Gio, but I didn't have my phone.

Chapter Sixteen

I had a new phone in my hands within a matter of days, much to my relief. It was not only my lifeline, but it was my connection to business as well. I could get emails on my laptop with no worries, but any incoming calls from clients would go directly to voicemail. Since my old phone was gone, I lost everything with it. It took me more than a day to set everything back up the way I wanted.

I called Gio as soon as I could, only to learn that he wanted me to stay put for the time being. If I was supposed to lie low, it wasn't working anymore. Someone knew where I was and wanted me out of the way. After two attempts, it couldn't be more obvious. The longer that I stayed here, the harder it became to face the facts that it would end soon. December was only a week away.

Gio assured me he was working on things and that he would let me know when he was ready for me to come home, but he warned me I would not be going to my house in Malibu. I would remain at the family estate. He was shady in telling me how long that would be, and I hoped he didn't think I would stay until the wedding. I could handle Gio all day, every day. I couldn't handle being cooped up for over three months.

I spent a quiet Thanksgiving with Cameron and Isabel, thankful that I had Cameron at home every night now. He had promised not to go anywhere and leave me alone. There had been no other mention of marriage between us. I assumed he was biding his time before he thought to bring it up again, especially after I admitted to him I loved him. I thought it was only a matter of time before he brought up marriage again.

December arrived with several bitter days, keeping us inside despite having a heated pool. Cameron worked on whatever business he had from the dining room table, but business was slow for me, so I spent a lot of time using the dance space upstairs. He forbade me from going to the boatyard without him, just in case, and I didn't need Melanie to have a conversation with him, so I didn't go in.

It was the second week in December when the dreaded call from Gio came through. Cameron had run out to grab groceries and supplies, the day nice enough for me to spend time on the deck in the sun. He locked the gate when he left, convinced that nothing would happen during daylight since there had been no other issues for almost a month.

Cameron assured me he would return before dinner, which was good because I wasn't the cook. He was much better at handling any type of food than I was. There was a beep from the intercom. Someone was at the gate. I wasn't expecting anyone.

I hurried from the deck into the house, stealing a glance up at the camera screen that showed me who was at the gate. It was a delivery guy. I pushed the button and asked him what he needed.

"Regan De Luca?" he asked.

From the camera, he looked young. Probably right out of high school. I hadn't ordered anything, which made this suspicious, but he did look rather young and harmless.

"Yes."

"I have a delivery for you," he said, holding the box up to the camera.

"Can you leave it there, and I'll come and grab it when I have time?"

"It needs a signature."

Damn it. "Okay."

I pressed the button to open the gates, observing the screen while the small van pulled into the driveway and stopped in front of the doors. I held my breath while I pulled open the door.

He gave me a lopsided grin, holding the signature device for me to scribble my signature on. Once I had signed, he handed me the package and bid me a good day. I watched from the doorway until he was back in his van and driving back out the gates before I pushed the button to close the gates and reactivate the alarm.

I looked down at the brown box, square and not big. There was no sign of who it could be from, which was odd. I wasn't sure if I should wait for Cameron to get home. I held it up to my ear to make sure there was no ticking inside while I walked over to the dining room table and set it down, debating.

Resigned, I opened the box while hoping that it was nothing that was going to blow up in my face. I had suffered two too many issues lately. This time might just be it for me.

Once I had the outer box open, I tipped it up with my eyes squinting in anticipation of a surprise. A dark blue velvet box landed on the table with a clunk. It looked like a jewelry box. I shook the box again and a small white envelope fell out, landing beside the box.

I grabbed the envelope, sliding the edge of my fingernail under the flap to open it. Please don't spew white powder at me, I prayed silently. I cautiously opened the package and peered inside with half-closed eyes to find a white sheet of paper. I removed the paper to discover a message scrawled in black ink. My hands shook as I lifted it up and read the card.

Regan,
It's my desire that you wear this to the Christmas Ball.
I very much look forward to meeting you and hope you feel
the same.
Your husband-to-be

My heart pounded. I set the card down on the table and picked up the box, slowly opening it to reveal an exquisite necklace that glittered with diamonds. I swore softly at the sight of it. Who in their right mind would send such an expensive gift without so much as a return address? It only served as a reminder of my responsibilities, a reminder of my status. Despite how costly it was, I wanted to dispose of it.

My head snapped up at the sound of the front door opening. After shutting the lid, I picked up the card and envelope and tucked them in my bathing suit. I couldn't control my breathing when Cameron walked in with a smile and arms full of groceries.

I blinked.

"Everything okay?"

"Yes! Here, let me help you." I hurried over to him, grabbing a bag and setting it on the counter. "What on earth did you buy?"

He shrugged. "Dinner."

"For ten?" I laughed, hoping that my shaky voice didn't betray me. I needed to dispose of the card before he found it.

"What's that?" he asked, setting down the other two bags and moving toward the box on the dining room table.

"A gift . . ." I blurted. "From my uncle."

I wanted to squeeze my eyes shut when he picked up the box and opened the lid, his eyes widening at the sight of the necklace, then moved back at me, his eyes still wide. "Your uncle sent you this?"

I nodded just as I heard my phone ringing outside. What now? I thought, heading outside to grab it without another word to

Cameron about the damn necklace.

"Gio," I said.

"Did you get the package?"

I looked back into the dining room from the window, watching Cameron putting the box slowly back down on the table before returning to handle the groceries. I let out a little sigh, hoping that he wouldn't question it further.

"Why would he send me that here?"

"It's time to come home."

I knew that this day was coming. It didn't make it less hard. "When?"

"The Christmas Ball is on the seventeenth. We'll announce your engagement."

"What about Pops?"

I wanted Pops there, but I didn't want anything to happen with him there. The same with Isabel. She shouldn't miss any more of my life, and this was pretty big.

"I haven't heard from him, but it can't wait. He gave me instructions."

I was silent. I didn't want to ask questions that Cameron might overhear. I would break his heart, I knew. I was breaking my heart. I just didn't want him to know why. I couldn't bear his hatred.

"Regan?"

"I'm here."

"Is this a bad time? Do you have company?"

"No, no. It's fine," I whispered, feeling the burn of the card just above my groin. "I'll check flights and let you know when I'll be home."

"Can you be home early next week? You'll need to prepare. Do not forget that necklace."

I glanced inside again. Cameron was putting groceries into the refrigerator. "Why would he send it here if I'm going to there soon? Couldn't he have waited?"

"What do you think of it?" He was avoiding my question.

"It's a necklace," I whispered. "It's presumptuous."

"He's thinking about you."

Damn it, I silently swore. "Well, I'm not thinking about him. This is presumptuous, and downright possessive."

"He was going to send you a gown, but I convinced him not to. I don't need to remind you of the expense of that piece."

"Of course not. This, though, this is crazy." I blew out my breath. "I've met someone here, Gio."

My admittance didn't bring an immediate reaction from him. He stayed quiet. He was the one that told me to have fun while I was here. I did that. I could almost hear him thinking on the other end of the line.

"Say something, damn it!" I shouted, stealing another glance inside to see Cameron turn and look straight at me.

Gio's voice was almost deadly. "You might be with someone else for the time being, but you belong to another."

"Pops didn't give me a choice." It was this or my career. Or Jake could get hurt. "I just didn't mean for this to happen."

I pinched the bridge of my nose.

"This is killing you," he whispered.

"It will end before I come home. I've got to go, Gio."

"Regan." Gio stopped me from hanging up. "He won't tolerate a side relationship. Neither will his family. He will expect you to be faithful to him, and always him."

"Likewise," I bit out.

"I've spoken with him. He's prepared to end any relationships he may have before the engagement being announced on Saturday. He promised."

"I'll be there."

"Did you find a wedding dress?"

"Yes," I bit out.

"Let me know when you expect to be back. I'll send a car."

"I will," I said. "See you soon."

I pushed the end button and set my phone back down on the table, staring out at the ocean. It was calm today, unlike the emotions that were rolling through me. Part of me wondered how I had gotten so caught up in this relationship with Cameron. I had known better.

"Going home?"

I whipped around to see Cameron leaning against the frame of the patio doors, hands stuffed in the pockets of his jeans and ankles crossed like he had been standing there for a while.

I shrugged. "I have to go home, Cameron."

"This is your home." His jaw hardened, and he pushed off from the door, coming over to me to cup my face in his hands. "My offer still stands, Regan. Marry me."

I pulled away from him, moving away so his body was not so close to mine. I would never survive doing this if he kept standing close to me. A headache was threatening, tears trying to force their way out of my eyes, and my heart was beating entirely too fast.

"I told you never to expect anything of me."

He scoffed lightly. "I didn't. At first. Now I want it all. I want you, and I will stop at nothing to have you." He moved toward me, and I moved back even when he stalked me.

I shook my head. "I didn't want this!"

It surprised me when he didn't fight back. "When do you leave?"

Tears threatened, despite his calm. I hurried around the pool, hurrying back into the house and slamming the door shut even though he opened it a second later and strolled in after me.

"I can't help what happened between us, Regan. I can't help what I feel for you."

I swiped away the tears. "I have no choice. I have to walk away. I *told* you this from the very beginning. I *told* you I didn't want a relationship."

He shook his head then, sadness washing over his face. "Will you at least wait until you leave before we end this?" he whispered.

My heart cleaved into two. The pain of this was so real that my body felt it in every part. I nodded my head; the words refused to come out. I knew it wouldn't be easier the moment I left his side. My heart would break more, but at least we would have more time.

And after I would leave this island and go home to heal. I wasn't sure how I was going to put on a smiling face next weekend, but I had to do it. There just wasn't a choice.

Cameron walked toward me, his hands sliding against my jaw to cup my face. "I never once lied to you. I love you, Regan. There is nothing in the world that is going to take that away. You will always have my love."

Chapter Seventeen

My flight home was the next day. Cameron and I stayed awake and in each other's arms all night. He wouldn't let me sleep. I wouldn't let him sleep. We used the time we had left. Before I got into my car the next morning, he held me for the longest time as though he didn't want to let go. I couldn't blame him. I didn't want him to let me go.

I waited until I was on the ferry before I cried. I didn't get out of the car at all during the ride. I cried until I thought I didn't have any tears left, then I cried more. Even when I landed in Los Angeles and began my ride home in the back of the car that Gio had sent, I cried. It felt like I was stuck in a never-ending cycle of tears and nothing would ever get better. I still had the dull ache in my heart, my stomach churning. I felt like I was going to vomit. It was a constant.

Gio had taken one look at me when I arrived home, at my red eyes and tear-stained face, and shook his head. But he hugged me. Something I had never remembered him ever doing. He hugged me and told me it was going to be fine. I went to my old bedroom, dumping my bags on the floor and collapsing onto my bed to cry more. My body felt cold, empty.

That had been a week ago. I stood looking out the opened doors of the ballroom, heard clapping echoing in the ballroom, and turned to see Gio walking across the shining floor. That evening, this room would be full of people. There would be my friends and family, and there would be friends and family of my intended. But no Pops. And not my mother. There would be people I had known my whole life, and there would be people I would meet for the first time. But not the people who mattered the most. The two people who had put me in this rotten situation.

The floor was so polished it mirrored the three large chandeliers overhead. The staff had set chairs on the far wall opposite the opening of the ballroom, and beyond the pool was a beautifully groomed, bright green lawn. There was a small portable bar that was set up in the corner near the doors leading toward the back.

Gio had yet to get ready for the evening, still dressed in a pair of tan dress pants with a black cashmere V-neck sweater. He had pushed the sleeves up mid-arm like he had been working hard. Gio always looked well put together.

I wondered how long he had been watching me dance, walking over to my water bottle, phone, and towel. I picked up the towel and pressed it to my face. I supposed he was coming in to tell me I better get my ass upstairs to shower and change. It wouldn't be long before limousines containing guests began the trek up the long driveway, that ended curled around a massive fountain in the center where they would enter at the front doors of the De Luca family home.

"I remember when your dad had this great idea of having a ballroom added on. And when you started dancing. You caught right on, despite not having started while you were young."

I dropped the towel back down onto the chair, putting my hands on my hips to face him. "I also remember him sending me to Vegas on a job that required some dancing."

Gio frowned. "And you did an amazing job. He was worried that you would take a liking to it and never come home."

I wrinkled my nose. Really . . . Pops didn't know me at all. "He was wrong. I will never do something so degrading again."

"You've done well for yourself."

"Right. I've done so well picking out men I'm being forced   to marry a stranger."

I couldn't help the edge in my voice. After crying for almost two days, the wrath and resentment oozed out. It was consuming me even more so than thoughts of Cameron.

"I'm sorry for that."

"It's not your fault."

"You deserve better than what your parents promised you into, but I understand why they did it, and I agree with it. You should get a choice, though."

I straightened. "I have a choice. I just didn't like the options Pops gave me as alternatives, and he made sure I wouldn't like them."

He tucked his hands into his pant pockets. "Should I even ask?"

"No. You know how Pops is. When he wants something, he gets it." Just like Cameron, I thought in the back of my head. "He made damn sure this would happen."

I closed my eyes. Getting heated with Gio when he had nothing to do with this was not the answer. He was only there to be the messenger, regardless of how he viewed the situation.

"You fell hard in Cape Haven, didn't you?" he whispered.

I shook my head, determined that more tears would not fall. It had been a week since I had last seen Cameron. "I don't want to think about him. I *can't* think about him."

Gio gave a nod of his head. Of all the people that understood me, I knew Gio probably understood me the most. "Regan, about tonight . . ." He paused for a minute, searching my eyes. "Please don't make a scene. Speak with him in private if you need to, but please don't make a scene."

The last thing that I wanted to do was make a scene. I wasn't the type of person to create scenes just for the sake of having all the attention on me. No matter what, I would be at the center. I think he meant not to let my anger over this situation blast out like it was now.

"I won't make a scene. But Gio . . . Do you know who it is I'm marrying?"

He had to know. Someone had to have told the man about this Christmas Ball.

He chuckled, but he neither confirmed nor denied it. "Just know you're perfect for each other. Meet him, spend some time with him. You'll see."

With a wink, Gio turned around to leave me alone, calling over his shoulder that I only had two hours to get myself ready before guests would start arriving. He knew it would take me over two hours to calm myself down.

I picked up my water, phone, and towel, following him out of the room. Before I left, I turned around to scan the room, knowing I would be in this room soon and dancing. Not as hard as I had just been, but dancing. Dancing with a man I couldn't picture. All I could picture was Cameron, and he was gone from my life. I had to move on, or I would forever be miserable.

I left the room, undertaking a big effort not to bump into any of the staff moving around in preparation. It was too bad Pops wasn't here. Even though he and I were not the best of friends, it would have been nice to have him here. Or my mom. They should be here to observe what they created.

I wound my way through the giant living room with windows from floor to ceiling, facing the expertly manicured back lawn, and stepped out into the foyer. The foyer was just as large, with the long winding stairway that curved up to the right of the front doors leading to the second floor.

I placed my hand on the black wrought-iron banister that led upstairs, looking up with a deep breath. My nerves were jumpy, even after trying to calm them by dancing. There was no sense in worrying about it. It was going to happen. It didn't matter if I was ready for it. I just wasn't sure I could mend my heart enough to keep an open mind. This marriage was bound to fail just for the simple fact he wasn't Cameron.

∞

Hours later, I took a deep breath and pressed myself against the door to my bedroom. My old bedroom, which was my current prison, faced the back lawn with a small balcony and sheer curtains that blew in from the breeze. The four-poster bed fit for a king was against the far wall, the blankets and pillows rivaling Isabel's hotel comforts. Two nightstands flanked each side even though I had never once in my life shared this bedroom with anyone else. The blankets and pillows were a deep red color. There was a tall dresser and my vanity, where I had only moments before finished the final touches to my makeup, was across from the bed.

The walk-in closet was in the corner next to the private bathroom. Most of my childhood possessions were still in the closet, but I didn't have much clothing left. I moved my stuff to my condo in Malibu immediately after I signed the papers at closing. Gio had Tatum gather some things from home to bring to me so I would have more than what I had when I was in Cape Haven, but I wasn't a person who needed much. The basics were enough.

After taking a lengthy shower, I dried myself thoroughly and started my makeup before sliding into the red gown that fit like a sheath, molding my body and flaring slightly at the bottom. It had just enough flexibility for me to move freely, any tighter would have suffocated me. The necklace had come last, my fingers shaking while I pulled it up to my neck and clasped it at my nape.

I had done my hair myself, against Anne's wishes to have someone come from the salon and have it professionally done. I curled my hair slightly and swept it into an updo, secured with sparkling clips. I could have called Tatum and she would have come over early to do it, but I wasn't ready to face her and her questions yet.

Tatum and Jazz had both called me daily since I had been home, but I wasn't ready to speak with either of them despite the insistent text messages I needed to answer. I settled for texting them both that I was home, but I was not feeling well. I would talk with them as soon as I was better.

I felt safe tucked away in my family's home without having to explain anything to anyone. I wasn't ready to tell them about Cameron. I couldn't cry any more than I already had. Crying wouldn't change anything, but I knew I would if they pressed me on what had happened.

I felt the door press into my back when someone tried to open it. I moved away from the door and yanked it open, coming face to face with Amber. Her reddish-brown hair swept up from her neck and she was wearing a very chic black dress with black heels.

"Going to a funeral?" I teased, pulling the door open more fully for her to enter before I closed it tightly. I could hear a lot of voices from below wafting up the stairs. Gio had given me precise instructions to stay in my room until most of the guests arrived. He knew I didn't like to be the center of attention. He was purposely putting me there.

I walked over to the balcony, sweeping the curtains away to see guests in formal attire standing around the pool. From the sound of it, most of the guests had arrived.

"Nervous?" Amber asked, checking her oval face in my vanity mirror. She ran her fingertip over the corner of her lips to ensure her lipstick was not traveling where it shouldn't be.

"No," I snapped, letting the curtains drop and moving towards her.

"Liar. This isn't your scene. I know that."

"It doesn't matter if this isn't my scene. It's where I have to be."

She turned, leaning her perky butt against the edge of the vanity while I lingered next to the bed, absently fingering the necklace that was branding my skin like I was property. I hated this necklace.

"That necklace is gorgeous. Is it from prince charming?"

I continued to finger it. "It is."

She raised her eyebrows. "Are you sure you aren't nervous? This is the first time you'll be meeting him, you lucky piece of shit."

"Bitch," I murmured with a smile.

"I've missed you, Reggie."

"How's school been?"

Amber had been attending school in upstate New York, not for business, but for medicine. She wanted to become a doctor and had worked tirelessly her entire life to have the best grades so that she could get into a wonderful school. She had quite a few years left, being only twenty-one, before she could graduate and begin her residency program.

"It's been hell," she said with a grin.

"But you've enjoyed it."

"I have, and I will continue to." She pushed away from the vanity and walked to me, sliding her hands into mine. "You know I have your back, sis. You give me the word tonight and we'll steal out of here so fast. We'll go to a club."

"Like this?" I laughed, waving at our clothes. She looked like she was ready to go to a club, not me.

"You're right. My mother would have a fit."

A knock at the door interrupted us. Amber groaned but went to the door to reveal one of the staff announcing Gio wanted me to come down. She closed the door and met my gaze.

"I mean it. I have your back. You just say the word."

I nodded, moving toward her. Amber, although she was not my blood sister, was still a sister. I had known her since she was nine. She aggravated me, but she was always there to talk to me when I needed to talk to someone. I was in high school by the time I realized it. She knew me enough to know when I wanted to talk and when to leave me alone. It helped that she was six years younger. There had never been a sister rivalry between us.

"Are you ready?" she whispered.

No, I screamed silently in my head. "If you go down the stairs before me, Gio is going to be pissed. If you want to go on ahead, I'll be fine."

We walked out into the hallway. The front staircase split the house in half, with two wings on each side. She turned to give me a quick hug before I watched her walk down the hallway and disappear down the back staircase, used primarily by staff.

I smoothed my hand down the front of my dress. There was no way to know who was going to be at the bottom of the stairs. I had to focus. I would do this, and I would do it well. There was never a time I was going to back down. Ever.

I walked toward the stairway, rounding the corner to see crowds below. My chin lifted a notch, even after I saw Giovanni at the very bottom looking up at me. I could see the pride in his eyes. After all, I was his only niece.

A hush swept through the foyer as I began my descent, eyes sweeping the crowd for a man who would be my husband in only a few months. There were unfamiliar faces and familiar faces, but none stood out to me. I smiled, demurely, as I focused my efforts on not stumbling and falling headlong down. The pressure was overwhelming, but I felt a bit more at ease when I reached the bottom and slid my hand into Gio's.

He kissed both cheeks, pulling my arm through his and placing my hand on his forearm. He guided me through the crowds, greeting people who I hadn't seen in so many years. It had been some time since Pops had thrown any extravagant parties here, and I was often away working when he did.

It was like being led through a jungle, except for skin, tuxedos and expensive gowns, and glittering jewelry instead of greenery. In all the years I had lived in this house, this was the fullest I had ever seen it. Staff in black uniforms skirted the crowds with champagne. As Gio swept me along toward the ballroom, I spotted Michael with a tall brunette on his arm. Who in the world invited him to this, and why?

I was about to ask Gio how he had gotten an invitation when Jack, one of my father's oldest friends and colleagues, came toward us with a giant grin on his weathered face. At six-foot- two, he was a handsome man with gray hair curling just above his ears. He reached out his hands to clasp mine, kissing each of my cheeks as Gio had done only moments ago.

"Ah! My lovely, Regan. It's good to see you, my dear."

"It's good to see you, Jack."

"Might I be the luckiest man here and claim your first dance?"

Gio gave him a brief bow, handing me over to him. I placed my hand on Jack's arm, allowing him to guide me to the center of the ballroom. There were already many couples dancing to the small disc jockey booth set up next to the bar.

"Are you certain you want to dance with me? Things could get interesting."

There was a twinkle in his cornflower blue eyes. "I welcome interesting things. I have the most beautiful woman in the room in my arms, and nothing can be more interesting than that."

I laughed. "You're too charming, Jack."

"If I were ten years younger, I would risk the wrath of your father and take you as my own." I blushed furiously. If Pops were here and overheard that, we would have problems. Jack was older than Pops, and even if he were ten years younger, he would be too old for me.

I sighed, wondering when I would meet the man of the hour. Gio had relinquished me rather quickly. I would have thought he would introduce me right away. Instead, he has me dancing already. I would never turn down a dance with Jack, though.

More people were pushing through onto the dance floor. Jack spun me around, but when I went to grab his hand to be pulled back, I reached out to nothing. It unexpectedly jostled me among the other dancers. My heartbeat kicked up for how many people were around me. I had never been claustrophobic; this was new for me to be overwhelmed until someone grabbed my hand and pulled me back in. I almost breathed a sigh of relief.

"Sad to see him go, are you?"

I gasped, looking up into another pair of the lightest blue eyes I had ever seen. This wasn't possible. There was a devil's gleam in his blue eyes; blue eyes I would recognize anywhere. It hadn't been so long ago that I had seen them. A week, to be exact.

Cameron swung me around, pulling me right into his arms and placing his mouth over mine before I could utter a single word. Reluctantly, my body seemed to remember the shape of his body and molded into it until I reminded myself of the severity of the situation.

"You look stunning in that gown. I should carry you away right now," he murmured, leaning down so his breath could tickle the curve of my ear. "And that necklace. Your *uncle* has exquisite taste in jewels."

I shook my head. "You can't be here. Why did you come here?"

He tried to take a nip at my lips, but I pulled away. "I missed you."

"You could have called me," I whispered, my voice urgent while I tried to scan the crowds for Gio. "You need to get out of here. You could be in danger."

He put a finger to my lips, then replaced them quickly with his mouth. He teased my mouth into submission, even though my head was screaming in alarm. How quickly I could melt away to his touch. I snatched my mouth away from his. He spun me out, then pulled me quickly back in, right back into his arms.

Despite the music, his lips were just next to the curve of my ear, and I closed my eyes in anticipation of feeling his lips at the sensitive spot just below. There was something about when he put his mouth there. My body turned liquified.

"You promised your uncle that you wouldn't make a scene."

"Cause a scene?" I jerked back as though someone had slapped me.

I stared at him in disbelief. Gio's words from earlier rang. *"Speak with him in private if you need to, but please don't make a scene."*

"It was you. You're the one I'm supposed to marry. You made me believe . . ." I choked on a sob, my heart hurting. "You made me believe I would never see you again."

Cameron swung me around, forcing me to be swept along in the dance instead of causing the scene while my head pounded and my thoughts raced. The music transitioned into another song and people left the dance floor. He slid his hand up to my neck, holding my head captive while his lips caught mine again. I was numb.

"Kiss me," he growled.

If I didn't comply with his command, I was in danger of causing a scene. I closed my eyes to allow it. To allow the one man I had thought about night and day since leaving the island, the one man who had caused my heart to shatter into a million pieces when I drove away, to kiss me. A man that I had been heartbroken over having to say goodbye to for months so that I could fulfill an arrangement to marry another. A man that I would marry, after all. I was confused, and hurt, and angry.

When Cameron pulled away from me and I opened my eyes, the entire dance floor was empty except for us. I looked around, becoming dizzy with my emotions getting the best of me. Cameron sank down to his knee in front of me, keeping my hand in his until he reached into his pocket and pulled out a stunning diamond ring.

"No matter what happens, I want you as my wife. I need you as my wife. You will always have my love. Marry me, Regan."

Chapter Eighteen

"Marry me, Regan."

He repeated, urgency in his voice. All I could hear was my heavy breathing and the pounding of my heartbeat in my ears. I looked down at him, his blue eyes silently pleading with me. Don't make a scene, I told myself. He didn't deserve it, and I didn't deserve it.

"Yes."

No sooner had the word slipped past my lips and Cameron had the ring slipped onto my finger. A straightforward, princess-cut ring featuring an enormous diamond. He stood quickly, pulling me to him while his lips sought mine. This was too much. I felt like I was going to pass out as an eruption of cheers, jeers, and clapping surrounded us. My head was spinning, and people were closing in on us with well-wishes, including our friends. I caught Jack's eye, and he blew me a kiss.

"Damn, old man . . ." I muttered under my breath, causing Cameron to look over at me with a frown. Gio had probably urged him to dance with me, knowing Cameron would find me on the dance floor.

Cameron turned to me. "Regan, I'd like to introduce you to my parents."

I looked up at a man taller than Cameron, but not by much, with the same dark hair but penetrating brown eyes and gray hair at his temples. The woman next to him was shorter than me, only coming up to him mid-biceps and she was looking at me with light blue eyes, the color of Cameron's except hers were biting. She did not appear to be enthused about this arrangement.

"Reno Moretti. And my mother, Orianna."

I reached out to shake Reno's hand, gasping when he crushed me in an embrace instead. The air whooshed out of my lungs, what little I had left. I was still stunned at what had just happened on the dance floor.

When he released me, Orianna offered her hand rather than hugging me. The feeling was mutual. I took her hand, not at all surprised that her handshake was limp. I smiled anyway. If this wasn't what she wanted, it wasn't what I had wanted either. This could have gone completely differently, and I would find out why it happened this way.

"It's nice to meet you after all this time, Regan," Reno said, his voice low, but his eyes sparkled. "We're deeply pleased that you'll be part of our family in only a few months."

I smiled. "Thank you."

Tatum and Jazz looked excited to talk with me, but Cameron took us away and we started dancing again with the others who had rejoined the dance floor. I stole a glance at Tatum, recognizing the pout on her lips, which quickly disappeared when Alex offered his hand to her.

Cameron's long fingers were possessively curled at my waist. The other one had crawled up my back and came to rest at my nape. I wasn't sure if I was angry or tingling with excitement. He was so possessive of me. That hadn't changed, and despite how things were now, I didn't think it would change.

"You lied to me," I whispered.

"I didn't lie to you," he countered.

I gasped at his audacity. "You knew. You could've told me."

"I didn't know either until right before I went to the island. Believe me, I was just as pissed as you were when I learned about this thing. When I heard from my buddy at the boatyard, there was a new owner. I had to find out who had convinced Mark McCarthy to sell. I was only going to meet you, then leave."

"How did you know I bought the boatyard?"

His eyes danced. "I'm a supplier, remember? Except, when I arrived and found out none other than Regan De Luca was going to the island, I was curious. Unlike your father, mine told me who I was marrying against his better judgement. And because I put up a fight about it."

Supplier of what? I thought. It wasn't boating supplies like I thought. Not now, not when I knew who he was. Who his father was. His father was like Pops. They ran things through businesses. That was a conversation for another day, though.

"I was supposed to lie low, like you. I went to the island to find out about the boatyard. I wasn't supposed to stay. But when I met you, I couldn't stay away. And then someone tried to drug you and I knew I couldn't leave you there alone. Someone knew where you were."

"Did someone know where I was because you were there?"

"I don't think so. According to what my father has told me, they were friends with a guy years ago before we were born and they were doing this big drug deal with a farm in Columbia but this guy got real bossy and weird about it and they got nervous about it so they cut him out of the deal. He got pissed and tried to ruin the deal, but it didn't work out that way. He's been trying to make their lives miserable ever since. And that means trying to get to us."

"Ludovico," I whispered. "That son of a bitch."

"I didn't intend on what we had together to get stronger and stronger. It just did, and I'll be damned if I'm going to let you walk away again. I put you in danger just by leaving. I won't make that same mistake twice."

"You aren't going to be able to protect me day and night, Cameron."

His smile was dazzling. "I will protect you. And to do that, I've decided we're going to have a quick engagement. Maybe we'll get married tomorrow."

My mouth opened, and he tried to swoop in to kiss me, but I pulled away. "No. I've spent the last week agonizing over having to leave you and marry someone else."

"Regan, you're getting angry. Let's talk about this later. Please."

I fully intended to talk to him about it later, but I had given Gio my promise that I wouldn't cause a scene and people were staring. This was a joyous moment. We were officially engaged. I wished I could feel better about it than I did, but my soul was hurting.

As soon as the dance ended, I told him I had to go to the bathroom and he let me go, but only after I had thoroughly ravished on the dance floor. It was an act of telling every man in the crowds that I was no longer available. Not that I had been to begin with. I was so angry and how my body reacted to him this way. Did he think this was a joke? I was wholeheartedly heartbroken, but he didn't know because he had known the entire time.

I made a dash for the bathroom. There was a short hallway before getting to the kitchens where there was a small bathroom. I was thankful it was vacant. I hurried in and locked the door, going to the vanity and looking at myself in the mirror. My face was flushed. The necklace sparkled from the lights over the mirror. This damned necklace.

"He was there! He sent it!" I cried out, then groaned, taking a swipe at a box of tissues. They flew off the counter and landed on the floor upside down. I didn't want to hurt myself, otherwise I might have punched the wall.

"Regan?"

I went back to the door, unlocking it and opening it for Tatum and Jazz. They rushed in and I locked the door behind them. They were full of sickening smiles, their eyes dancing in delight at the turn of events. Tatum was the one who noticed my flush and stopped smiling, followed by Jazz.

I took another deep breath, not wanting to cry.

"He was there," I bit out. "He was there right after they delivered this necklace. He had it delivered to me, knowing he knew about me and I didn't know about him."

I covered my face in my hands, burying my hurt as though my hands would absorb it all and make it go away. I felt two sets of arms come around me in comfort. But it wasn't going to comfort me. I didn't know what would make me feel better. I just knew for the rest of this night I would have to put a fake smile on my face and get congratulations from people.

"I don't know what to do," I said, moving away from them to lean against the vanity. "I don't think I have been more confused in my whole life than I am right now. He was lying, and he knew I was lying!"

Jazz leaned against the wall while Tatum sat down on the closed toilet. "But you know what? It worked out. You're head over heels in love with him! You still are. Because he's the same man."

"It's true," Tatum said.

"You're supposed to be my friends!" I shouted, then lowered my voice so no one on the other side of the door could hear. "I couldn't stop crying for two days, thinking I would never see him again! My heart is still hurting from it."

"But that's changed."

I pinned Jazz with a glare. "You're damn right it's changed. My heart broke, and I felt. Every. Piece. Of it. I thought I was dying. I haven't been able to eat. I haven't been able to sleep."

"Would you rather it truly be someone else? A stranger?"

Good God, but Jazz was smart. I looked at her with a lopsided smile. "I am so sorry." I held out my hand to Tatum. "And you, Tatum. What a horrible friend you must think I am."

"Not at all," Tatum said. "You've been through hell these last few months. It's going to get better. You just need to sit down with Cameron, away from prying ears and eyes. Alone."

I nodded. She was right. I needed to have this out with Cameron before I felt any better about it. "I'm going to go up to my bedroom. Can you find Cameron and tell him where I am?"

"What about your guests?" Jazz asked.

"We won't be gone long enough. I just want to talk with him away from everyone. Please, can you do this for me?"

They agreed, and all three of us slipped out of the bathroom. I went toward the foyer while they went out in search of Cameron. It took me more than just a few minutes to get through because of people stopping to congratulate me all the way toward the stairs. I hurried up the stairs to my room, as quickly as my dress would allow, excited for some quiet for even just a few minutes.

It was several minutes later when my bedroom door opened slowly. I was looking out over the backyard, standing amidst the billowing curtains when he stepped in, but I turned. He closed the door and turned the lock.

"Why did you lock it?"

"So you can't run away from me." I gave him a look. "No one can interrupt. People are going to be looking for us."

I stared at him. "By all means, let's talk about how you deceived me. Made me think I was falling in love, and loving someone that I could never have."

He crossed the room to me, ignoring my words. "The sooner we get married, the better. Now that it's announced, the danger is worse."

"Where's Pops?"

He frowned. "I don't know where he is. Do you think I know where he went?"

I folded my arms in front of me so he couldn't try to pull me in with his wily charm and seductive caresses. It was my invisible shield. Why did he have to look so damn handsome in a tuxedo?

His eyes were glittering with concern and love.

"Oh, come on. Where would he go?"

"I don't know. Maybe he went overseas."

I nodded.

"I truly don't know where he is. I know I shouldn't have gone to the island and inserted myself into your life. I didn't mean to walk into it and fall in love with you."

"Put yourself in my shoes," I whispered. "You meet this great guy and try you your absolute hardest to dissuade him from anything serious and all, but tell him you have no future together, only to fall headlong into love with him."

I let my arms fall to my sides, giving him the opportunity to sweep me up into his while his mouth sought mine in a mind-blowing kiss that left all my anger in shambles. I tried to hold on to the anger so I wouldn't be heartbroken all over again.

"I'll never give you another reason to doubt this," he said, his teeth nipping at my bottom lip. "I did what I had to do. And I'm glad I did, since someone found out where you were."

His voice cracked with emotion, and sympathy washed over me. I didn't pull out of his arms, but I ran my hand up to his biceps. I was putty in his hands.

He let his forehead fall against mine. "It nearly killed me to let you go."

I couldn't respond. My heart felt like it had crawled up into my throat and stopped there. He pulled away and our eyes connected. Anguish flooded his eyes, and I knew he was telling me the truth.

"You're still in such danger. I can't lose you again."

"What about you? Don't you think we're both in danger? Especially if we continue with this plan to get married?"

He flinched as though I had slapped him. "Are you considering not marrying me?"

I didn't respond to him. My heart belonged to him, and I never thought it would change. Becoming his wife and spending each morning with him was something I couldn't resist. What I was considering was that I, or we, could be in danger even after marrying. And *I* couldn't lose *him*.

"Regan, I can't protect you if I'm not with you." His voice was gravelly, shaky even. "I can't lose you again. Please."

"I said I would, and I intend to. I'm confused right now. I'm hurt, and I'm angry."

"Let's just enjoy the rest of the night."

I nodded, trying to pull out his arms so I could smooth down my wrinkled dress. He pulled his arms tighter around me until the length of me pressed against him. I sighed as his fingers danced over the line of my jaw, the pad of his thumb coming to rest against my bottom lip while his eyes bore into mine.

Dear God, but my body felt like it had dissolved. I melted in his hands any time he touched me. He ran his thumb over my lips, pulling it away just before his mouth pressed softly against mine. There was no urgency, no demands or possession. It was simply love.

It seemed like time had suspended while his lips pressed against mine, moving softly until I was responding. His mouth picked up urgency, and I knew beyond a doubt if this continued, we weren't going to make it back to the party.

He pulled away from me slowly, keeping his arm swept across my lower back and running the backs of his fingers over my cheek before withdrawing his arm. I concentrated on breathing in and out, smoothing out the front and sides of my dress before he linked his arm within mine.

"I like your room," he said with a wink, closing the door behind us without moving his arm from mine or breaking any contact.

I rolled my eyes. "It *was* my room. My house is in Malibu. I'm only staying here because Gio insisted."

"I'll have my things brought up later, after people have gone."

My eyes turned to him quickly. "What are you talking about?"

"You don't think that I'm ever going to leave your side now, do you? Oh, no. I'm staying with you, and you won't be sleeping alone again, Regan."

I should have known better, but I didn't argue with him because it would be pointless to dissuade him. Or Gio. As we walked down the stairs, I caught Amber's stare. She wagged her eyebrows at me, causing me to chuckle under my breath and Cameron to tighten his arm against mine.

"Oh . . ." Amber said, sliding over to us as we got to the bottom step. "Introduce me, sis, to this beautiful man."

"That's my fiancé you're talking about, *sis.*" My lips had thinned in a line. "Cameron, this is Amber. Amber, this is Cameron. And you will *not* be hitting on him. Find your own."

Amber's lips turned into a pout momentarily before she smiled and inclined her head toward Cameron. "I would never dream of it. Do you have brothers?"

Cameron laughed. "One's already married, and the other you would do well to stay away from. Other than that, I believe I may have some cousins around here." He pointed across the room at a blond-haired man in a white tuxedo with a neatly combed mustache. "There. My cousin, Adams."

"Adams?" she asked.

"Yes. His name is Adams."

"Not Adam?"

"Not Adam. Adams."

I stopped myself from laughing at the bizarre look that came over Amber's face like a cross between confusion and absurd delight. Without another word, I watched her leave us and make her way toward the man. I shook my head. He isn't going to know what hit him with Amber. She would have made a talented daughter for Pops. She was cunning, and she almost always got her way. Amber would have been the tool he was looking for.

Cameron guided me back into the throes of the party, stopping periodically to introduce me to people and stopping so I could introduce him to the people I knew. We talked in a group with Tatum, Jazz, Bryce, and Alex, trying to schedule something for the six of us to do without the threat of danger. If I could return to living in my house, we could hole up there for a while, but I would need to work on Cameron for that to happen.

My family's estate was by far the most secure place to be if someone was trying to kill you, with my condo a pale comparison. There was no gate, even though I had a security system. As I found out on the island, someone could easily disarm it. I had more than a bat in my bedroom, but I would be more afraid of waking up startled and shooting someone like Tatum in confusion. No, going back to my condo probably wasn't the best decision.

We danced more, and we danced so much that I realized the crowds were thinning out after a while. He politely excused himself and went to speak with some of his maternal uncles he had already introduced me to. His siblings did not make it to the party, but that was okay. I had met enough people to set my head spinning.

I accepted a glass of champagne from a server and stepped out into the coolness of the night, spotting Michael on the other side of the shimmering pool. He noticed me and raised his champagne glass to me in greeting.

I had thought it very odd for him to be here to witness me get engaged to someone else. I hope he didn't think that there had been someone else while we were seeing each other.

I gathered a bit of my dress into my hand as I stepped down the few steps that led to the enormous swimming pool, releasing it when I walked around the pool freely, without having to worry about falling in.

Absently, I fingered the jewels at my neck while I stepped over to him with an apologetic smile. His hand cupped my elbow with ease while he leaned over to kiss my cheek.

"You are entirely the most beautiful woman here, Regan," he said, his brown eyes twinkling. "I shouldn't have let you go so easily."

I cocked my head to the side. "I could've sworn I saw you with a brunette earlier this evening."

He sighed. "I just met her, but . . ." He leaned down to whisper to me. "She's quite flighty. She said she was getting a migraine and took a cab home. I'm not sure it's going to last long."

I smiled. "If she's flighty, well, maybe not for you."

"I agree." His eyes searched mine. "I miss you."

I missed him, but on a different level. Time together would have been so infrequent that I couldn't see anything else but us drifting apart, eventually. I wasn't even sure how it would work with Cameron, but it would have to.

I held onto his arm, leaning down to remove my heels. They had worn out their welcome on my feet and I needed them to be off. He grabbed my arm, even after I had leaned back up, pulling me a little toward him. I hoped he wasn't trying to lean in to kiss me. That would be incredibly stupid, and he wasn't a stupid man.

"Michael," I breathed. "Whatever we had is done. It's over."

Out of the corner of my eye, I saw Cameron coming down the stairs toward us, and I hoped he wouldn't be jealous and make a scene. Michael and I were not together and hadn't been for several months. I hadn't lied about not seeing anyone when he had asked me, more than once.

"That's—"

"Your fiancé," he finished for me.

"Yes."

Cameron was eating up the distance with his long legs. I really did not want there to be a scene. He had shed his tuxedo jacket and bow tie and wore only the white shirt, the first button undone, and the sleeves rolled up.

I smiled graciously, even when he reached us and snaked his arm around my waist, a clear intent to stake his claim on me, even though asking me to marry him in front of an audience earlier had already done so.

"Cameron, this is Michael. Michael, my fiancé, Cameron."

Cameron, without releasing me, held out his hand for a firm

handshake. I sensed he wanted nothing more than to pull me away as quickly as possible.

"You're a lucky man."

"I am."

"Congratulations to you both. I wish you nothing but happiness."

I smiled at Michael, hoping that he would find his own happiness soon. He was a great guy and had always been thoughtful toward me during our times together, but that was where it would have to end. Cameron, despite recent events, still had my entire heart and there would not be room for anyone else in it.

"There are guests that are leaving and would like to pay their respects to us," Cameron murmured down to me.

"I also must be leaving," Michael said, leaning over to kiss my cheek again despite Cameron's still having his arm around my waist. "You look beautiful, Regan."

Cameron's arm tensed so much that I could feel his muscles digging into my lower back. He did not like the interchange or the fact that Michael had kissed me, even though it was only my cheek. Knowing Cameron, even the cheek would be too comfortable. To his defense, he did not know Michael either, although kissing my cheek and telling me I look beautiful—again—may have been to get a rise out of Cameron. And it worked.

"Goodbye, Michael. I hope your date feels better."

Cameron waited until Michael had walked away from us and was almost at the house before he scooped me up in his arms, intent on walking back to the house carrying me.

"I don't like him."

"You don't have to like him. He's not the one I'm with."

At the patio doors, Cameron set me down on my feet and I moved to rejoin the party ahead of him. There were very few people still left lingering in the ballroom, and even fewer in the living room and foyer. The music was still going but very low now. No one was dancing any longer, and there were only sounds of whispered voices and quiet laughter. The conversations that had been buzzing in my ears all night were no longer there.

I had to admit I was exhausted, yet my body was humming. It was probably the champagne. I could handle a fair amount of wine, but champagne did something entirely different, and I knew I had imbibed more than I normally would.

Cameron caught my wrist just before I reached the foyer, pulling me back into a spin that landed me against him. He tipped my head back with his finger to my chin and pressed his lips to mine. I surprised myself by opening my mouth to his and sliding my arms around his neck. Without another moment's hesitation, he pulled his mouth away and swept me back up into his arms to carry me up the staircase.

I could have sworn that I heard Gio call out goodnight to us before we disappeared up the stairs and around the corner.

Chapter Nineteen

"You knew who he was. You could have told me."

I strolled into the dining room the next morning, catching Gio at the head of the long mahogany table set for three. The breakfast bar behind him was full of fruit, eggs, bacon, sausage, toast, and muffins, along with juices and coffee.

Sunlight was filling the already brightened room. I almost had to squint while passing the windows to get to the breakfast bar. Gio lowered his daily newspaper as I passed him. He carefully folded it and placed it beside his own plate of food, picking up his coffee to sip it while waiting for me.

I set my plate down and slid into the chair next to him, giving my chair a couple of hops to get closer to the table before picking up my coffee and taking a tentative sip. He leaned back in his chair, looking at me.

"Careful, Reggie. I hardly knew more than you did. I knew you were perfect for each other. That's all I knew."

"I agree with your uncle."

My head snapped over to see Cameron walking into the room, his presence as commanding as his voice was. I couldn't stop the shiver from going up my spine if I tried, thinking about how I had yielded to him last night without even realizing what I was doing. I blamed the champagne. He had taken full advantage, and I hadn't stopped him. It was as though the week apart had melted away, and we were together like nothing had changed. Except he was gone when I woke this morning. I presumed to use Pops' office to take care of some business.

"We already hashed this out last night," he reminded me. "Can we get past this? Please?"

I shook my head. I wanted to get past it. I needed answers to soothe my hurt still. "You knew that I had met someone. You could have told me it was him."

"I didn't know who they set you up to marry. I didn't know you met him already. I didn't know any of this. Please, don't blame me for something I had no part of."

He was right. Gio didn't deserve my wrath. It was best directed toward Pops and my mom. Then I looked over at Cameron while he loaded up a plate of food. I took my time watching him, admiring his firm backside in a pair of blue jeans. I was a lucky woman, no matter what the situation was. He was a handsome man, and he treated me like there was nothing in the world that mattered more to him than me. I couldn't complain, but I would never admit it. I could marry a stranger as they had led me to believe for months. Instead, I got to marry him.

"Regan."

When he said my name like that, shivers shot across the surface skin. It was as smooth as melted chocolate, and it caressed me when it shouldn't. I watched him settle into the seat across from me and spread his napkin out on his lap before digging into his food, piercing a piece of melon, and bringing it to his lips.

"You need to consider getting married sooner."

"I'm not buying it. What's the difference if we get married? Isn't the entire issue that we were born to who we were born to? The danger will never be gone."

"Listen to yourself," Gio interjected. "You're still getting married. You're talking in circles because you're hurt, and we get it."

I slumped. "I feel duped. You knew me for who I was, but I

didn't get that luxury."

"I didn't lie to you though," he said, even though a smile curved his lips. "I asked you if you were seeing anyone, and you said no. You could have told me you were engaged. It might have prompted some different conversations."

I would have kicked him in the chin had he been closer. "Technically, I wasn't engaged. And I told you from the beginning I wasn't interested in a relationship."

Cameron calmly set his fork down and brought his napkin to his lips to dab the corner, replacing it just as calmly before looking up at me. "Let's move past this."

I nodded. He was right. We could have handled things differently between us both, and they weren't. I needed to swallow my pride. "Who is trying to kill me, and why? Is it Ludovico?"

"I've been trying to find that out while you were on the island. It could be anyone. Ludovico included."

I looked at Gio, fully convinced that it was Ludovico. But he was right, Pops had many enemies. As did Cameron's father, Reno. So long as Pops and Reno were who they were, and they did what they did, we would always be a target for them. Getting married made a bigger mark.

"We need to get married," Cameron interrupted. "I'm not waiting until March."

"It doesn't matter if we get married now or in March," I pointed out. "Besides, the save-the-date cards have gone out. That's what Anne told me."

"I meant a small ceremony to make it legal. I won't deprive you of the big splashy wedding in March, but we would keep it quiet."

"There haven't been any attempts on your life?" I asked Cameron, but he shook his head. I slapped my hand down on the table, earning a raised brow from Gio. "Isabel. Please tell me she isn't in danger."

"Isabel will be fine. No one knows about her except you two, me and your father." He looked at me pointedly, his eyes serious. "Is there any chance that you're pregnant?"

"Gio!" I gasped. "Of course, I'm not pregnant."

Gio looked at Cameron. "Get married in a small ceremony, get her pregnant, then you hide out until the baby is born."

"Are you out of your damn mind?" I shouted. "I'm not getting pregnant. Having a baby isn't going to stop this. It just puts our child in danger."

"He's right."

"You're talking about the possibility that if I'm pregnant and someone takes me out, your child, your own flesh and blood, will go with me. To hell with this arrangement. That's what's going to get me killed!"

"Arrangement or no, we're getting married."

I hadn't really wanted to back out of the engagement, but it was really aggravating me. I had never been one to back down from a fight, but this was unnerving. I was a prisoner in my family home, not even allowed to go to my house, and Cameron was pretending as though there was nothing at all wrong, even though I knew he was aware as much as I was, probably more.

I did the only thing I could. After eating my breakfast, I stopped talking. Gio resumed reading his paper, but Cameron watched me. When I finished, I stood up and threw my napkin over my plate just as Cameron stood up. It was as though he had timed it.

I walked out of the dining room, mindful that Cameron was on the other side of the table, matching my pace until we both reached the door at the same time. He leaned into me, pulling my hand into his and brushing a strand of hair away from my face with the back of his fingers.

"I really like the thought of you having my baby," he whispered.

I would have punched him if I hadn't thought the same thing myself already. I would love to have his baby. The thought of a little boy with his father's eyes and dark hair made my heartbeat kick up slightly. Now was not the time. They had to know that it was dangerous. I didn't want to die, and I didn't want to die while carrying another innocent person. Especially not Cameron's innocent little person.

"We aren't even married yet."

"We'll be married within the next month. We, or you at least, need to stay put for the time being. We can apply for the marriage license and as soon as we get it, we're doing it. I'm not waiting until March."

I didn't like the thought of being stuck here for a month. I knew I would go stir-crazy in another day or two. I wasn't used to sitting idly. Amber was busy seeing friends while she was home from break, and she would soon leave. I would rather not sit with Anne and have conversations with her because it was all about wedding stuff, and Gio and Cameron were busy working on whatever they were working on.

I pulled my phone out of my pocket when it vibrated, frowning at the caller. I looked back up at Cameron, who had raised his eyebrows at me in silent question about who was calling.

"It's Tate," I blurted.

"I have work to do. I'll be in the library."

He leaned down to kiss my cheek, rounding the corner to cross the foyer toward the library that was on the other side of Pops' office. I accepted the call, putting my phone up to my ear and hurrying into the living room for some privacy with this call. No one could know who I was about to talk to.

"Hey," I whispered, looking around once again just to make sure no one was listening. I opened the doors out to the backyard and slipped out, ensuring that I would have total privacy.

"Regan," Jake said. "How're you?"

"I'm fine. What's wrong?"

"Nothing. I wanted to hear your voice. I heard you're engaged. Congratulations."

I frowned. News travels fast. "I told you about that. It's official now."

"My father heard about it."

My suspicion of Ludovico doubled. "And?"

"Naturally, he doesn't want the two families to merge."

"Why would he even care? He has his own drug business, and whatever else, and seems to do well enough if I remember the size of his house and the number of associates he has."

I walked around the pool, settling down in a lawn chair well away from any prying ears. It was good to talk to Jake, even though it was incredibly risky for him to call. I wasn't sure if Pops knew I was still in contact with him, and I wouldn't know how to explain it to Cameron. I knew I should tell Cameron. There shouldn't be secrets between us. But Jake was a friend, and he wasn't a threat. After how he acted toward Michael, he would see Jake as a threat.

If anything, I should have a personal vendetta against Ludovico. He was the one who tried to take out my mother. He was the reason she had to go into hiding most of my life, missing out on everything that I had gone through, giving up her husband, even to another woman. The list of his personal crimes against me and my family was endless. We should all be going after him. Who was he against two powerful families?

"There was a reason he kidnapped you when you were twelve, Regan." His voice was incredibly low, leaving me to strain to hear what he was saying. "He-"

Nothing. Silence. "Jake?" I asked, then more urgently. "Jake?"

"I have to go. I'll call you when I can."

Click. I stared down at my phone. Damn it. It was too risky for him to call me now. I knew the reason he had kidnapped me. I glanced up at the house, contemplating what to do. Ultimately, my heart won out.

I sent him a message on social media: *Don't call. Too risky. Will talk when we can, but do not call.*

Oh, Jake, I thought. He was my first friend, my only friend, for a long time. Even though we hadn't talked much while we were both growing up in two separate lives, he was still there whenever I needed him. I knew he disagreed with most of what his father did, but I still didn't want him to put himself in danger. Ludovico was not someone to mess with, and I knew it wouldn't stop at getting rid of his only son if need be. He was that much of a bastard.

Chapter Twenty

"We need to talk."

I looked up from the floor of the ballroom where I was stretching in preparation to dance, almost the same spot where Cameron had swept me into his arms and I realized he was here not because he had snuck in, but because he was the one Pops had intended for me to marry. I wondered if I had found someone else years ago, if things would have turned out differently. I still suspected that of the relationships I had, other than Michael, Pops had interfered. And he had done so for this very reason.

Cameron was strolling across the floor, wearing a pair of cargo shorts with a white t-shirt. My mouth went dry. I hoped I would always look at him this way. The confidence in his walk, the gleam in his eyes. And he was all mine.

"Should I be worried?" I quipped. "When someone says something like that, it usually means that a break-up is coming."

"That's not happening, but I want to talk to you about some things, now that you know who I am and who my family is."

He stopped next to me and sat down, stretching out his long legs and leaning back on his arms. How a man could look so relaxed and self-confident at the same time astonished me.

"If you're supplying drugs through the boatyard, it stops now," I said. "I bought the boatyard free of Pops so I wouldn't have a dirty business."

The smile that curved his lips confirmed my suspicion. Damn it, he was running dirty businesses like Pops and like his father. And I was going to get pulled into the throng as an unwilling participant. Not only that, but Pops had also chosen him as a shield. A shield for me. If Cameron took over this massive enterprise between the two families, it would put an enormous target on his back and someday I would lose him to it.

"Yes, I have been. I supply it, the build manager runs it." I shook my head. "But that changed when you bought Mark out."

"Did Mark know?"

"No."

"What else?"

He sat up and reached out to me, but I slapped his hands away. The only thing I needed to know was what else Cameron was into, and what he was planning. It wasn't just his future now. If what he told me was true, and he didn't learn about this arrangement until just before we both arrived on the island, he had decisions to make. I couldn't lose him again.

"Regan, when I met you, something changed." I gave him a sardonic look. "Not that day. I realized at the club that night when someone drugged your drink. I realized I couldn't lose you. I knew then you were my person, and I was fine with that, but you didn't know it. And I wasn't fine with that."

"Then why didn't you tell me?"

"I didn't want to put you in more danger. I wasn't supposed to be there. If someone knew where I was, it would put both of us in more danger. I couldn't tell you, and it was the chance I had to take."

"Okay, so the incident at the club happened. What changed?"

"When I was growing up, I was fine taking over the family business. Whatever my father was into, I could do. My father raised me to do it. Drug trafficking, racketeering, smuggling, loan sharking. The last few years have been different since Caleb was born."

"Your nephew?"

He nodded. "Peter isn't a banker. He's a loan shark. Both he and Stefan work for my father. The older I get, the more I realize I want to have a family like Peter, and I don't want to live that kind of life. I don't want to worry about my wife and kids being in danger because of my dealings. The businesses that I own, except a few, are clean. There's nothing dirty."

I hadn't noticed the steady increase of my heartbeat until I realized during the incident at the club, his life may have flashed before his eyes. He knew about me even though I hadn't known about him. He knew I would be his wife. And the threat in my life had been real.

"Is this why you had trouble with past relationships?"

He laughed. "No. Like you, traveling a lot usually would put a strain on things. None of them I could ever picture as my wife, though."

This time, when he reached out, I let him take my hand. He didn't try to pull me into his arms or lean over and kiss me. He just kept my hand within his, tangling his fingers in mine.

"So, this is your fatal flaw?" I asked. "You're running some illegal shit? Making lots of money doing it?"

He shrugged. "Making lots of money, yes. Giving lots of money to charity, yes."

I perked up. "You give money to charity?"

"Kind of like you giving money to people in need, like Melanie. I like to give money to good causes. Causes that mean something. Causes that mean something to me or mean something to someone who means something to me."

"Like?"

"Did you know that only fifteen states have stolen dog laws?"

"You mean when someone takes someone else's dog?" He nodded. "Do people still do that? I thought that happened a lot of years ago. I didn't realize it was still happening so much."

"People steal certain breeds to either ransom or sell to dog fighting rings." I showed my disgust, and I hoped my face expressed it. "Out of fifteen states, including California, there are only five that have specific stolen dog statutes for people that steal dogs."

"What does this mean? What do you give money to?"

"I have a friend named Riley who rescues stolen dogs. She tracks stolen dogs down and uses whatever means necessary to take them back and return them to their families."

I raised a brow. "She?"

"She's like you, except you think she's a big softy at first, but she's tougher. Tougher than some men I've met. I think once you meet her, you would get along with her well."

"Did you date her?"

He pulled a face, still flirting with my fingers. "No."

"What is it you do for her? You give her money?"

"I fund a lot of her activities. She does a lot of traveling and she has a lot of expenses. Travel arrangements, accommodations where she is staking out the stolen dog, food for her, food for the dog. Some dogs need care, which is expensive."

If she didn't have a past relationship with Cameron, she had my interest in what she was doing, and I wanted to meet her. Someone who would dedicate her life to rescuing these defenseless animals was a friend of mine.

"Any other charities?"

"That's the main one. It takes a lot of money to run it. Riley didn't come from a family with money like we did. I give to some other smaller charities, like women's shelters. And I give to some places for women trying to get out of prostitution. You know it's legal where I grew up."

I laughed, scooting closer to him and throwing my arms around his neck. My face pressed against his chest. "Can't you have one terrible thing about you? You really can't be this perfect. I mean really."

He laughed. "What I'm about to tell you next will do it."

Immediately, I withdrew and moved back to where I was. "Why?"

"This is not my doing, and I don't agree with it. We're having an engagement party on New Year's Eve at your Pops' country club."

That didn't sound like a good idea. "Has anyone heard from Pops?"

"No, not that I know. Gio is meeting with a potential dealer from Columbia, interested in getting into bed, so to speak with your dad. He's coming up to meet with Gio, and they thought the engagement party would be the best place for it."

"Why the hell would they think that?"

"It's public, not likely to have something go wrong there." He held up his hand, knowing my trepidations on it. There was enough going on without having one more thing to worry about. We shouldn't be having parties and splashy balls. None of us should congregate in one area together, no matter how public it was.

"Will this ever end?"

"I hold on to hope every day."

Chapter Twenty One

I stepped out of the long, black limousine in front of the De Luca Country Club main entrance. The building was shockingly white, with several bushes in front of rows upon rows of windows. The clubhouse was a two-level building built into the side of a hill with the main level containing the bar and restaurant and the lower level with a pro-golf shop and several private rooms. A row of golf carts lined up out the back windows.

The glow of the sunset behind the clubhouse took my breath away with its beauty, almost the entire horizon awash with burning red and orange swathes. It was evenings such as this that made me stop and give thanks for life. It may not be a perfect life, but it was still life.

"Miss De Luca?"

I looked at the doorman, holding out a white-gloved hand to me. Pops made the ridiculous policy that the doormen had to wear these odd hats that looked like they belonged on a toy soldier, not a grown man. The valet people didn't have to wear any hats, the wait staff and bartenders didn't have to, only the doormen. I gave him a smile along with my hand, allowing him to pull me up the step to the entrance while Cameron stepped out behind me. I felt his hand press against the small of my back, urging me forward while the doorman's hand fell away from mine.

I pulled the light shawl around my arms closer, even though

the heat Cameron radiated was enough to keep me warm. Again, he looked entirely too handsome in his black tux as we joined the engagement party. I would have thought the Christmas ball was a party enough for our engagement. Here we were. I hoped Gio knew what he was dealing with at this meeting.

"Regan!"

We were no sooner stepping through the doors than Amber waved us down from the spot she'd claimed next to the bar. Dressed in a long, gold shimmering gown that had no straps and clung to her breasts, she looked like she was on the prowl. Hair swept up into a coiffure, and diamonds dripped from her ears and neck. I knew her dad hadn't been in the picture her whole life, and medical school was expensive. Pops took care of her and Anne, despite not having a legal claim to do so. He did bad things, and sometimes he didn't. Deep down, he was a good man.

Cameron followed closely behind me, standing alert, and looking around with heightened awareness while I leaned down to kiss Amber's cheek. "Finding anyone to take home to your mother yet?" I teased. "Or did you hit it off with Adams?"

"Adams is . . . nice. But no, didn't hit it off quite that way. I'm too far away. You're late, by the way."

I shrugged. "I had issues with my dress."

Amber's eyes passed over my long silver dress, the bodice sparkling with gems. It was also void of sleeves and didn't quite reach the floor where my matching heels peeked out. She rolled her eyes, not believing my excuse. She was right, of course. Cameron and I had been otherwise occupied and lost track of time.

Gio was confident about the party, while Cameron and I were less than thrilled, even if it was a private event at the club, but it was New Year's Eve and if we were together, we would get through it.

The bartender, recognizing me when I came in, handed me a glass of champagne while Cameron asked for a bourbon.

Champagne again, I thought. This ought to be a fun night.

"Did you make up with him?" Amber wagged her eyebrows.

"You're a little shit," I said, a smiling curving my lips. "There wasn't anything to make up for. We're getting married. That's why we're all here."

"I'm happy for you." She leaned over to whisper in my ear. "Cameron seems to be an excellent catch. You're very lucky."

I couldn't disagree with her. Cameron accepted his glass of bourbon and took a sip of the amber-colored liquid slowly, swirling it around in his low-ball glass while looking around. His parents had left immediately after the Christmas Ball, and although he seemed adept on his own, I felt bad for him. I knew Alex would be here because Tatum had told me he was bringing her. I was almost certain that Jazz would be here, too, but I wasn't sure she would bring her girlfriend. I hoped Bryce would make a showing. Cameron needed his friends, just like I needed mine.

I hadn't heard another word from Jake. He had read the message I sent him, but heeded my advice and stopped contacting me. It worried me what he was about to tell me, but I tried to put it out of my mind. Had there been more to my kidnapping than Ludovico had told me? I hated lying to Cameron, but I didn't think he would have been understanding if I was taking calls from another man and especially one whose father was Ludovico Mancini.

"Regan?"

Amber waved her hand in front of my face. "Sorry . . . I don't know what's wrong with me tonight. I think I'm jittery. This is dangerous. We shouldn't be here."

"It is too dangerous," Cameron said, his lips very close to my ear.

"What can we do?"

He shrugged. "Let's just try to have a good time, but be extra cautious."

It felt strange being in Pops' country club with such a damning feeling. I thought maybe it wasn't a good time to be drinking, but as Tatum and Alex arrived, more glasses of champagne were in my hands and more frequently. Jazz arrived with her girlfriend, Kara, as midnight grew closer.

The club, much smaller than our family home, swarmed with people. Everyone appeared to be having a good time. I had to make sure that I stopped drinking champagne and kept a clear head. Cameron, I noticed, was also sipping his drinks slowly. We were both uneasy, and that emotion fed off each other.

The champagne was going right to my head, and it wasn't even midnight yet. Escaping the buzzing of the party, I inched my way down the staircase leading toward the lower level, which stemmed in two directions. Left led to the shop and private rooms, while going right led to a patio that had a pretty fountain with three mermaids sitting in the center.

I pulled my shawl closer; darkness having chased away the pretty sunset hours ago. The wind from the ocean was cold. I desperately needed to clear my head. I walked around the fountain to face the darkness as the waves against the shore sang softly.

"The view is breathtaking."

The sound of his voice slid over me, much like his hands had earlier, slowly and tentatively, like he was looking for something. He stopped just behind me, his hands settling on my hips and his lips at the side of my neck while he pulled me against him.

"It is beautiful."

"I was talking about you."

I laughed softly, leaning my head against his chest while his arms came around my waist and locked me in. Together, we listened to the gentle caress of the waves and said nothing else. We just sat in silence; enjoying each other and enjoying the moment.

It was several moments before I turned around, looping my arms around his neck and watching his hair get ruffled in the breeze. He looked at me like he wanted to devour me. I hoped that he never stopped looking at me that way. He tucked his bow tie into his pocket and undid the first couple buttons of his shirt, just a peek at his chest. I leaned forward and pressed my lips against the hollow at his neck just before his chest began.

His arms moved, drawing me even closer to him.

I felt the ground move, thinking that he had me so wrapped around his finger he was making my world shake until the ground really moved. The ground shook and suddenly threw us apart, and I heard something falling, realizing that it was the building.

It threw me onto my side, but I recovered quickly, trying to find Cameron through the smoky haze. I covered my head, realizing that the building was falling around us, searching for him. Dear God, someone had tried to kill us both, was my first thought.

"Cameron," I whispered, halfway turning and sitting up with my palms on the pavement to see that it ripped my gown in multiple places and I had blood on my arms from the debris.

I waved my hands to clear the smoke in order to see. We had been right next to each other one minute and ripped apart in the next second. He couldn't be far from me. I didn't know which way to find him, so I felt with my hands, not caring that my fingernails were breaking because of how much concrete I had to move.

I gasped as soon as I touched flesh, pulling myself over to where Cameron was laying. There was blood on his forehead, his eyelids closed as though he were in a peaceful sleep.

"Dear God, no . . ." I murmured, picking up his hand and moving over his chest to feel the faint rise and fall of his breathing. I laid my hand down on his chest. "Cameron, please. Wake up."

His hand moved within mine, then his arm drifting up to slip around me. I laid my head down on his chest, the feel of his hand moving up my back reassuring that he would be okay.

"I thought you were dead."

"Are you hurt?" His voice was low and scratchy, barely there.

"Nothing but some scrapes, I think. You have blood on your forehead."

He brought his fingers up to his head, pulling away his fingers with blood. A faint smile curved his lips. "Looks minor, but my head is pounding. Something must have hit me. What happened?" He pushed himself up onto his elbow, waving his hand to clear some of the smoke like I had tried to do.

"I don't know. The ground shook, then the building was coming down around us like rain." He put his hand on the curve of my face, carefully. "When will this stop?"

"It will stop. Marry me, Regan."

"I told you I would."

"Marry me sooner."

"Will it stop then?"

He looked at me but didn't respond. He didn't have a response any more than I did. Who knew if anything would stop even if we married? We didn't even know who we're fighting against.

"We need to get out of here. I smell smoke. The building could be on fire."

"I don't know which way is which," I said as he pushed himself up, bending down to help me up. "I don't want to go the wrong way."

I heard sirens in the distance. Whatever had happened, it was bad. We crept around the patio, finding the concrete half-wall that had enclosed the patio and working our way until we could find the steps leading up toward the parking lot.

Cameron kept my hand firmly in his, leading the way up the stairs, and I was right behind him, clinging to his arm like I was going to be left behind somehow. I had never been this dependent on anyone in my life, but I was frantic to find out who else had gotten hurt in whatever had happened.

As we reached the top floor, the smoke was clearing away slowly and I could see fire trucks, ambulances and police cars flooding into the parking lot, the blue, red and white lights like a fireworks display. People came out of the club in streams.

Cameron brought me straight into the crowds, hoping to find that everyone had made it out alive. Firefighters were running toward the building with the fire hoses to distinguish any fires that had started while the police began talking to those coming out. Paramedics were coming out with people on stretchers.

I felt Cameron's hand squeeze mine as he stopped a police officer. "What happened?"

"From the sounds of it, a bomb."

I immediately paled. They hurt people. Because Pops had to make one more deal, one more goddamn way to make more money, as if he didn't have enough. This was getting out of hand.

Cameron and I wound our way through the crowds. I cried out when I saw Tatum and Alex, both looking as rumpled as Cameron and I were, but otherwise fine. Lots of people had gashes in their head and wounds on their arms, and faces. I started watching the stretchers that were coming out and held my breath.

"Jazz?" I asked her. "Amber? Gio? Anne?"

She shook her head. "I'm not sure where Jazz and Kara were when it happened. I just know that Alex and I were about to head outside to get some air, and then we were both basically thrown clear of the building."

I looked up at the front of the clubhouse. There were holes in the side of it, like someone had thrown things clear through, but the front was intact, which meant that wherever the bomb went off was probably inside somewhere. I desperately wanted to go inside, even moved away from Cameron toward the entrance.

His hand tensed, and he pulled me back. "No," he said. "Absolutely not. Let the paramedics and firefighters do their jobs. We can look at the damage tomorrow if it's safe enough."

"I have to . . . see."

I gasped when I watched Gio wheeled out on a stretcher. To stop the scream, I slapped my hand over my mouth. There was a white towel pressed to his head and I could see the part of his face not covered was black and blue. His tuxedo was in shambles, and he had a neck brace on.

I tugged my hand away from Cameron, running over to Gio. He wasn't conscious, but I looked up at the paramedic with pleading eyes. "My uncle," I said. "What happened?"

"He's got some burns and we're taking precautions with his neck and spine. We're taking him in as quick as possible to make sure there are no internal injuries."

Cameron's arms came around me, but I shrugged them off, trying to run into the clubhouse to see if Amber and Anne were in there. Jazz and Kara. My mind screamed. How could this have happened? How could we have *let* this happen? If I knew the way to the Mancini house in Santa Barbara, you bet your ass I would be jumping in a car and hightailing it right to his front door. *Kill me, you bastard, but don't you dare take anyone I love just for the satisfaction of your own revenge.*

Cameron grabbed me again, throwing his arms around me to immobilize me despite my pushing against him. "I have to . . ."

His voice whispered in my ear. "We will. Just let them do their jobs."

I stopped struggling, realizing that it was futile to continue to fight him. There was still imminent danger inside with the structure and fires. The professionals were doing all that they could to get anyone out they could. I saw people being brought out on stretchers, covered in sheets, and I couldn't help myself.

I buried my head in Cameron's chest and bawled like a baby. He ushered me over to a concrete parking block, helping me to sit down while he kept my face pressed against his torn tuxedo. His comfort meant everything to me then. Tatum and Alex sat down next to us to wait. Wait for news on any survivors. Wait for news on those who had died in the blast.

"I'll kill him," I whispered, looking up at Cameron. "I'll kill that bastard if he's the one that did this. I promise you."

"Who?"

"Ludovico Mancini. If he was behind this, I'll kill him."

"I can't just sit here," Tatum wailed. "I need to find out about Jazz and Kara."

I watched her slowly get up, Alex right behind her as she wound her way back through the crowds. Firefighters were ushering everyone to get as far away from the building as possible. I didn't care. I wasn't moving.

Paramedics attempted to assist us, but Cameron waved them away, telling them to treat others first. We were fine other than some scrapes and a likely concussion. We would go to the hospital later and get thoroughly checked out.

"We're not doing any good here," Cameron said. "We should go to the hospital. Maybe we'll get more news there on survivors."

I nodded. "What do we do? Hail a cab? Call an Uber?"

Cameron called over Alex. Alex was in decent enough shape to drive, so we all piled into his Nissan and drove to the nearest hospital. Many of the ambulances had already pulled in, the emergency room a mess of people in fancy gowns and tuxedos.

∞

There was a knock at my bedroom door, and I looked up from my book in annoyance at the intrusion. I sat cross-legged in the middle of my bed, deeply engrossed in a book that was assigned at the tail end of the school year. Instead of failing all my fourth-quarter classes, the school administration was allowing me to do the work over the summer for credit. It was highly non-standard, but I would take it and I would do it. The last thing I wanted was to repeat a grade and have even more whispers about me. After all, I did most of the year. It wouldn't be fair to make me repeat the entire curriculum.

The housekeeper, Mary, opened the door and stuck her head through. I laid my book upside down on the bed and looked over at her, pursing my lips in guilt for my annoyance. I liked Mary.

"Your daddy is requesting you in his study."

Mary had come from the deep south after graduating from high school and her southern twang never slipped away or even dulled in the fifty years since. She'd worked for my family ever since I could remember.

"Come along now. Don't keep him waiting."

I dogged-eared the page and tossed the book aside. Mary opened the door wider while I hopped down from my bed. I stopped in front of her, looking at her gray, springy hair pulled into a bun behind her head. She wore the worst imaginable shade of pink lipstick against her alabaster skin. But I liked her, so I didn't say anything.

"What does he want?" I asked as we walked down the hall.

"If I knew, I wouldn't be comin' to get you."

"Why didn't he come get me himself?"

"Your daddy is a busy man, child. I reckon he would if he had the time."

We lapsed into silence as we walked down the curving staircase. At the bottom, Mary left to continue her other duties while I went into the study across from the end of the staircase and to the left. It was the one part of the house I rarely went into. There was no need to venture this way.

The double doors were closed when I stopped in front of them, and I was hesitant about whether I should knock or just open it. He was expecting me, but that didn't mean he wanted to be interrupted. The door suddenly opened, and Frank looked down at me. He smiled, ushering me into the room before closing the door again.

Pops' study was extensive, facing the circular driveway with enormous windows across from the doors and a massive desk to the left of a wall covered with books. The wall of books extended into the adjoining room, which was the library. Across from the desk was a sitting area with a brown leather couch, matching chairs, and tables on either side of the couch and one in the middle.

I stepped into the room, my feet going oddly slow as I looked over at Pops sitting behind his desk smoking a cigar. Frank sat down on the couch, resting his forearms on his knees with his legs splayed while Ezekiel sat in a chair in front of the desk, his ankle crossed over to rest on his knee.

"My darling girl," Pops said. "Sit down, please."

I hadn't talked to Pops since I came home only a few days ago. Mary and the other staff pampered me. The personal shopper took me shopping, and they whisked away the clothing that I had been wearing in disgust. Everyone talked in hushed tones around me like I was supposed to be shielded from knowing anything was going on.

I slipped into the chair next to Ezekiel. He gave me a wink.

"How've you been?" Pops asked.

How have I been? I screamed inside my head. Why haven't you talked to me since I've come home, or even asked me what happened? Why have you been ignoring me? The silent questions raged in my head, afraid if I had such an outburst, he would send me back to my room.

"Fine," I answered.

His blue eyes stared into mine, penetrating as usual. He wasn't a man who liked to be kept waiting or not getting his questions answered truthfully. He had a knack for knowing when someone was lying, and he knew I was not being straight with him. But what could I say? I have night terrors, reliving when my finger pulled the trigger? That I found a friend in Jake, his adversary's only son, who had provided me with comfort and friendship, maybe a little love, while I was there?

"Tell me the truth."

I lifted my chin a notch. "I'm fine. Absolutely fine. I'd do it again if I had to."

I watched his lips below his mustache curl up. He took another puff of his cigar; the smoke circling over his head then disappearing. He tapped the ashes from the end into a small rectangle ashtray. My answer had made him proud.

"Where is Nicco?" I blurted, letting his pride in me get the better of my mouth.

"Nicco will no longer be driving you. Pollo will do so from now on."

"You fired him?"

The three men exchanged glances before Pops' eyes came back to meet mine. I knew. The bottom of my stomach felt like it had fallen out. My heart thundered in my chest and the palms of my hands began to perspire and itch. My breathing raced.

"You killed him," I whispered, my voice shaking. I didn't want to believe it. But I knew beyond a doubt. "You killed him because he let me get kidnapped."

"Regan . . ."

"No!" I clamped my hands over my ears. I didn't want to listen to what he had to say. I didn't want Nicco to be gone. He would have never let me get taken. Someone had purposely made him late that day, and it hadn't been his fault he wasn't there in time. Pops had killed him anyway.

I slowly withdrew my hands from my ears, staring at Pops so he would know the true extent of my anger. It wasn't anger. I was furious. I would never forgive him for this. Never.

"You killed him," I repeated, my voice deadly quiet, no longer shaking, and shocking me at how sinister it sounded. Two could play this.

"Regan."

I opened my eyes to horrible florescent lighting overhead, slowly realizing I was at the hospital in the emergency room waiting room. The waiting room was so full that people from the party were sitting and lying on the floor. Many of them I recognized. I was curled into a most uncomfortable chair with my legs pulled up beside Cameron, whose arms and chest provided a cushion and warmth for me. I must have dozed off during the agony of waiting. My heart was beating fast, my palms wet with sweat. It had been so long since the last flashback. I thought they had stopped.

"They're ready to take you back," he whispered. "I'll meet you back there. I have to complete some paperwork."

I shook my head. "You should go first."

"No."

He pulled me up from the chair, walking with me to where the nurse was waiting. He wasn't about to argue this with me. I looked at the nurse with a small smile. She was very pregnant. Her blue scrubs stretched over her swollen belly, with dark smudges beneath her eyes. Instantly, I felt bad for her. She looked positively miserable. What could have been a slow night, allowing her to take some breaks and put her feet up, had turned into a flurry of activity and one patient after another. We had caused this.

My smile slid away while she walked me back into the swarmed emergency room, leading me into a private room instead of one that was only isolated by a curtain. There were so many people that some didn't even have that. There was someone lying on a bed in the hallway. She asked me to state my name, date of birth, and even though I didn't need to say it, that I had been among those at the country club.

"Quite a mess, that one," she said, waving me to the bed.

I sat down and lifted my legs onto the bed, reclining back. "There are still missing people. Do you know if anyone died?"

"Sorry," she said, grabbing a blood pressure cuff and sliding it onto my arm. "I haven't heard anything. I only know that the most critical are in surgery and there is a steady stream of the rest waiting."

I laid my head against the small pillow at the top of the bed, looking up at the ugly lights and drop-in ceiling panels while she took my blood pressure, continuing to ask me questions about any symptoms I was having.

My questions were automatic. I hoped if Gio had been critical; he was in surgery and would come out of this unscathed. I hoped Anne, Amber, Jazz, and Kara were among them as well and not . . . I couldn't even think about it. I squeezed my eyes shut, and when I opened them, Michael, dressed in blue scrubs, was walking in. When he saw me, he stopped and stared at me for an expectant moment before turning to close the door.

"Regan?"

"That's me."

"Your party at the country club, I presume?" he asked, giving the stool on wheels a kick to send it sliding away from him, pulling the stethoscope from around his neck.

He was so proficient, yet the way he moved was calm, comfortable, and confident. "It's a long story. What are you doing here? You haven't done a residency here for years."

"They called and asked me to come in. I couldn't say no."

"You never could."

The door opened and Cameron strode in, his tuxedo jacket bunched up in his hand. The same hand clenched around the fabric when he saw Michael standing over me with his stethoscope pressed over my heart. He came to my side, picking up my hand and placing a featherlight kiss to my scraped knuckles.

Michael watched the entire interchange between us while trying to listen to my lungs. He frowned, pulling away from me.

"Your heart rate is elevated," he said. "It wasn't a minute ago."

I noticed the sly smile on Cameron's lips. "What's her prognosis?"

"She's scraped up a bit, that's all." He nudged his chin toward Cameron. "You need that gash on your head looked at. You may have to get stitches."

"Yes. Please look at it," I said, sitting up and sliding off the bed so Cameron could, albeit grudgingly, take my place.

Michael swung the stool over to me so I could sit down while Cameron hopped up on the bed, refusing to lie back to be tended to. I watched the makeshift bandage peel away with a grimace. Michael wiped a bit of the blood away but was scrutinizing the wound with practiced hands and eyes. If there was any male rivalry going on, I couldn't tell from Michael. He was nothing but professional.

"Yep, maybe three or four stitches here. I've got others to check on while Lydia takes your vital signs and gets the sutures prepped."

Michael gave me a wink and stepped out of the room, leaving us alone with the nurse. Cameron looked over at me with a look that said that he still didn't like him, but Michael had done nothing but his job. I scooted close enough to stay out of Lydia's way, sliding my hand into his and lacing my fingers with his while she took his blood pressure.

"Any word on anyone else?" I asked him.

I was eager to find out who else had survived. There had to have been fatalities with as much damage as I had seen when most of the smoke had cleared.

"No. I'm sure we'll hear something soon."

I looked at him. Now was not the time to shield me from hurt. I hoped he was being honest. I had to know. I would go crazy if I didn't know, and soon. It was Pops' damn meeting that had us all there in the first place with a stupid excuse for an engagement party.

"Tatum and Alex both checked out and are fine. Other than that, nothing. I'm sorry I couldn't find out anymore. I know you're worried."

"It's not your fault," I whispered. "I'm thinking . . . that if we stay together, more people are going to get hurt."

"Hey." He leaned over to me, earning a dirty look from Lydia, who was attempting to clean up his head. "Stop that. We're going to get through this." He picked up my hand to show me the ringer on my finger. "See? You said yes."

Despite myself, I gave him a small smile. I loved him. There hadn't been any doubt about that even now. I just wanted to stop having to look over my shoulder. I wanted Pops to come back, and I wanted to make sure no one else got hurt.

The door jerked open, causing me to swivel the chair around to see Tatum. Her eyes were frantic, tears streaming down her flushed cheeks, and I knew. I shook my head, bringing my hand to my mouth as I choked. No . . .

"Jazz."

She hurried over to me, falling in front of me, and laying her head in my lap as sobs wracked her body. I looked up at Alex, who looked about as distraught as Tatum was.

"You can't be in here," the nurse snapped.

I turned to look at her, eyes wide and fighting tears. "She's fine. I understand you have a job to do, but . . ." I choked again, willing the tears to stay where they were.

Not Jazz. No, I thought. She had such a bright future. Kara and she had been so in love, and Jazz was so talented. The lump in my throat grew bigger, especially when I felt Cameron's hand on my back moving slowly in comfort. I laid down my head on the end of the bed and let it all out. I didn't even care when Michael came back into the room to see two women bawling their eyes out, but he didn't say anything until we had stopped crying.

"Who?" he asked quietly.

"Jazz."

Thankfully, Cameron had answered him for me. I wasn't sure I could speak right now. My heart was falling into the hollowness of my stomach. I couldn't believe it. I didn't want to believe it. And I didn't want to face anyone else that might have died. This had to end.

Chapter Twenty Two

I had been to the funeral of someone only one other time in my life, and I didn't remember it. It was when we buried my mother, except now I knew we hadn't buried a body. Or if we did, it wasn't hers. I paid for all costs of Jazz's funeral a week later without hesitation, since both of her parents had died when she was younger. Jazz wasn't the only loss. Many others had died, and most had suffered injuries. Gio had pulled through with a broken leg, concussion, and some burns on his face and arm. Amber and Anne had also been fine, with injuries that were not as critical but more than minor. Kara was in a brief coma but had come out of it and could come to the funeral. She and Jazz had been close to where the bomb had detonated.

It was what she had said to me after the funeral that would stay with me forever. The anger she had from losing Jazz was understandable. Taking it out on me was not. She approached me just as Cameron and I were turning to leave, a bandage still covering part of her head.

"You think your money is going to take care of this?" she asked, her voice scathing and her eyes accusing. "Just because you paid for this does not absolve you of guilt."

Cameron's arm tightened around me, silently telling me not to take the bait. Let it go, let her mourn in her own way and don't spit back. And he would be right, as he usually was.

"I paid for this because Jazz was my friend. Other than you, she had no one," I breathed. "I'm sorry you lost her, Kara. But I lost her, too."

"You self-righteous bitch. You get to live. You get to live happily ever after with your prince charming, while I live out the rest of my days alone. She was the love of my life."

"That's enough," Cameron said.

I watched Kara limp away from us, but her words stayed with me. They were still with me even now, weeks later. The guilt was with me. I hadn't paid for the funeral because of the guilt. I did so because it was the right thing to do.

By the beginning of February, I was exhausted, depressed, and I felt sick all the time. It had been a steady stream of calls and things to do since then. The country club was a total loss and would need to be rebuilt. I was barely eating or sleeping, even after Cameron insisted upon trying to manage my life for me while I managed everything else.

Cameron had convinced me at the end of January to get married by a district judge. Our witnesses, Giovanni and Anne, were the only ones who knew. No one else knew, and no one else would know about it. Not until we were ready for people to know. We would continue with the wedding in March as a renewal of our vows in a more proper setting.

Thankfully, Anne had recovered and continued to wedding plan with the help of a wedding coordinator. She asked very little of me, and I was fine with that. I truly did not give a damn if the place settings were white or patterned, the cake was three or four-tiered, and I didn't care what color the flowers were.

With a heavy sigh, I flung my magazine onto the table between Tatum and me. We were taking advantage of the warm sun, lying next to the pool in lounge chairs, listening to a local pop music station in the background.

Tatum's head lifted. She was lying on her stomach, dark sunglasses hiding her eyes, which had been about as red as mine over the last few weeks. "What's wrong?"

"I need to get out of here."

"Ha! That's not going to happen, and you know it." She pushed herself over until she was lying on her back. "And I don't blame Cameron. You need to stay put."

"Until March?"

She shrugged. "If that's what it takes, I guess. If it helps, we miss you at home."

"You and Alex?" I teased, knowing that was what she meant. "It's going well then? At least so far?"

Tatum smiled. "Yes. I was hesitant to let him stay with me, being that we haven't been together for very long, but he ended up staying more nights at our place than he would at his own. It just ended up this way. I hope you don't mind."

"I don't mind. If I'm being watched, they know I'm here, but I'm glad Alex is there with you. Do you think he'll ask you to marry him?"

"I don't know. None of my past relationships have been like this. It's so easy."

I rested my cheek on my hands, looking at her and how happy she was when she talked about him. They were good for each other. I wanted to see her married and happy.

"I'm happy for you, Tate."

The patio doors opened from the living room and Cameron strolled out, a pair of loose, tan cargo pants with a black t-shirt. He removed his sunglasses from his pocket and slipped them on. My breath hitched every time I watched him walk. It was a cross between a swagger and a saunter, smooth and deliberate.

With a hand on my hip, he rolled me over so he could sit on my lounger. He looked serious, even though he greeted Tatum happily. I knew he was happy that she was here to keep me company. I'd been working with Melanie via phone and video chats on manager training throughout the month of January, sneaking in some work on the side for some clients in consulting.

The good thing about both was I could do them both remotely. Melanie was doing so well. I didn't have any qualms about her continuing without regular check-ins. It delighted her when I called her and asked her to contact me if she had questions or problems, but she would be on her own. There was no need for me to watch over her shoulder. When I told her Cameron and I were getting married, she screamed in my ear with excitement.

He tucked a wayward strand of hair behind my ear. "We need to talk."

"Gotta go!" Tatum rolled and quickly came to her feet, the magazine still in her hand. "I'm going to the kitchen for a snack."

Neither Cameron nor I responded before she skipped away, literally skipped across the concrete patio and up the stairs. I shook my head at her overflowing personality. I hadn't been lying. It was good to see her happy. Loss of Jazz aside; she was doing well. We were both healing slowly, grieving in our own ways.

I looked back at Cameron. Whenever he said we had to talk, I became overcome with nerves. We had been married for a week, and although it wasn't an ideal honeymoon, it had been blissful for me. I was almost positive he wasn't going to ask me for an annulment.

I sat up, pulling my knees up to my chest and laying my cheek on them to look at him. "Having second thoughts about marrying me?"

He smiled. "Nothing in this world would make me give you up. Nothing." He sighed, looking away from me for a moment. This wasn't going to be good if he was hesitant to tell me.

"You have to leave."

He nodded. "To Italy. I'd take you with me, but I'm going to be busy and there are many people there that don't like Moretti or De Luca family members. I'll be too busy to protect you."

I nodded. After all, I understood the drawbacks of running a business, even multiple businesses. There were people to run them, but that wasn't always ideal to be completely remote. There would be a time I would need to get back to the boatyard.

He let out a big breath. "Please listen to me first before you immediately say no."

"You're scaring me."

"I want you to go stay with my family."

"Cam . . ."

"My father would protect you with his life. You *are* part of the family now. They just don't know it yet." He passed his hand over his face. This was worrying him. "I wouldn't ask this of you, but I'd feel better if you were there. It's more remote, and it has the very best security."

Jesus. That wasn't asking a lot of me, I thought sarcastically. To travel to an unknown place and live with strangers for an undisclosed amount of time was asking a lot of me. It wasn't a horrible way to get to know them, like he had said, we are family now.

I sucked my bottom lip between my teeth. "When do you leave?"

"In the morning. I have an early flight. If I can get you a flight out around the same time, we can go to the airport together." He picked up my hand, pressing a kiss to my palm. "I wouldn't ask if I didn't think this was the best choice."

"What did Gio say?"

"I haven't talked to him, but he'll agree. He knows, as your husband, I'll do whatever I need to do to protect you."

Husband. The word, when he said it, sent shivers up my spine and spread warmth through my chest. I smiled. There was hardly anything I would not give him, and if this gave him peace of mind, I would do it.

"What about your family? Are you sure that someone inside your own family isn't trying to stop the wedding?" He was about to answer, but I put a hand on his arm. "I'll go. But I guarantee I'll fight with everything I have if I'm in danger there."

His eyes darkened. I could tell he was worried about leaving me. The last time he left me, I had almost died. Another month and a half and we'd be married for the second time and in front of hundreds of guests. Anne had already announced that the wedding would be here, on the back lawn beyond the pool. Security would be at maximum, just in case, but it convinced Gio that any danger was not because of us getting married. It was merely the interest, which means it would always be there until we took out the person who was causing it.

"How long will you be gone?"

"I have a return flight scheduled a week out. I'm hoping that it doesn't take that long, and I can get an earlier flight back. We'll see how much I can accomplish while I'm there."

"Don't get killed, or I'll never forgive you."

He smiled and pressed his forehead against mine. "I love you."

"You might feel differently after a week away from me."

He growled. "Not a damn chance."

I leaned back, still watching him. Both of us had spent as much time outside as we could instead of being cooped up inside the house, and his skin had a nice tan. He was already handsome with his dark hair, albeit long from the lack of a haircut, and his blue eyes. I reached out to tuck back the hair that had fallen over his forehead. Damn him, he was going to make it impossible to say goodbye, even for such a short time. We had been inseparable since the Christmas Ball.

"Will it always be like this? Both of us traveling all the time?"

"No." He was firm about it. "I'm going to turn over the ownership of my businesses in Italy. My uncles are taking them over as joint ventures between them. Once it's done, I'm washing my hands of them."

I liked that idea. I had a feeling those were the culprits of his dirty business dealings, but I couldn't know for certain, and I didn't ask him. The further we both got from the shady side, the better I would feel. I trusted him to do what he had to do.

"We'll talk about our future when I get back."

I nodded. We hadn't talked about where we would live after the wedding. I had my condo in Malibu and my house in Cape Haven. He had his house in Cape Haven, and he had said it was his only house. I would be happy anywhere, so long as it was with him. I just didn't want my children, the grandchildren of not only one gangster but two of them, to have the same childhood that I did. My children would be safe, even if they had to live on the island. That sounded better the more that I thought about it. They would spend time with their grandma, Isabel.

"What're you thinking about?" Cameron whispered.

"Our kids."

He leaned back in surprise. "Are you . . ."

I shook my head quickly. "No."

"What, then?"

"Where we'll raise them. I had a hard life being the daughter of Gavriel De Luca. I had no friends. People whispered about me. I don't want my kids to go through that."

He kissed my forehead. "They won't. We'll make sure of that."

Chapter Twenty Three

Cameron had prepared me enough to know that the house was bigger than the De Luca family home and he hadn't been lying. Several palm trees tall and short flanked the tall iron gates on each side. Inside the gates were dark green bushes and vibrantly colored flowers. The driveway split in two directions at a courtyard with an enormous fountain in the center.

I rolled down my window as we drove to the left, sneaking a peek at the other driveway that had a two-car garage. When we stopped, I noticed that there was not enough room for the limousine to fit into the second driveway. The driver opened my door, and I stepped out onto a driveway that was made entirely of orange-tan bricks. I looked overhead at a walkway that connected a detached two-garage with a room above it to another two-car garage that was attached to the house. I wondered how many people could live here that they needed space for six cars. It was like a small community.

The courtyard was the most beautiful that I had seen, with a three-part fountain with an enormous pool in the center with turquoise water, flanked by two smaller pools. I crossed the courtyard and stepped up into a covered entryway, stopping in front of a double door made of oak.

I hadn't even had the chance to knock when a small, bald man I assumed was a butler opened the door. He had a tiny gray mustache like Charlie Chaplin in the roaring twenties did. I stamped down the bubble of laughter that threatened to escape.

"Miss De Luca?"

Mrs. Moretti now, I thought to myself. "Yes."

The driver came up behind me, carrying my suitcase plus a smaller bag I had used as my carry on. I hoped it would only be a week before Cameron was back, or I was going to need to go shopping. Shopping in Las Vegas would be something I could look forward to.

"I am Retton," he murmured, his voice tight. "I'll bring you to your room."

He opened the door wider for me. The driver set my luggage right inside as soon as I stepped in before quickly beating his retreat. I didn't blame him. As I entered the foyer, I could see up to the second level vestibule. I was only in the foyer, and the size of this house astonished me. It was at least twice the size of my family home.

"This way. Someone will bring up your luggage shortly."

I followed him in, half listening to what he was pointing out while I was looking around with wide eyes. The parlor was ahead of us, also open to the second floor, with an exercise room off to the side. I followed him up a curving stairway to the left, my mouth still gaping when I looked down over the railing to the first floor.

We stopped at the first room past a game room, and he swung the door open to a large bedroom, including a large walk-in closet and private bathroom. If this was the guest bedroom, I would be curious about what the master suite was like.

"What's down there?" I asked him in the hallway that followed the walkway I had seen connecting the two garages.

"The guest bedroom."

"There's another bedroom? How many bedrooms are there?"

"Six," he said in a clipped tone. He didn't disguise the fact that he was a stereotypical butler.

"Why don't you put me in the guest bedroom?"

"It's reserved for guests."

He put an odd emphasis on the word 'guests'. "I'm a guest."

My questioning was irritating him. The frown was enough to know that, but when he purposely ignored my questioning of where my room would be, I knew for certain. I wondered if Cameron teased him when he was home. It would be hard for him not to. Retton was so rigid.

"This is Master Cameron's room. I was told you would be here." I opened my mouth to say something else, but he cut me off. "Dinner is at six. Promptly at six."

"Where would that be?"

He was already turning to leave me in the bedroom, not bothering to answer me, which meant that after I got settled in, I would need to find my way around, or I would probably be late for dinner. I looked at my watch. Two hours before dinner. But I was stronger than they thought. I would manage just fine. I had faced the worst types of business owners, some that tried and failed to intimidate me, then there were those who tried to get me to sleep with them. I did not include extracurricular activities when hired for a consulting job.

I was closing the door when I heard someone calling from down the hallway. I waited to close the door to see a man hurrying around the corner with my suitcase and bag.

"Miss! Your bags."

He was out of breath when he reached me, and I wasn't surprised. This was nothing but a maze of rooms, and the house clearly lacked nothing. I hoped there was a place where I could dance. If not, I would settle for poolside.

"What's your name?" I asked as he wheeled my suitcase into the room, just inside the door, and set my bag on the floor next to it.

"Bradley."

"Thank you, Bradley." I smiled. "Do I tip you? Sorry, I'm used to hotels."

"No. Mister Moretti pays my wages."

"Okay, thank you again for bringing them up."

He gave me a nod before retreating down the hallway from where he came, but instead of closing the door, curiosity pulled at me. I left my luggage and went through the walkway, impressed at the windows that lined each side. I could see the courtyard down on the left, and to the right there was nothing but a wall higher than the floor of the walkway and a lot of green trees. There was a door, then another short hallway to the left. Upon further investigation, the short hallway led to a set of stairs that went down. Presumably to the garage.

The door, when I opened it, opened to a simple bedroom and private bathroom much smaller than my room at the De Luca home. Nothing special, just a guest room. Just as Retton had told me.

I was just about to turn to leave when the smell of Pops' cologne assaulted my senses. He had worn the same cologne for as long as I can remember. There was no mistaking the smell. I walked further into the room. It wasn't so much different from any other room with a bed, nightstand, and dresser. It had only one window that overlooked the entrance beneath the walkway, and the walkway itself, and another small window in the private bathroom overlooking the long driveway from the extension of Lake Las Vegas Parkway.

I wondered if I was imagining this. It was odd to smell it, though. Was I so exhausted that I was imaging things? I moved back toward the door, stopping in my tracks. There was something on the thin carpet that I stepped on. I moved my foot, looking down at the small object near the bed. It was nearly under the bed. Reaching down, I picked it up and placed it in the palm of my hand. It was a cuff link. Not just any cuff link. A cuff link that was etched with a large, scrolled D.

I turned back around and returned to Cameron's bedroom, my

chest heaving as though I had just run a marathon, the cuff link clutched in my hand so tightly it would leave an imprint. I leaned up against the closed door and closed my eyes.

What. The. Hell, I thought. If Pops wasn't here now, he was at one time. There was no doubt about it. Someone was lying to me, and I prayed to God—something I hadn't done for a while—it wasn't Cameron who lied to me.

There wasn't much I could do about it right now, even though my mind raced with unanswered questions. If Pops was here, why wouldn't Cameron have told me? Why wouldn't Pops have told me? I knew who I was marrying now. Why the big secret? Maybe he was moving around.

"Where are you, Pops?" I whispered to myself, pinching the bridge of my nose.

I opened my eyes, looking around Cameron's childhood bedroom. It was simple, yet masculine, with a four-poster bed at the farthest wall from the door with a dark brown duvet and several pillows. Windows flanked the bed on each side. The walk-in closet and bathroom were one way, while a tall mahogany dresser was on the other side.

Across from the bed was a desk and chair, not huge by any means, but big enough to handle light work. I imagined Cameron as a kid doing his homework there with a smile. I put my suitcase on the bench at the foot of the bed and unzipped it. I wasn't sure unpacking my clothes would be conducive if he would be back within a week, although he hadn't said when we would leave here.

In the end, I decided that unpacking my clothes would be for the best. The walk-in closet was mainly empty except for a few shirts, a couple of suits, and some dress shoes. After I hung up what I could, I found a spot in the drawer for the rest. I unpacked my toiletries and settled down on the bed, curling up to breathe in the smell of Cameron. I missed him so much that I ached, and it hadn't even been twenty-four hours since we had said goodbye at the airport.

I dozed off quickly. When I woke, it was ten minutes after six. Swearing, I jumped up from the bed and rushed out of the room, quickly getting confused where I was. I followed my way back toward the game room and as soon as I saw the foyer; I knew I was close to the staircase.

A dark-haired girl was coming toward me, and I had a feeling she was Cameron's sister. Her hair was black, I presumed from hair dye, and she had dark-lined eyes wearing a black jumpsuit with a black and red striped shirt underneath it. She smiled at me. "Regan?"

"Zoey?" We both laughed. "Cameron has told me so much about you. He's worried about you, you know. Since he can't be here as much as he'd like to be."

"Yeah, yeah. Big brother crap and all that. I'm doing fine." I didn't see her roll her eyes, but I heard it in her voice. "He texted me you'd be coming. Said to keep you company 'til he gets back, but I'm on my way out."

"You aren't going to dinner? I was hoping you'd show me to the dining room. I don't know my way around yet."

She slid me a knowing smile. "Dinner started fifteen minutes ago. You're late."

I nodded, sucking my button lip between my teeth, and pressing my top teeth into it. "Shit. Is that bad?"

"Normally it would be, but probably not since you just got here. I'm heading out anyway, so I'll show you on my way."

We walked side by side toward the staircase. We hadn't passed more than a few sentences between us, but I liked her already. She appeared to be headed toward the Goth look. I wasn't sure if it was rebellion or if she had just fallen into that crowd, or maybe that was just what she liked. Either way, I liked her immediately.

"So. You and my brother, huh?"

"Yeah," I breathed. "Me and your brother. Your oldest brother, that is. I understand you have three older brothers. That must be rough."

"Stefan." This time, she rolled her eyes. "He's not here. He's a creep. And Peter. He's here right now, but I'm not sure how long."

Yeah, I liked her a lot. Sixteen or twenty-six, she was not boring to talk to. "Why do you think your brother is a creep?"

"He's mean to me. And he hits on all my friends, even though he's in his twenties."

As we stepped down to the lower level, I figured I should have talked to her long before coming here. She was giving me a total unbiased opinion of her family, whereas Cameron was too nice to do that. It was abundantly clear that Zoey spoke her mind without reservation.

At the bottom of the stairs, I remembered the master suite was to the right, and continued following her to the left. Once we started down that way, she waved her hands to the doors on our left.

"Wine cellar, or something like that, kitchens . . ." she said, then waved her hand toward the end of the hallway, which rounded the corner but didn't really end. "Down there is another small eating area that overlooks the pool, the family room, and another bedroom. Also, there's a bathroom that we consider the pool bathroom since it's right by the sun deck, but the bedroom shares it."

We stopped in front of an open door to the right, and the uneasy feeling of being the center of attention immediately assaulted me. It was a dimly lit room, furnished with darkly red painted walls and a long mahogany table that seated at least twelve people. There was a side table to the left that didn't have any food on it but had unlit candle tapers in the center. Servants were bringing food for each person.

"Regan, so nice to see you again," Reno said from the farthest end of the table. He was wearing a black button-up shirt with the sleeves rolled up to his muscular forearms. That was where Cameron had inherited his nice muscles. "Zoey, you're late."

"Actually, I'm going out. See ya, byeeee!"

"Zoey!"

He had risen from his chair, but she was already gone. I smothered a laugh with the back of my hand, pretending to cough, while he sat back down with an ominous look on his face. At only sixteen, she must be rebelling more than anything. I couldn't say that I blamed her. Hadn't I done the same thing around that age?

"Regan, sit down. We've set a place for you. Tomorrow, you'll be on time."

Reno was a man that would not abide unruliness. I wasn't sure how Zoey had gotten away with it, but I knew for certain I wouldn't be late to dinner tomorrow. He had a commanding personality. Very much like Cameron. I looked at Orianna, sitting to Reno's left, and wearing a whimsical dress that parted just above her cleavage where a long, gold necklace dipped low. She barely glanced at me while I walked toward her. Across from her was a man with hair the color of honey, and eyes that were brown like Reno's. He was staring at me, his eyes hard and his lips tilted up. Nice try, I thought. It was one of the most fake smiles I had seen.

I nodded my head at him in a silent greeting and he said nothing, just watched as I pulled out my chair next to Orianna. A small light garden salad was in front of me before my ass had even touched the cushioned chair.

"How was your flight, my dear?"

"Boring, but a short," I said, meeting his eyes.

"Cameron shouldn't be long in Italy, at least."

"Cameron may want to stay a bit," Orianna interjected, her voice slightly above a whisper. "It's been so long since he's been home."

"He's a grown-ass man, ma." My gaze whipped to Peter. "And he's busy. He'll come home when he does and stay for as long as he can. I'm sure that he and . . ." He waved his fork in my direction.

"Regan," I said between my teeth.

"I'm sure he and Regan have things to do before their big day next month."

In that moment, with three grown sons and a daughter who seemed like she might be gone more than she was home, I felt sorry for Orianna. I had judged her without knowing her, something that I always strived to avoid doing. I may have judged her wrongly. She was probably lonely.

Was this what Isabel would have turned out to be like had she not been a target and stayed with Pops? I shuddered. I would never turn out like that. I would insert myself into my kids' life so much they wouldn't be able to shake me off. I hoped Cameron and I would stay involved with each other rather than him running off to work all the time.

Speaking of Pops . . .

"I want to know where my father is," I said to Reno, staring at him with anticipation that if he knew anything, he would slip up. There had to be a reason I found the cuff link.

"I wish I could tell you that, my girl."

Dead end. "You and he must have been good friends for many years . . ."

He leaned back, having finished his salad, and waited for the next course. For a moment, he looked like he was staring right through memories.

"Many, many years." His fond smile told me everything I needed to know. "We've been friends since we were boys in Italy. Gavriel, Ludovico, and me. Gads, but we were a troublesome trio. All three of us got our fair share of thrashings."

"Ludovico . . ." I whispered.

"Did your father never mention him?"

Pops never talked about his history as a child or otherwise, and Isabel couldn't say anything without telling me her secret. I was just as caught as I had been when I found out that I was going to marry a stranger.

"No."

"What do you know of Ludovico?"

I sat back, placing my fork upside down on my plate. "I know that he's the bastard that kidnapped me when I was twelve. And could be behind the two attacks on me in Cape Haven. Maybe why Pops is taking an extended, very secluded vacation."

Peter and Orianna remained tight-lipped throughout our exchange, but Peter was looking at his father like he was eating up every word. Orianna looked as though she wanted to drift away. Maybe she was drunk.

"I would like to share with you our story, but perhaps now is not the time. I want you to come to my office in the morning. Will you?"

I nodded, but I wasn't sure I could wait that long. I needed answers. What Reno shared with me might give me the missing information I needed. And maybe not. But I had to know. Ludovico was still my suspect, but I had no evidence of it, and I could be totally wrong. I didn't have evidence that he was behind the bombing at the country club, either. I hadn't heard from Jake, but I couldn't take the chance of sending him a message. Not now.

Reno waved to Retton, who poured wine for each of us. Thank God for alcohol, I thought. I might survive this after all. I wasted no time in picking up my glass and taking a drink, letting the red liquid with hints of black cherry and redcurrant slide down the back of my throat.

"How's your mother?"

My eyes widened briefly. This could be a way to extract information from me that shouldn't be out, or he really knew what had happened to my mother and wanted to have a conversation about it.

"My mother died when I was young," I said, staring into my wine while I swirled it around in my glass.

Reno smiled. "I know. I was at her funeral."

"Then why do you ask?"

"You need not pretend with me. I know just as much as there

is to know about your family. Gavriel is my best friend, after all. That, and I make it my business to know, especially since you will by my daughter-in-law in only a month."

I swore I heard a grumble from Peter, but his eyes never lifted, even when the main course was being served. Filet mignon with roasted asparagus that was sprinkled with sea   salt. Simple yet paired well with the wine.

"I hope you are not a vegetarian or not of those that won't eat anything animal-related people."

"Vegan," Peter offered.

"No, I am not vegan or vegetarian. I enjoy steak, if it's prepared well."

Reno picked up his steak knife and fork, digging into his meal with gusto. "About your mother . . ."

"She told me. And she was fine when I last saw her. I hope she remains that way. It's too risky to contact her right now."

"She told you about Ludovico and the falling out we had?"

I cut into my steak and took a small bite, quickly chewing and swallowing, followed by a sip of wine. "She didn't tell me enough."

He nodded his understanding and said no more. We lapsed into silence. I focused on eating while Reno and Peter resumed their conversation in hushed tones. Orianna said nothing, eating her dinner painstakingly slowly.

I couldn't wait to be finished and return to my room. I hoped Zoey would be around in the next day or two so she could show me the rest of the house, but I was certain that she would have school. Once the main course was done, dessert was served. A delicate slice of vanilla cheesecake with a drizzle of chocolate.

These people ate well. Not a large amount, but they had style. I supposed they needed to when they lived in a house this extravagant. It wasn't too bad of a meal to sit through, but I was looking forward to my discussion with Reno tomorrow. I hoped fervently that Peter wouldn't be there.

I excused myself just after the dessert, finishing the last of my wine quickly. Reno was the only one to bid me goodnight, and I hurried back to the staircase. I waited there for a minute to see if Orianna would come out next so I could speak with her.

It was futile. No one came out for a few minutes and once I saw Retton, I hurried up the staircase without looking back. I slowed once I got to the top, purposely walking close to the railing to look down at the open parlor below, but no one was there. It was just as well. I was tired after such an eventful day and the wine had helped dull my senses.

Chapter Twenty Four

I could smell his cologne as soon as I stepped into the foyer, which meant that Pops was still awake and I was in trouble for being out past my curfew. Damn. Still, there could be a way to get in without him knowing. I closed the front door as quietly as I could, as futile as it would be. His office was right there. He would see me cross the foyer to get to the staircase.

Maybe there was another way . . .

"Regan."

I closed my eyes, hearing the unmistakable disappointment in his calm, never irrational voice. I stopped where I was. If I just stood here, maybe he would think he had mistakenly heard me come in.

"I know you're there. Come here."

That was disappointment in his voice alright. Laced with an underlying tone of not messing around this time. I had done my best to be a horrible teenager lately. I think it was years of him being too busy for me catching up. When I had come home after being kidnapped, he increased my dance lessons and put me in martial arts classes. Not self-defense. Fighting. During the summer was not a big deal, it meant less time spent at home. During the school year was brutal. Class all day, then hours of classes afterwards, plus I had dance classes. He didn't have to worry about me getting into trouble if I was too busy. Joke was on him though.

"If I have to come and get you, you'll not like it."

The clip of his tone, still calm, was enough to get me walking toward his office. The doors were open, and I sauntered in until I filled the doorway. His office was dark, only the small lamp on his desk lit. He was sitting in his chair, smoking his cigar. It seemed like all he did. He sat behind his desk, smoking his cigars. Usually, Ezekiel and Frank were with him. Tonight, he was alone. Of course, it was well past midnight.

He waved me in with his fingers, a beckon. A summons.

I had done this enough to know that I was about to get yet another lecture that I would ignore. Tomorrow I would sneak out again. I needed to find a better way to get back into the house without being caught.

I sat down in the chair, watching him take a puff and blow the smoke leisurely into the air before turning his eyes on me. I wasn't going to be the one to speak first. What would I even say? I was out taking a walk? He would never buy it. He was always onto me.

"You're sixteen, my darling girl. I don't remember allowing you to leave tonight. And you're far too young to be sneaking into the house after curfew, don't you think?"

"You're right," I said. "I should be able to come and go whenever I want."

He sighed. "It's not safe for you, or should I remind you of the time that they kidnapped you right from your school?"

How dare he bring that up? I lifted my chin up defensively but remained silent. I wasn't in the mood to battle this out with him. I really didn't care. He thought it was unsafe, there was more reason to do it.

"I could remind you I killed two men getting away."

His eyes blazed with shock. I had back-talked to him. The line of his jaw hardened, and he took another puff from his cigar. "I could have you sent away."

"Do it. I don't care what you do to me."

We stared at each other, the battle between us raging. If he sent me away to a girls' school or just a school far away, it wouldn't change anything about my life or anything that had happened in my life. All it would do was make sure he didn't have me around. Something I thought he would prefer.

"I know you've been hanging around Jacob Mancini."

Heat scorched my face. How did he know that? No one should know that. Jake and I were careful when we met up because we knew it was dangerous for us both. I opened my mouth to say something, but words failed me.

"You think I don't have you watched at all times?"

"I'm not one of your thugs! They shouldn't be watching me!"

The sharp intake of his breath was unmistakable, but still he remained calm. "It's apparent you do, if you're going to sneak around to meet with dangerous people."

"Jake's not dangerous."

His eyes narrowed. It was pointless to convince him otherwise. Jake was Ludovico's son. Pops would believe nothing good would come from that family. Nothing I could say would sway him.

"If Ludovico learns of this, he'll kill you this time and send your body back to me in pieces. There is a reason he kidnapped you."

"I know why he kidnapped me," I snapped. "You made some deal years ago that you didn't include him in, then when you made one when I was twelve, he wanted a part of it."

"And do you know what happened after you saved yourself and took yourself out as a bargaining chip from the exchange that night?" I shook my head. "You will stay away from Jacob Mancini from now on." He stared at me, as though staring at me was going to whip me into behaving better. "Or I will have you sent away."

"Would Mom want you to do that?"

His fist slammed down on his desk. It was the first time I had ever seen him angry, making me and everything that was on his desk jump. "Do not speak to me of your mother. If she was here, you wouldn't be doing this."

I wasn't sure how to answer that. I never knew her. Before she died in a boat accident, I never knew her. I was too young to remember her. My parents had gone for a cruise in the Pacific off when a storm had hit. She had fallen overboard. I wish I had known her. Maybe I would know the answer to his question that hung, pregnant, between us.

"I don't know," I whispered.

He sighed again. "What do you want me to do? What would make you happy enough to stop this reckless behavior?" I shrugged. "What are you doing when you are going out with Jacob Mancini?"

"It's not always with Jake." I shrugged. "Sometimes meeting friends."

"What friends?"

He hadn't meant it as though I didn't have any. I had very few friends at school. He had meant for me to tell him who exactly I was meeting. This made me twitch. I didn't want to throw out any names. He would probably start calling parents.

"Just some kids from school. We aren't close. We just hang out."

"Are you drinking?"

"No." I rolled my eyes.

"Are you doing drugs?"

"No, Pops. I am not getting into trouble other than sneaking out. We don't drink and we don't do drugs. It's not cool to do those things."

His eyes narrowed. "You aren't having sex, are you?"

"Pops! I'm not talking about this with you. I'm just going out with friends. We talk and just hang out like kids do."

He seemed to have relaxed after that. How horrifying to have to talk to your Pops about having sex. I was only sixteen. He *didn't know that I had already, but it truly was not an experience I wanted to repeat soon. It was painful and embarrassing.*

"Can I go to bed now?"

He set his cigar down on the edge of the ashtray, folding his arms in front of himself while he considered lecturing me more or allowing me to escape this interview. "If I give you a little more freedom, will you promise me you'll not drink or do drugs? Or have sex with anyone?"

I grimaced at the last question. Didn't have to promise that one. I wasn't in a rush to do that again. "I promise."

He nodded. "There'll be rules, and if you break them, the freedom will end. Understood?" I nodded, eager to gain more freedom. "I'll think about how we can make sure we're both happy and let you know. In the meantime, no more sneaking out."

Which meant that I wouldn't be able to get to see Jake tomorrow. Darn it. "Fine. I won't sneak out again. You'll let me know soon, though, right?"

"I will. Now go to bed. It seems to me you have dance class tomorrow."

I didn't answer. I was already up from the chair and hurrying out of his office, the deep musk of his cologne following me out. Ugh. Did Anne really like that he put on so much cologne? He never used to smell so strongly of it when I was a kid. I took the stairs two at a time to get to my room, just in time to message Jake that I couldn't meet him tomorrow, but I would let him know when.

∞

"Why did he send her here?"

It was midmorning, and I thought it was a perfect time to see if Reno was available to continue our discussion from last night. The doors to the library were open just enough for me to hear the derision dripping from Peter's voice. It could be I was going crazy. I could have sworn that I smelled Pop's cologne again on my way downstairs. If he was in this house, I would know it. Maybe I was going crazy.

The way Peter was talking made me think that part of me wasn't. He was making it obvious he didn't like that I was here. Did Zoey mean to tell me that Peter was the creep instead of Stefan? Maybe she had mixed up the names. Maybe they both are. I remembered Cameron telling me that Peter was a loan shark, but he was also married and had a little boy.

I was hoping to see Zoey on my way downstairs. I wanted to see the rest of the house, but wasn't sure I wanted to do it alone. It might be better to do it alone, though.

"She'll be your brother's wife. You will respect her, or you'll answer to me." I heard Reno answer. His voice contained every bit of hardness that Cameron had sounded like when he refused to be questioned. He would not entertain any arguments.

Warmth spread through my chest cavity. Cameron had been right. Reno would protect me. Even against his own children. The fact that he didn't know me, or that I could fight for myself, was something I respected in him. He would get to know me in time. Family above all else. That was how it should be.

"Why here?"

Peter was really pushing it.

"This is the safest place for her."

"I think they could call off the wedding, and we should keep our families separate. We don't need the De Luca's."

I tensed, holding my breath while I waited for Reno's reply, and I wasn't disappointed.

"I'm going to say this one time." His voice chilled me. If I ever thought Pop's smooth voice could be cool at the sign of an issue, Reno's was ten times more. Maybe because his tone was deeper. "Our families will benefit from this marriage. What Gavriel and I started almost thirty years ago will become one massive enterprise. If you want to go head to head with me, you will regret it."

That was what they wanted from Cameron and me getting married, and we had fallen right into it. Reno wanted Cameron to take over this enterprise, and Pops was backing him up to make sure I would be well-taken care of the rest of my life and all the money he's made wouldn't go to waste.

I didn't hear anything else, though I waited. I realized that maybe the conversation was over, and I was about to get caught redhanded for eavesdropping on them. Whirling, I sprinted across the foyer to get to the staircase, one hand on the banister and one foot on the first step, when I heard his voice.

"You must be looking for my sister."

I froze. From behind, he thought I was a friend of Zoey's. Slowly, I turned around to face Peter and whatever he would say to my face. Instead, it was a different man dressed in a dark gray suit. He had blue eyes and dark blond hair, a cross between Cameron and Peter. He was tall and appeared to be just as muscular as the other men in the family, but there was a hardness in his eyes. It was uncanny how much he sounded like Peter.

I stiffened when his eyes took leisure in looking me up and down like a child would eat a popsicle, but with his eyes. I felt thoroughly undressed by his eyes. Zoey had been right, after all.

Stefan was a creep.

"Yes, I'm looking for Zoey."

Whatever possessed me to play along with the game he was playing, I wasn't sure, but I wanted to find out how far he would go. Find out how much of a creep he was. The fact he thought I looked as young as a sixteen-year-old was a compliment, even though I didn't take it as one.

"Stefan," he said thickly, even though I hadn't asked for his name. "My bedroom is just upstairs and to the left."

Was he inviting me to his bedroom? I suppressed a shiver. The fact his bedroom was near mine gave me a glaring warning that I should lock my door at night. Zoey had been dead right about her brother. She should have warned me further about him, though, unless she thought warning me he was a creep would be enough.

"Ah, Regan! I was hoping you would come down soon."

Reno's loud voice carried across to me, and I had the intense pleasure of seeing the realization on Stefan's face that I wasn't a friend of Zoey's. I was his brother's fiancé, or wife rather, who he had just been hitting on.

His eyes hardened. "Regan De Luca," he murmured.

I stepped past him, nearly brushing against him, my eyes never wavering from his. I smiled at Reno, and he swept his arm out. When I entered, it rendered me speechless.

This wasn't an office. This was an open, two-story library with wall to wall books, all except for the far wall with the large window. Books reached a ceiling as tall as the house was. Had I been able to explore the rest of the house, I would have found this room at the opposite end of the house, presumably close to Zoey's bedroom. I would have been able to look down into his office.

Jesus H. Christ, I thought as I walked in and looked high above me. It was everything I expected a library to be, and then some. Dizzy, I dropped my eyes. There was a desk in front of the window, situated like any other office with chairs in front of it, but the room was so large that it had a couch and some chairs, not necessarily around each other. There was a table that was small but looked like it belonged in such a place with four chairs around the perimeter. A reading table, maybe. Right now, it looked as though there was a map spread out on it, but I couldn't tell what the map was of, even when I walked more fully into the room.

This was how you do it. I smiled when Reno closed the door behind us. It was peculiar to have a door when the whole second level was open. If someone was upstairs, they would hear every single word. There was a ladder on each side to reach books way up there, and a walkway around the perimeter of the three walls.

"Impressed?" he chuckled, coming around next to me, and lightly cupping my elbow in his hand to guide me over to his desk. The room held me captive in the loving embrace of knowledge.

"That's not even close," I said. "I like to read, but this is . . . this makes me want to escape entirely from reality."

"You are welcome in here any time while you're here. I have a separate office adjoining my bedroom that I use for more private conversations. Even if you see me here, you are welcome to come in. Please," he waved to the chair, "have a seat."

I sat down in a chair. It was leather, and it swiveled. I resisted the urge to spin around like a giddy little girl. Reno sat down behind the desk, watching me closely. Did he recognize my euphoria?

"I want to apologize."

"Apologize? To me?"

"First, for what you just overheard. I meant what I said. Disrespect of you, Cameron, or the sanctity of your marriage, I will not tolerate."

I smiled. I liked Reno. He was proving to me that although I wasn't probably liked by either of his two younger sons; he was a reasonable man, and he had my back. Especially while Cameron was away.

"The second is rather delicate. I lied to you last night." My smile dissipated. "It's about your father . . ."

The grip that I had on the arm of the chair tightened until my knuckles were white. What about Pops? He knew where he was. I hadn't heard the door open behind me. Reno picked up his hand and waved his fingers like he was motioning someone into the library.

I turned to see who was about to come in, leaping from my chair with a gasp to see the familiar dark head with a graying mustache. There wasn't a cigar between his teeth, but he still leaned on the black cane with the head of a ram as a handle.

I ran to him, feeling like it was a great distance between the desk and the door, throwing my arms around his neck and nearly knocking him off balance when I finally reached him. I breathed in the deep smell of his cologne, vowing to never again make fun of how much he put on. I hadn't been going crazy.

"My darling girl."

"Pops . . . I've been worried sick about you! Why are you here?" I whirled to face Reno. "Why would you lie?" I turned back to Pops. "Why weren't you at dinner last night? Where've you been since I got here yesterday?"

"Let's sit down, shall we?" he said, avoiding my questions.

I returned to my chair, waiting with teeming patience about to spill over while Pops took the seat beside me, and Reno sat back down. I tapped my foot while I watched them each light a cigar.

"Smoke later and come out with it."

Pops looked at me, his eyes admonishing. "Patience, girl."

I gripped the arm of the chair again, leaning toward him. "I have spent the last six months worried sick about you. Patience be damned. I want to know now. Have you been here the whole time?"

"No." He leaned back, puffing away on his damn cigar. He was insufferable.

"May I?" Reno asked Pops, answered by a simple nod. "Regan,

after you thwarted Ludovico by killing his men and ruining the exchange that would have allowed him into the deal your father and I had with a Columbian farmer, he was under suspicion from the FBI and he fled the country."

"And now he's back," I guessed.

"He's back. Just in time for us to strike another massive deal with another farmer in Columbia. Except now, he knows that there is to be a wedding between our two families."

"He did plant that bomb," I mumbled to myself.

"Yes."

"Either way, Ludovico is beyond angry at the turn of events, always in our favor. He was always very jealous. Reno had his private plane waiting at LAX to bring me here. I had you go somewhere safe, and Reno had Cameron lie low." Pops looked at me. "Except Cameron didn't lie low as he should have. And you. You were not supposed to tell anyone where you were."

"I didn't," I said. But I had. Tatum and Jazz how known where I was. I grew uneasy, thinking either of them would have had anything to do with the incident at the club. "Tatum?"

Pops shook his head.

"Jazz?"

He shook his head again.

"Pops, I didn't tell anyone else where I was."

"You didn't speak with anyone else on the phone."

"I broke it off with Michael, but I didn't tell him where I was." I frowned. There was no one else I had told. Had not spoken with anyone else other than Gio. And Jake. My eyes snapped up to meet Pops. He was staring at me. "I talked to Jake one night, but I didn't tell him where I was."

"No, you didn't. But somehow Ludovico knew where you were, so either he was having you followed, or his son knew where you were. We don't know. You are lucky to be alive."

Jake wouldn't do that to me. I had known him for years, trusted him for years. If he had any part in his father's treachery, he could have killed me many times over. He wouldn't have had to wait until now.

"And where were you last night?"

"Stefan and I took a trip to Columbia."

Which explained the smell of his cologne in the hallways on my way down to speak with Reno. I was thankful that I wasn't going crazy after all. Pops had been staying in the guest room. I slumped in my chair, digging into the tiny pocket on the inside of my leggings.

"Regan?" Pops asked. "Are you unwell?"

I waved my hand nonchalantly and pulled out the cuff link and handed it to Pops. It surprised him to see it, but accepted it from me. "I found this in the guest room." I looked at Reno. "That's why I asked you last night if you knew where he was. You were lying to me, and I should have known. I know why you threatened me for years to find me someone to marry, but what about this contract, or arrangement? Why?"

I didn't add that Isabel had given me the answer. I wanted to know if it was the same answer between them. An arrangement such as this, at this day and age, was off the wall.

"Why not, I would ask. We were both growing our enterprises quickly, and while your father wanted someone strong to take over for him and keep you safe, I wanted a strong woman for Cameron to take over for me."

I wasn't exactly dumbstruck. Isabel had basically said the same thing, in a roundabout sort of way. Pops had built everything, so I didn't want to marry someone and throw it away.

"After Ludovico kidnapped you, and you took it into your own hands to get out of the situation, I knew beyond a doubt Cameron would love you. You aren't about to take any shit from anyone."

I couldn't help but smile, even though I tried to hide it. "He would have been, what, thirteen or fourteen? How would you have known? Why didn't you just keep getting Cameron and me together and see if it would naturally happen?"

"I wasn't leaving it to chance," Pops huffed. "Are you saying that you still aren't willing to go through with this wedding?"

I don't remember Pops asking me my opinion of anything. Now, he was asking me if I wanted to bow out of the wedding after Cameron and I have already been married? Not that I would have backed out. We just needed to figure out how to get out of this big enterprise our fathers were trying to push us into. From the sounds of it, they invested Stefan in it.

I scoffed. "Invitations have already gone out."

"It's never too late."

I frowned at Pops. "Are you changing your mind about Cameron and me getting married?"

"No, don't mistake me. I want nothing more than this to happen. I feel as though perhaps pushing you to do so was unkind."

"You mean not giving me a choice? Not giving him a choice?" I wanted to stand up and pace, but I stayed where I was. "Lucky for you, both of us are rule-breakers and we met each other before we were supposed to and actually formed a connection."

Reno finally spoke up. "I believe now, more than ever, especially after seeing you and Cameron together, you're supposed to be together."

If he thought that was a sign, I hadn't done an outstanding job of being angry at Cameron that night for his role in the deception. I recalled being horrified that someone would hurt him—namely my unknown fiancé—then to find out that he was my unknown fiancé after having spent almost three months unintentionally leading him on. And then I was angry. And then there was the relief that I was marrying the one person I *wanted* to marry. He had even asked me!

Dear God, what a crazy six months it had been. Except for me being drugged, then attacked at home, then a bomb nearly taking us both out. Instead, innocent people lost their lives.

"Ludovico is doing this," I said. "That's what Mom said. I mean

. . . Isabel."

I had never seen Pops' face soften so instantly when mentioning her before. As I had grown up, there was no mention of my mother. No pictures, no fond memories to share. It was as though it had wiped her from our lives. Looking at him now, I realized he still loved her. Then I knew the reason there were no pictures or memories. It was painful for him.

"I'm not hiding out the rest of my life because of one man. What are we doing about this? Do we know where he is? Do we know what he's planning?"

"We don't know that for sure," Reno cut in. "Cameron is usually one step ahead of everyone else, but he hasn't been able to find anything out except that Ludovico is in his home in Santa Barbara."

I grasped the arms of the chair. "I have to go see him."

"No!" Both Reno and Pops burst out together in the same raised tone. Jesus, they really were best friends.

"You will do no such thing," Pops said. "He will kill you."

"Cameron would kill us both if we let you do that," Reno said, his voice low. He looked straight at me. "It would kill him if he lost you. Kill him."

Those words warmed me, but it still convinced me that if I went to speak to Ludovico that I would get my answers. I wouldn't be going to get answers. I'd be going to kill him.

"I forbid you to leave here," Reno said. "We'll come up with a plan when Cameron comes home. Despite what you think, my son is much stronger than I am. Promise me, Regan. Promise me you'll not attempt to leave."

I was probably going to regret saying it. "I promise."

We sat there, in the library full to the brim with books, and I heard about the history of Reno, Ludovico, and Gavriel. They had grown up in the tiny town of San Gimignano, a village that was tucked between Pisa and Florence, within the Siena province. They were all about the same age, Reno being the oldest, followed by Gavriel, then Ludovico.

Ludovico was the second son of a farmer while Reno and Gavriel had grown up closer to the town, both first-born sons of merchants. The rift that had grown between the friends many years later stemmed from the fact that Ludovico was jealous not only of the wealth and intelligence of his two friends but their devilishly good looks. When Ludovico had met Isabel Iacono while she was visiting her cousin, Elena, at a neighboring farm for the summer, he had been instantly smitten.

Isabel hadn't been instantly drawn to Ludovico as he had been with her. Until he introduced her to his good friends, Reno and Gavriel. Isabel's attention turned to Gavriel, the attraction to him much stronger than it had been to Ludovico. He was soft-spoken, gentle, persuasive, and equally taken with her.

Ludovico had been beyond angry with both Gavriel and Isabel, but he overlooked it because the three friends were making the biggest deal with a coca plant farmer in Columbia. The deal was going to give the three of them a way into the drug smuggling trade when they made their move to America, settling on the west coast. Everything was going smoothly, even after they moved–all settling into different areas purposely not living too close to each other–but Ludovico grew bossier, and got more agitated with Gavriel and Reno, accusing them of leaving him out of discussions. They couldn't persuade him there were no side discussions happening, that he was involved in everything along with them. In the end, Gavriel and Reno had no choice but to cut him loose or lose the entire deal.

Chapter Twenty Five

After my first two days at the Moretti family home, I finally made use of the pool. Like the house, it wasn't an ordinary pool. There were two reflective ponds, one in front of the pool and one behind it, next to a shelf wall where water from the pool spilled over into a waterfall haven. There was also a spa connected to the pool near the back reflective pond and a lounge pool that was separated by the cutest little bridge to cross directly to the spa.

The sun was plenty hot, and no one else was in the pool. Zoey, who was harder to track down being seventeen, was at school during the day and usually out with her friends afterward or holed up in her room with homework. Since I had been there, she had not joined us once for dinner. But she hadn't been kidding when she said not to be late for dinner. Peter had been late one night, and Reno nearly told him to not bother joining. I had been lucky to avoid Stefan except at dinner, where he sat across from me. Every chance he had, he stared.

Part of me had avoided the pool because I wasn't sure what Orianna's schedule was, but since I rarely saw her, I believed she was a recluse and maybe stayed in the bedroom she shared with Reno. Zoey had told me that her parents' master suite was one entire side of the house on the other side of the library. Attached to the bedroom and a master bathroom the size of a bedroom, there was a private garden nearest to the courtyard and Reno's private office, which overlooked the pool in a small circular alcove that stuck out almost to the lounge pool.

Perhaps that was why I suddenly felt like I was being watched. I finished my lap and stood up in the pool, wiping the water from my face and looking around. There was a door to Reno's private office, but it was closed. I couldn't see in the windows to see if he was looking out at me. I looked up at the sun deck on the second level, but no one was there. Turning toward the covered lanai on the side of the house where the family room and dining room were located, right outside of the family room, is where I saw Stefan strolling toward me.

I pulled myself out of the pool, grabbed my towel to pull around my body before he reached me. He wore a pair of dress pants and a white button-up shirt. Other than the expensive watch he wore on his wrist, he was the opposite of Cameron. Stefan was all business.

I was reluctant to resume my conversation with him now that he knew who I was. My door had remained locked at night, and even then, I woke up sometimes to strange noises. My saving grace was Pops was just down the hall. I watched him, and he looked me up and down, leisurely. I couldn't wait until Cameron returned.

"You think you have my brother wrapped around your finger," he murmured, moving around me to sit down in a chair next to the small round table poolside. I shuddered when he purposely brushed up against me.

"You don't know anything about me," I murmured, turning to look at him. "To tell me what I think is presumptuous. And rude."

I truly didn't want to be at odds with anyone in his family, but I wasn't going to be intimidated by anyone, and that included his brothers. It wasn't going to happen. But being nice wasn't going to kill me, and perhaps it would make him act kinder.

I tucked the corner of the towel in so the towel would shield me from his roving gaze and planted my hands on the table next to him while looking right at him.

"Don't think for one minute that you can push me around."

He leaned back, the side of his mouth twitching. I hoped by showing him I wasn't going to cower made him move away from him. Having Cameron wrapped around my finger was not true, nor was it a goal. And I didn't want to be wrapped around his finger, either.

"You don't like me."

"I don't know you," I shot back.

"You get to know someone by talking to them."

"Well, you don't get to know someone by telling them what they think."

I could do this all day long if I had to. I wouldn't be swayed by his false sense of entitlement. Zoey's words echoed. He was a creep, and while I couldn't take her word for it, I had discovered that myself when he thought to hit on me without knowing who I was.

A woman in an apron came out with a tray of iced tea and two glasses. She set them on the table and poured us each a glass without asking, while we stared each other down. I had dealt with men much worse than Stefan. I could stare at him all day and not budge.

"I like you," he finally said.

"Do you?"

He picked up a glass of tea, taking a drink before setting it down again. "I do."

I crossed my arms in front of me. "You come out here and presume to know what I think, and now you suddenly like me? I'm curious about why you *think* you like me."

"I've heard a lot about you."

"Try again."

He laughed, his voice low and borderline sinister. "That's why I like you. You aren't going to skirt your way around any conflict, and you say exactly what you're thinking."

"I would have thought differently yesterday when I overheard you telling Reno that we should call off the wedding. It seemed abundantly clear to me you do not want, or welcome, me in this house."

He stared at me as though he was trying to think of what to say to me, his eyes hard and unyielding. Instead, he stood up almost toe to toe with me, still not saying anything. If this was a staring contest, I would win.

"Stefan," I heard Reno's voice behind him.

Stefan took a step back from me but kept his eyes on me. He didn't need to tell me this wasn't over just because Reno interrupted us. I doubted Reno could handle Stefan, since he had not heeded his words about respect. Or maybe this was his way of showing it. I didn't know enough about him to know what the hell was going on.

Stefan didn't say another word before he strode away from me. Reno must have been coming from his office, and I turned to smile at him as though unfazed by the conversation with Stefan. His hand touched the back of my arm while he came around.

"Everything alright?"

I nodded. "It's fine."

"Regan, what did he say to you?"

I sighed and then gave him a shaky laugh. "I'm not sure. I think . . . he was trying to intimidate me, but I wasn't backing down."

Reno swore quietly, sitting down in the chair that Stefan had been sitting in. He ran his hand over his face, agitated by something having to do with Stefan. I sat down in the chair next to him, drinking my iced tea while waiting for him to say something.

"Stefan is a hard man to understand."

Was that what he was? That wasn't the impression I got from him. I understood perfectly well what he was trying to do, and when it didn't work, he tried to exert his masculinity at me by towering over me.

"Reno, I don't want this family to be at odds because of me."

"It isn't. Stefan has a history of being quite nasty to anyone outside of the family, but you . . ." He reached over the table to take my hand in his. "You're family."

"And Peter? It doesn't seem like he's fond of me, either."

"Peter is a little more amicable than Stefan is. They'll both come around. It's just going to take Stefan longer. You won't be here long, and after the wedding, when you are legally married, they'll come around."

I wanted to tell him I was already legally a part of this family. He was Cameron's father, and one of two in the family who wasn't against this. Hell, it was part of his idea that we do this. But I knew it was safer to keep this quiet.

"There's something you should know about Stefan."

It piqued my interest. I knew something was odd about him, but I didn't know him and couldn't judge him with my experience yet. The way he had treated me spoke volumes, both this time and when he had hit on me.

"Cameron is twenty-nine." I nodded. Nothing surprising about that. Cameron had told me that at one time. "Stefan is five years younger than him. Peter is three years younger than Stefan. And of course, Zoey. The difference in their ages led Stefan to believe we adopted Cameron."

Laughter erupted from me. I rocked back into my chair at the absurdity of it, even when Reno wasn't laughing along with me. He was serious. Stefan believed Reno and Orianna had adopted Cameron. I sat back up, mirth gone.

"He's still convinced that we adopted Cameron. Stranger things have happened. Many couples have adopted, only to get pregnant years later."

"Cameron looks just like you."

Reno shook his head. "Stefan has a delusional jealousy. We tried to get him help when we began seeing signs of issues when he was younger, but it did little good. Cameron is the head of the family after me. That has never sat well with Stefan, so he concocted a theory that would discredit Cameron so he couldn't be the head of the family."

I immediately regretted my outburst of laughter. This was serious. Much more serious than I had originally thought, which didn't give me an excuse. Now, I understood, and I wanted to help Stefan.

"Why can't Stefan take some of it?"

I didn't want to say too much for Cameron. He would need to have conversations with Reno himself about his future. If Stefan had gone with Pops to Columbia, it meant had a vested interest in this business.

"He will. I've had discussions with him about it."

"He wants it all."

He nodded. Stefan's jealousy ran that deep that he wanted Cameron to have no part of it. It was fine with me; I would rather leave everything about this behind, but Cameron may have his own feelings about it. Discussions we would need to have, and soon.

"They'll both be leaving here soon. Try to stay away from him."

"I'm trying. He was hitting on me yesterday when you came out of your office. He thought I was one of Zoey's friends."

He shook his head. "Out of all my children, he's the one that's the most trouble."

"Not Zoey?"

"Zoey's an angel compared to Stefan. She's had her moments lately. She's finding her way in life, but she isn't into any trouble that I know of. And I have a lot of eyes around this town."

"Not a big town."

"I mean Las Vegas."

That was good for me to know. I had given my promise to Reno that I wouldn't leave and the last thing I wanted to do was betray him. There had to be a loophole in what he had asked me to promise.

Promise me you won't leave, he had asked. No, he had asked

me to promise that I wouldn't attempt to leave. I wasn't *attempting* to leave. I was just going to do it.

I smiled. He had a lot of eyes around town; I think I could probably handle that part of it. I just had to figure out how to get out of this house without being detected. I wasn't locked in like at the Mancini house with heavy gates around the perimeter like before. There were gates here, yes, but there were a lot of trees and bushes too. And cameras, I was certain. Someone wasn't going to put me in a car until it was time to leave.

"When are Peter and Stefan supposed to leave?"

"Peter is leaving tomorrow. Stefan, I think he's due to leave this weekend." He looked at me curiously. "Why do you ask?"

"I want to know how long I should avoid them," I blurted.

"Stefan. You should avoid Stefan. Peter is more reasonable. He may listen to what you have to say, and why this is going to work."

"Why does Peter stay here? Doesn't he live in Henderson?"

Reno's eyes flashed, impossible for me to tell what emotion. He guarded himself, then softened. "I'm sure Cameron told you his brother married young." I nodded. "They have their problems now and again. Sometimes he needs to walkaway for a few days."

I couldn't say I understood, not being in that situation. They got married young and had a child almost immediately after. Anyone in that situation may struggle. Then again, there may be couples that were so in love, they didn't. Everyone was different. There was one thing I knew. I needed to get to know his family better, including his brothers.

It was a risk, but it was possible to speak with Peter about my idea of leaving the compound. I wasn't sure how much he knew about the situation, but maybe he would help me. I wasn't sure I wanted to leave, but it was a chance I needed to take. Pops could be right. Ludovico could kill me this time. I just knew I was tired of hiding, and it didn't sound like it would end.

Reno left me a short time later, retreating into the house. He was spending time with Pops while he was here, as I should be doing. I wasn't sure how long he had been overseas, but since they were best friends, I would think they were smoking cigars and talking business.

I was taking extreme risks upon myself by thinking about leaving here. I didn't want Jake involved, otherwise I would ask for his help in this. I just needed to do it soon, otherwise Cameron would be back, and I wouldn't have the chance. After dinner, I would try to corner Peter.

Chapter Twenty Six

My thoughts, as I lay in the backseat of Peter's Mercedes-Benz, were that of I was crazy for doing this. If I survived this, Cameron was likely to be furious with me. That was if I survived. Ludovico could kill me.

I had cornered Peter after dinner. He wasn't thrilled with getting in the middle of this, but I think he disliked the idea of me in Cameron's life, so he said he'd help me.

I was crouched under a blanket in the backseat, the edge of the car seat digging into my shoulder. It seemed the most inconspicuous spot to hide. It was this, or the trunk, and it horrified me to think of being in there. He had told me he needed to put his bags in there and it was already full of his golf clubs. Other than the front seat, that didn't leave much choice.

This worked out only because the stairs that I discovered on the other side of the guest room led directly down into the garage where Peter's car was. If I had walked outside to get to the garage, they would have caught me on camera. He had promised to take me to the airport. I had no intention of getting on a flight. The longer I had to wait, the more risk there was of being discovered. Especially since Reno had a lot of eyes in this town.

The front door opened and felt the car shift as Peter slid into the driver's seat, shutting the door behind him. I waited, my breath held, until the garage door opened, the car started, and we were driving out. As I was blind to how far we'd gone, I stayed under the blanket. If I was making a mistake, it would be too late to turn back now.

"You can take off the blanket now."

I threw the blanket off, taking deep gulps of air like I was hyperventilating. I hadn't realized how little air I had while under it, and now I felt like my lungs were bursting with it. There really wasn't anywhere for me to go between yet, so I just stayed where I was.

"You can come up here now."

The car pulled over to the side of the road, and Peter jumped out to open the back door and help me out. If any cars were passing by, they would have thought this was the weirdest thing to see. I stood and stretched my aching legs for a minute before hurrying over to the passenger side and sliding into the cool gray leather.

When we resumed driving, I looked over at Peter. He looked back at me. "I appreciate you doing this. I know you were hesitant."

"Hesitant? Is that what you call it? This is downright crazy. You know that if Ludovico is tracking you, you won't come back. If what you told me is true, he'll kill you."

I guess I hadn't got the impression that he cared before, but now the tone of his voice was telling me that maybe he cared a little. "You . . . you think maybe I shouldn't be doing this?"

"If Cameron finds out that I helped you do this, he's going to kill me, so yeah, I think you shouldn't be doing this."

"He won't kill you. You have a wife and a kid."

He barked out a laugh. "My father is nothing compared to my brother. Cameron is going to be irate if he finds out that you aren't where you should be."

My stomach sank all the way to my toes. If this backfired, and I really was being followed, I knew this was going to hurt Cameron. I knew it would hurt Pops. There was no other way that this was going to end.

"I have to do this," I whispered, looking out my window at the desert passing by.

It was still early enough. No one would know that I was gone for a while yet, so I got a head start. I would be in a public place, briefly, then get an Uber back. Only then would Reno and Pops find out that I had left.

"You don't. You know you don't, Regan."

"It won't stop unless I do."

"You don't know that! You are trying to take it upon yourself to manage the situation. What if Cameron already has it managed? What if, by doing this, you are putting him in danger?"

Damn it. Peter had a good point. One that I hadn't thought of. Was that why Cameron had left? He had told me he had to transfer his overseas businesses out of his name to his uncles. Had he been lying to me?

"Do you want me to turn around?" Peter asked me, his voice soft.

I shook my head. "No."

"You're making a big mistake. I don't think it's just Cameron at stake here. You're already a part of this family."

My head snapped up, our eyes meeting. Did he know? Did Cameron tell him we had gotten married already? "Why . . . why do you think that?"

"My dad has never defended Emma the way he's defended you, and we've been married for almost four years. Not that he doesn't love Emma, he does. And he absolutely dotes on Caleb. But not the same way he does you."

"He hardly knows me."

"You're missing the point. If you die, this is not only going to crush Cam, but my dad, too. He's put a lot of stock in you as his daughter-in-law and future matriarch of the family."

"What about your mom?"

He laughed. "She wanted Cam to marry her friend's daughter,

Megan. That would have never worked. You can hardly get two words out of Megan. She's quiet, reserved, and easily swayed. Not you. You are bold, but you are intelligent, which is why I don't understand why you are doing this. I don't think you've thought this through."

"I've thought this through. It's the only way."

"It's not." His palm smacked the steering wheel. "But I'll drop you off at the airport, and you'd better be quick about it and get back before anyone realizes you're gone. For all our sakes. We need you and Cam in this family, at the head of this family, for the legacy of our children. Everything that our two families have worked to build. Cameron is strong, but he can't manage it all on his own. He needs you."

My heart squeezed like he had physically reached in and grabbed my heart with his hand. I had thoroughly misjudged him. That was exactly why I tried not to judge people before getting to know them. And this is the second time that it's happened. Shame on me.

When I watched Peter drive away after dropping me off, I still felt that squeeze in my heart. I turned and walked into the airport, almost numb. I stopped; a lump was stuck in my throat, lodged there momentarily while the back of my eyes burned with the threat of tears. I pulled my phone out of my pocket and looked down at it. I couldn't do this to Cameron. I couldn't do this to any of them.

I went to sit on an empty bench, my mind racing. Regardless of whether I had promised Reno that I wouldn't attempt to leave, I had. It had been pointless. I couldn't make the call to Jake. I couldn't put him at risk.

I jumped up from the bench and hurried outside, hailing an Uber. When the car stopped in front of me, I jumped into the backseat and studied the driver carefully before closing the backdoor. Now that I had abandoned my original plan to contact Jake well away from the Moretti house, I needed to get back quickly and safely.

I gave him the address, and we lurched into motion. Cautiously, I watched my surroundings as we drove away from the airport to make sure we were going in the right direction. I wasn't satisfied until we were on Las Vegas Parkway and the gates were opening.

As soon as the driver pulled into the driveway, I ordered him to stop and held out a wad of cash to him and told him to get out immediately. When I stood outside of the car, I waited until he pulled back out, and the gates closed before I fully breathed again. I had made it, and I had made it alive.

I ran across the courtyard to the front door and flung it open, hurrying into the house. If Reno was looking at the cameras he would have seen me come in and was likely cursing right now.

"Regan," I heard from the library. "Come here."

I was sixteen all over again, except instead of Pop's smooth voice that was about to lecture me into submission, it was Reno. And his voice was hard. I turned into the library, stalking forward and eating up the distance from the door to the desk, ignoring Pops and Stefan.

Reno stood up from the chair, slowly setting his cigar down on the edge of the ashtray. Pops was going to say something to me, halfway out of his chair as well, but Reno held up his hand and he sat back down.

"You promised me you wouldn't leave." He slammed his hand down flat on his desk, but it didn't faze me. "You promised me!"

"I promised I wouldn't *attempt* to leave. That wasn't an attempt. I just left."

Reno wasn't fazed either as we faced off. "Do you really think that it matters? You left, knowing what I said to you. Knowing how Cameron would react if he found out."

"Cameron doesn't need to know."

"I don't?"

I experienced a chill to the core of my body when I heard

Cameron's voice coming from behind me. I felt the blood drain from my face, but I slowly turned around to look at him while he sauntered in, looking fresh as summer. My mouth turned dry.

I would have run to him, thrown my arms around him, and kissed him if he hadn't been looking at me like he was truly furious. He was. There was no mistaking that he was angry. I had not a second ago told his father that we should withhold information from him. I was in deep shit.

"Cameron, listen to me."

He strolled right up to me, and I saw Stefan move to the edge of his chair for a front-row seat to whatever action was about to come. I had never seen Cameron look like this. He looked lethal. He came right up to me, looking down at me, but not touching me.

"Do you have any idea," he said in a low voice, in a tone I had never heard come from his throat, "what it's like ... to come home. And find that your *wife*. Who should be here. Is not. That your *wife*. Took it upon herself. To go to the very man. Who is trying to kill her."

I took a step back, but his hands shot forward and grabbed me. Not by the arms—he knew better than to do that to me— but by my elbows. Not harshly, but not exactly gently. I didn't even know what to say. It wasn't true. I wasn't going to Ludovico. I wasn't crazy. And then I realized he had just let everyone know I was his wife. Not his fiancé. Wife. I was his wife.

"Do you?"

This time, I jumped at the tone of his voice. I couldn't tell him why I had really left. I hadn't gone to confront Ludovico. I had gone to call Jake away from this house. In the best public place I could think of. "I wasn't going to go. I changed my mind," I whispered.

I wasn't sure if he was going to believe me or not, but it was worth a try. He looked down at me, then his mouth came down on mine so quickly that I didn't have time to close my mouth. I felt one hand curl around the back of my neck, holding my head from moving away, the other hand sliding from my elbow to the curve at my hip. His mouth was eager, punishing yet yielding when I returned his kiss.

It hadn't been close to even a week since we had parted ways at the airport, yet I felt like it had been months since I had last seen him. It felt good to be in his arms again, even if he was furious with me.

Reno cleared his throat. Cameron dragged his mouth away from mine, the burn still imprinted on my lips. He kept his hands behind my neck and on my waist, obviously not in a hurry to release me.

"I would like to hear the rest of what she has to say," Reno said. "And how you even got out without being seen?"

I didn't want to betray Peter, but he had been the one to get me to change my mind, even though I was already at the airport when I did. If he hadn't been brutally honest with me, I wouldn't have changed it.

"I hid in Peter's car."

"That son of a bitch."

"Cameron, let her say her piece."

"Peter gave me a ride. He didn't want to, and the entire ride he tried to talk me out of going to do what I had planned to do. In the end, when he dropped me off, I couldn't. I couldn't do that to Cameron. Or Pops. Or Mom. I couldn't do that to anyone. I came immediately back."

Cameron's hands softened, his hand falling away from my neck to curl around the other side of my waist. "Is that true?"

I nodded. Cameron returned his gaze to me, lifting his hand to tuck my hair behind my ear. Stefan made a puking sound, pushing back into his chair now that the excitement was over.

"Never do that to me again. Swear to me, promise me, you will never purposely search for Ludovico."

"I swear to you."

"Swear that you will not search for any loopholes in your

promise."

"I swear I won't. I shouldn't have this time. We need a plan. If Ludovico is the one, getting married isn't going to stop him. He's got a bigger vendetta."

"Speaking of which . . ." Pops finally spoke up. "Was I mistaken in that you referred to my daughter as your . . . wife?"

Cameron grinned down at me. "You're not mistaken. Regan is my wife. We got married a couple of weeks ago."

Pops smiled. Reno smiled. They appeared to be pleased with the new revelation. Stefan sneered, even when Cameron tipped my face up toward his and pressed a simple kiss to my lips.

"What was the goal?" Stefan asked.

"I didn't want to wait to make her my wife," Cameron answered.

Warmth flooded my body. I hated the fact that I had made him worry. The way he had come in, and what he had said, not to mention how he had said it, made me think it was more than worrying. Reno had said that it would crush him. Did I really mean that much to him? I was his wife, but we'd only been together since September, and even then, I was trying to push him away. Was his love for me that strong? Because I knew I felt that way toward him, and if the roles were reversed, it would devastate me.

"That's why I changed my mind. Not because I don't want this to end, and not because I'm a coward. Because I couldn't do that to the people I love."

"No one has ever thought of you as a coward," Reno said. "Never that."

"I agree," Pops murmured. "No one who kills two men at twelve years old is a coward. If anyone is a coward, it's Ludovico. If you had gone there, he'd be so protected by his soldiers and associates that it would have been easy for him to kill you. Or have someone do it for him."

"What's everyone doing in here?"

We all turned to Zoey's sweet voice in the doorway. She wore mostly black again, this time with huge baggy pants covered in chains, zippers, and large pockets, along with a simple black tank top with a red flannel shirt tied around her waist and a pair of red combat boots.

"Cam!" She brightened when she saw her brother, hurrying over to him to throw her arms around his neck.

I knew enough to step back when she did so as Cameron's arms came around her, and he lifted her off her feet in a bear hug. It was heartwarming to see the love between these two siblings. I had a feeling that it wasn't that way between him, Peter, and Stefan. Stefan looked painfully bored now.

"Did she tell you?"

Cameron set her down and looked over at me. "Tell me what?"

"After you get married, I'm going to come and visit."

Zoey was more excited now than when I had asked her yesterday in passing. She and I had seen so little of each other since I'd been here, and she had rarely seen Cameron in the last six months or longer, so I thought it was a good idea. She merely told me it would be cool, but here she was, nearly bouncing up and down with excitement over the news.

Cameron's mouth turned up at the corners, giving me a knowing smile. I was confused. I didn't have siblings other than Amber, and I didn't know any better. This family was odd. They were all so very different from one another.

"Are you going out?" I asked her.

"I was, but since Cam is home, I might have to dip." She looked up at him, a full grin on her face still. "Are you home for a while at least?"

"Couple of days. Regan and I have wedding stuff we need to do, since it's not too far off." Her smile turned to a pout. "Go with your friends now and we'll spend some time together tomorrow. I need some time with Regan."

"Fine," she said, annoyance clipping her voice, but the smile returning. "Where are you going to live after you get married?"

Cameron looked at me, his eyebrows up. "We haven't talked about it yet."

"We should," I prompted.

"Yes, we should." He looked around at everyone. "As much as I'd like to stay and chat, I'd like to spend some time with my . . . fiancé."

I wasn't sure why he hadn't told Zoey that we were married already when everyone else in the room knew now, but he would have his reasons. She seemed to have a lot of friends and you could never be too careful.

He gave her a little push, and she skipped out of the room before Cameron took my hand and pulled me out of the room moments after the front door shut. Instead of bringing me into the parlor, or even toward the family room, he pulled me up the staircase.

Chapter Twenty Seven

"Regan."

"Jake?" I asked.

We were sitting on the hood of his car in the vacant parking lot of the Performing Arts Center. I had my legs pulled up and my cheek resting on them while I looked at him. The way he had said my name was a cross between a question and a whisper. I was seventeen, almost eighteen, and had more freedom, since I didn't have to sneak out anymore. We had been meeting here on and off for more than a year.

By now, I knew how to lose my followers. Pops still had me followed, even though he hadn't specifically told me he was. The threat of never seeing Jake again had not come up, but it didn't need to. When he said something once, he expected it to be followed. Except I wasn't about to stop meeting Jake. Which meant I had to be smart about losing those who were on my tail.

"I like you."

He said it much like the time he had said it when we were sitting with our feet in the pool at his house, when his fingers had touched mine. When his mouth had accidentally run into mine. My first kiss. This time he wasn't touching me, and the way he said it was almost like an ache.

"I like you, too."

"No, I really like you. I have for a long time."

Oh. Oh, no. I continued to look at him, with my cheek pressed to my knees. I didn't want him to like me like that. He was a friend. And I had a boyfriend named Xavier. I couldn't imagine having a Romeo and Juliet relationship with Jake, although that was what we were doing now. As friends. Pops and Ludovico would never accept us together like that. Even if I did like him that way, I just couldn't. I would be eighteen in less than a month, and I'd still have to sneak around.

"Say something."

I wasn't sure what I could say that wouldn't hurt him. There was no other way around it. "You can't," I whispered. "You can't like me that way, Jake. I won't let you."

"You're all I think about, Regan."

"Well, stop," I snapped, jerking my head up and straightening out my legs in preparation to jump off the car. "It can't ever be that way between us, Jake. You know that."

He sighed, looking up at the scattering of twinkling stars across the inky black sky. "I know it would be hard, but we could."

That did it. I slid off the car, coming to my feet in front of it and looking at him. "No."

He smiled at me, not a grin or even a friendly smile, but a sad smile. "How did you get to be so smart? Way smarter than me."

"I'm not smarter than you, Jake. I have more common sense. Your father would never let that happen, and neither would mine."

"But if they could come to a truce."

"It hasn't happened in almost twenty years! It won't happen now. Just don't think about me like that anymore." I leaned over the vacant side of the hood, my torso pressed along the warmth of the hood while I looked up at him. "Okay?"

"Okay."

He had said it, but I didn't believe him. He resigned himself to the fact that I wouldn't let it happen, not so much that he would stop thinking about me that way. He was eighteen, and I was almost eighteen. We were both going to college in just a couple of months. It wasn't far away. We could still meet up.

"Are you looking forward to college?"

I flipped over, keeping my feet firmly on the ground while arching my back flat on the hood. He didn't say anything, and I looked over, expecting to see him crying. He wasn't crying, but he wasn't answering me either.

"Jake."

"No. I'm not looking forward to it. Are you?"

"Yes! I can't wait to not have to see those brats anymore with their rich parents, enormous houses, snooty clothes, and fancy cars."

"You have a rich parent. And you live in an enormous house."

I pulled a face. "It's not the same. I don't act like I'm rich. Besides, I'm not rich. Pops is. He provides for me, but he doesn't hand over his money to me."

"You're an only child. Whatever he has, you'll inherit someday when he's gone."

I hadn't thought about that. I didn't even know what I wanted to do in college, didn't know what I would focus on. Business, I suppose. I wasn't interested in being a doctor, or a nurse, or a lawyer. But I also wasn't interested in working a menial job or one I would have to sit in a cubicle with no windows. No, if I was going to do any office work, it would be in a giant corner office with lots of windows. I would be the boss.

"What are you studying?"

"Business, what else?"

"You don't want to do that, though. You told me you want to be an artist. You let your dad cow you into studying business?"

He shrugged. "I'm his only son. There really wasn't much choice."

"This is bullshit. We should be able to do whatever we want instead of what our dads want us to do." I sat up straight again, miffed more that he was being made to do something he *didn't want to do.*

"Regan . . ."

I turned to look at him. "Jake?"

"Can I kiss you?"

"Jake, stop!"

If he wasn't going to give up this crazy pursuit, I was going to get seriously mad, and I didn't get mad often. Pops was usually the one I got mad at. Never at Jake. He was looking at me, staring at me with twinkling eyes. Did he think by kissing me I would change my mind?

"Just to see . . ."

I groaned. He wasn't going to give up unless it satisfied him that kissing me would be like kissing his sister. "Fine."

He slid down from the car, coming to stand right next to me. Jake was an entire head taller than I was, so he would need to lean down to do it. I turned slightly. This wouldn't be cheating on Xavier. This was only a test.

Jake's hand slipped around my waist while his other hand pressed against my jaw while he leaned down into me. When his lips pressed against mine, my first thought was this would be what it would be like to kiss a brother if I had one. But when he moved his lips against mine, coaxing my lips to open to his and his tongue swept against mine, I lost the feeling in my legs. He tasted like the Coca-Cola he had been drinking, sweet, his mouth and tongue warm against mine while he explored slowly.

I pulled away abruptly, nearly stumbling back away from him with wide eyes. His hand stayed poised where it had just been against my cheek, his eyes just as wide as my eyes. This wasn't good.

"I have to go," I sputtered, hurrying over to my car parked right next to his.

I pulled the door open, but Jake was there in an instant, blocking it with his hand so I couldn't open it enough to slide in. His eyes were pleading with me not to run away from him now.

"Please don't leave."

I looked at him. He wasn't on the verge of crying, but he was apologetic without verbally telling me he was sorry. Maybe he would say it, maybe he wouldn't but I was flustered, and I wasn't sure if I could stick around.

"I'm sorry. It won't happen again."

Inwardly, I sighed in relief. I didn't want this to happen again, but after that I kind of did, and that was the most dangerous thought about Jake that I had ever had, and I didn't like it. The way he kissed me wasn't anything like how Xavier kissed me. The way Jake had kissed me made me feel like kissing Xavier was like kissing a brother if I had one. I wouldn't be able to kiss Xavier again.

"It can't happen again," I whispered.

"It won't. I promise."

I looked down at my phone, the message glaringly clear. It was a message from Jake, but it was a message that had alarms sounding so loudly in my head I hadn't heard what Anne had said. Since Cameron and I had gotten home from Vegas, it had been a steady stream of wedding preparations. The wedding was only a week away.

"Regan, did you hear what I said?"

I looked up at Anne from my phone, not sure whether I should put it down or keep it in my hand. No one could see this message. "What?"

"Put your phone away and listen to me. Please."

I didn't want to put my phone away. If this message was true, I couldn't put it away. I would need to do something. If it wasn't true, I'd be in trouble. I wasn't sure if I could risk ignoring it.

"I need your input on the final seating." Anne continued. Her voice had an edge of frustration even though she, along with Pops, wasn't one to leap to anger. "And I need you to review the set list for the DJ. Then I need you to go up and try on your dress again if you can manage it alone. Otherwise, I can help you."

I wasn't sure why she needed my input on those things, other than trying on my dress one more time. I had tried very hard not to lose any more weight, but I wasn't sure I had put any weight on. If the dress didn't fit, I would have to fly Jane   in from Myrtle Beach.

"Why do you need my input?"

"Regan, this is your wedding. Honestly..." She shook her head, her big blonde curls shaking even though her hair was up.

"You've done everything, and thank you for doing it."

She bit her lip. "Oh, I hope you love it. I want you to have the most magical day. You and Cameron..." She sniffed, pressing her fingertip to her eye to stop tears from coming. "You deserve the very best."

I looked at her, sad for her. I had often wondered why Pops had never married her. Now I knew why. Maybe she was happy, just as they were.

I wondered what would happen if Isabel ever returned. Would Pops kick Anne to the curb? I couldn't tolerate her for long, but I didn't want her to get hurt. Amber either. They had been in my life for so long.

"Are we done?" I asked.

"No! Can you please just look at this seating chart for the reception?"

She slid the long piece of paper toward me, complete with a map of the dance floor, DJ set up, and more tables than I could count. I didn't even know who was coming! How should   I know where everyone would sit?

I pretended like I was looking at it when I was really panicking about what to do about Jake's message. I needed to do something. Pops, Gio, and Cameron had all gone to deal with country club issues with rebuilding. Apparently, wrong building supplies had come in. I wasn't sure why it took all three of them, but I knew Anne wanted me for a wedding talk, anyway.

"This looks perfect, Anne."

I pushed the paper back toward her, noting that she was beaming from ear to ear that I had said it was perfect. With Anne, everything about the ceremony and reception would be perfect.

"I'm going to trust you in the music. I really don't care what we dance to. I don't care what I walk down the aisle to. I just don't have an opinion on that, and I trust you implicitly."

"Can you at least go try on your gown? We need to make sure it fits."

"Yes, I can do that."

"You and I should probably purchase your lingerie. They are essential to your wedding night," she said, her eyes twinkling.

"I'm not supposed to leave."

"Please? You cannot go without."

I shrugged. I could go with nothing under my wedding gown. Cameron wouldn't mind. "If you can get permission from Pops and Cameron, I'm all yours. I wouldn't get your hopes up."

"Challenge accepted!"

I would have laughed if I wasn't trying to figure out how I could break away from her, assuming she would get permission. Holding my breath on it would be dangerous, but I wished her luck with it. I looked back down at the message. If anyone had an inside angle on what Ludovico was up to, it was Jake. And it looked like he was up to trying to nab the next best thing to me. And I'd be damned if I was going to lose one more person to his games.

"Why did you and Pops never get married?"

She stared at me for a second and I thought maybe I should not have asked such a personal question. "When we first met and started seeing each other, he told me he would never remarry and that I should never expect it."

"And that was that?"

"Yes. He's always provided for me. And Amber. It never entered my mind."

"I suppose you don't have to be married to be committed to someone. An unspoken agreement, of sorts."

Now she was really staring at me. "Don't think for one second that you're going to get out of this, Regan De Luca. I have worked far too long, and far too hard."

I put my hand on her arm. "That was not where I was going."

"Go try on your gown. Tell me if you need help."

"I won't need help."

She nodded. "Go on now."

I stood and went to the staircase, glancing at the door to the office to make sure that no one was there. Once Pops had come back, Gio had moved into a place of his own to make room, but he was here a lot still. There was the country club to contend with. Every minute that it wasn't open, we were losing money. They had torn the shell of the clubhouse down, and the building would need to be rebuilt. Gio was handling most of that, Pops still trying to keep out of the public eye, not draw notice. Many issues had come up lately, which commanded their attention, and they had brought Cameron into the mix. I suppose he would need to know since we were married.

I hurried up the stairs and into my bedroom, closing the door behind myself and leaning up against it while I focused on my breathing and closed my eyes. My phone vibrated again, and I was sure that Jake had sent me another message.

"Please" was it said, but it was a resounding 'please' in my head. Something was wrong and my heart lurched, but I could not go running off to meet Jake. I couldn't even tell Cameron about my relationship with Jake, not yet. Not until we dealt with Ludovico.

There was a knock at the door, and then it pushed against my back. I moved out of the way enough to see Anne stick her head around the door. "Good news! Your dad said we could go, but we have to go now, and we have to make it quick!"

I heaved a sigh of relief as the door clicked shut. I would need to try on my dress later. If Pops was granting me enough leeway to go shopping, I would need to do that first. Anne seemed like she was absolutely bursting with happiness at getting to go with me.

I rolled my eyes. My phone vibrated again, so I texted him back to let him know I was on it. No need to text me back. I sent a text to Tatum next. If all was alright, she would reply to me and I would recognize there was no need to take any risks.

∞

It was exhausting with Anne and her constant chatter. I liked Anne, I really did, but she was the type of person who didn't stop talking. She talked about everything, and anything, and it went on and on. We found lingerie, and I went with simple but sexy against her, wanting to get me some knockout red ensemble. Hell no.

When we finally got out of the store with our bags in hand, the sun was setting. We had been out for a long time. Too long. I checked my phone. No text from Tatum. Now I was worried. We walked down the sidewalk toward where Anne had parked, but she got sidetracked by a jewelry store. I wasn't keen on having to go to another store.

"Wait here, then. I will only be a second."

When she ducked into the store, I took my shot and hailed a cab. As I slid into the backseat, I sent a text to Anne and apologized for ditching her, but I had to take care of something quick before going home.

The drive to my house on the beach in Malibu took longer than it should have, but it was because my nerves were on edge. Every two minutes I was looking at my phone, watching for Tatum to text me back. Even if she was at work, she would have taken two seconds to shoot me a text that said she was fine. But she wouldn't be at work this late. The taxi had barely rolled to a stop in front of my quaint condo on the beach, and I was handing the driver some cash and jumping out. The garage under the house faced the street, and mine was one of the middle units. I rushed up the stairs to the door, attempting to open it before entering the code in case it was unlocked.

It swung open, surprising me. Usually, regardless of if we were home, Tatum and I kept it locked. It was a habit. The hallway led into the kitchen with the open dining room and living room to the right. I could see the kitchen counter from the hallway, clean just like I liked it. The house was quiet as I closed the door with a soft click behind.

Now would have been a good time for me to be carrying my gun, I thought while I crept toward the kitchen. I looked at the open windows in front of the dining room and living room, hoping for a glimpse of a reflection of what might be around the corner, but there was no such luck.

Then I heard it, a muffled scream. I rushed around the corner and came to a skidding halt, seeing Tatum tied to a chair with her mouth taped. Alex was next to her, but he must have put up a fight because his face looked pretty beat up. There were two men I didn't recognize that were standing, waiting. Waiting for me.

Tatum tried to scream again, but I shook my head. There was no reason for her to get worked up. I held up my hands to the men, hoping to show them I wasn't armed. It wouldn't have been lying. Idiot me had gone running blind right into a trap. A trap that Jake had set. It had been him the entire time, and my heart ached with the reality of it.

"We've been waiting for you, Miss De Luca."

I looked at the taller of the two men. He had his hands on his hips, letting me know he had a gun at his waist. As if I was stupid enough to think they weren't armed. He slicked back his dyed blond hair, and his jaw was covered with a fine stubble.

"I don't doubt it," I said. "What's the plan?"

He stepped toward me, while the other kept close to Tatum. Tatum wasn't going to do anything, even if she wanted to. Her eyes were wild with fear, and there was nothing I could do to assure her everything would be fine. I wasn't sure they would be. In fact, this time I was certain they wouldn't be. But I would just as soon get it over with.

"We're going to go for a ride. There's someone who would like to speak with you."

I barked out a laugh. "Is that what he wants to do? Let's not keep him waiting."

Both men were walking toward me now, the other one looking back at Tatum. I hoped they were at least untying them, but it wasn't looking good. The smaller one with the droopy eyes motioned for me to raise my arms to be patted down. Huffing from having to be searched, I raised my arms and let him run his grubby hands over me.

Satisfied that I wasn't armed, they pushed me back toward the hallway, but not before I cast one more look back at Tatum. I hoped they could get themselves out of this and get help. I wasn't sure where I was being taken, but if they could get word to Cameron, he would know that I messed up. The despair in the pit of my stomach had sunk low. This wasn't how I wanted to go out. I would have much rather gone out fighting. Maybe it wasn't too late.

As soon as we stepped outside, a black Cadillac pulled up on the street in front of my house and stopped. The windows were all tinted. The men pushed me forward and tossed me into the back seat, the taller man sliding in next to me. He grabbed me and I struggled with him when he tried to put a piece of cloth over my mouth. I fought even harder, holding my breath so I didn't breathe in anything that was on the cloth, but it was too much. I was suffocating, then I slipped into darkness.

I came to while still in the car, groggy enough so that even when the door opened, I couldn't climb out of the car myself. Hands were on my arms, pulling me out into the fresh air, which I gulped in like I was still suffocating. They were pulling me toward a house, a house that I recognized all too well.

"Let me at least stop and get the feeling back into my legs," I snapped. "Obviously, there's nowhere for me to go."

Abruptly, the hands released me, and I crumbled to the ground, wincing when my ass hit the concrete. I wiggled my feet and stretched my legs while taking deep breaths. If I was going to be confronting this man, I was going to be of sound mind.

Using the short wall around the landscaping, I pushed myself to my feet. I straightened my back as much as I could and jerked my head toward the door. "Let's get this over with, then. Wouldn't want you two to lose your jobs, or your lives, because of me."

They both stood behind me, large burly men that were packing heat in chest holsters. They weren't moving until I proceeded into the house in front of them, not trusting me. I couldn't say I blamed them for that.

I opened one of the two front doors myself, passing through the familiar foyer and into the large living room. It hadn't changed at all since I was here last. The same furniture, albeit newer, the same décor. It was just as ugly as it had been before.

Ludovico sat in the same chair he had sat in when I met him for the first time. He looked the same except for the gray at his temples. He was not looking at me with kind eyes, but with intense anger. I couldn't blame him for that. After all, I had killed two of his men after the last time we had seen each other, besides thwarting his grand plan of cracking into Pops and Reno's drug smuggling enterprise. We stared at each other and continued to stare at each other even when he stood up and walked around the coffee table toward me.

It probably wasn't the smartest thing that I had ever done, but I had been training my entire life for this. Pops had made sure that I could defend myself. I curled my hand and punched him in the face so hard that he stumbled back against the coffee table, his legs catching the edge and pitching him into the end of the couch. It didn't take but two seconds for his thugs to be on me, each holding me by the arm while four others stepped into the perimeter of the room.

Ludovico, spry for his age, pushed himself up and came up to me, but now he held a Beretta 92fs pistol and he had the barrel at the center of my forehead, not quite touching me. They released me, but he kept the gun pressed against my head.

"You don't want to fuck with me, little girl."

I nearly laughed at his words. I had been thinking the same about him. He really didn't want to fuck with me. And I wasn't a little girl anymore. I was not in the mood for this.

I lifted my hand quickly, my fingers curling around the barrel and pulling the end of the barrel up against my forehead until it touched. I kept my eyes trained on him, narrowed and challenging. At least I knew if I died, it would be quick.

"Do it," I spat, not recognizing my voice. It should shake in fear, but it was strong.

I kept my eyes on him, waiting for him to call my bluff. Was I bluffing? Would I even hear the pop of the gun if he pulled the trigger and killed me? I wasn't sure it would last long enough for me to register before my soul left this body. My family, and Cameron's family, would avenge me.

"No!"

I heard Jake's shout, even though I couldn't see him. He must have come through the front. Ludovico kept the gun pushed firmly against my forehead, my fingers still holding it there.

"Don't kill her."

Ludovico stared at me; his eyes were just as hard as mine were. Two could play this game. And I was ready to play. He made no move to pull the gun away from me, and I made no move to let go of it, even when Jake came around to the back of the couch, not daring to approach both of us. If this was going to be done, I want it done now. He was the one who had been behind all of it, and I was done with the games.

"Do it," I growled.

"Regan, no!" Jake jumped over the couch to stand next to us, his eyes pleading with me like he had done so many years ago when he had asked me to not go. Why did he care now? He was the one who had set me up for this. He was the one who had betrayed me in Cape Haven.

I didn't care. This ended now.

Slowly, Ludovico pulled the gun away from me and my hand fell away, but he kept it trained on me. I liked it better when he had it aimed at my head. Death would have been instant. Now, it would likely be painful.

"She'll marry me," Jake blurted.

"No!" I shouted.

"What?" Ludovico said.

"Jake, you're out of your mind if you think I'm going to marry you."

He ignored me. "There is another way out. Nobody has to die. She can marry me, and we will join the De Luca and Mancini families. Think about it."

I was about to spew another hateful and very resounding no. Was this his plan? Is this why he betrayed me? No one knew that Cameron and I were already married. No one would betray our secret that we didn't wait until the ceremony. I knew Cameron would never sign divorce papers. Neither would I. He would have to kill me first.

"Things should have been much different, many years ago," Ludovico snapped. He pointed the gun at me again.

"Don't," Jake said.

Ludovico lowered the gun again and looked at him. "You could have convinced her years ago that you were the one for her." I saw Jake wince, my murderous eyes going back to Ludovico. "It wouldn't have mattered. She did what she did, leaving Gavriel and Reno open to finish their deal while I had to flee the country."

It was true. Ludovico had been hell bent to make someone regret leaving him out of yet another deal. Except this time, it was my fault because I was the one who caused him to leave the country. Had I not created the mess with killing his two men, he might not have been under scrutiny and stayed in the country, although I doubted Pops and Reno would have let him in on their Columbian deal. There was a reason they cut him out. I could be wrong. Maybe they would have given him a second chance.

"You have five days to convince her, or else I will kill her personally and send her lifeless body back to her father."

Chapter Twenty Eight

I have five days until they kill me. They left me to my own thoughts in the same room as the last time. They had literally thrown me in. I landed on the floor, and the door closed with a bang behind me with the lock turning with finality. I laid on the floor for a minute, resting my forehead on the carpet, thinking *here I was again*, except this time I didn't think I would be leaving. I wouldn't be in a car to go somewhere again. The only way I was leaving was in a body bag because I would not be marrying Jake.

I pushed myself up from the floor, walking toward the window to look out at the ocean. It was dark, and I knew that by that time Cameron would know. I prayed Tatum and Alex had freed themselves. I was sure Anne had been frantic when I didn't return home, feeling guilty that she had gotten sidetracked and left me alone. If it hadn't been this time, it would have been another time. I wasn't sure they would know where to look for me.

Jake eventually came to the door, but I wasn't interested in whatever he had to say. I didn't want to hear what he had to say. All I could think of was how I had trusted him all these years. I wondered how he knew I was in Cape Haven. Had he hired Justin himself?

God, I felt so betrayed. He had been my friend. I gave him strong words, but he had no reply, leaving me alone with my thoughts again. This time, I wasn't thinking about how I could get out of this. There was no way out. And I hoped no one came here to my rescue, or there could be the chance of more innocent deaths at my hands, and I wasn't having it.

Night came and went. They brought a tray of breakfast in the morning, but kept the door locked. Lunch came. Dinner came. This was torture. There was nothing to do in this room other than sleep, which I did a lot of. I was tired most days, and I had a suspicious feeling about why. The last month had been crazy enough for me, but while Cameron was in Italy and I was with his family, I suspected I was pregnant.

The doorknob to my prison cell jiggled, and I immediately sat upright from the middle of the bed, on high alert. I stared at the door. I had no friends here.

The door opened, and Jake slid in, closing the door. He wore a pair of black jeans with a wrinkled blue button-up shirt. I had two thoughts. My first thought was he was he was here to convince me to marry him. Only I knew it would never happen. The second was he was going to apologize for throwing me under after I trusted him. I didn't want to listen to whatever he had to say.

"We have a real conundrum here, Regan."

Of course, we were in a conundrum, but I wasn't about to relent. I knew this time was different. He was going to kill me unless I married Jake. Or so he had said. This wasn't a problem, it was reality.

He walked toward the bed, sitting down next to me. He was a grown man now, and he was good-looking. There was always a bad boy look about him, like he'd wear a leather jacket and biker boots, but he was my friend. Since he had kissed me when we were younger, I had stayed clear of those thoughts toward him. It would never happen.

"No, we don't. He'll kill me, and I've come to terms with that."

His hand came to rest on my knee, and I eyed it cautiously, then lifted my eyes to his. If I could have read his thoughts, I would have foreseen what would come next.

He grabbed me with both hands, pulling him toward him before I could react. His mouth pressed to mine, his hand moving to curl around my neck. I reared back despite his attempt to keep my head steady and slapped him.

He jumped away from the bed quickly, stabbing his fingers through his thick, dark hair and looking away from me in shame. I swiped the back of my hand across my mouth as though ridding myself of him.

He spun back around, sitting on the bed next to me, resting his arms on his knees, and burying his face in his hands. I didn't move. I didn't want to comfort him after what he just tried to do. I could understand his reasoning for trying, but I don't think I could forgive him for what he did.

"I'm sorry."

I sat back, crossing my legs under me. "You're going to tell me what that was about, but first I want you to tell me why you betrayed me. Why would you tell him where I was? Did you hire Justin yourself to come after me and try to kill me?"

Jake stared at me. "What are you talking about?"

"I'm talking about the text message you sent me yesterday that said Tatum was in trouble. I called you in September and shortly after that, somebody put something into my drink at a bar, trying to kill me. The other people checked out who knew where I was. Except you. And you put Tatum in danger and texted me to draw me out."

He still stared at me. "I didn't know where you were in September. You didn't tell me. And I didn't text you yesterday. How would I know if Tatum was in danger?"

Confusion assaulted me. Jake was a good liar, or he wasn't the one who betrayed me. But it couldn't have been anyone else. There was only him. He had texted me yesterday and told me Tatum was in trouble. Without his text, and her response, I wouldn't have gone to my house. I knew it was risky.

I frowned. "You didn't text me yesterday."

"I swear to you. I've been trying to not to get in touch with you. My father has been crazy lately, almost delusional. I didn't want to take the chance in messaging you."

"The text I got was from you, Jake."

"Someone is texting using my number." He shook his head. "And if you think I knew where you were in September, someone was listening to our conversation and guessed where you were. I didn't know where you were. Still don't."

It had to be his conniving father. That relieved me to know he hadn't betrayed me as I thought. It was a tremendous relief. "What about kissing me? How's that going to change this situation?"

He stayed where he was while I waited for him to give me an answer. I deserved an answer. I deserved to know. After a minute, I thought he wasn't going to answer me.

"I thought it would change your mind, and you would marry me."

I didn't laugh. I wouldn't hurt him that way. Not like he almost did to me. Instead, I pushed to my knees and brought my arm around his shoulder and the other around the other side of him in a sort of sideways hug. His head lifted, and he turned his face toward mine, his lips catching mine.

His kiss caught me. It was just as it had been all those years ago, and he wasn't trying to force me this time. I didn't pull away at first. He pulled my arm, so I fell into his lap, cradled by his arms.

No. I wouldn't do this to Cameron. I turned my head away, breaking the contact of our mouths. Tears gathered in my eyes, one sliding down my cheek and falling heedlessly down. Tenderly, he smoothed the pad of his fingers over my wet cheek.

"I can't marry you, Jake."

I slid to my feet, moving away from him enough to create distance between us. I needed to think, and I couldn't be near him to do it. He thought this would make a difference. I pinched the bridge of my nose.

"You don't have a choice. He's going to kill you this time," he said, his voice thick and hoarse. "I wouldn't be a terrible choice for a husband, would I?"

I debated whether I could trust him. I knew he said it wasn't him who texted me, or who knew where I was when I called in September. It wouldn't matter, anyway. It wouldn't save my life. If anything, it would hasten my death.

"I'm already married."

His hand snapped up, his eyes meeting mine in surprise. "How?"

"What do you mean, how? Cameron and I were married by a judge at the end of January." I moved back toward him, sitting down next to him again. "There's more, Jake. I think I might be pregnant. Cameron doesn't know."

He jumped up. "Sweet Jesus!" He ran his fingers through his hair again, clearly agitated with this new information. "What're we going to do?"

"*We* aren't going to do anything, Jake. I said, I *think*. I'm not sure. And this is my issue, not yours. There's only one way to end this."

"No. I don't accept that. I won't let you die."

"You will. Your father will kill me this time, you said so yourself. I can't marry you, so that's it."

He looked at me in horror. "You've got to be out of your damn mind if you think I'm going to let that happen."

I would have winced at the vehemence in his words, but I'd known Jake for a long time and even though no one else knew of our friendship, I knew what he said was true. He was forever trying to protect me, even against his father.

"Jake," I whispered. "Let me go."

"No!"

I tucked my legs under me. "You know why he had to flee the country, don't you?"

He looked at me. "I don't care."

"You know he won't let me live after what I did."

Rather than sitting down next to me on the bed, he sat down on the floor next to the bed. I think he didn't trust himself to keep his hands to himself, so I was fine with the distance between us.

"Why did you talk to me through the door all those years ago?"

He cracked a smile then. "Because I didn't have many friends."

"I still don't have many."

He sighed. "I took the opportunity for myself. I didn't know why he'd taken you then. But when I saw you for the first time . . . I thought you were the most beautiful girl I'd ever seen."

"You were thirteen. I was a shiny new toy. Of course, you thought that."

He shook his head. "No. I thought you were beautiful. Still are. And then we started hanging out after dinner in the evening by the pool, talking to each other, learning about each other and I loved you. I carried that with me even when we were teenagers."

"Right before you went away to college," I whispered.

"Yes, all those years and then . . . we kissed. Really kissed. I thought I had died and gone to heaven with you in my arms. Despite what my father wanted, I had to have you. I wanted you, and that was all that mattered to me."

"Except we couldn't be together."

"Regan . . . I've loved you since you were twelve." I opened my mouth, but he held up his hand to stop me from interjecting. "I know you didn't feel the same way I did, but it never changed my feelings. That still hasn't changed."

"This is it then? That's why he gave you five days to convince me?"

He nodded. "Something I have to figure out. I'll figure out a way to get you out of here."

"No. I already lost one of my best friends. I'm not losing you, Jake."

"You can't put yourself at risk."

I rolled my eyes. "We're going to continue to go around and

around with this, Jake. You think one way, and I think the other. We aren't going to agree."

His head snapped up. "What about Cameron?"

"What about him?"

He pushed to his feet, suddenly animated with whatever plan he had up his sleeve. He was pacing, mumbling to himself. I thought he was going stark-raving mad.

"I need to get to Cameron."

"You're putting yourself in danger if you do that. If he finds out you're Ludovico's son and that I'm here now, he may kill you. Jake, I didn't tell anyone about us."

"You'd at least be alive! I need to go talk to him and your father. They need to know where you are. Maybe we can come up with a plan."

I looked around, not really at anything. "In this fortress?"

"There are ways in, just as there are ways out."

I smiled. Maybe there was a way, after all. If Jake could get to Pops and Cameron, and explain everything he had explained to me, and everything he knew, maybe there's a chance. He gave me five days. Tomorrow will be day three. I was running out of time, and Jake needed to act fast.

"I'm almost positive Reno is on his way, too. I'm his daughter-in-law, and he is most protective of me."

Jake nodded. "Where's your phone?"

I grimaced. "I think they took it after they knocked me out. Make sure you don't get followed when you go."

"I'll be taking every kind of precaution."

I still had a bad feeling something bad would happen. If this worked, it would be too easy. Nothing was that easy. There wasn't another way, though. This was all we had.

"If your father intercepted your phone number. You can't contact him on your phone."

"I'll go buy a burner phone. Either way, I'm doing this." I smiled then. "You're a good friend, Jake."

"Thank me later."

"Don't tell him . . . please. That I might be pregnant. I don't know for sure."

"I'm not telling him that. Hell no."

My eyes glistened. "I don't have much time left, Jake. Less if your father gets suspicious of anything or decides that five days was too generous. If there's a chance that I can live, make it so."

Chapter Twenty Nine

The fourth day arrived, one day until I was a goner. Jake showed up late last night to let me know he had connected with Cameron and was assembling with Pops, Reno, and Gio to figure out a plan to get me out of there. It helped to know Cameron had said he would storm the gates himself, but Jake assured him it wasn't a reasonable way to get in. There were too many armed men surrounding the house. At least with Jake, they would have inside intel on where Ludovico had his guards stationed and how to get in.

I worried about Jake, and how his family would react to knowing he had helped the enemy. I knew that Ludovico's motive behind was irrational, and his own doing, but deep down, I think he wanted to kill me just because I had one-upped him. I think the loss of the two men that I killed years ago had really pissed him off, and I think he knew I wouldn't hesitate to do it again. And he would be right.

I was feeling incredibly frazzled by the fifth day. Jake hadn't been around since he had told me he contacted Cameron, and I didn't know when Ludovico would summon me for the reckoning. It wouldn't matter. I wasn't going to let him kill me without a fight. Or would I?

Wasn't I afraid of dying? Yes. I was afraid of dying, but I was more afraid of what Cameron might do in retaliation. Or Pops, or

Reno. It was them I worried about in all of this. It wouldn't be over until someone took a stand, and I would do it. After all, Ludovico had started this all years before I had been born.

The waiting was wearing on my nerves. Noon passed, then dinner passed. Jake hadn't come around, but I thought maybe that was good. Maybe he was still planning. It occurred to me that Ludovico had reconsidered, or he was giving Jake more time, but then I thought that would be absurd. He wasn't the type of man to give any flexibility.

It was nine by the time I heard the key in the door, dark having fallen already. I leaped from the bed, my heart thundering in my chest. Would he come for me himself, or send his thugs to drag me down again? I had to stop overthinking. I was ready for this.

The door swung open to two tall, very armed men with scowls on their faces. One had a scar that ran nearly the entire length of his chin. He was the shorter of the two, but dangerous. The other one had dark, hard eyes. Mean.

I lifted my chin and moved forward. When they went to grab me, I pulled away from them with narrowed eyes and an edge to my voice. "I can walk myself. I know where we're going."

The shorter one still reached out, but I slapped his hand away. It wouldn't take much to push them both, grabbing a gun in each hand and blowing them away in a single shot. That would just hasten my demise.

I pushed between them, walking down the hallway without bothering to see if they were following behind. I was certain that they were, even when I started my descent down the staircase and arriving moments later in the living room.

Ludovico sat in the chair where he usually was while Vicky stood behind him and off to the side. I met her eyes, only to find that hers were sad. She didn't know me, but she didn't want this to happen. I could tell by the way she was studying me.

"Ah, Regan . . ." Ludovico stood up, his hand coming to rest on his beloved Beretta, but not removing it from its holster at his hip.

He wore a fancy pinstripe suit, and I resisted the urge to laugh. Was he trying to be an original gangster? Because that wasn't going to happen. He was a second-rate criminal and no more. His own sick jealousy drove him to do it. Jealousy of Pops and Reno.

"Things could have been different between us," he said. "I am sad to see that it hasn't gone my way in that. Jake tells me he tried to win you over, was even close to winning you over, but you were ever so stubborn."

I watched him, and as he strolled around the living room, my eyes tracked his every move. There were two men stationed at the back of the room, the two men that had brought me down from my prison cell standing at the ready behind me, and one on each side of the room. Those were only the ones I could see. There was no way of knowing how many were patrolling the perimeter.

Ludovico was pacing, or stalking rather, around the room. He was trying to intimidate me even though I wasn't the one with the gun. If I had a gun, this would have ended already.

"I've tracked you. You didn't know that, did you?"

"Of course, I knew it. Jake wouldn't have done that to me."

He stopped behind his chair, pressing his palms into the leather back. "It didn't take much to figure out where you were. I could hear waves on the beach. I knew you had been in Miami, and I knew you got on a ferry. Didn't take much after that for one of my men to track you down."

"That's four of your men I've taken out," I whispered softly.

He stared at me. "If you hadn't killed my men and screwed up the entire deal, you wouldn't be in this position."

"That's not true, and you know it. This started years before I was born because they cut you out of a deal. And that was your own doing. You're shifting the blame to someone else."

"That was Gavriel and Reno's doing."

I lifted my chin, not willing to give him the satisfaction of begging for my life or sharing anything about my life with him. Being that he was following me, I wondered if he knew I had married Cameron. But he wouldn't have given Jake time to convince me if he had known.

Ludovico stayed where he was, pulling out the Beretta from the holster. He gave one heavy sigh, then aimed it at me. He could have at least given me the courtesy of being closer to me. My heart was pounding in my chest, drumming in an intense tempo, and like it was trying to get out of my chest. A tear slipped from my eye. I was being selfish, but what else could I have done? Even if I had said I would marry Jake, that would have only bought me a little more time.

I wanted to close my eyes, but I wouldn't give him the satisfaction of the fear in anticipation of having a bullet rip through me by closing them. I prayed it was quick. His aim would be true, but he may want me to suffer first.

"Stop!"

I closed my eyes a fraction, not sure I should move. Ludovico still had the gun aimed at me, even though Jake's voice had stopped him. I didn't dare turn around. When he brushed back past me, I thought my heartbeat would slow down, but Jake stepped in front of me. Ludovico's eyes widened.

"Jake, no . . ." I whispered. "Don't."

"I'll shoot you," Ludovico said. "I'll shoot you, then I'll shoot her. And then I'll shoot those who you've allowed into my home."

Ludovico didn't waver. The gun in his hand was steady. He shook his head, but he wasn't looking at me and he wasn't looking at Jake.

Slightly, I turned my head over my right shoulder to see Pops. Cameron had to be behind him. I turned my head over my left shoulder to see Reno. They each had guns in both hands, one on each of the men that had brought me down from the bedroom and the two men that were on the side of the room. That still left two men that were armed with guns pointed at them. If anyone pulled the trigger, this would be a bloodbath.

Ludovico laughed again. "If you shoot me, I'll kill them both.

This bullet should get them both in one shot. Is it worth your daughter's life, Gavriel?"

My eyes widened when Cameron stepped in from the door behind Ludovico, a gun in each of his hands, one on Ludovico and another aimed at the man standing closest to the door he had come through. He scanned me to make sure they had not hurt me, but he clenched his jaw and I could see the fear in his eyes. Gio came out of the other door, his guns pointed at the other man and Ludovico.

My heart had no chance to slow down, it was beating so hard. My eyes were on Cameron. I wouldn't stand for him to be hurt any more than I would the rest of them, but I was ever so glad that they were here.

"She should have been mine," Ludovico said, his voice punching the air.

"I never would have been."

A jolt shot through me when I heard Isabel's voice behind me. She strolled in casually, as though she had been waiting in the car and had been impatient. I saw her wink as she came around to the side of me and Jake, then she turned to Ludovico.

"Move on, Leo. Gavriel and Reno didn't want to cut you out of the deal. You gave them no choice but to do it."

"Isabel," he whispered. "I killed you."

"You thought you killed me."

Like a flash, he moved the gun away from Jake and me and pointed it at her. I gasped, not ready to lose the mother that I just gained. I looked at Vicky, who had tears in her eyes with her fist in a ball. This was her husband's first love, the one that he had never gotten over. I couldn't feel bad for her. Not now. Not after five days of hell with no help from her.

"What are you going to do, Leo? We've disarmed your men, and we have a lot more outside. You aren't going to win."

"No!" I shouted, rushing toward her without a thought that Ludovico's bullet could hit me. "I'm not losing you again."

"Regan, no," Cameron said through a clenched jaw. He could do nothing to stop me unless he removed his guns from where they were. To do so would take a chance.

Isabel tried to push me out of the way, but I wasn't moving even though his gun still aimed at me. She didn't have a gun, or if she did, she didn't have it out. Someone was going to die, even though everyone in the room was holding their breath.

"Kill me, if that's what will satisfy your revenge," I said.

"Regan . . ." Cameron moved toward me; his guns still drawn and aimed. "Move out of the way."

Ludovico cocked his head to the side. "You're right, of course. Killing you will satisfy my revenge for what you did to Santino. I had to flee the country after that, losing out in a lot more than I had before you were born. I'll get the satisfaction of your mother's heartbreak when I kill you."

I wasn't going to back down, and I wasn't going to close my eyes this time. There was a loud pop, the sound of a single gunshot. I looked down to make sure I didn't have a bullet hole in me. No one was moving. Vicky was standing with a gun in her hand, her hands trembling ever so slightly while still aimed at where Ludovico had been. He had fallen to the floor and was no longer moving. I didn't have to guess her aim had been true.

Cameron ran to me and wrapped his arms around me so tightly that I thought time had stopped and he would never let me go. My heart was still pounding, my breath coming in gasps from how close that had been. He was shaking, or I was shaking. Maybe both of us were shaking. We had been so close to losing each other.

I watched Jake rush over to Vicky and take the gun out of her hands before she slumped down on the couch. He pointed it at the two men Cameron had been covering and motioned for them to drop their weapons. Without hesitation, they threw their guns to the floor.

"I'm so glad you came," I whispered into Cameron's chest.

"He's lucky I didn't kill him," he ground out.

After making sure Vicky was doing okay, Jake approached us. I smiled at him, lifting my head from Cameron's chest and dragging myself out of his arms. It was Jake I had to thank for everything.

"Jake . . . if you hadn't offered to marry me . . ."

"I would have married you even if your life wasn't in danger. You know I would have. I've loved you for longer than you think."

"Jake," Cameron growled.

"Let him finish."

"I see the way Cameron loves you, and I understand why he loves you."

"I love you in my own way, Jake. And you'll always be my friend."

Chapter Thirty

The white wedding gown fit perfectly as I stared at myself in the mirror. Anne had been beside herself with emotions not only for the safe return of all of us, but for those last-minute preparations. Amber had flown back for the wedding and was steering clear of her mother.

"Oh!"

I turned, not having heard Isabel open the door to come into the bedroom. I smiled while she walked toward me and grabbed both my hands before throwing her arms around me.

"You're so beautiful, my daughter," she whispered. "I'm fortunate to be here today."

"Today wouldn't have been complete without you."

She took a few steps back and adjusted the veil, which was attached to my crown, then she moved toward the window and drew back the curtains. "It's a full house. Are you ready?"

I sucked in a deep breath. "As ready as I'll ever be."

We walked toward the door and moved into the hallway. It took some maneuvering to get the door shut without my train getting closed in. We laughed while she grabbed at the bunches of fabric behind me and held them while we walked together down the staircase.

"Anne has really outdone herself. It is just perfect."

"Is she . . . treating you well?"

"Oh yes, she's been wonderfully understanding."

"Are you and Pops . . ." I gave a shaky laugh, not believing I was going to get involved in their business. "Are you going to get back together?"

"I'm not sure. Your father and I have talked a lot over the last few days. And then there's Anne. She's very understanding, especially when he insisted I stay here. I have a life in Cape Haven though."

I nodded. I understood what she was saying. Maybe they would get back together, but it would take time and a lot to consider. Either way, I was happy to have her in my life and even happier that she had never truly left.

The house was eerily vacant while we moved through to the ballroom, the doors open to the beautiful day outside. There was an altar set up on the back lawn beyond the pool with rows of white chairs in front of it. Cameron stood in front of it talking to Reno. Warmth flooding the length of my body. The way he looked in a tuxedo brought back memories of the Christmas Ball.

I could see Pops just beyond the doors, looking sharp in his black tuxedo. He was looking at his watch when we came across the ballroom. Isabel relinquished the train of the gown to the two young women the wedding planner had hired. They spread out the train behind me, keeping a hold on each end as I stepped out the door into the sunshine. Pops turned. The smile that he gave me filled me with a sense of pride.

Isabel kissed me on the cheek, wishing me luck before she hurried down to take her seat in the front row. Pops held out his hand to me, and I slipped my hand into his. He looked at me for a full minute, just looking at me.

"Have I told you how proud I am of you?" I shook my head. "I haven't always been the best dad. But I've always been proud of you."

"Thanks, Pops."

"Let's get you down to your groom. He was impatient to see you this morning when we told him he couldn't. He's even worse now. It's bad luck to see the bride, you know."

I laughed. "We're already married."

He sniffed, pulling my arm through his until our arms linked and pulling me beside him while we walked down and around the pool toward the white runner leading up to the altar.

As we came around the shrubs on the other side of the pool house, Cameron came into view and my breath caught. He stood tall next to the officiant, his arms behind him, watching me with hooded eyes. I was just about to step forward when Pops squeezed my arm, stopping me from moving.

"Are you happy?"

Now was not the time to ask me such a question. "I'm happy, Pops."

With that, we began walking down the aisle. All the people that stood on each side were blurring, my attention all on Cameron at the end of the impossibly long aisle. Anne couldn't have just invited a few people. She had to squeeze in everyone she could think of, including everyone from Cameron's side.

Cameron and I made eye contact while I focused on taking one step at a time, Pops' arm providing me with support. I opted for simple flats rather than heels, which proved to be a wise decision as I walked on the soft lawn. When I reached Cameron, his eyes never left mine, even when his lips curled into a devious smile.

Pops handed me to Cameron and reached to shake hands with him, but I could see the wrinkle in a frown on his forehead. "I'm not sure I like the way you're looking at my darling girl," he whispered.

Cameron laughed. "You're too late."

He wasn't wrong. Pops was far too late for that warning. Without another word, Pops turned and took his seat between

Anne and Isabel. I looked at the other side of the aisle, at Reno and Orianna. Reno was smiling and Orianna, well, she always looked like she had a pained look on her face, but I was up for the challenge of getting to know her. The rest of his family were all seated in the front row, including Emma and Caleb, who I had only met that week.

While we stood in front of him, listening to the officiant, Cameron and I couldn't keep our eyes off each other. Everything and everyone faded into the background, including the officiant, as though the words didn't matter. They didn't, really.

"I have to tell you something," I whispered, too eager to wait.

"Now?"

He looked alarmed, and I didn't want him to be nervous. "Yes, now." I swallowed the lump in my throat. I hope he didn't run screaming down the aisle. "I'm pregnant."

His eyes widened, a flush rising to his cheeks. Suddenly, I was afraid I'd given him a shock. Maybe he wasn't ready for this. I wasn't sure I was ready for this. We hadn't been careful enough. Without warning, he pulled me into his arms and his mouth was on mine, eliciting several gasps and murmurs from our audience.

"I haven't said that part yet," the officiant leaned over to tell us.

Cameron didn't seem to mind, his mouth moving against mine without letting up. His arms came around my waist, pulling me up against him and creating a warm flush throughout my body. It took a few moments before he finally broke his lips away from me, still keeping his arms around me and pressing his lips against my neck.

"I think my heart is going to burst," he said against my neck.

The officiant cleared his throat, and Cameron straightened, but kept his hands at my waist. It thought to a moment he was going to put his hands on my stomach, but he stopped himself. There would be a time and place to announce it to everyone else.

The rest of the ceremony continued, but neither of us were paying any attention. We kept our eyes locked the entire time, not willing to give our devotion to anything else in this world apart from us.

We recited our vows in a lifeless tone, having already done this, and when he finally gave Cameron the go-ahead to kiss me, Cameron didn't hesitate. His lips pressed against mine so softly. For several seconds, they were against mine, not moving, just pressed against mine, until his arm slipped around my waist and pulled me against him.

I smiled, and he smiled before he slowly withdrew. We hurried back down the aisle amidst cheers and clapping, those that had attended hopefully happy for us and our new journey. The journey wouldn't end like I thought it would. I caught Jake's eye when we passed by, giving him a wink. He elicited an invitation from Cameron, and Cameron couldn't deny him. Had it not been for Jake, I wouldn't be alive.

The wedding reception immediately followed the ceremony, with round tables covered with white tablecloths on the other half of the lawn, along with a portable dance floor and DJ booth.

Bright yellow and red flowers decorated each table, along with crystal glassware, white dishes, and sterling silver. We skipped the receiving line because of the number of guests that had attended. No one would have been able to eat. The plan was to go directly into dinner, but so many people wanted to talk with us that Cameron and I soon found ourselves pulled away from each other.

The first person to grab me was Tatum, and I couldn't say I blamed her. Other than ensuring she was fine and letting her know I was safe, there wasn't much time to talk. It had taken hours of effort, but in the end, she and Alex got free.

"What did you say to Cameron during the ceremony?"

I smiled. "I do."

She took a swipe at my bare arm. "That's not what I meant. When he started kissing you right in the middle! He shocked everyone."

I looked around, making sure no one was listening to us. "You won't tell anyone?" Who was I kidding? She wouldn't be able to keep it to herself. I leaned in toward her. "That I love him."

"Regan! Tell me!"

I shrugged. This was mine and Cameron's secret to hold on to for a while. "I don't know what to tell you, Tate. I love him." I found him in the crowd, and our gazes locked.

"You're going to tell me."

"I just did," I said and whirled away from her, running right into Stefan and Peter.

"I heard I missed a hell of a fight when you got home from the airport," Peter said. "And I got an earful from my brother for it."

Guilty, I gave him my most apologetic face. "I had no intentions of doing what I told you I was going to do. He knows that now. I'm sorry for putting you in the middle of it."

He grabbed my hand, looking down at my wedding ring. After more than a month of not telling anyone, I could finally put it on. "I'm happy you're my sister."

Not sister-in-law. Sister. I threw my arms around his neck and hugged him. Reno had been right about him all along. Peter came around. I eyed Stefan, standing awkwardly next to us with hardened eyes. It appeared he wanted to say his piece as well, and he was family, so I needed to have it out with him. When I parted from Peter and he went on his way to dance with his wife, I stood my ground with Stefan.

At first, we stared at each other and didn't say anything. He took a step toward me, but he knew me well enough to know I wasn't going to step away from him. Instead, I swept my arms wide. In Ludovico, the devil confronted me himself, who had a gun aimed at my head. What would Stefan do?

"Peter may be soft on you, but not me."

I sighed. "Stefan, this is supposed to be a happy day. Can't you just let whatever it is you have against me go?"

"I don't have anything against you."

"Can't you let whatever it is you have against Cameron go?"

"You have me pegged all wrong."

Exasperation was setting in. And hunger. I desperately needed to get something to eat, and soon. Stefan must have been able to tell I was getting weary of this feud, or apprehension, between us. Whatever this was. I looked up at him.

"Would it help if I let you know I talked with Reno about you assuming more?"

His eyes lit with surprise. "You did what?"

"Do you think I haven't noticed how big of a role you play in this business? You want it. I don't. And I'm not sure Cameron does either. Cameron has his businesses that he owns, and now I have one. We are busy enough."

"Why would you do that?" He was suspicious.

"Because she's having my baby." I felt Cameron's arms slip around my waist as he came up behind me, resting his face against my neck. I could feel his smile, and it made my heart flutter. "And I want to be around for our kid. So, you take it over, little brother."

For the first time since I had met him, Stefan smiled. I couldn't believe it. A few well-chosen words could make him smile like a young boy. He strolled away from us, him and his smile, and I turned in Cameron's arms, looping my arms around his neck.

"Have I told you how much I love you?"

"It can't possibly be as much as I love you," he whispered back. "What you have given me this day, I can never give back to you."

He dropped to his knees, hands at my waist, while he pressed his face into my stomach. I laughed, sifting my fingers through his dark hair. I think he was happy. More than happy. He looked up at me, eyes shining. Things in our lives would be very different now. Nothing would stop our next journey together.

Acknowledgements

There are so many people I want to thank for making this book come to fruition. I couldn't have done it without the steadfast support of my husband, Joe. The need to sit and write instead of doing, well, anything and your patience with that has not gone unnoticed. But to say you've created a monster is an understatement because now it won't ever stop.

To my beta readers of this book–Scott, Jessica and Tonya– without you, I might not have taken the leap. Without your unbiased opinion of it, I wouldn't have known what I have created.

I am incredibly grateful to everyone who has supported me throughout this process. Those who are planning on buying it without knowing what the book is about, those who aren't big readers, and those who have faith in my writing abilities. Thank you sincerely. I am humbled by your support.

I am proud of this book. Even though my heart lies in historical, this one would not leave me alone until I wrote it and I'm glad I did. I had fun with this one, in all its plot twists and maddening emotions. My next two book releases will be historical fiction, but don't worry . . . My fourth novel will be a romantic suspense and could include a reunion of certain characters from *The Gangster's Daughter*.

Find more books by
Jodie Leigh Murray
by scanning the QR code below

Books are also available through:

Amazon

barnesandnoble.com

Bookshop.org

Tertulia

Select Bookshops